CHUNKY

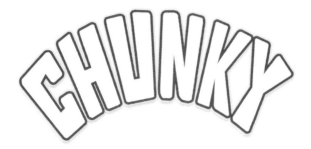

This book is dedicated to
drama teacher Mrs. Miller

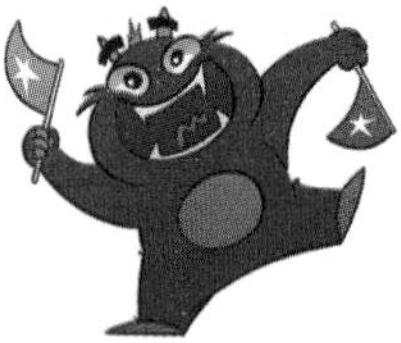

Katherine Tegen Books is an imprint of HarperCollins Publishers.
HarperAlley is an imprint of HarperCollins Publishers.

Chunky
 For information address HarperCollins Children's Books, a division of HarperCollins Publishers, 195 Broadway, New York, NY 10007.
www.harperalley.com

Library of Congress Control Number: 2020949371
ISBN 978-0-06-297279-8 – ISBN 978-0-06-297278-1 (pbk.)

The artist used Adobe Photoshop to create the digital illustrations for this book.
Typography by Yehudi Mercado and Laura Mock
22 23 24 25 NGS 10 9 8 7 6 5 4 3 2 1
❖
First Edition

YEHUDI MERCADO

CHUNKY

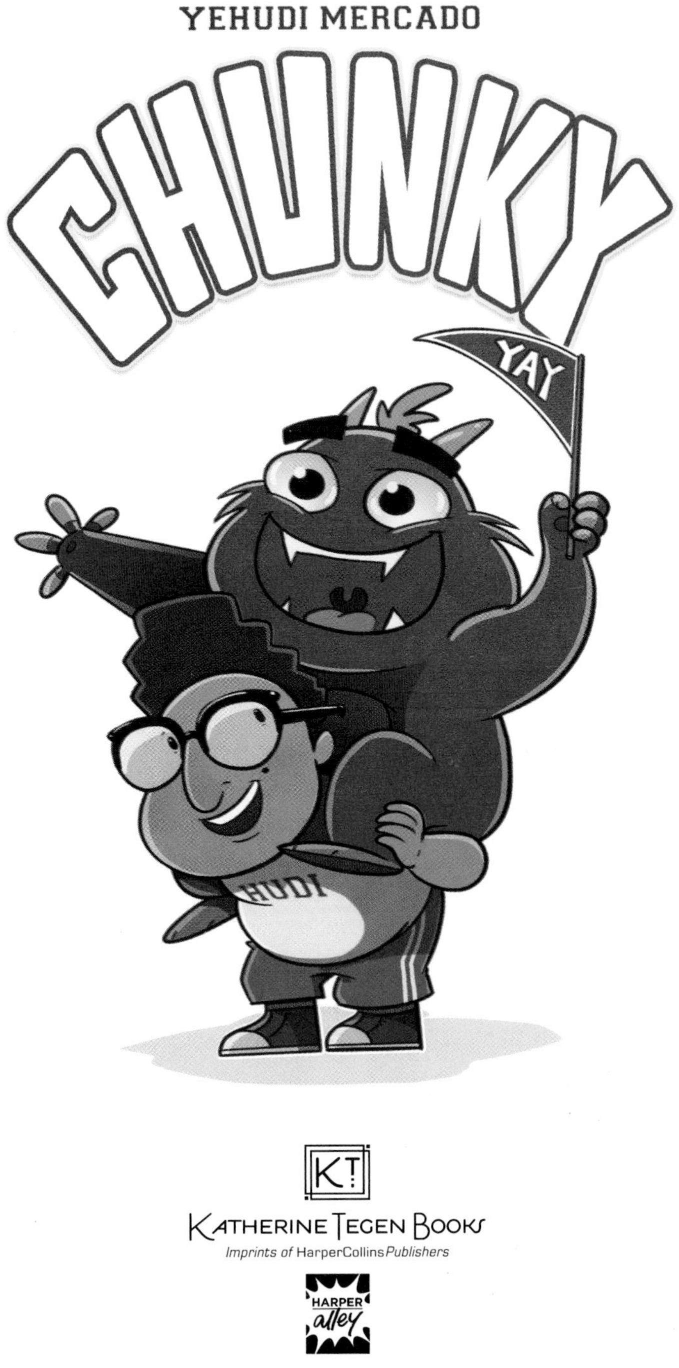
YAY
HUDI

KT
KATHERINE TEGEN BOOKS
Imprints of HarperCollins*Publishers*
HARPER alley

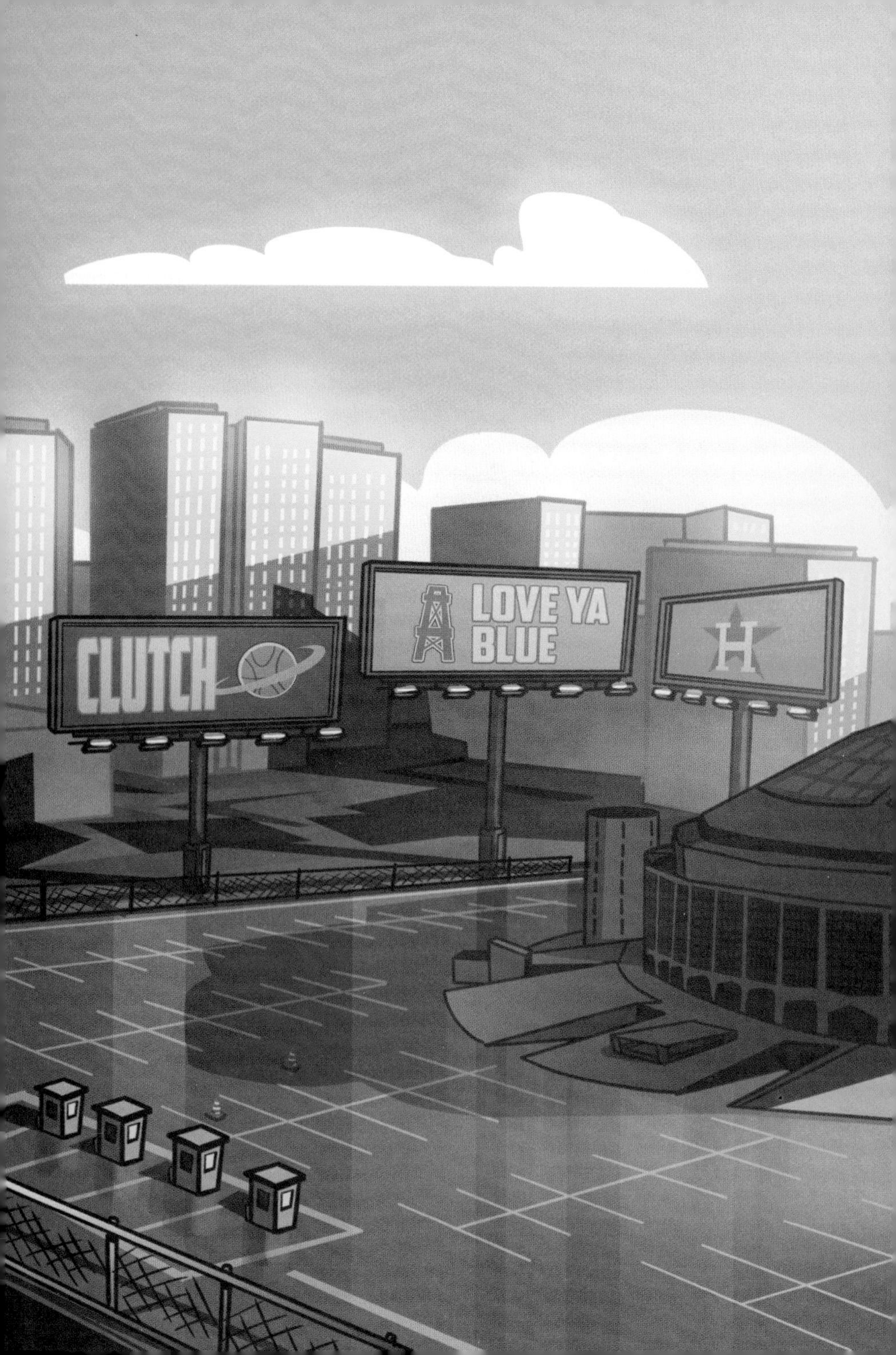
CLUTCH
LOVE YA
BLUE
H

CHAPTER ONE
Pregame

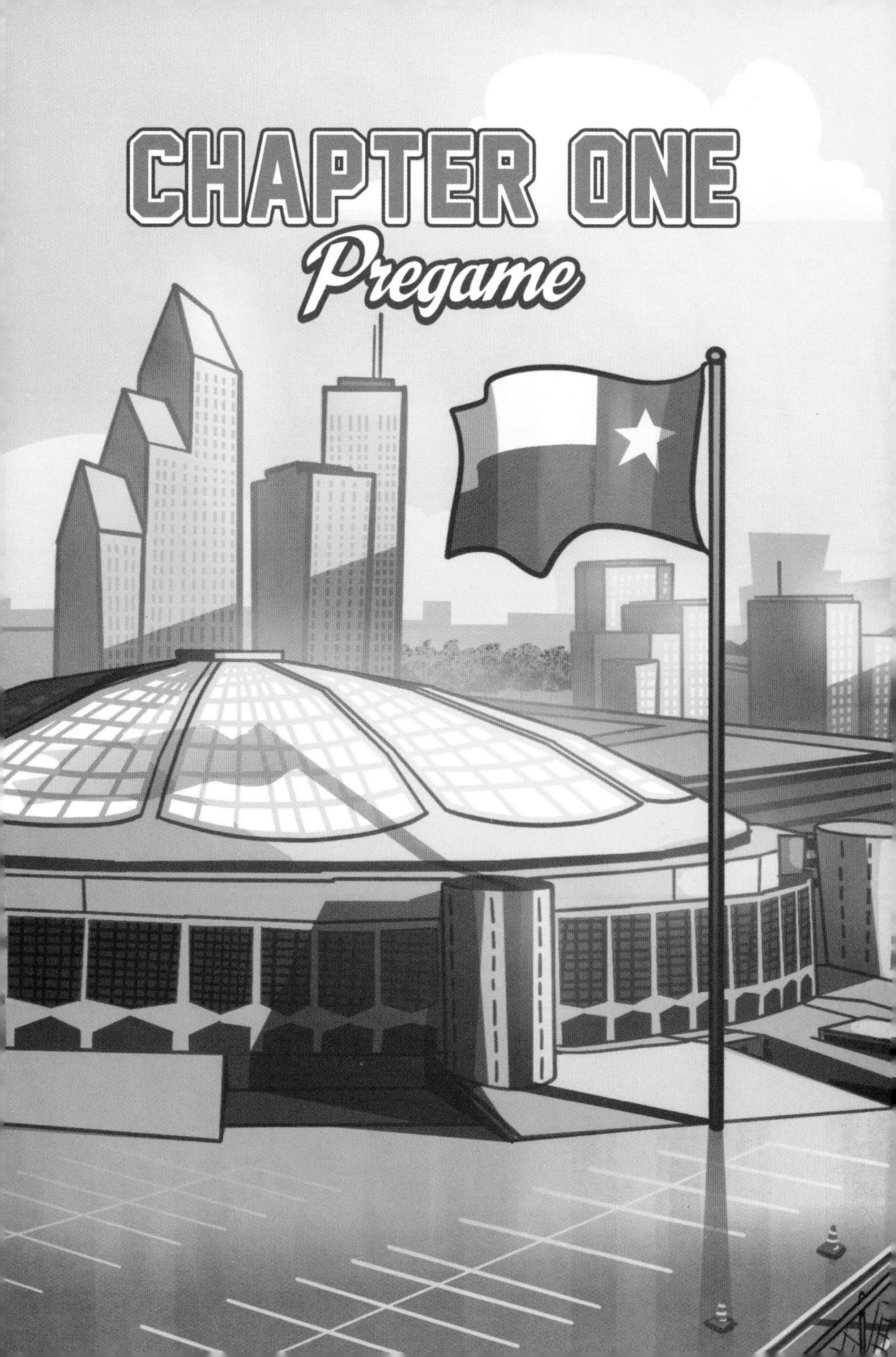

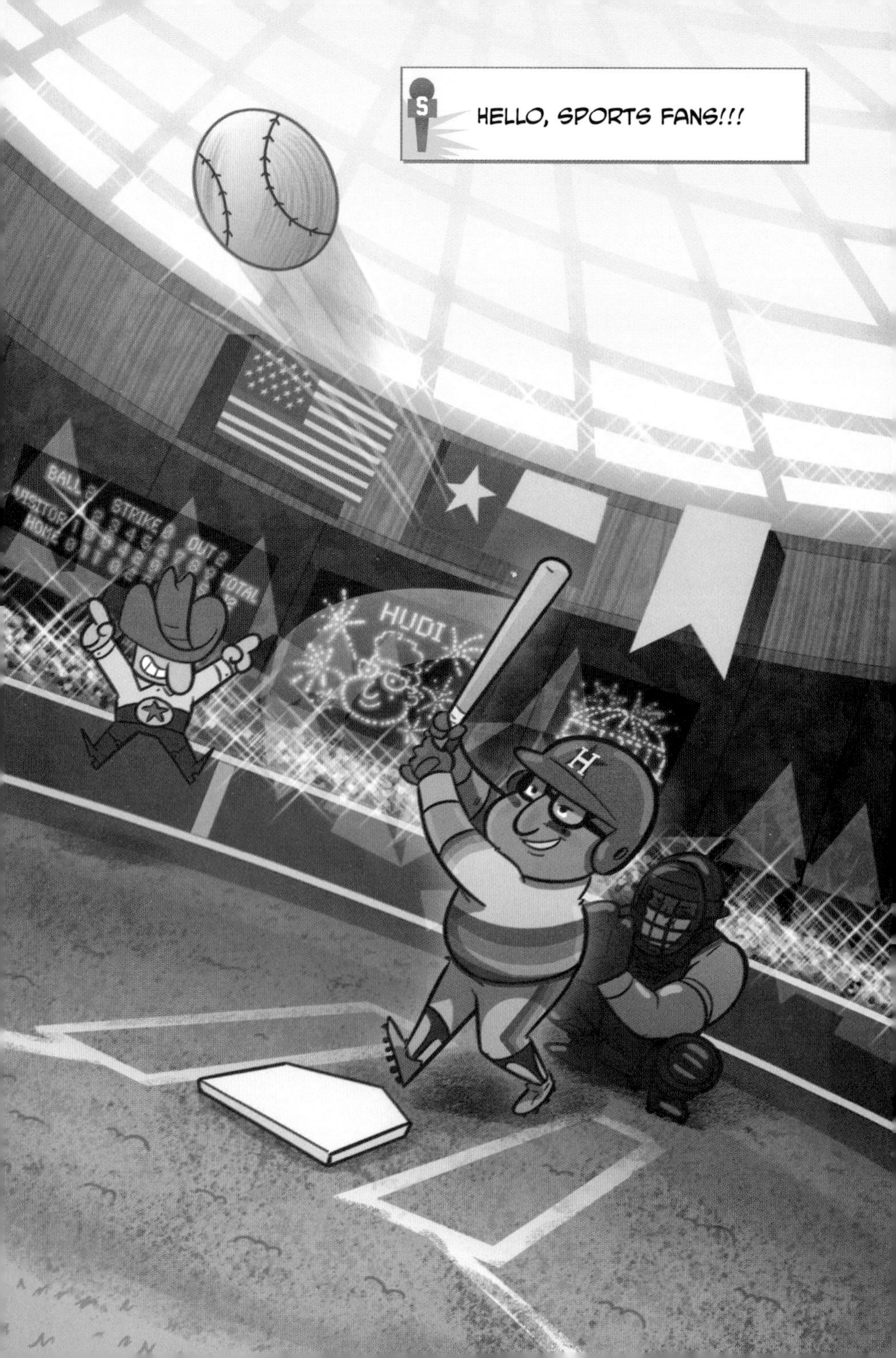
HELLO, SPORTS FANS!!!
BALL
STRIKE
OUT
VISITOR
HOME
TOTAL
HUDI
H

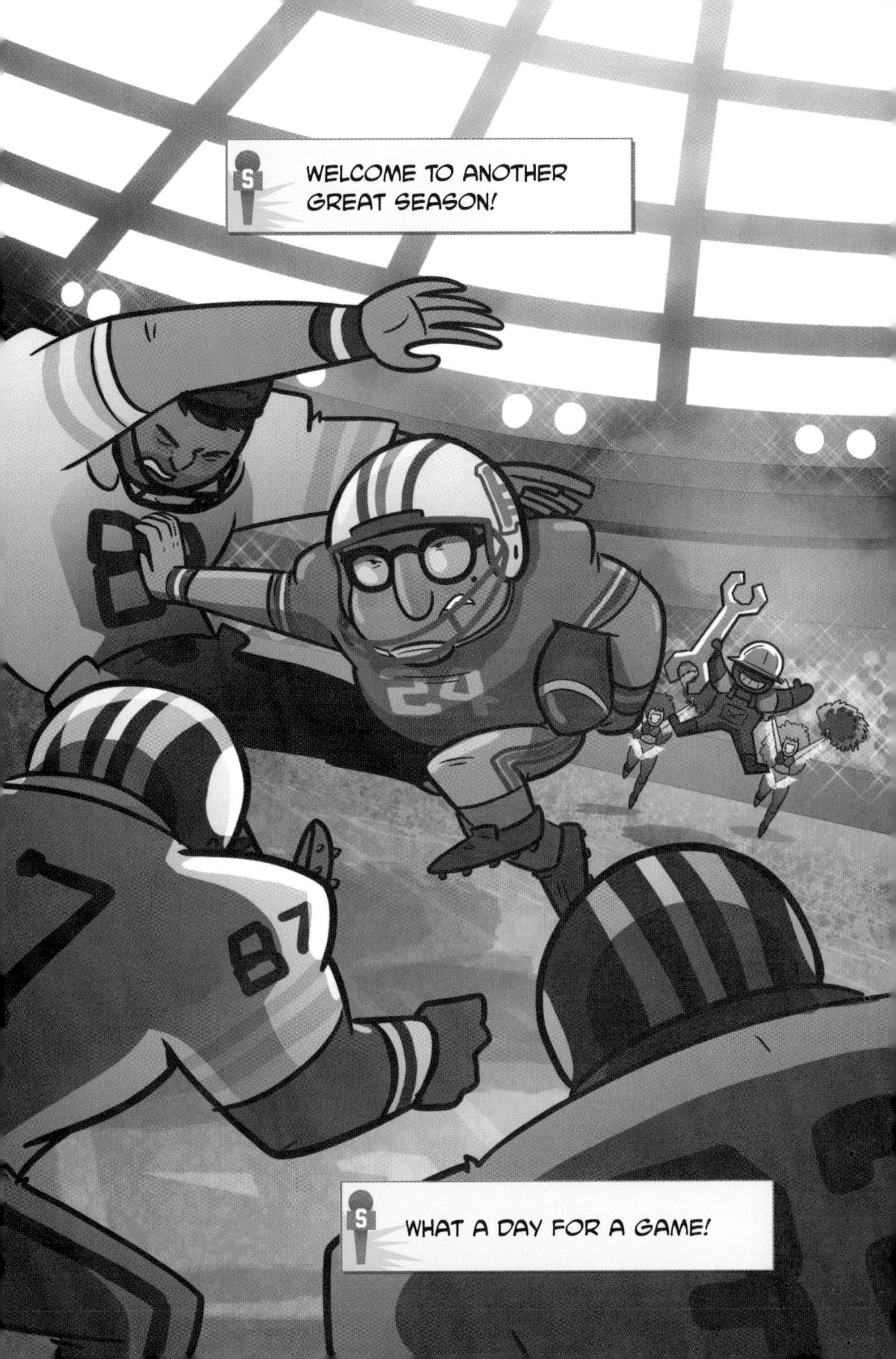
S
WELCOME TO ANOTHER GREAT SEASON!
S
WHAT A DAY FOR A GAME!

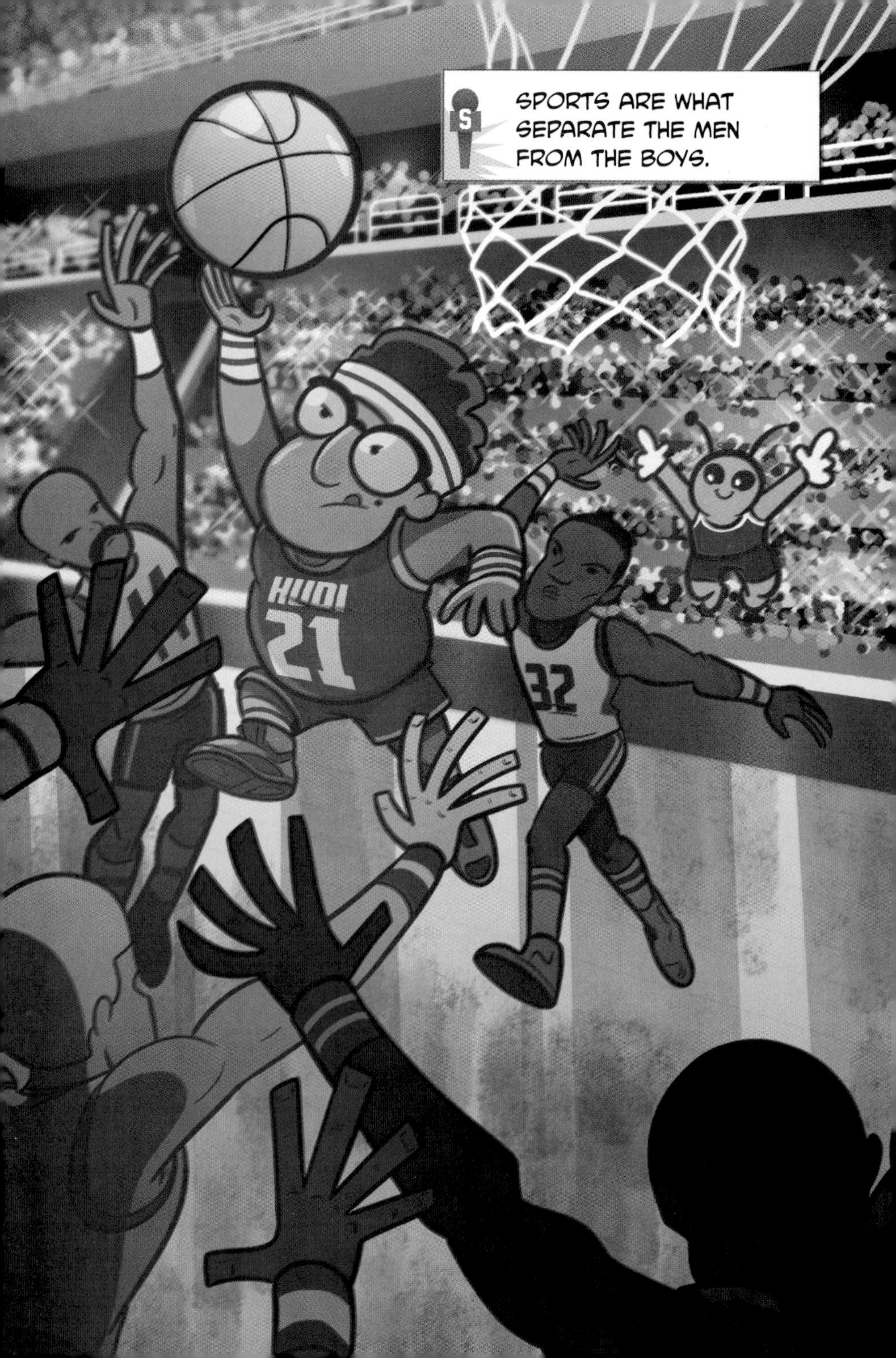
SPORTS ARE WHAT SEPARATE THE MEN FROM THE BOYS.
HUDI
21
32

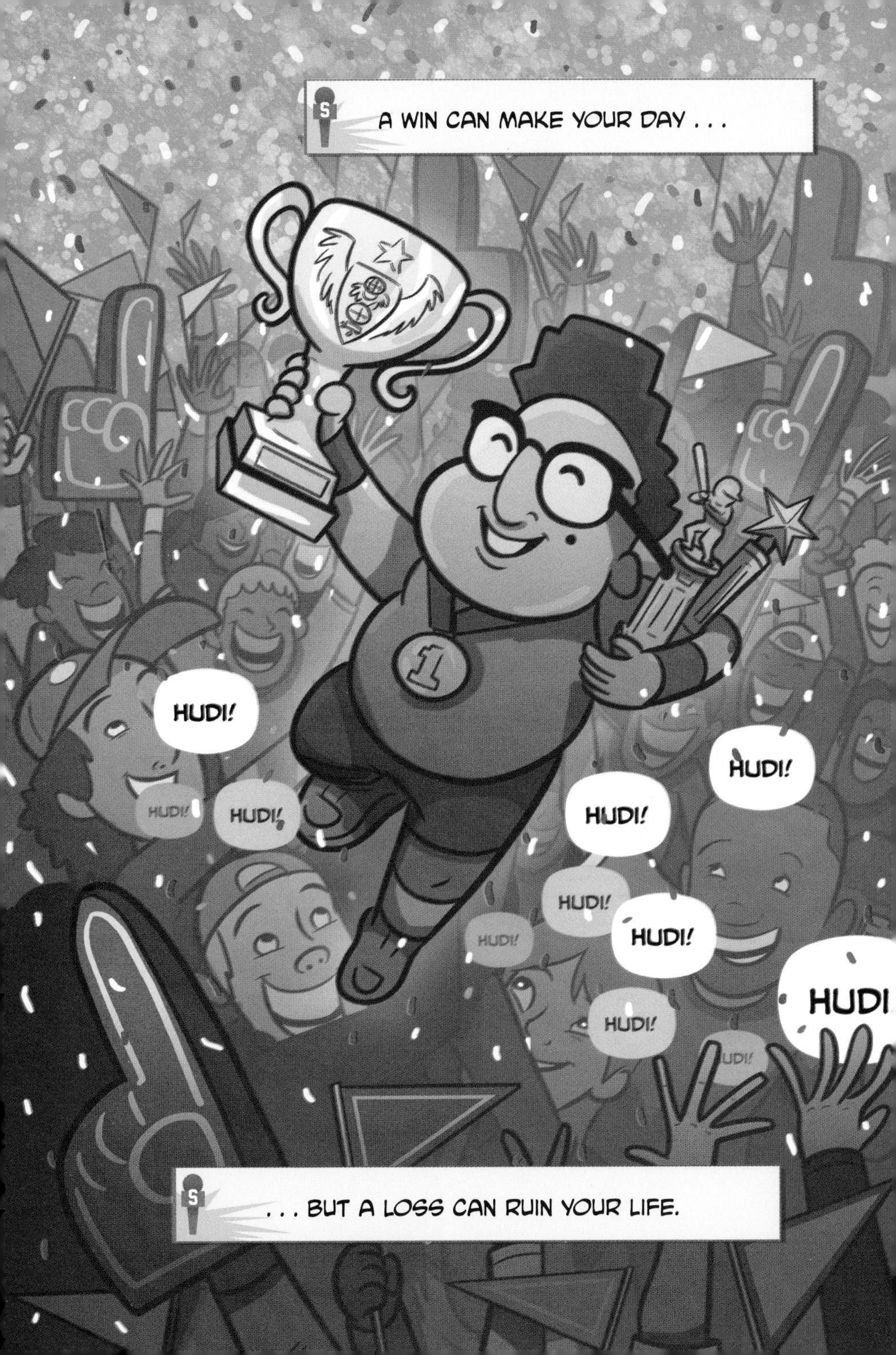
A WIN CAN MAKE YOUR DAY . . .
HUDI!
HUDI!
HUDI!
HUDI!
HUDI!
HUDI!
HUDI!
HUDI!
HUDI!
HUDI
. . . BUT A LOSS CAN RUIN YOUR LIFE.

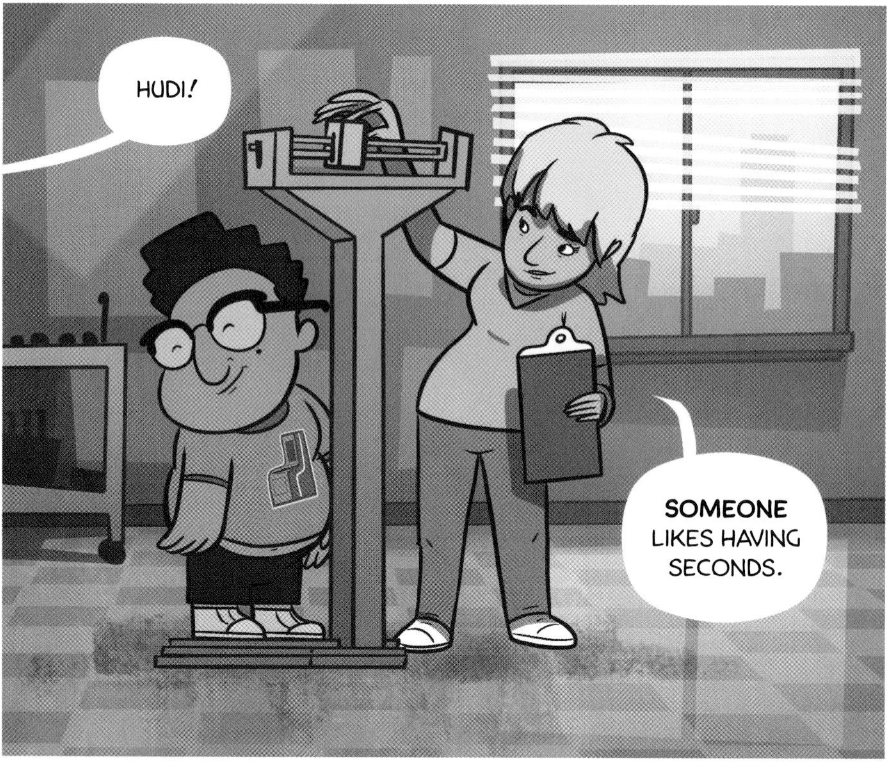
HUDI!
SOMEONE LIKES HAVING SECONDS.

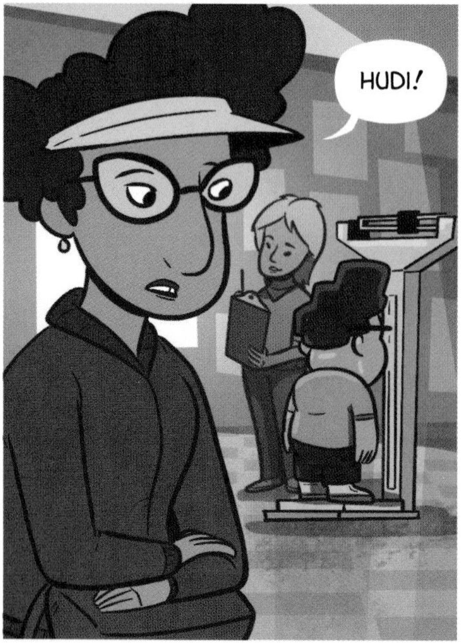
HUDI!

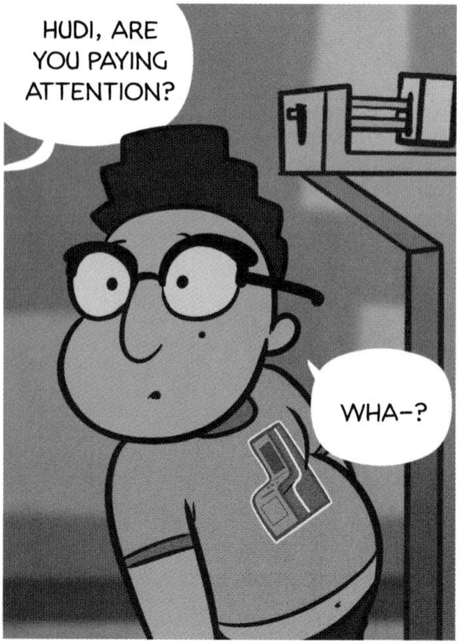
HUDI, ARE YOU PAYING ATTENTION?
WHA-?

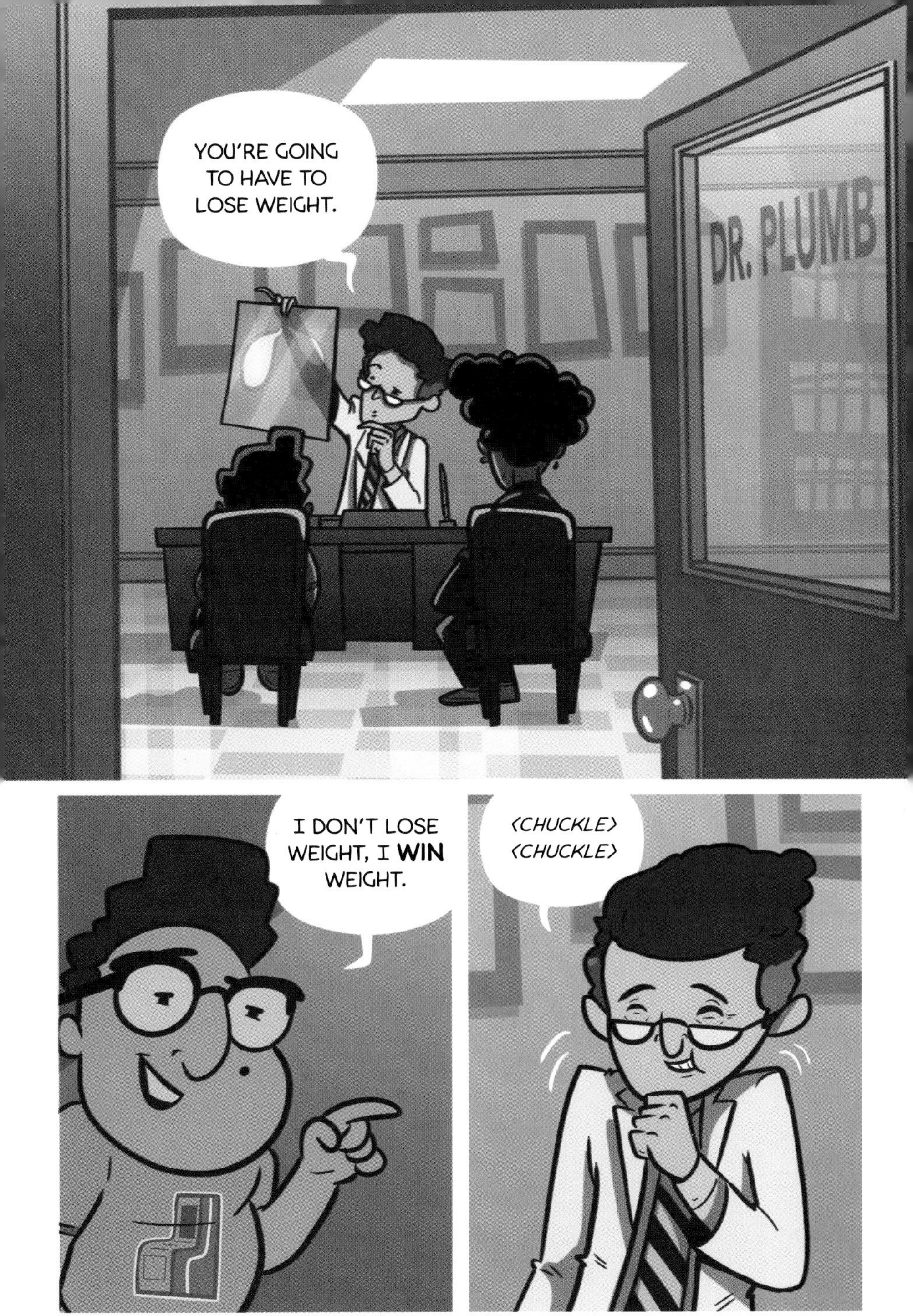
YOU'RE GOING TO HAVE TO LOSE WEIGHT.
DR. PLUMB
I DON'T LOSE WEIGHT, I **WIN** WEIGHT.
<CHUCKLE> <CHUCKLE>

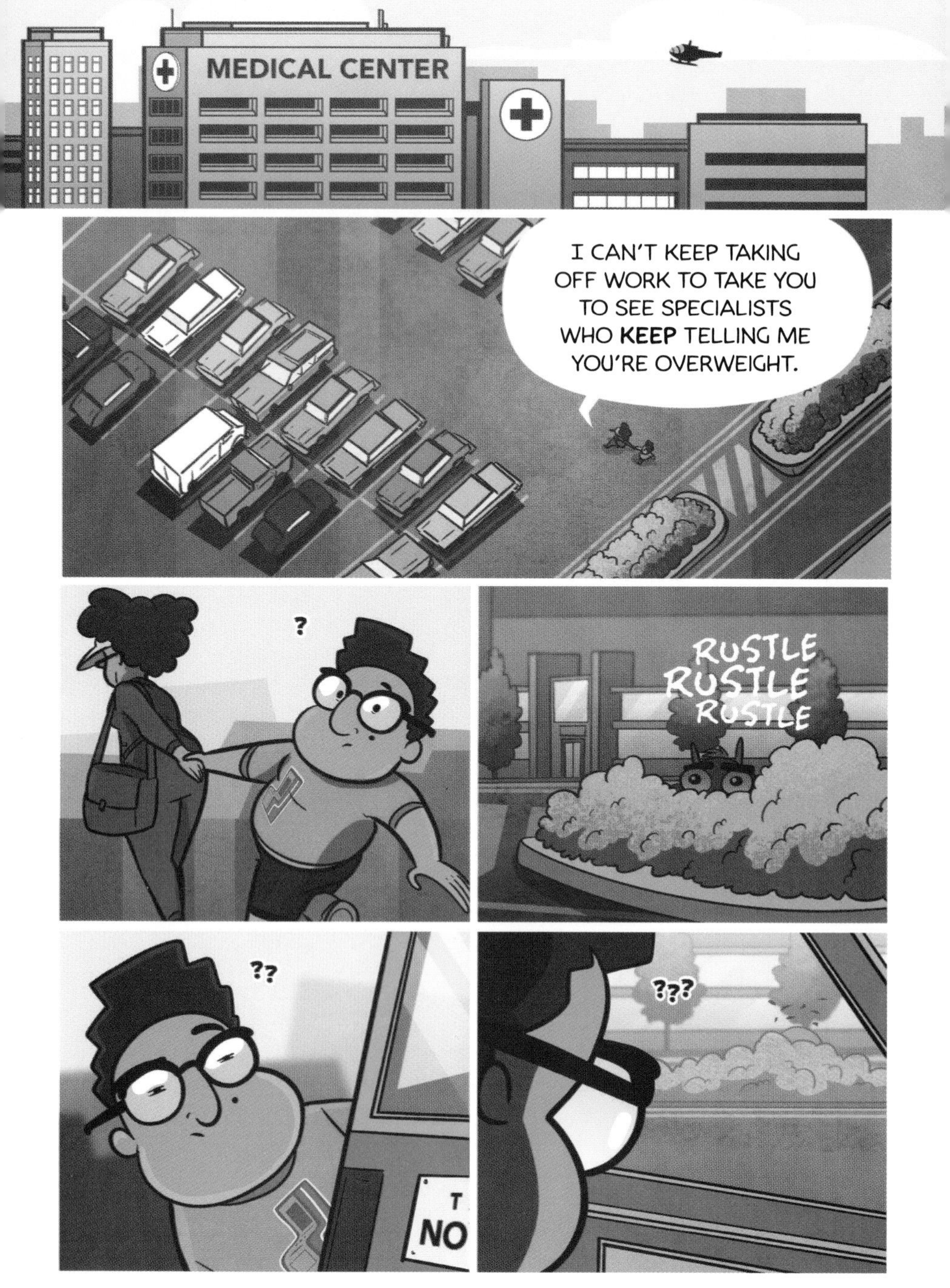
MEDICAL CENTER
I CAN'T KEEP TAKING OFF WORK TO TAKE YOU TO SEE SPECIALISTS WHO **KEEP** TELLING ME YOU'RE OVERWEIGHT.
?
RUSTLE
RUSTLE
RUSTLE
??
???

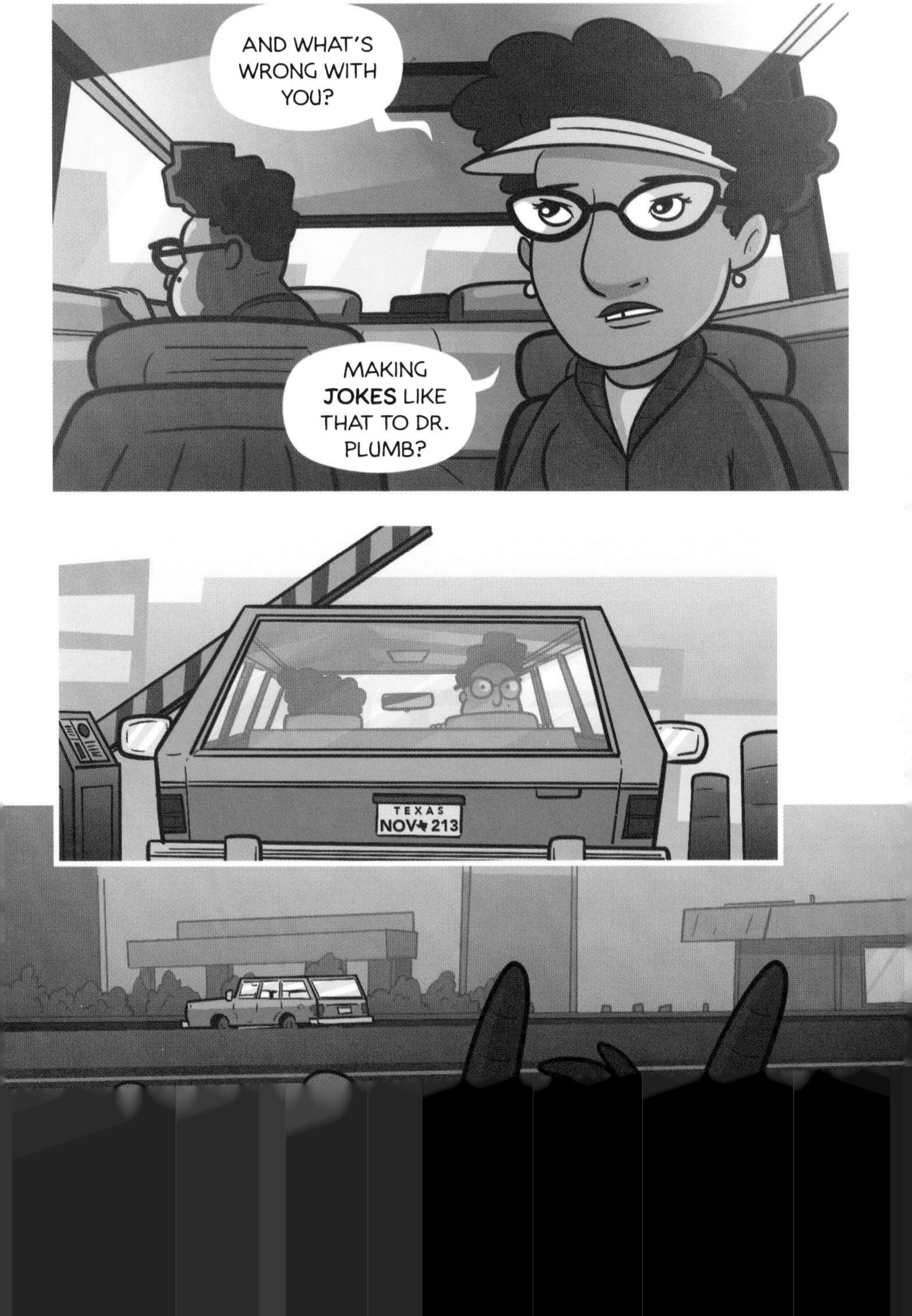
AND WHAT'S WRONG WITH YOU?
MAKING **JOKES** LIKE THAT TO DR. PLUMB?
TEXAS
NOV 213

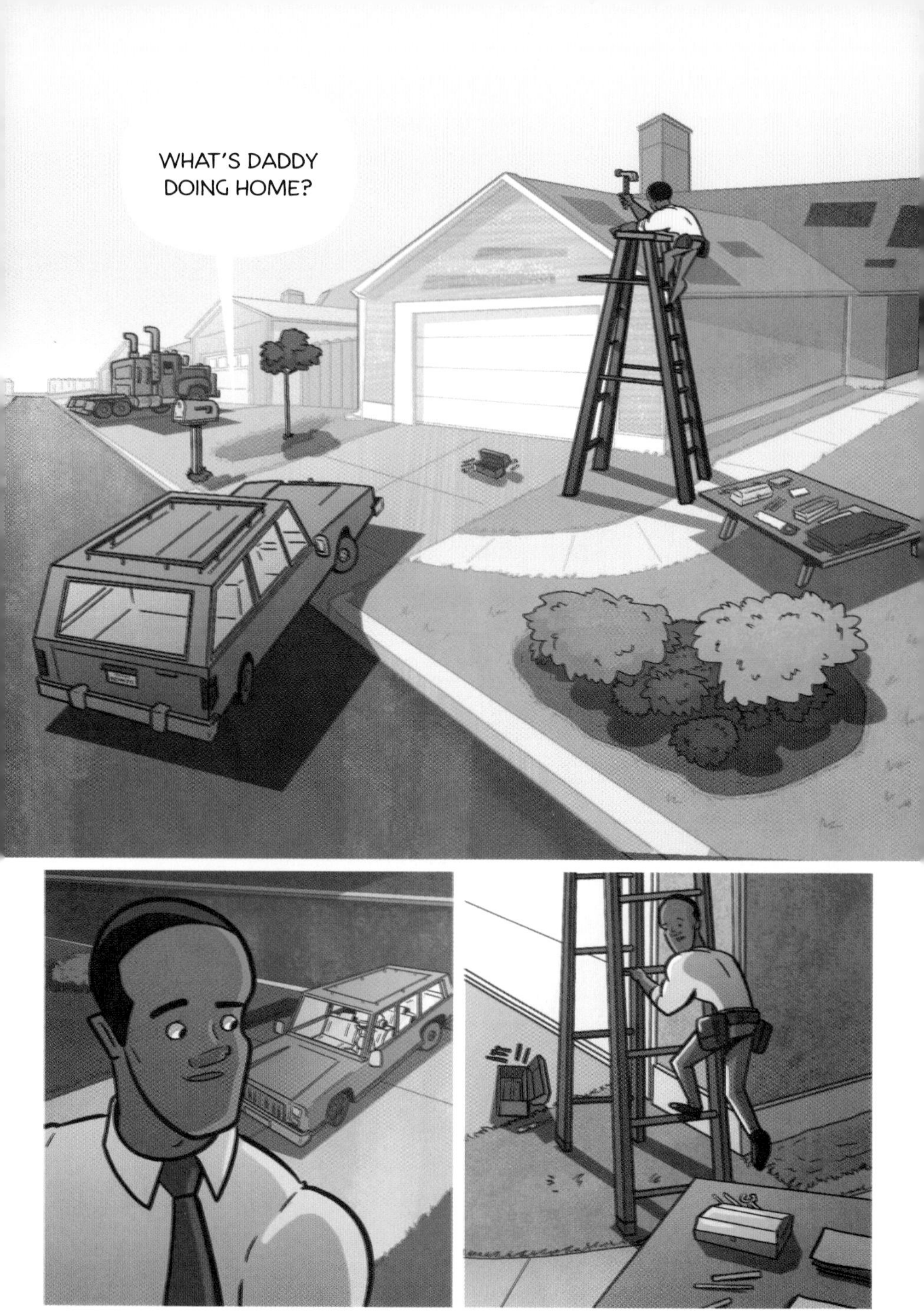
WHAT'S DADDY DOING HOME?

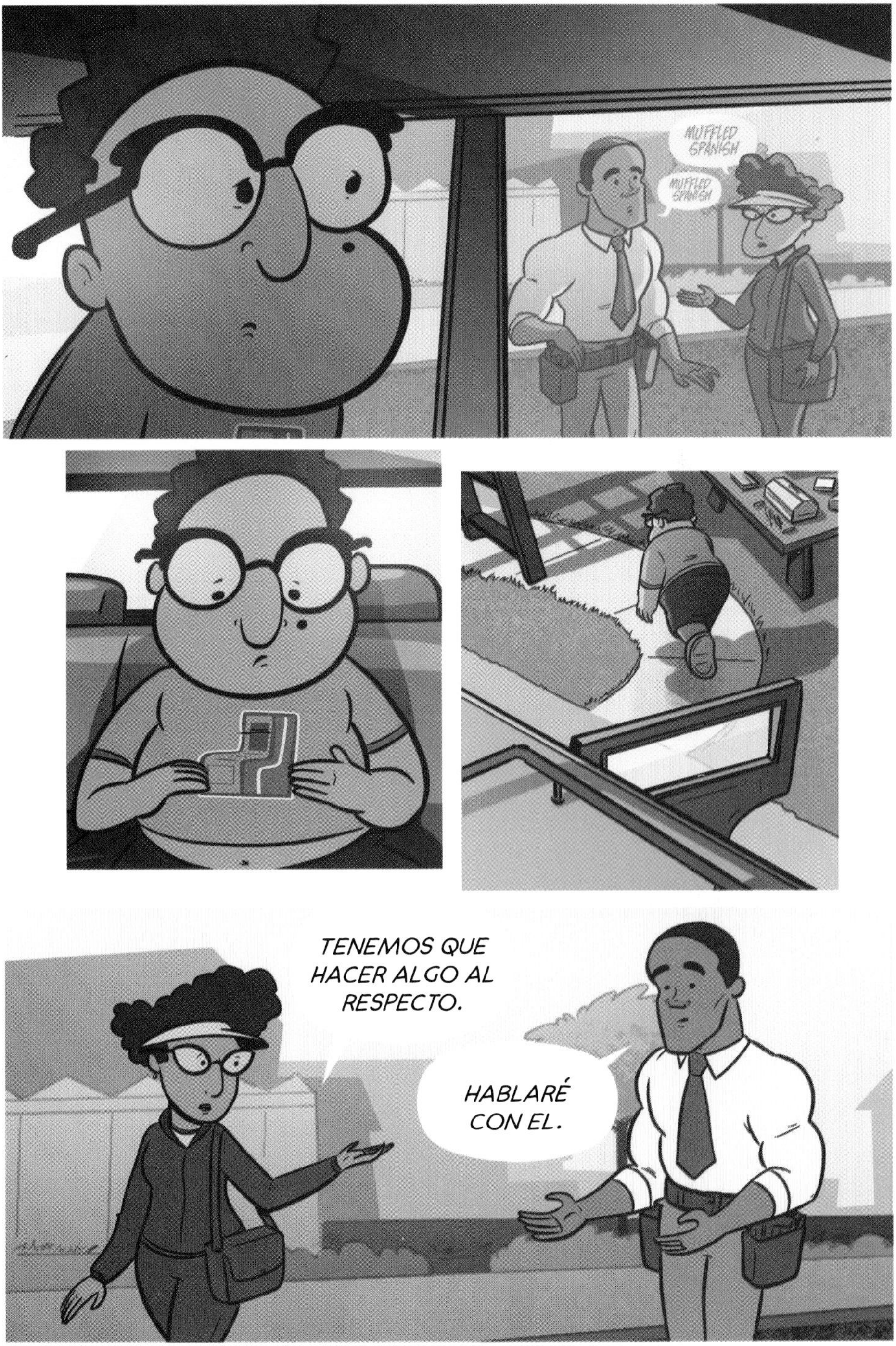
MUFFLED SPANISH
MUFFLED SPANISH
TENEMOS QUE HACER ALGO AL RESPECTO.
HABLARÉ CON EL.

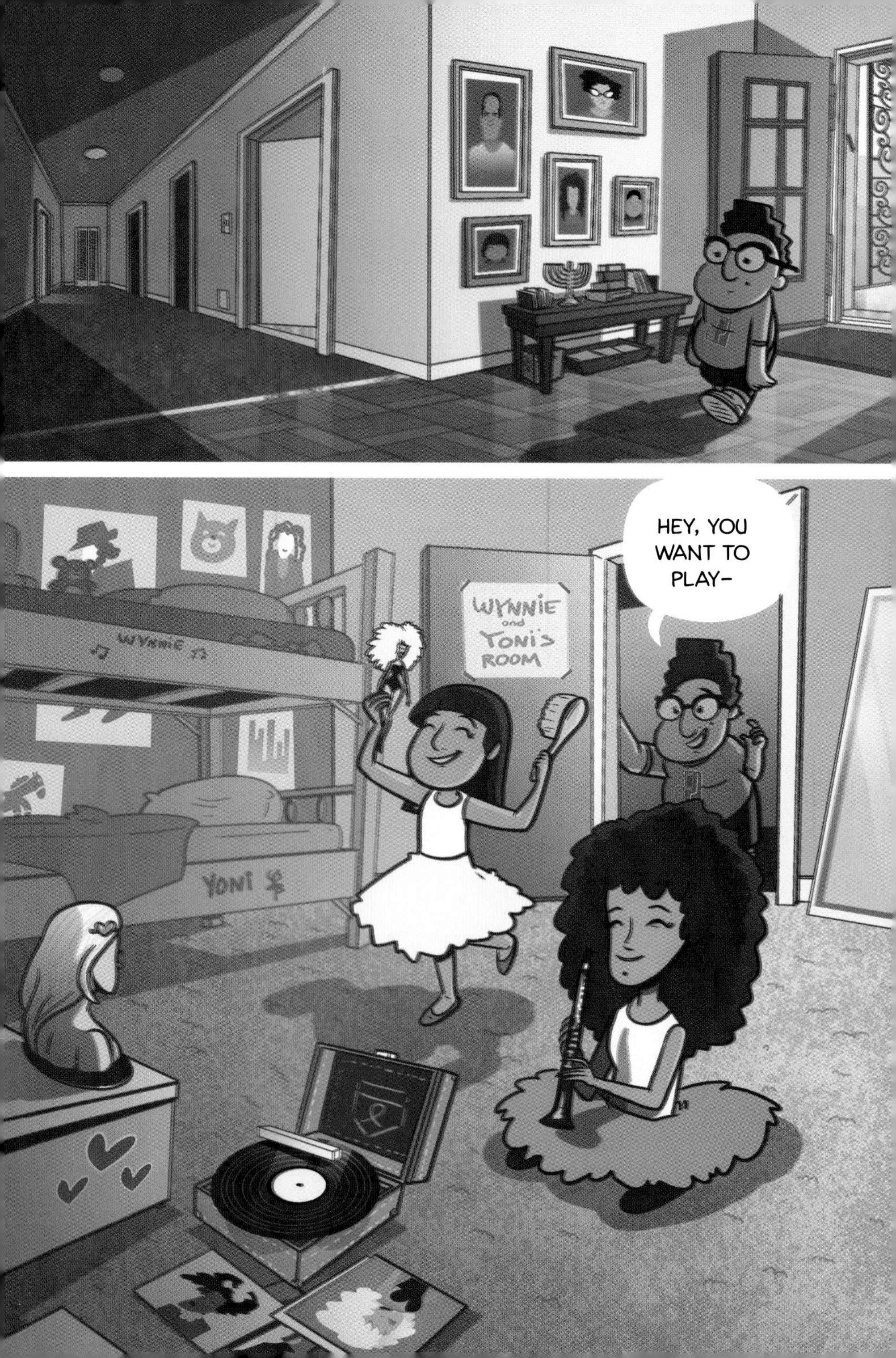

WYNNIE
and
YONI'S
ROOM
WYNNIE
YONI
HEY, YOU WANT TO PLAY-

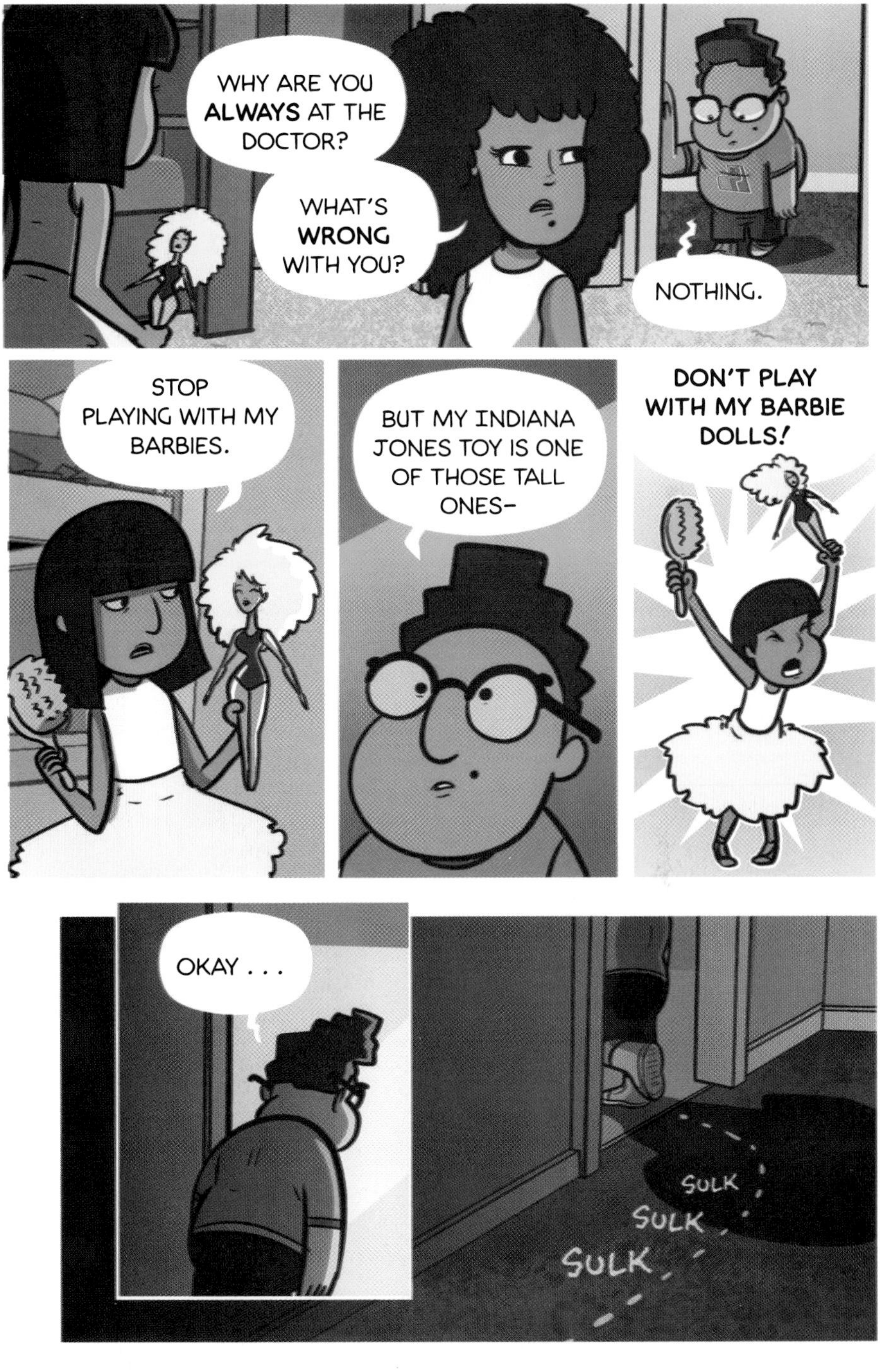
WHY ARE YOU **ALWAYS** AT THE DOCTOR?
WHAT'S **WRONG** WITH YOU?
NOTHING.
STOP PLAYING WITH MY BARBIES.
BUT MY INDIANA JONES TOY IS ONE OF THOSE TALL ONES–
DON'T PLAY WITH MY BARBIE DOLLS!
OKAY . . .
SULK
SULK
SULK

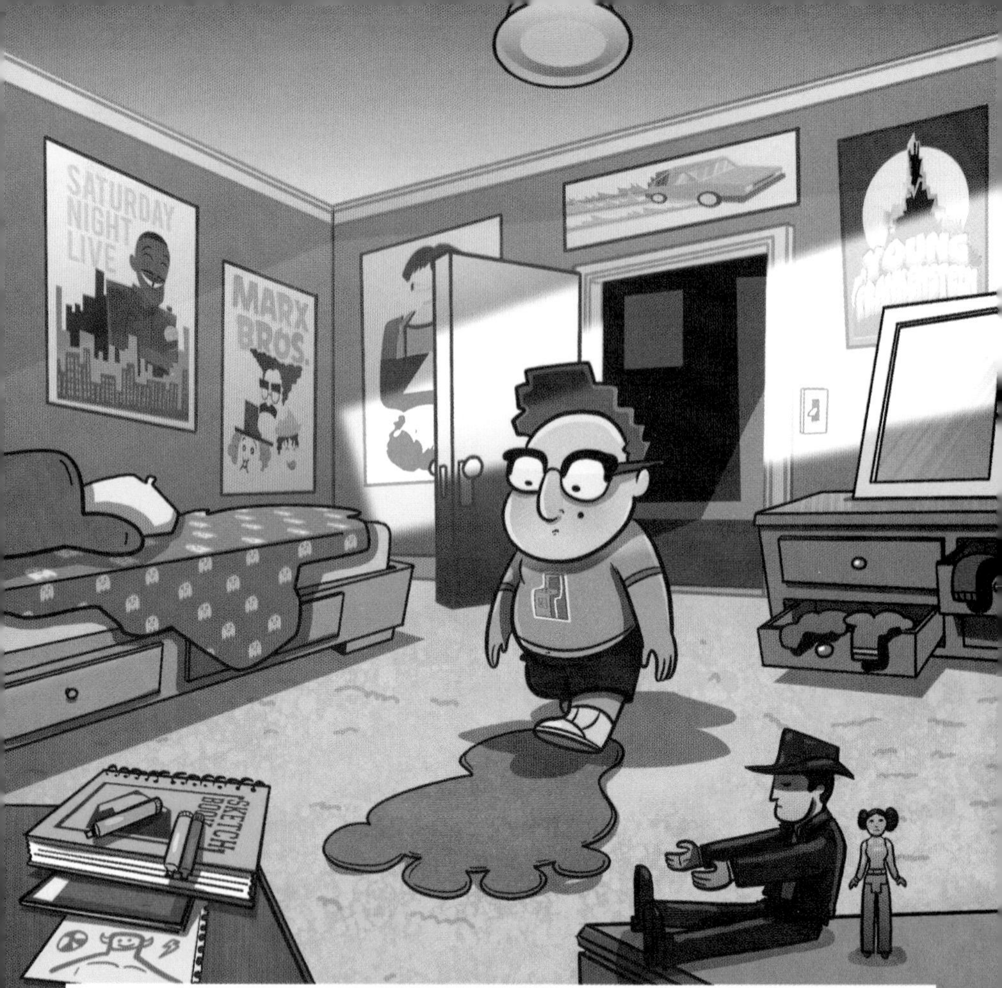
SATURDAY NIGHT LIVE
MARX BROS.
SKETCH BOOK

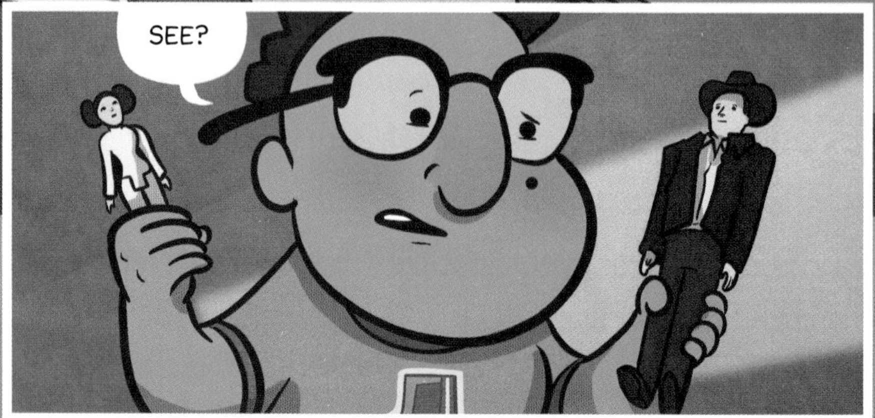
SEE?

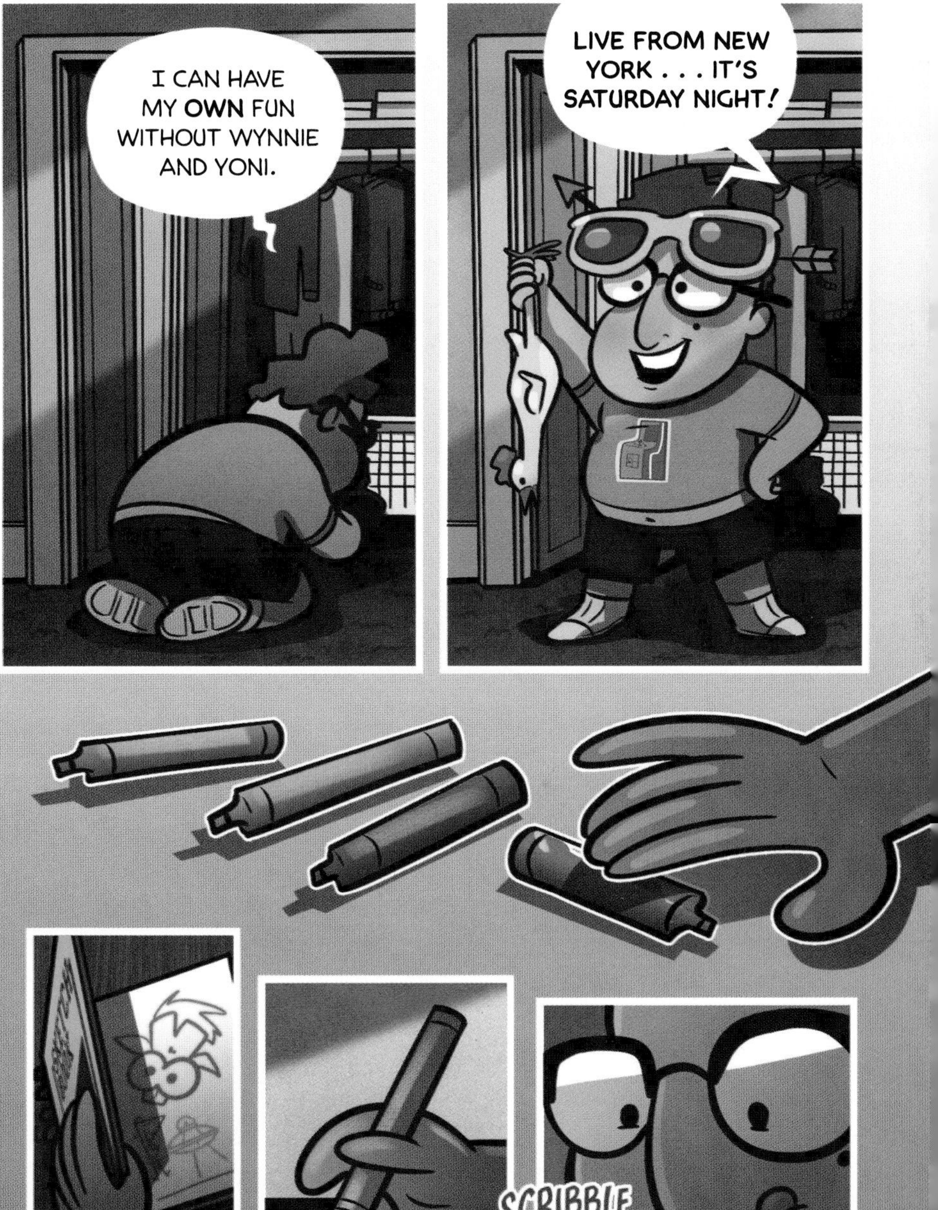
I CAN HAVE MY **OWN** FUN WITHOUT WYNNIE AND YONI.
LIVE FROM NEW YORK . . . IT'S SATURDAY NIGHT!
SCRIBBLE
SCRIBBLE
SCRIBBLE

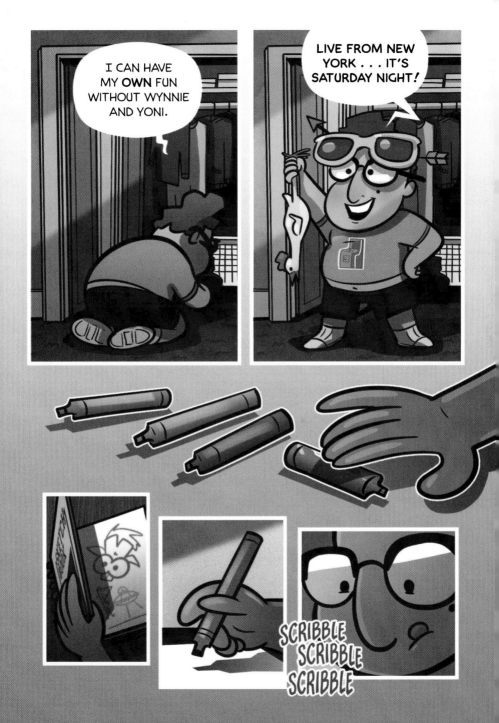

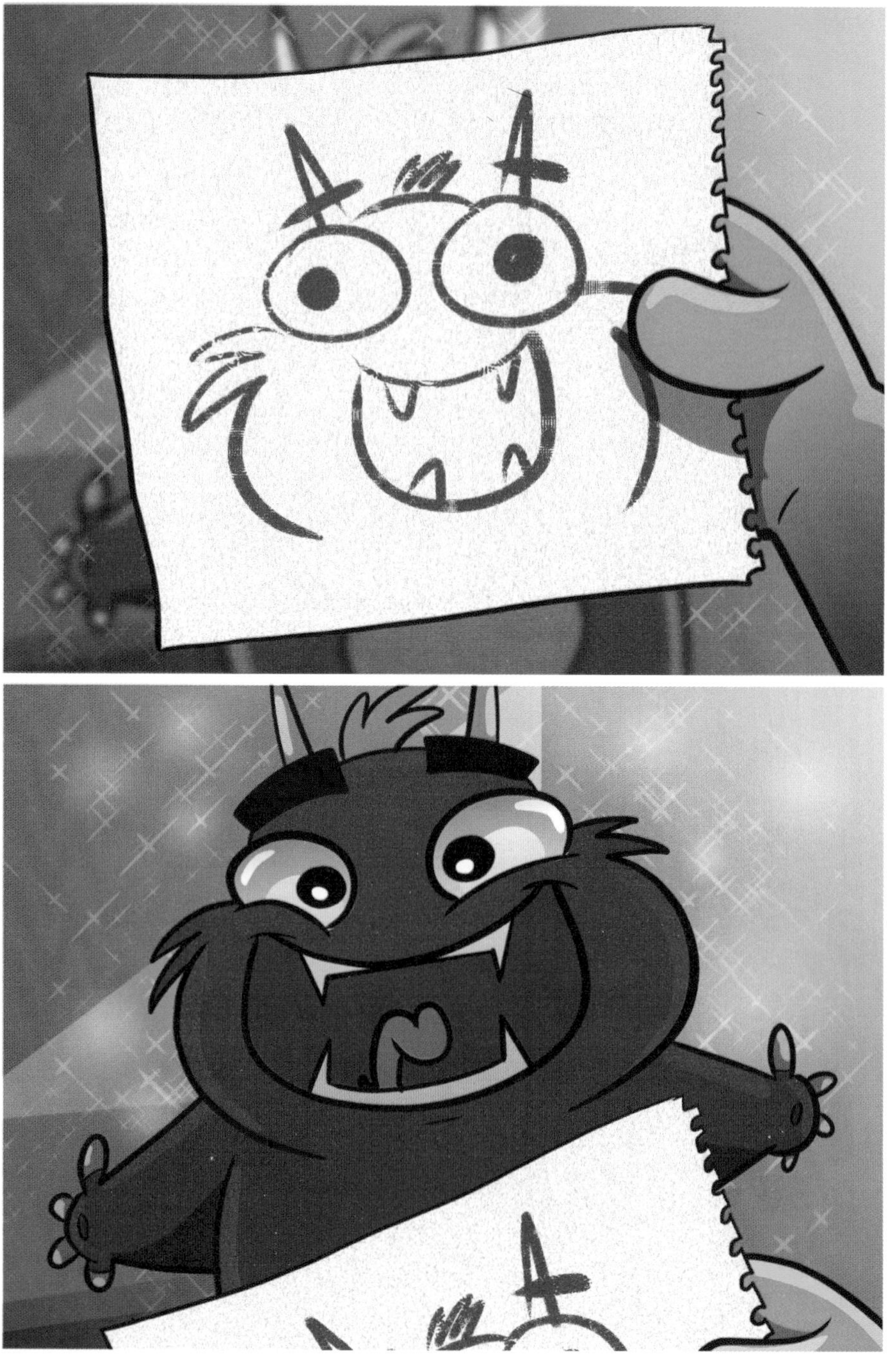

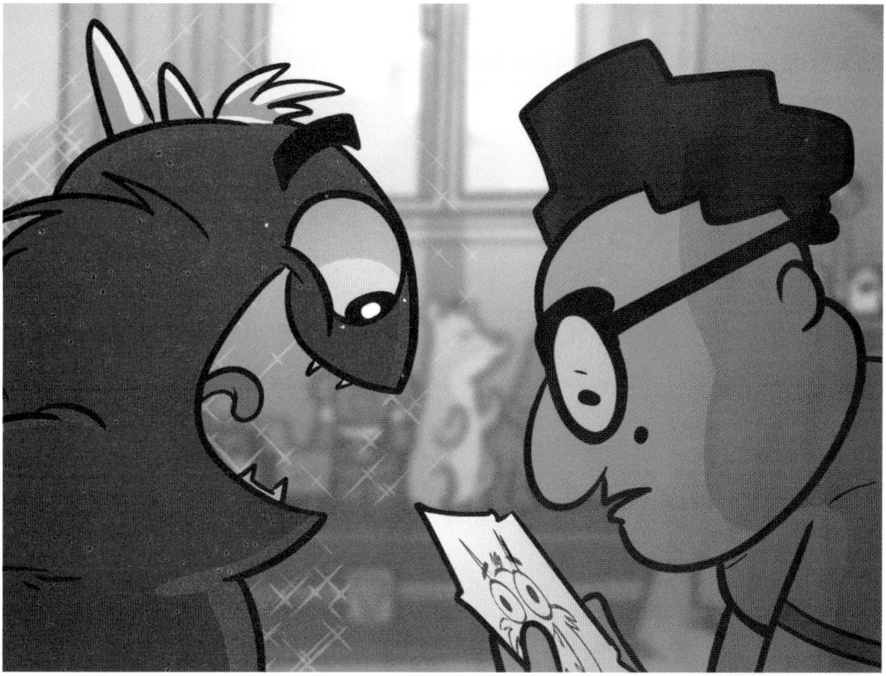

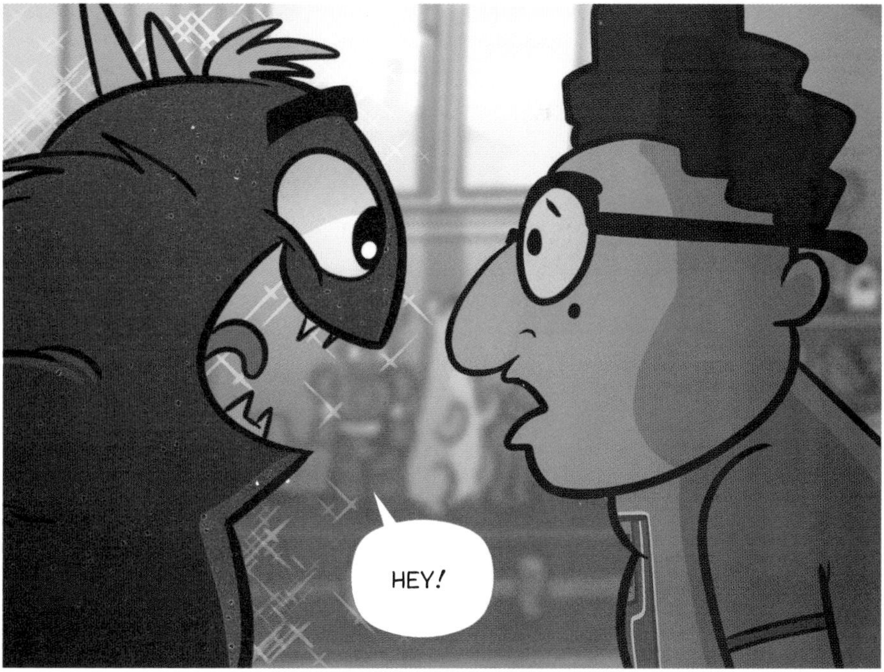
HEY!

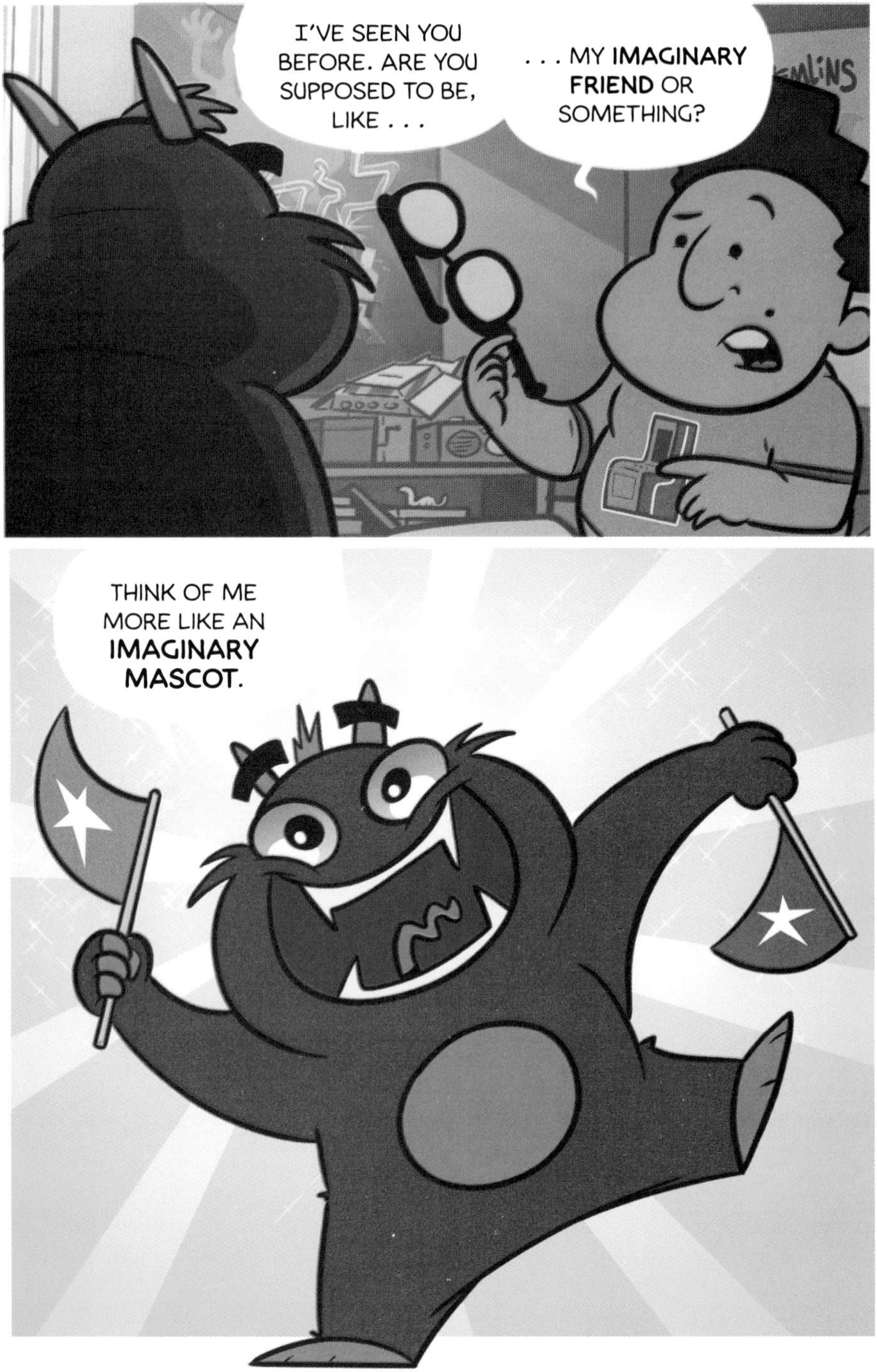
I'VE SEEN YOU BEFORE. ARE YOU SUPPOSED TO BE, LIKE . . .
. . . MY **IMAGINARY FRIEND** OR SOMETHING?
THINK OF ME MORE LIKE AN **IMAGINARY MASCOT.**

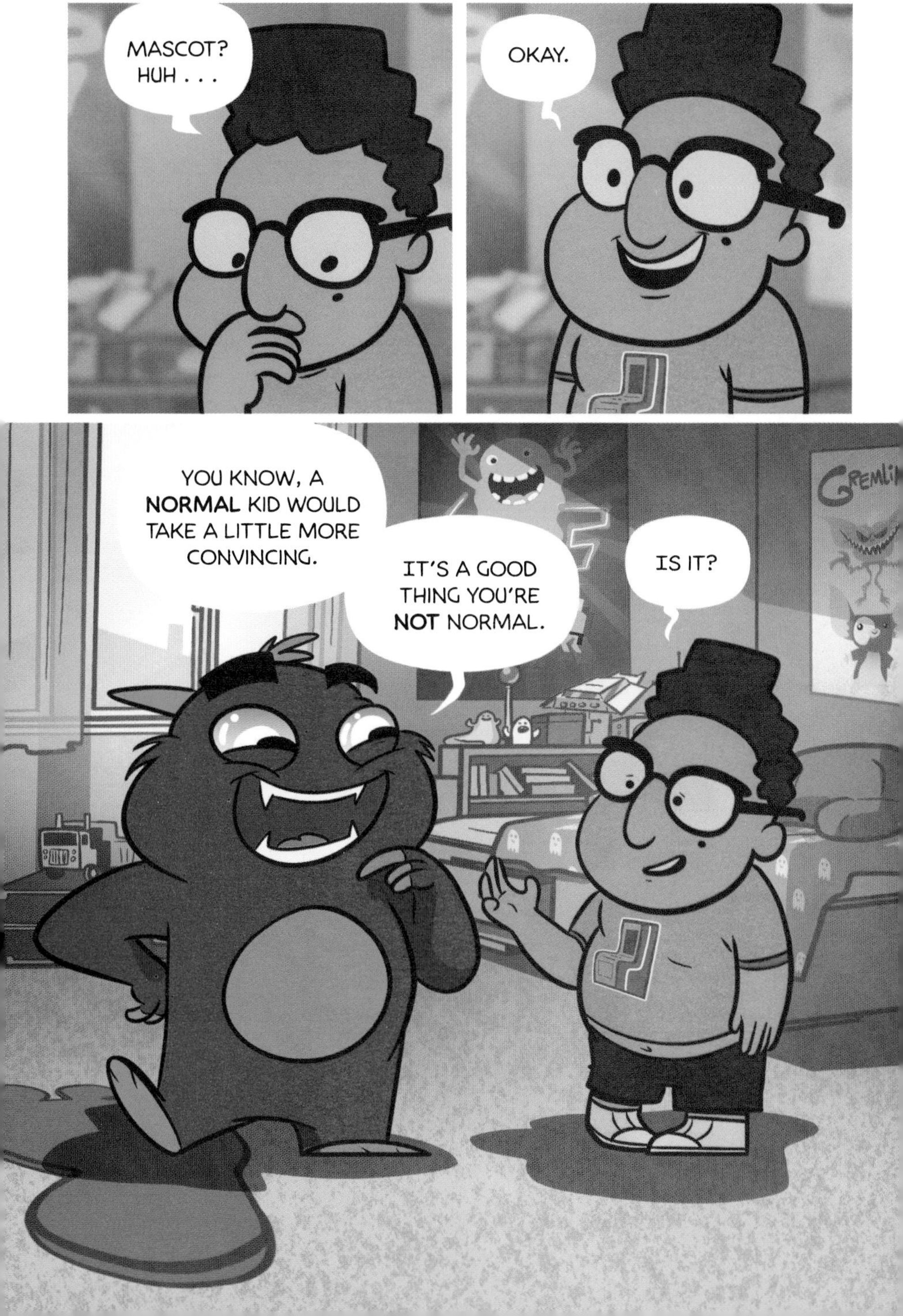
MASCOT? HUH . . .
OKAY.
YOU KNOW, A NORMAL KID WOULD TAKE A LITTLE MORE CONVINCING.
IT'S A GOOD THING YOU'RE NOT NORMAL.
IS IT?

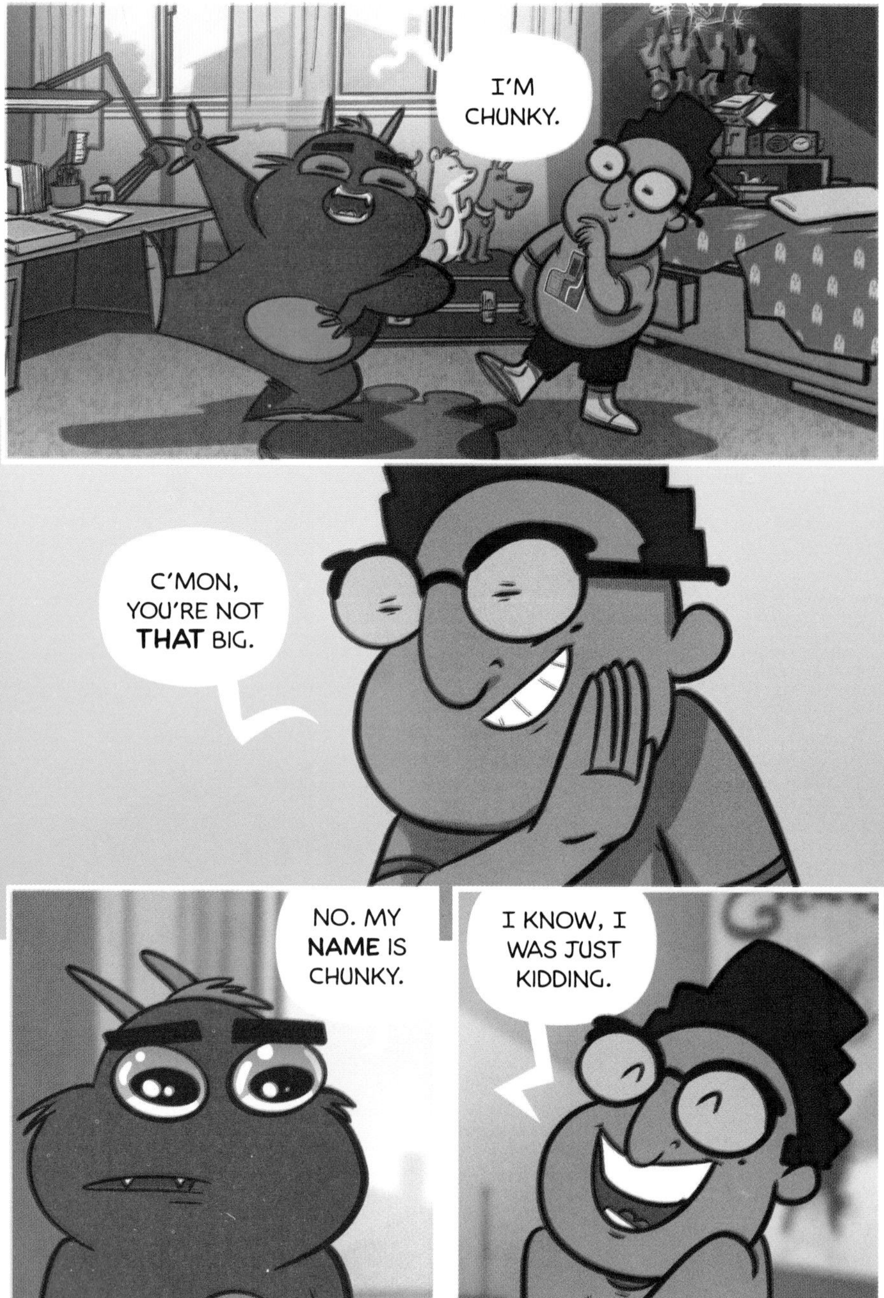
I'M CHUNKY.
C'MON, YOU'RE NOT **THAT** BIG.
NO. MY **NAME** IS CHUNKY.
I KNOW, I WAS JUST KIDDING.

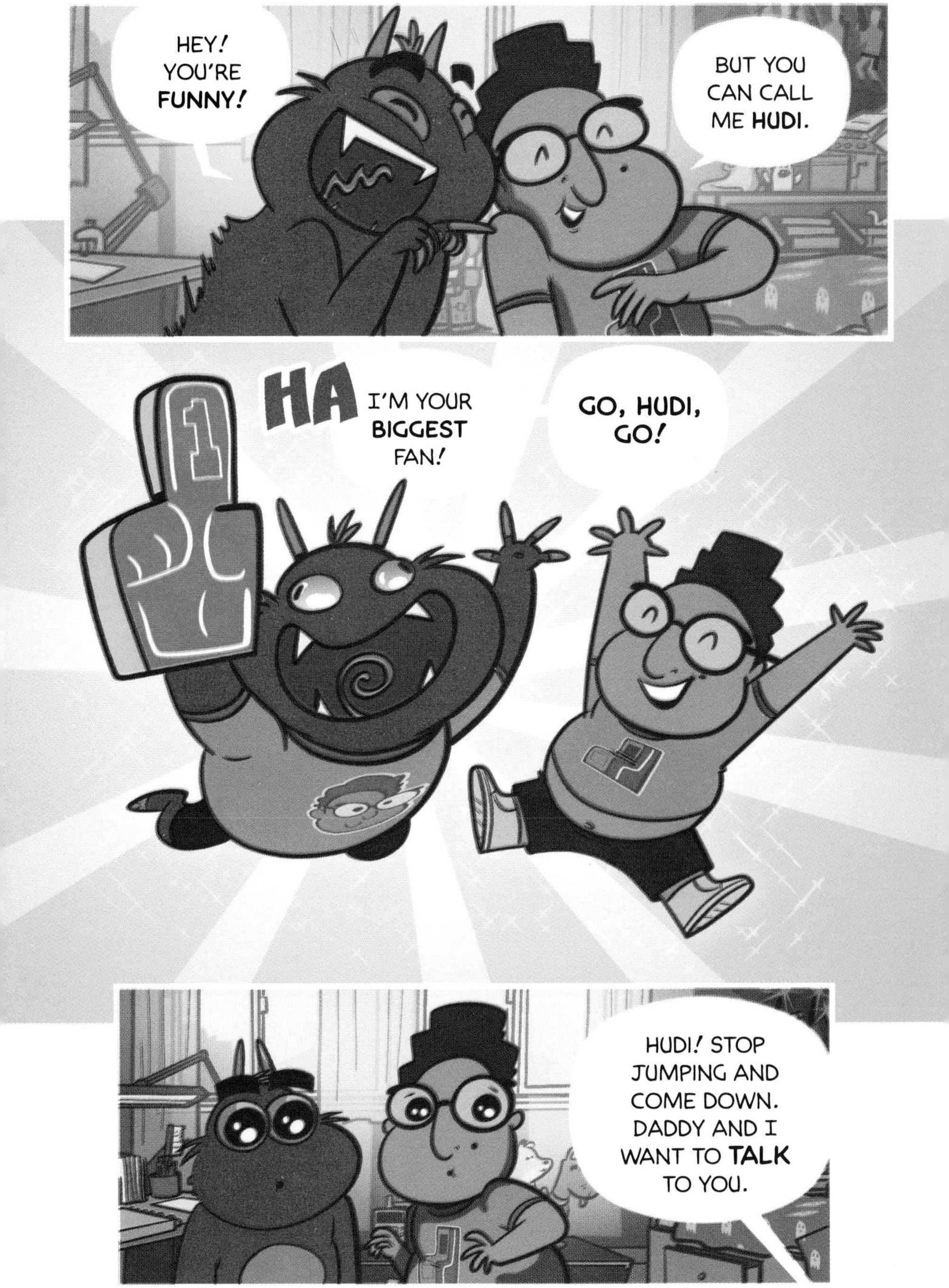
HEY! YOU'RE **FUNNY!**
BUT YOU CAN CALL ME **HUDI**.
HA
I'M YOUR **BIGGEST** FAN!
GO, HUDI, GO!
HUDI! STOP JUMPING AND COME DOWN. DADDY AND I WANT TO **TALK** TO YOU.

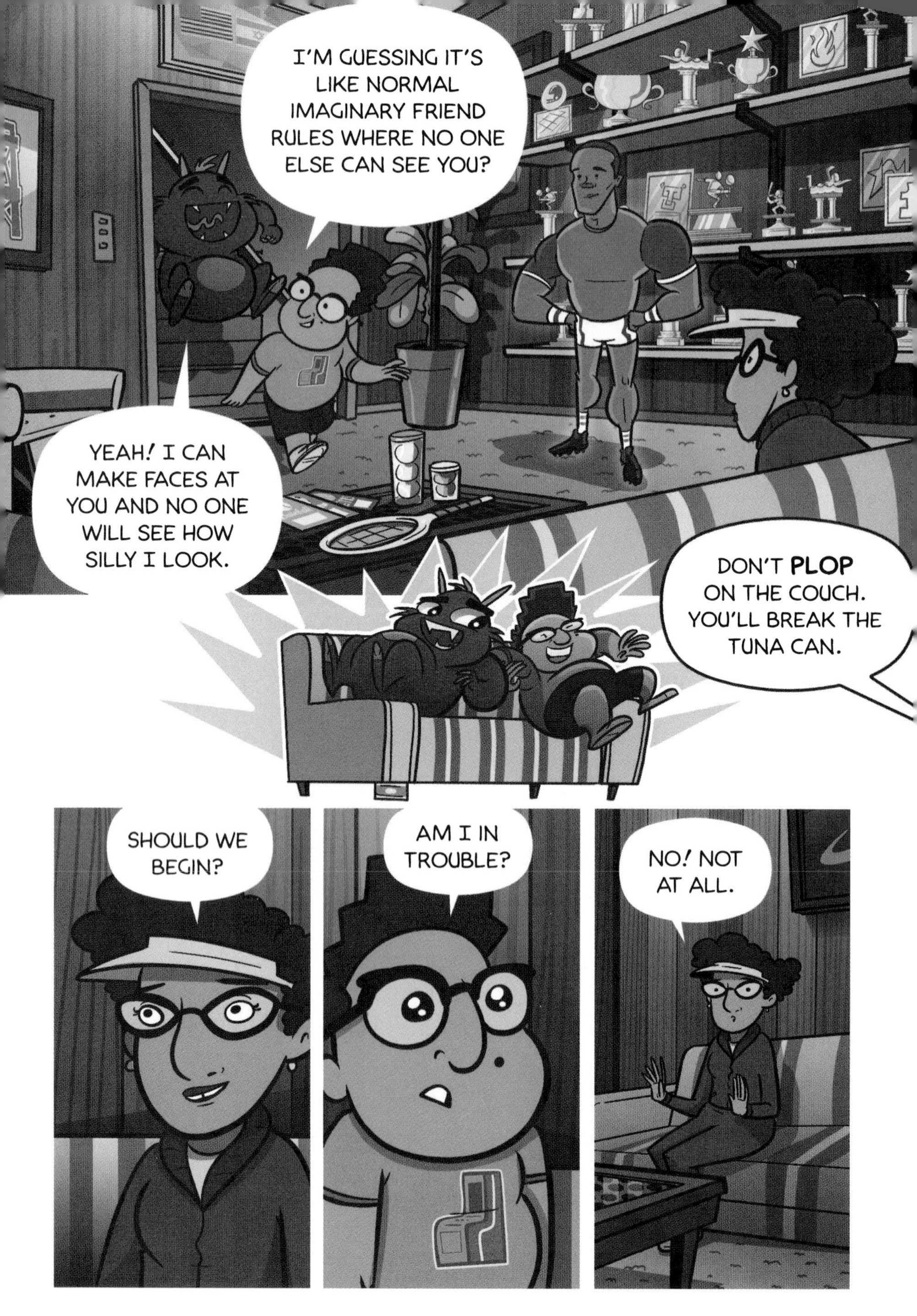
I'M GUESSING IT'S LIKE NORMAL IMAGINARY FRIEND RULES WHERE NO ONE ELSE CAN SEE YOU?
YEAH! I CAN MAKE FACES AT YOU AND NO ONE WILL SEE HOW SILLY I LOOK.
DON'T **PLOP** ON THE COUCH. YOU'LL BREAK THE TUNA CAN.
SHOULD WE BEGIN?
AM I IN TROUBLE?
NO! NOT AT ALL.

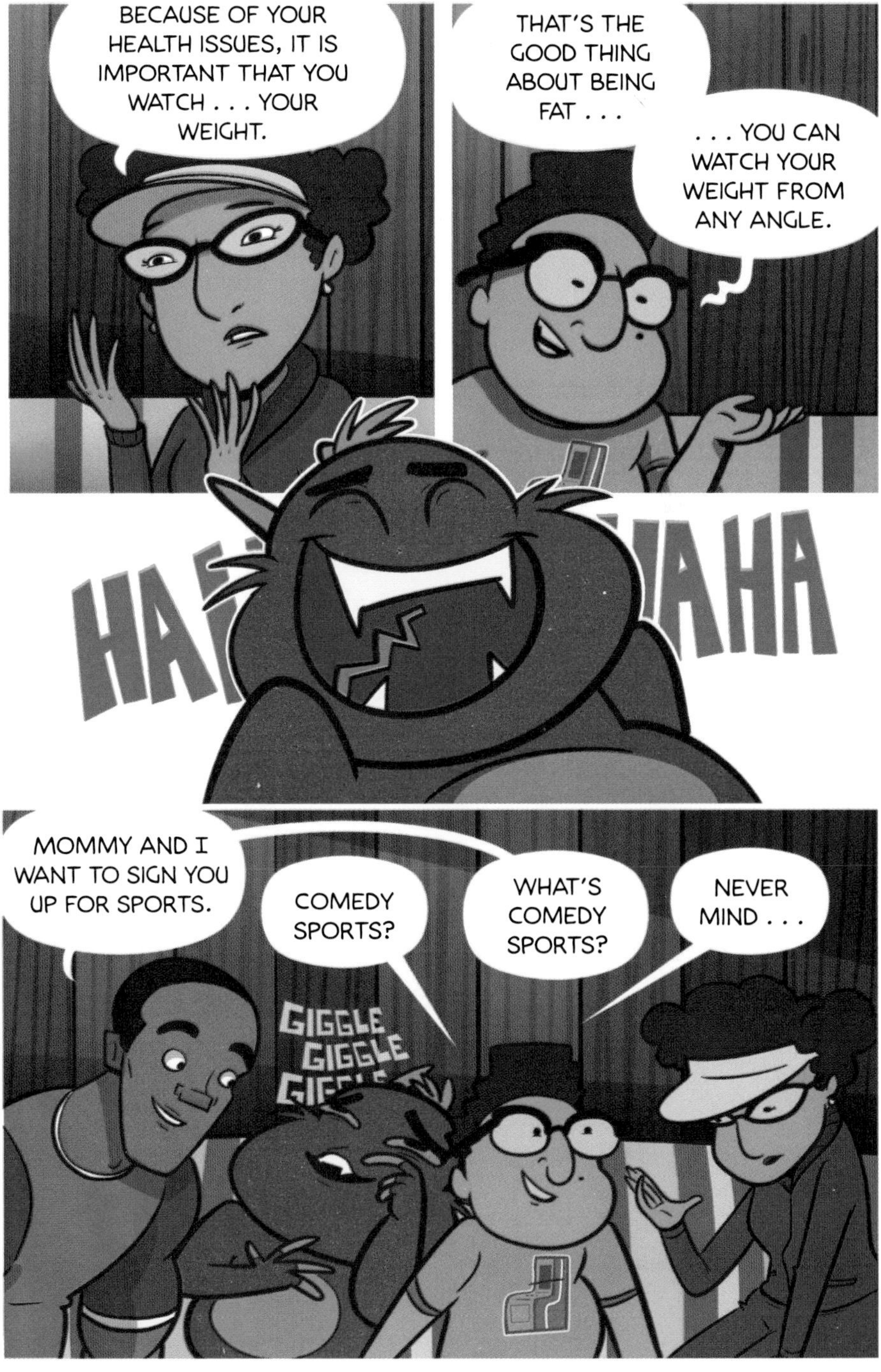
BECAUSE OF YOUR HEALTH ISSUES, IT IS IMPORTANT THAT YOU WATCH . . . YOUR WEIGHT.
THAT'S THE GOOD THING ABOUT BEING FAT . . .
. . . YOU CAN WATCH YOUR WEIGHT FROM ANY ANGLE.
HA
HAHA
MOMMY AND I WANT TO SIGN YOU UP FOR SPORTS.
COMEDY SPORTS?
WHAT'S COMEDY SPORTS?
NEVER MIND . . .
GIGGLE
GIGGLE

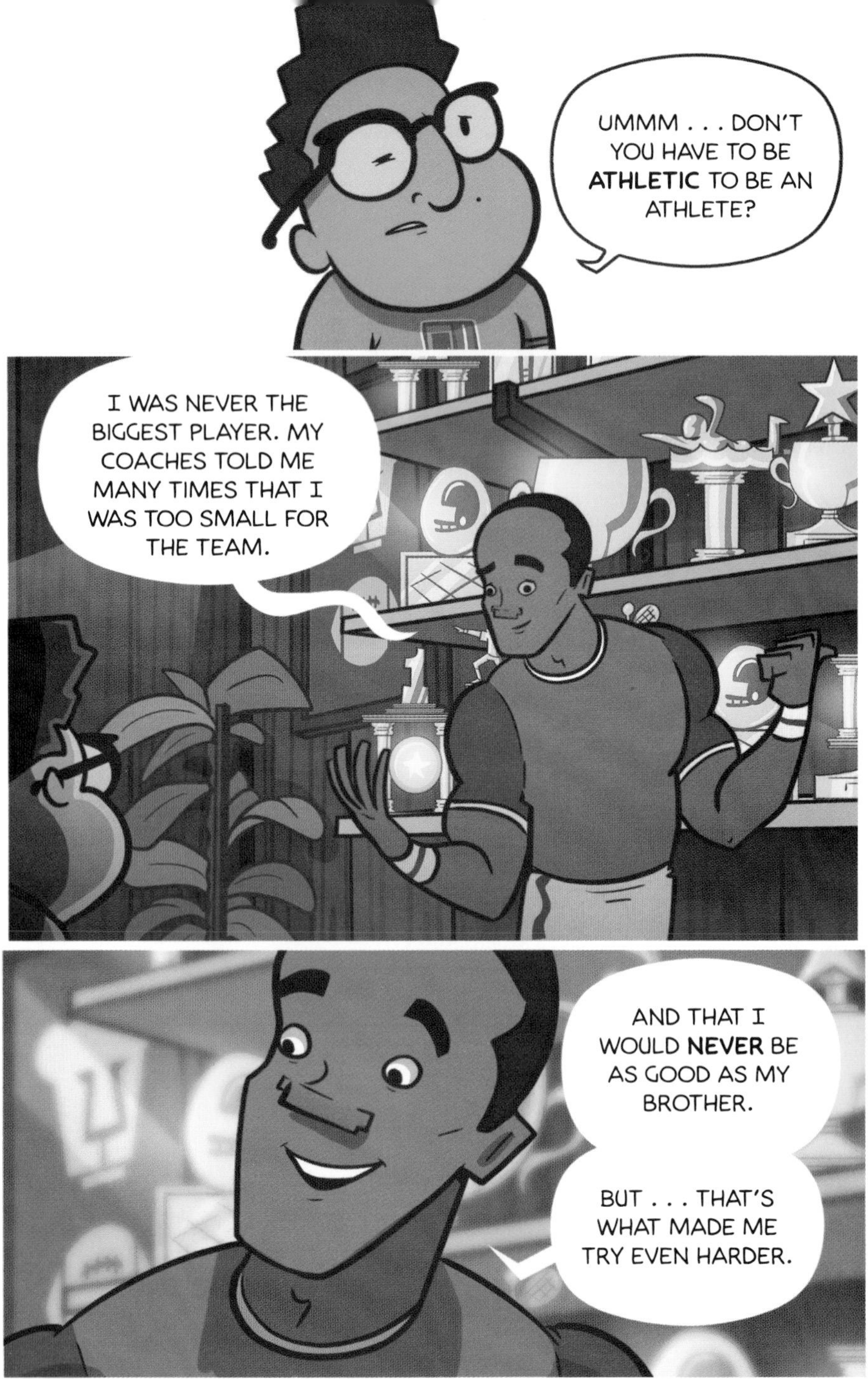
UMMM . . . DON'T YOU HAVE TO BE **ATHLETIC** TO BE AN ATHLETE?
I WAS NEVER THE BIGGEST PLAYER. MY COACHES TOLD ME MANY TIMES THAT I WAS TOO SMALL FOR THE TEAM.
AND THAT I WOULD **NEVER** BE AS GOOD AS MY BROTHER.
BUT . . . THAT'S WHAT MADE ME TRY EVEN HARDER.

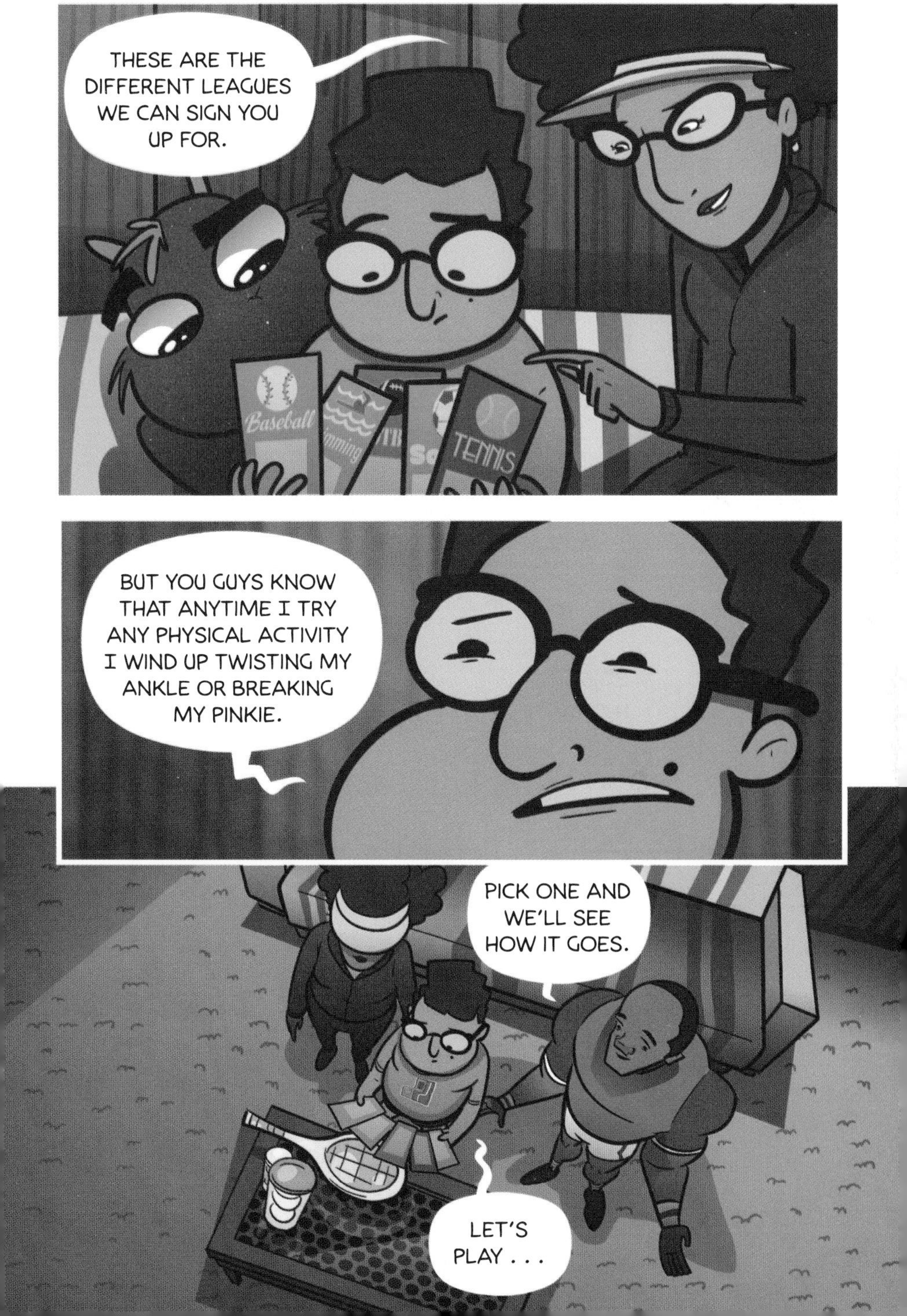
THESE ARE THE DIFFERENT LEAGUES WE CAN SIGN YOU UP FOR.
Baseball
TENNIS
BUT YOU GUYS KNOW THAT ANYTIME I TRY ANY PHYSICAL ACTIVITY I WIND UP TWISTING MY ANKLE OR BREAKING MY PINKIE.
PICK ONE AND WE'LL SEE HOW IT GOES.
LET'S PLAY . . .

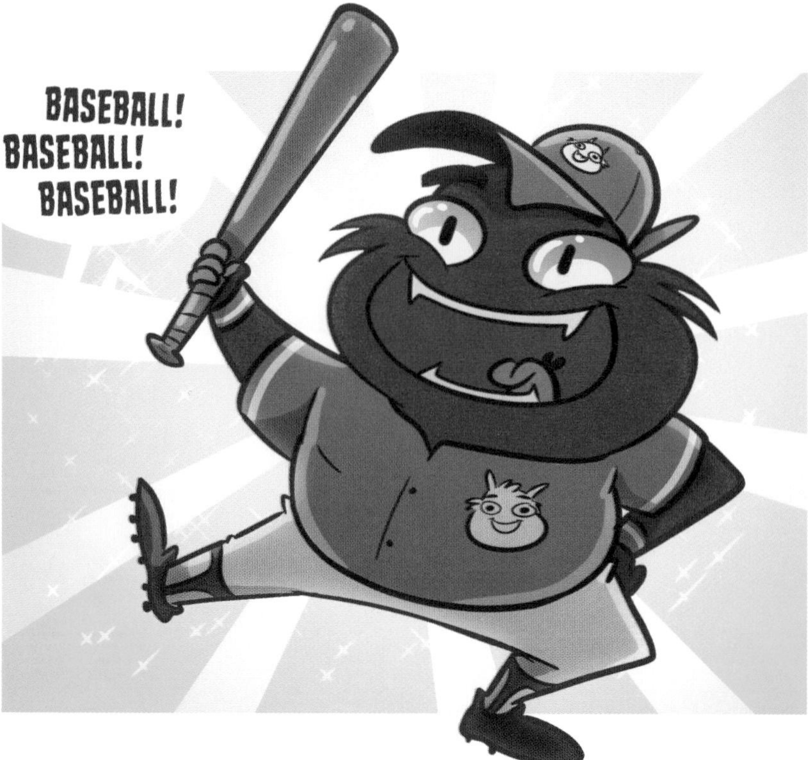
BASEBALL! BASEBALL! BASEBALL!

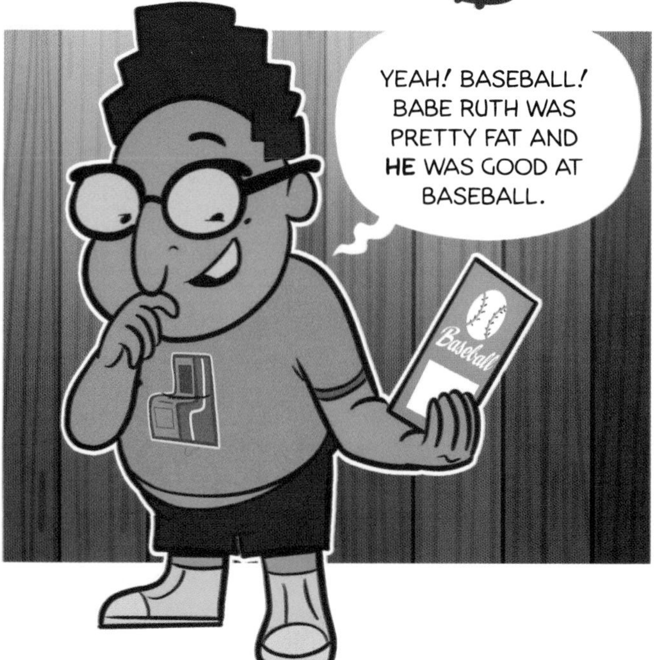
YEAH! BASEBALL! BABE RUTH WAS PRETTY FAT AND **HE** WAS GOOD AT BASEBALL.
Baseball

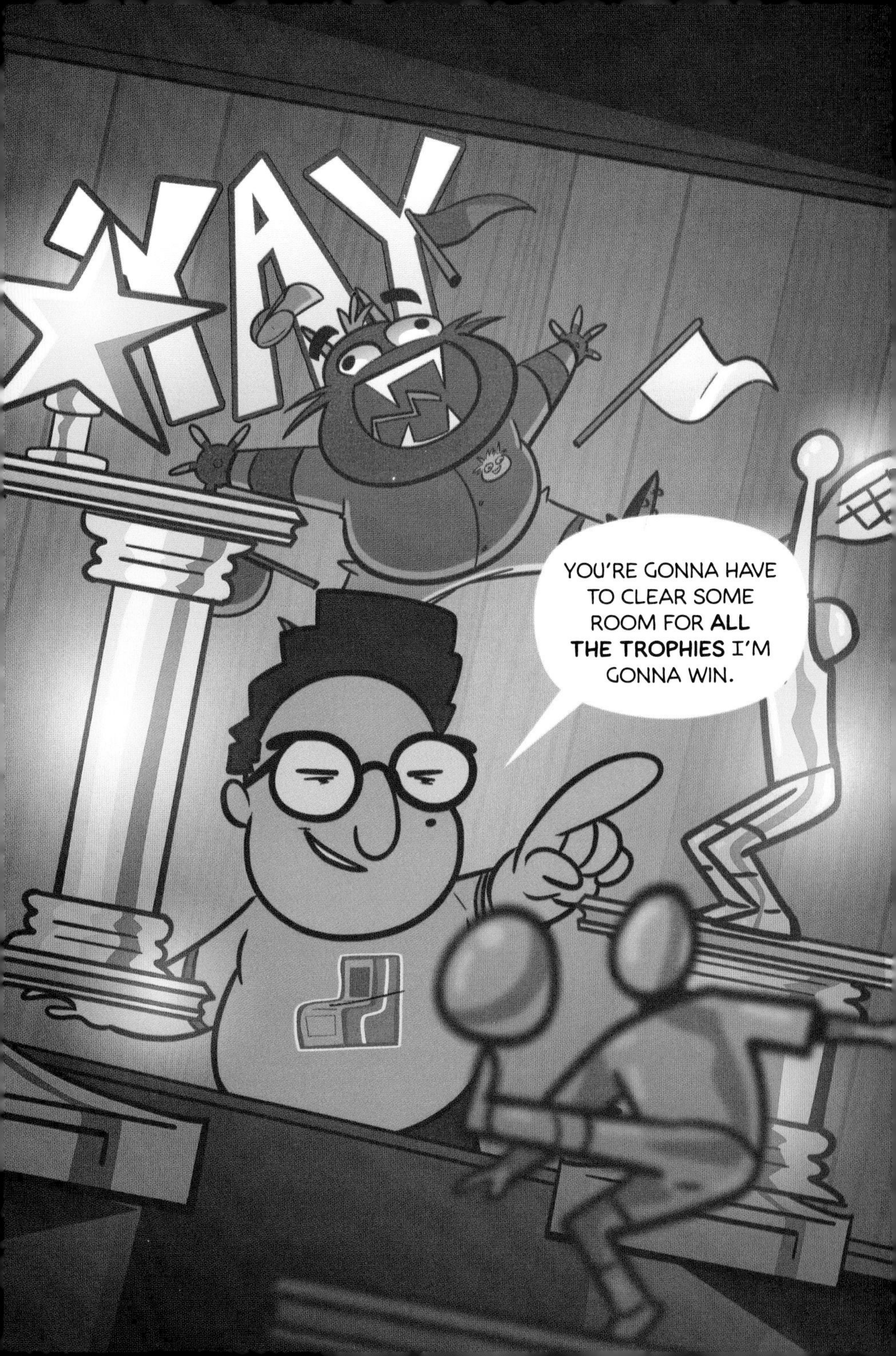
YAY
YOU'RE GONNA HAVE TO CLEAR SOME ROOM FOR **ALL THE TROPHIES** I'M GONNA WIN.

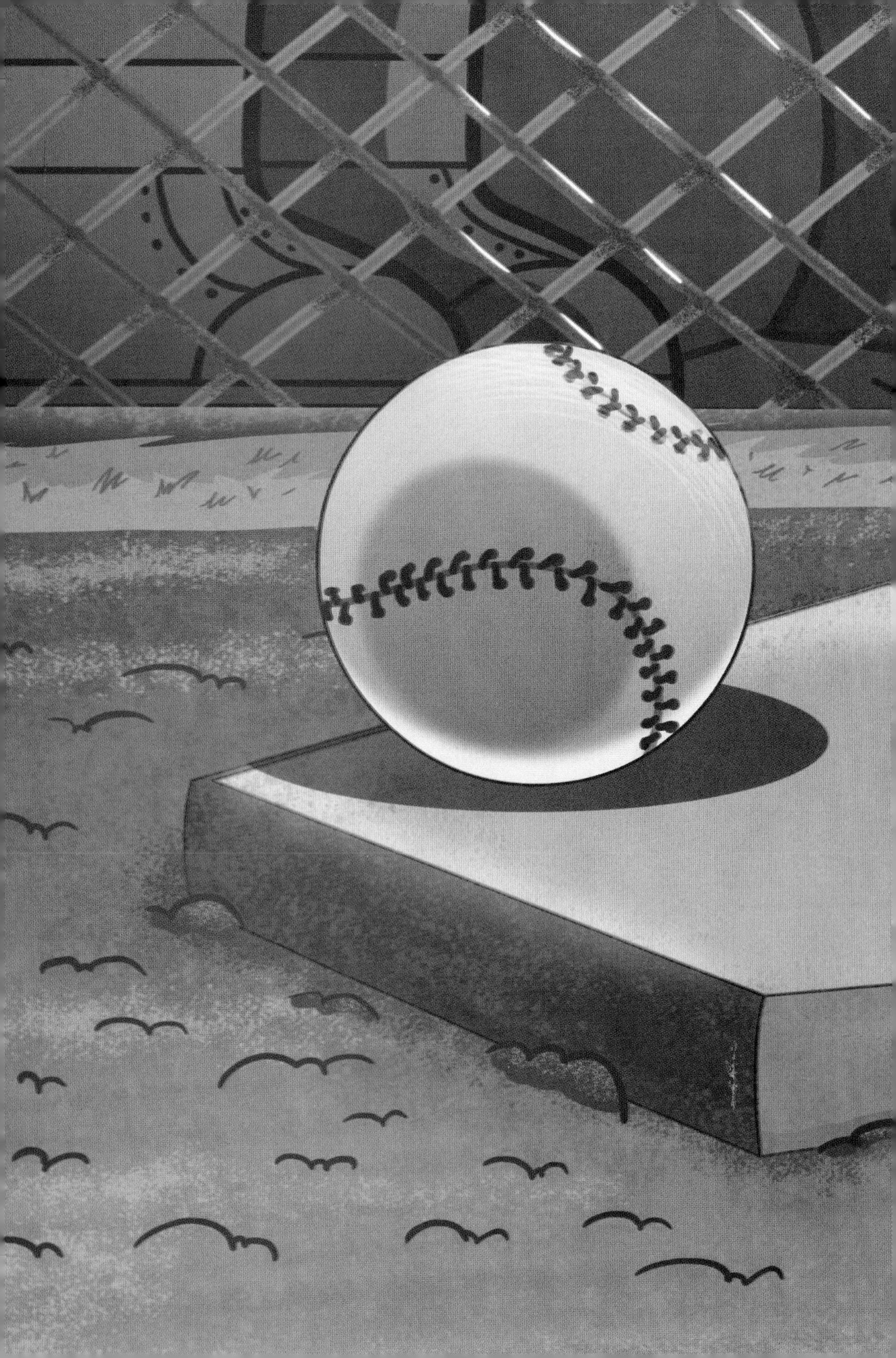

CHAPTER TWO
Baseball

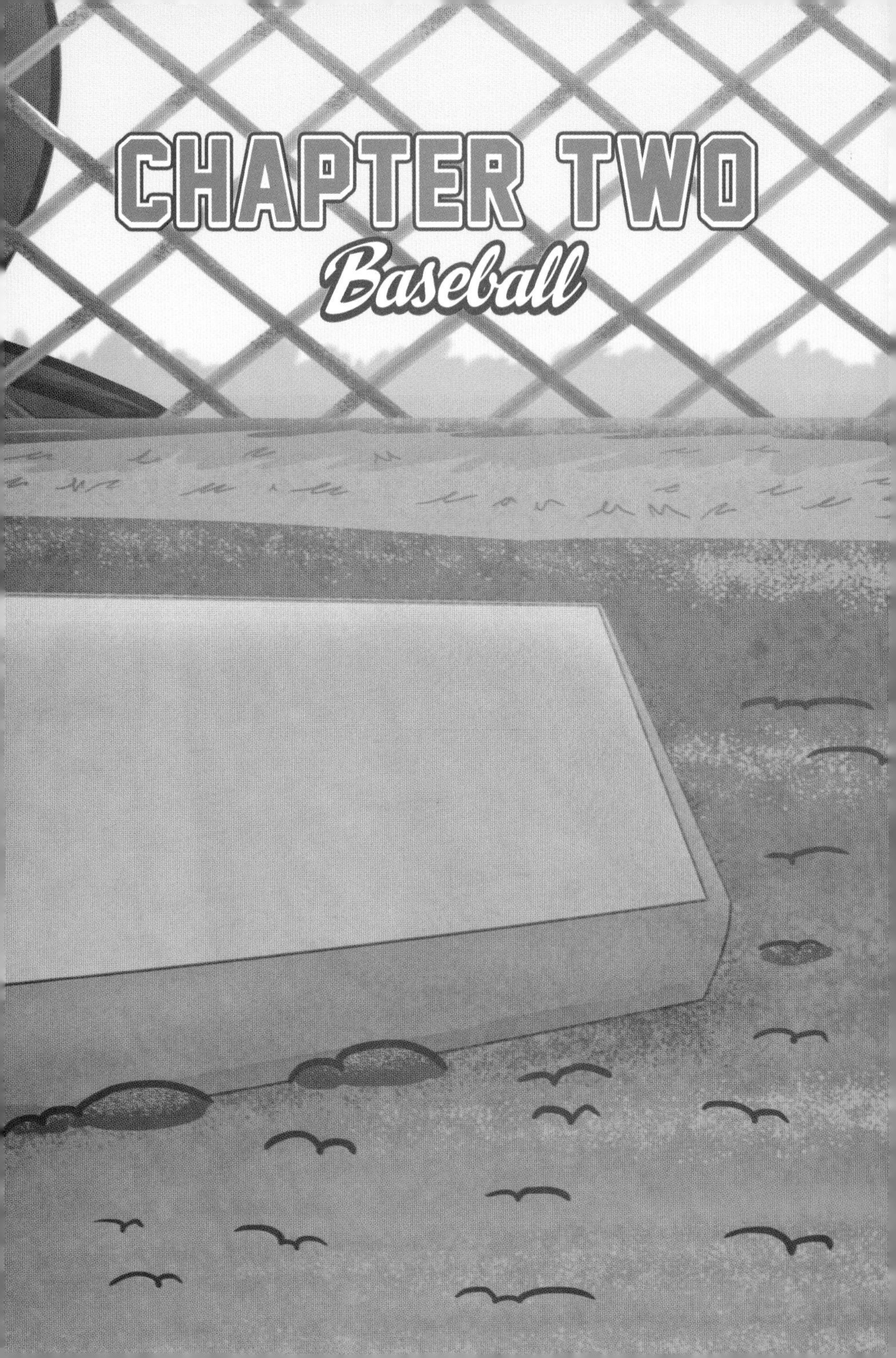

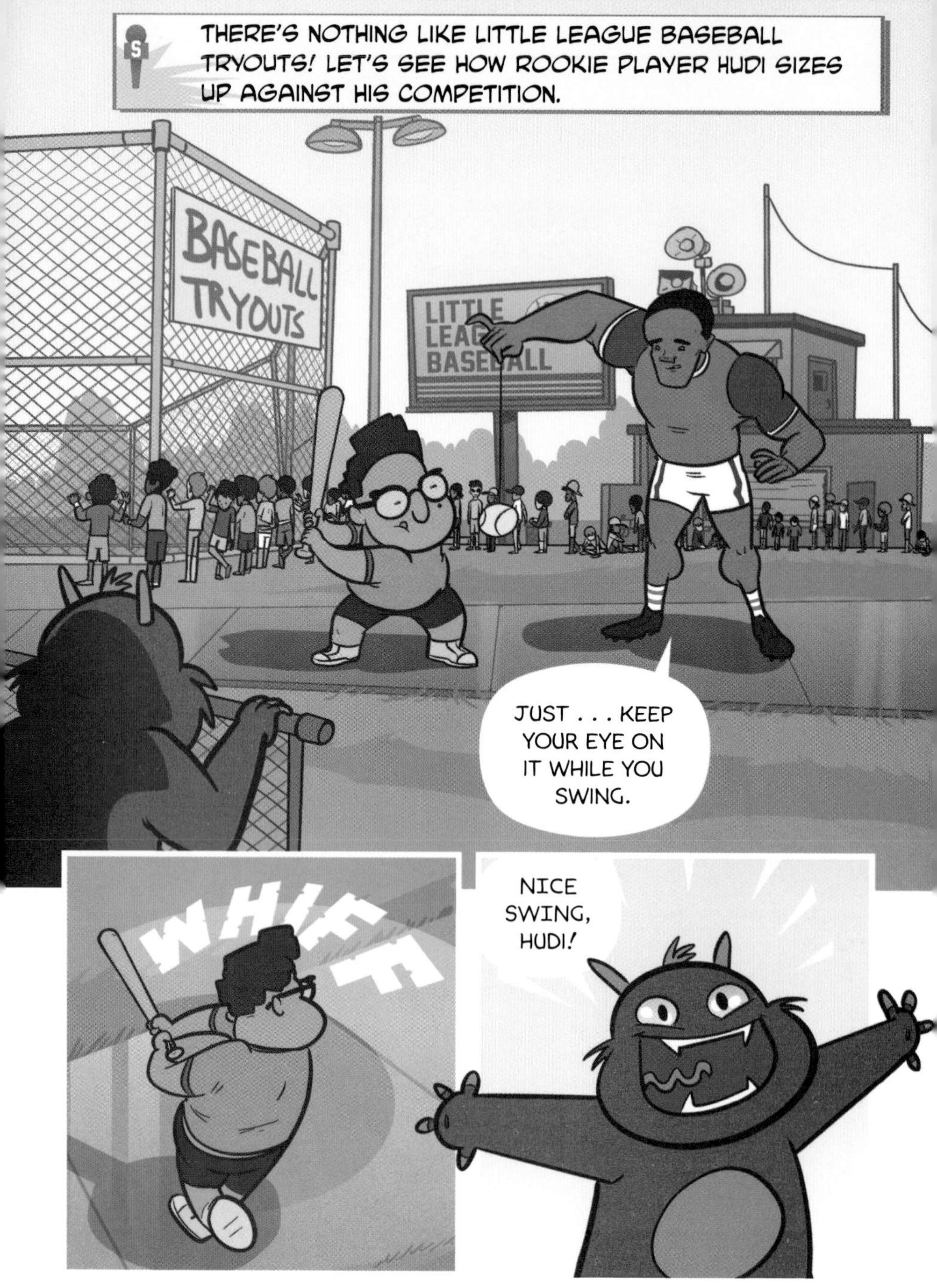
THERE'S NOTHING LIKE LITTLE LEAGUE BASEBALL TRYOUTS! LET'S SEE HOW ROOKIE PLAYER HUDI SIZES UP AGAINST HIS COMPETITION.
BASEBALL TRYOUTS
LITTLE LEAGUE BASEBALL
JUST . . . KEEP YOUR EYE ON IT WHILE YOU SWING.
WHIFF
NICE SWING, HUDI!

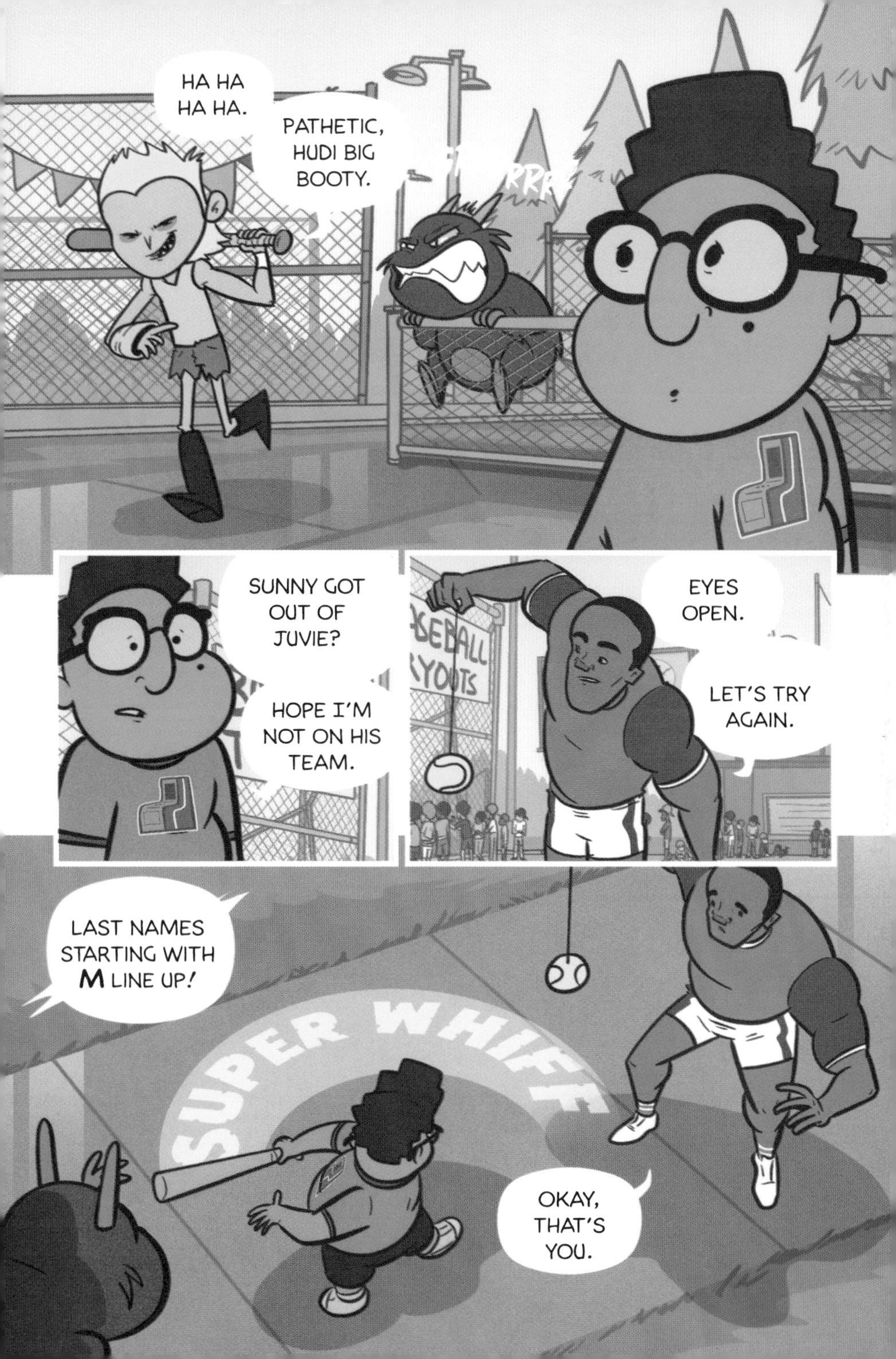
HA HA
HA HA.
PATHETIC, HUDI BIG BOOTY.
SUNNY GOT OUT OF JUVIE?
HOPE I'M NOT ON HIS TEAM.
EYES OPEN.
LET'S TRY AGAIN.
LAST NAMES STARTING WITH M LINE UP!
SUPER WHIFF
OKAY, THAT'S YOU.

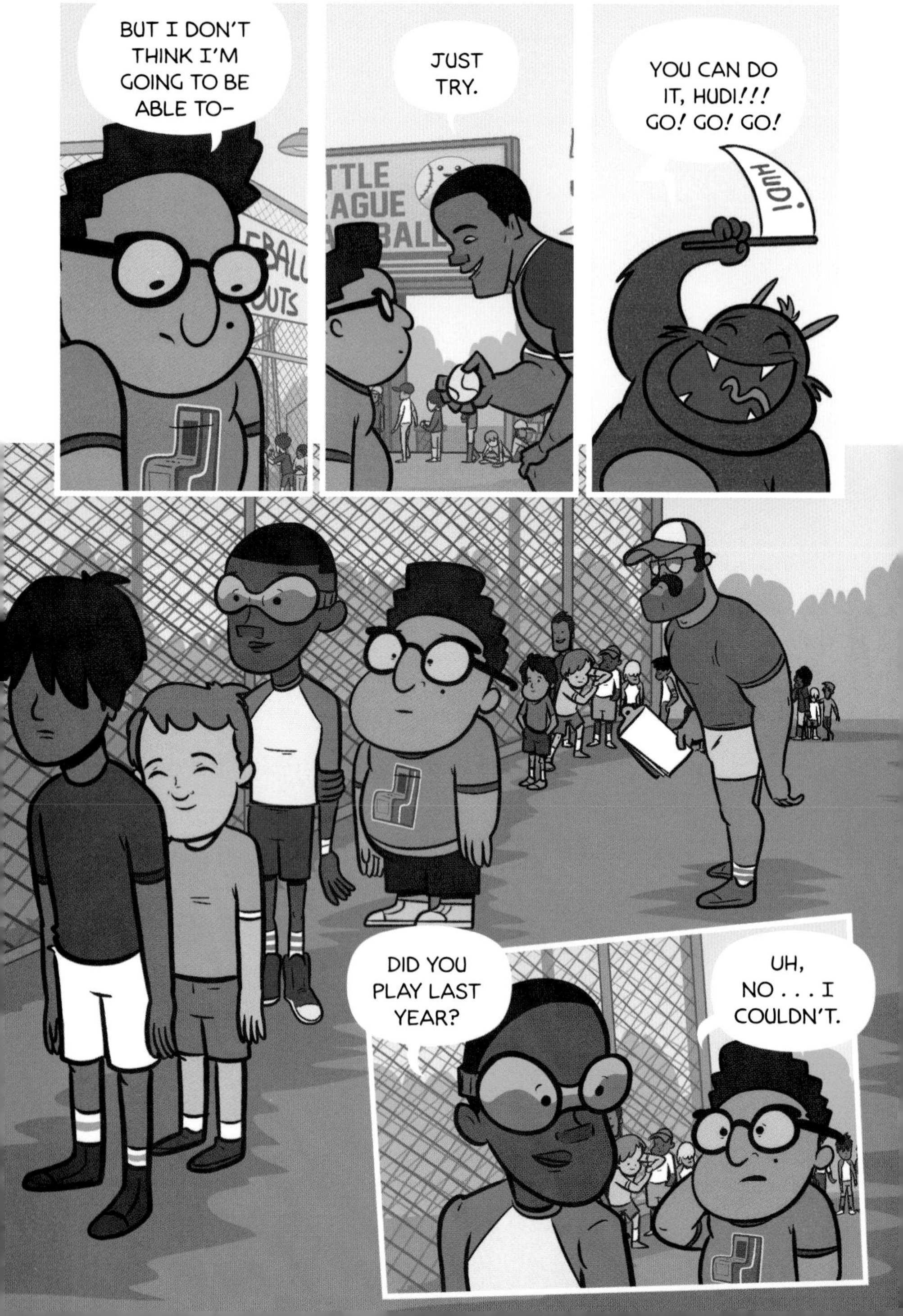
BUT I DON'T THINK I'M GOING TO BE ABLE TO–
JUST TRY.
YOU CAN DO IT, HUDI!!! GO! GO! GO!
HUDI
DID YOU PLAY LAST YEAR?
UH, NO . . . I COULDN'T.

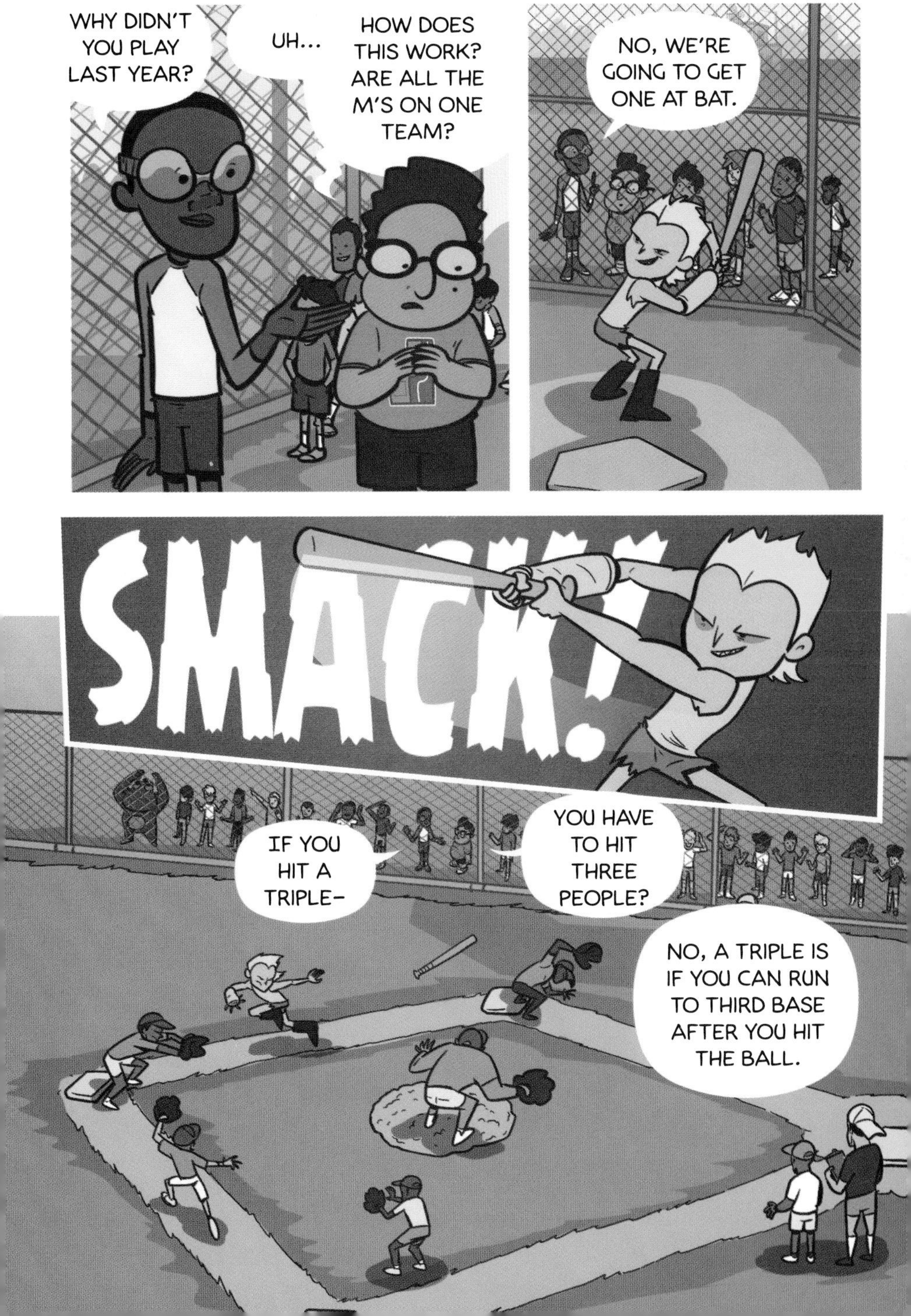
WHY DIDN'T YOU PLAY LAST YEAR?
UH...
HOW DOES THIS WORK? ARE ALL THE M'S ON ONE TEAM?
NO, WE'RE GOING TO GET ONE AT BAT.
SMACK!
IF YOU HIT A TRIPLE–
YOU HAVE TO HIT THREE PEOPLE?
NO, A TRIPLE IS IF YOU CAN RUN TO THIRD BASE AFTER YOU HIT THE BALL.

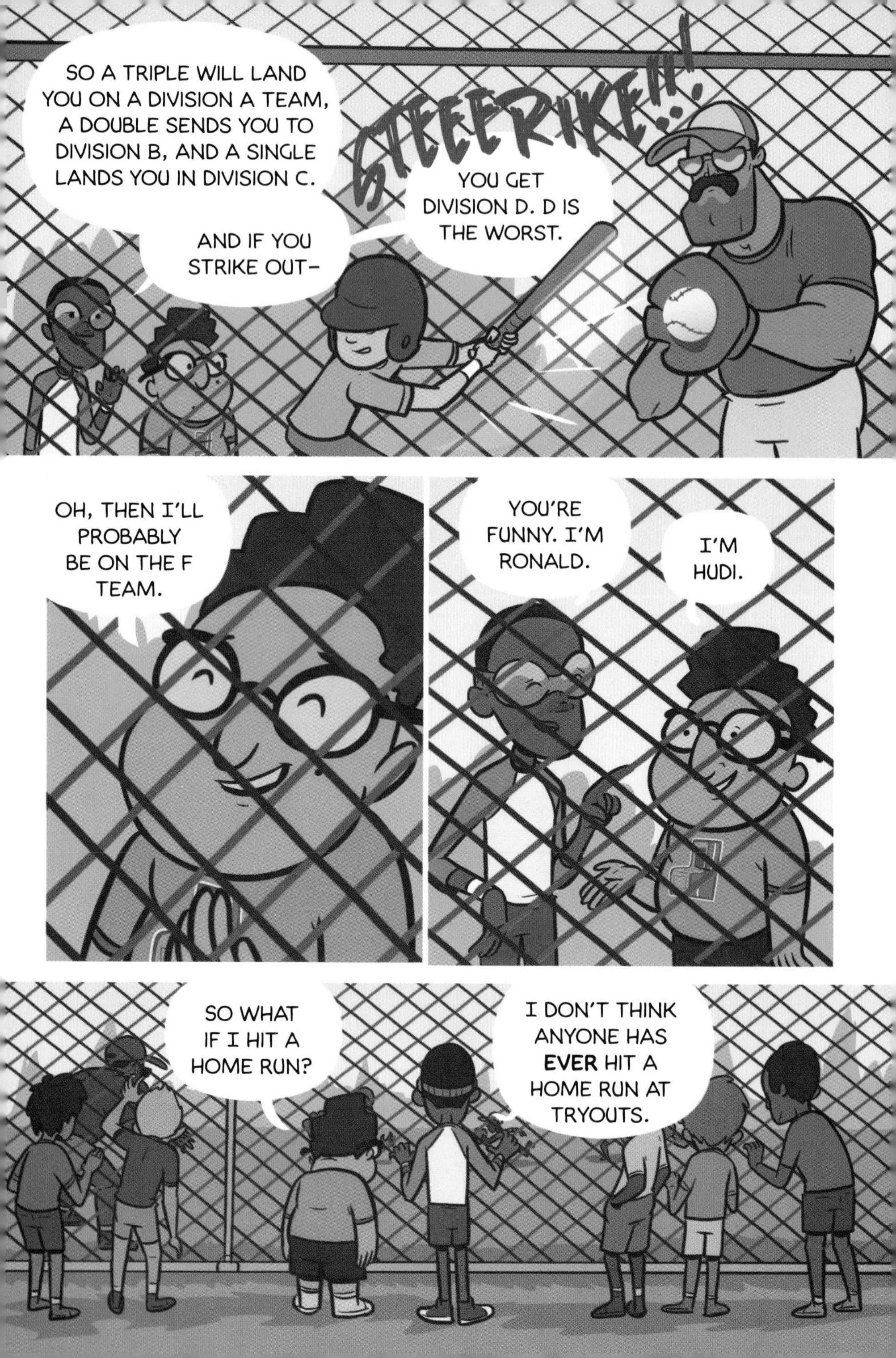
SO A TRIPLE WILL LAND YOU ON A DIVISION A TEAM, A DOUBLE SENDS YOU TO DIVISION B, AND A SINGLE LANDS YOU IN DIVISION C.
AND IF YOU STRIKE OUT–
YOU GET DIVISION D. D IS THE WORST.
STEEERIKE!!!
OH, THEN I'LL PROBABLY BE ON THE F TEAM.
YOU'RE FUNNY. I'M RONALD.
I'M HUDI.
SO WHAT IF I HIT A HOME RUN?
I DON'T THINK ANYONE HAS **EVER** HIT A HOME RUN AT TRYOUTS.

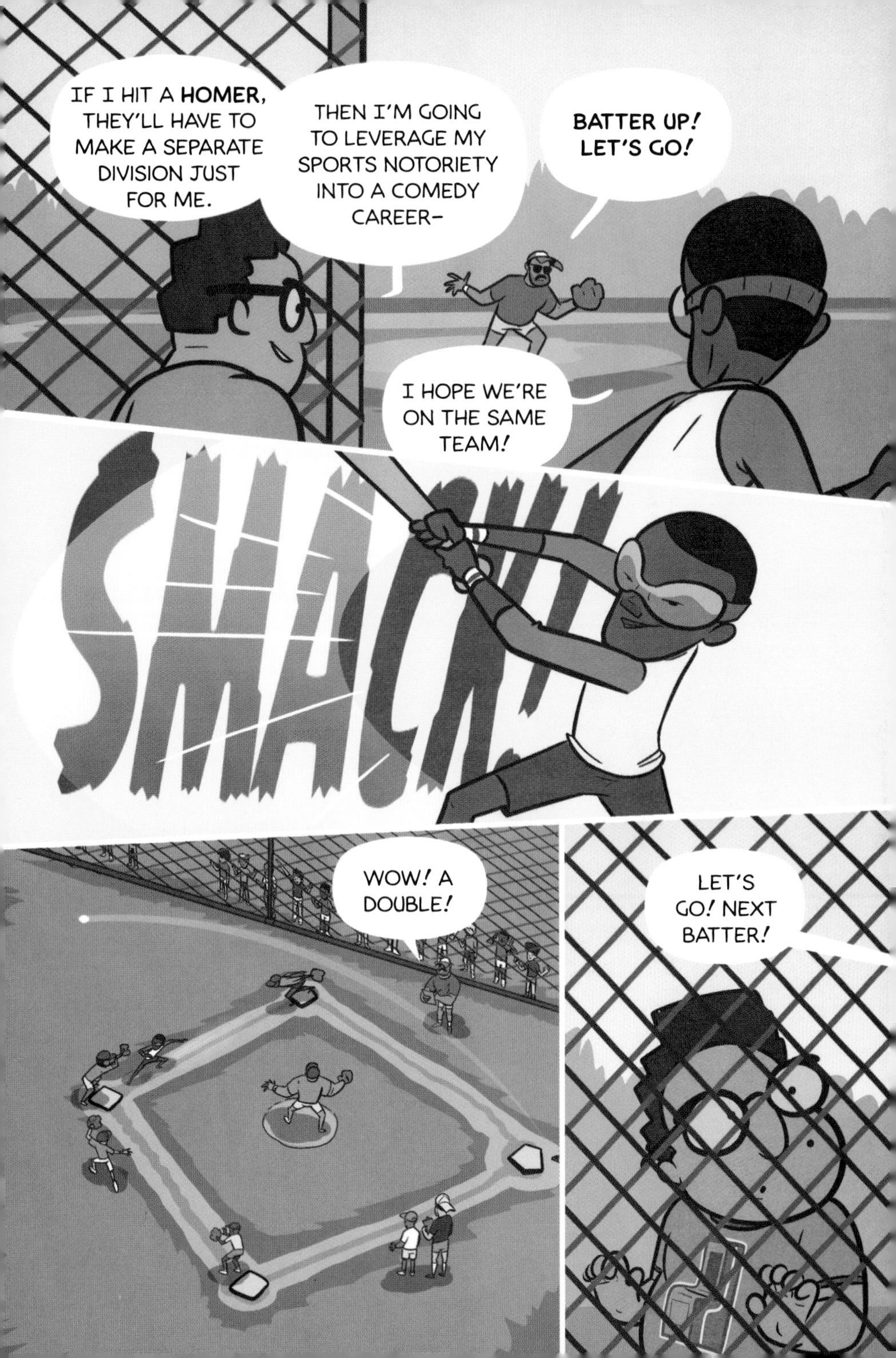
IF I HIT A **HOMER**, THEY'LL HAVE TO MAKE A SEPARATE DIVISION JUST FOR ME.
THEN I'M GOING TO LEVERAGE MY SPORTS NOTORIETY INTO A COMEDY CAREER–
BATTER UP! LET'S GO!
I HOPE WE'RE ON THE SAME TEAM!
SMACK
WOW! A DOUBLE!
LET'S GO! NEXT BATTER!

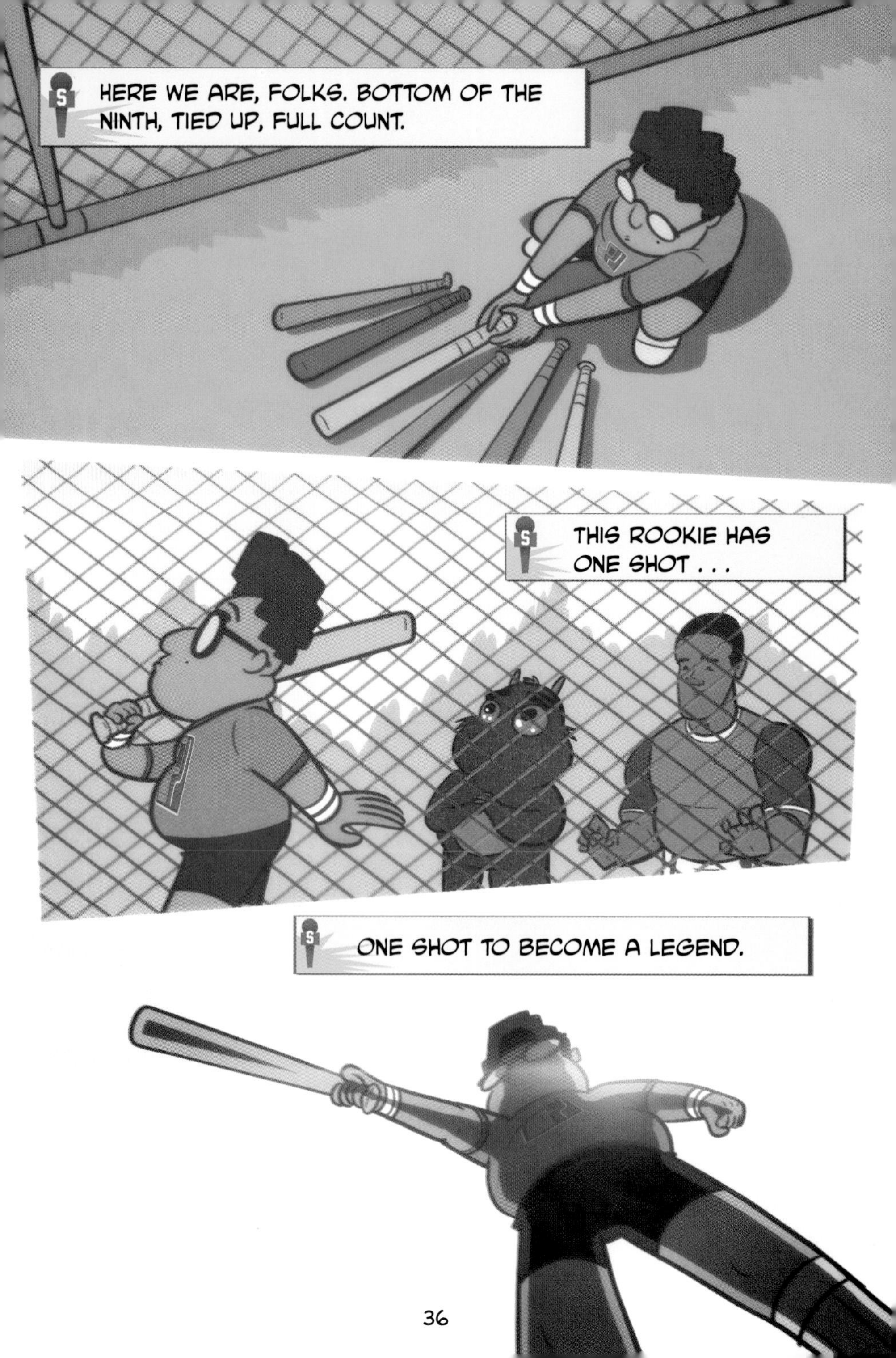
HERE WE ARE, FOLKS. BOTTOM OF THE NINTH, TIED UP, FULL COUNT.
THIS ROOKIE HAS ONE SHOT . . .
ONE SHOT TO BECOME A LEGEND.

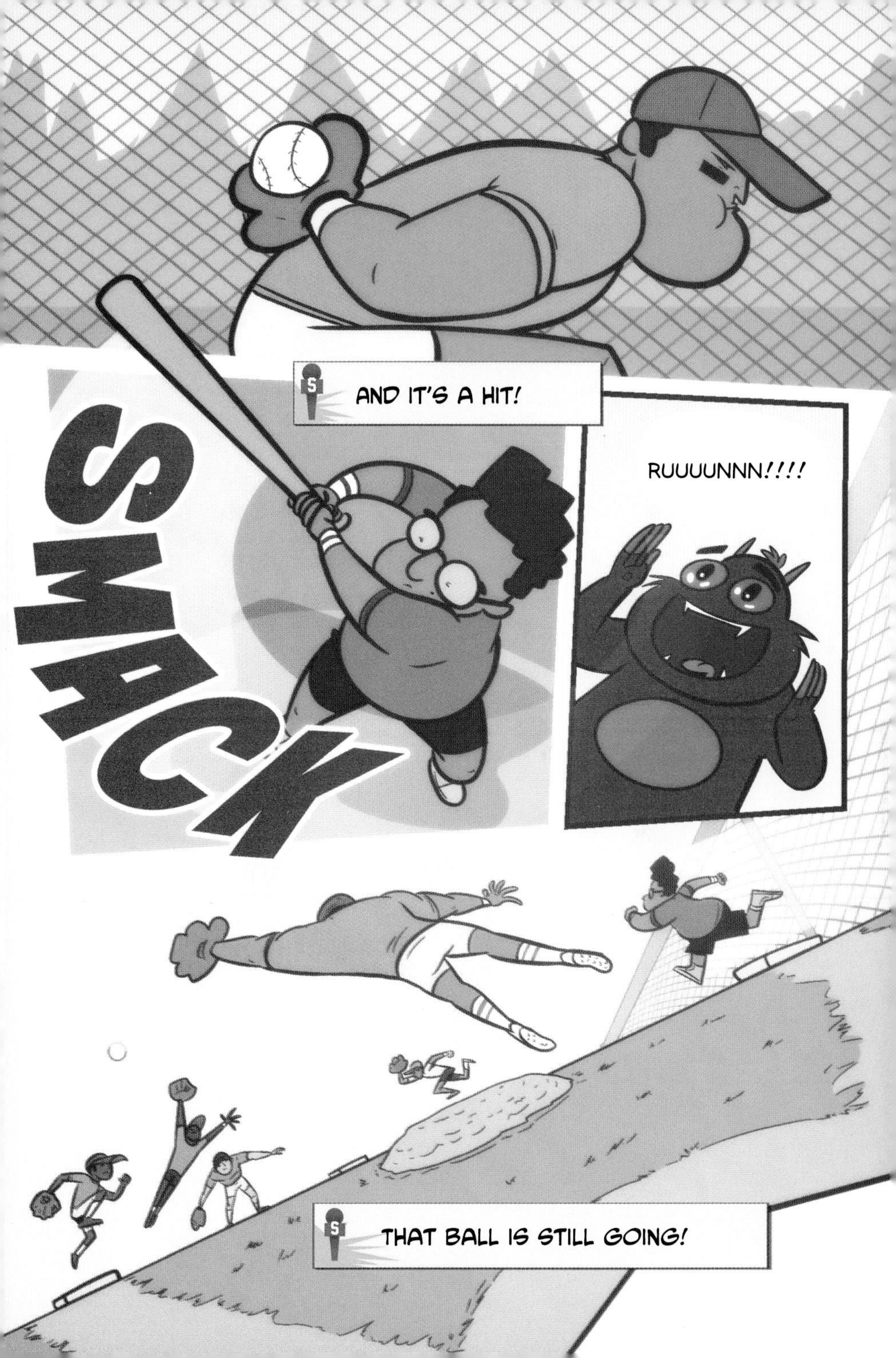

AND IT'S A HIT!
SMACK
RUUUUNNN!!!!
THAT BALL IS STILL GOING!

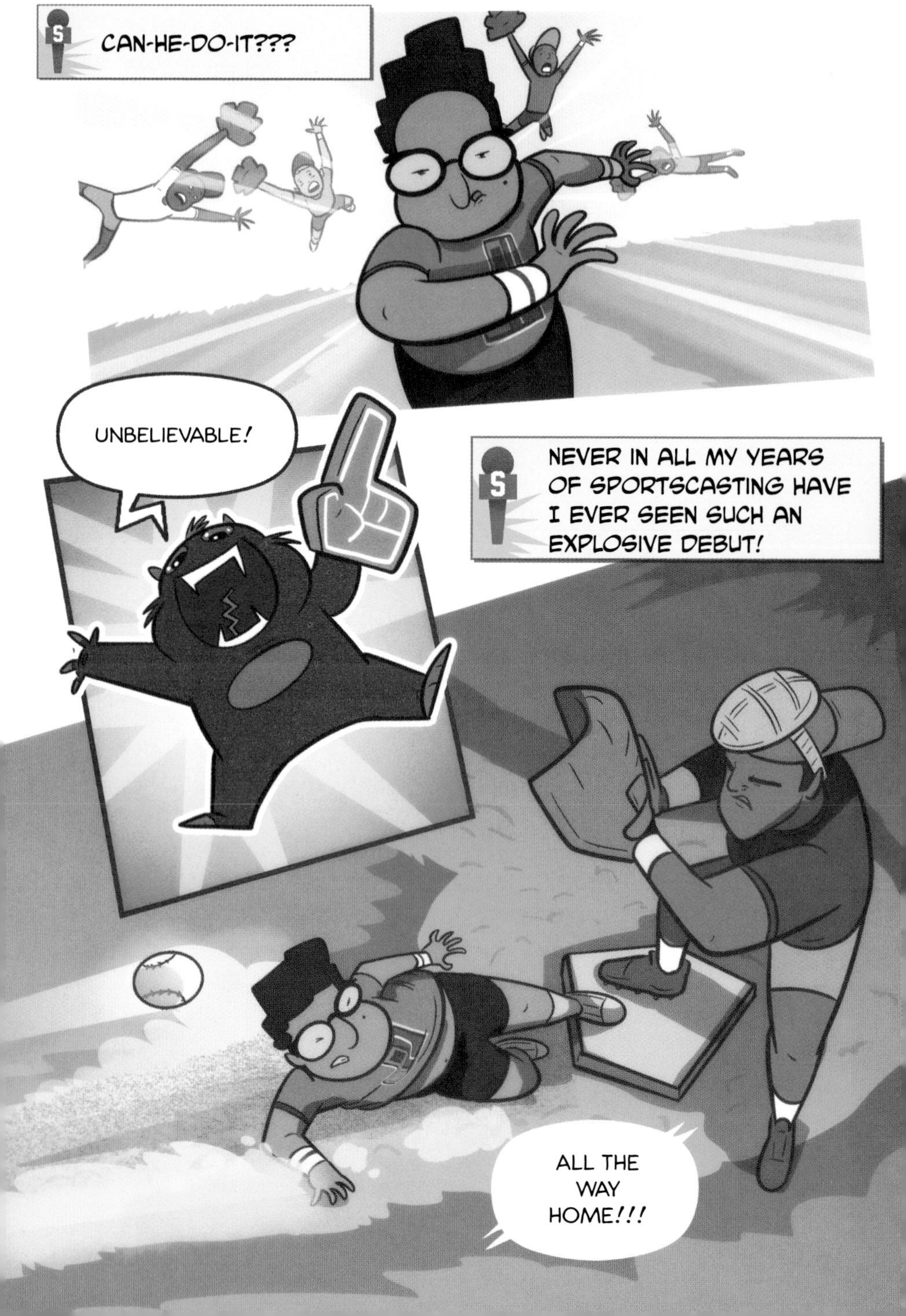
CAN-HE-DO-IT???
UNBELIEVABLE!
NEVER IN ALL MY YEARS OF SPORTSCASTING HAVE I EVER SEEN SUCH AN EXPLOSIVE DEBUT!
ALL THE WAY HOME!!!

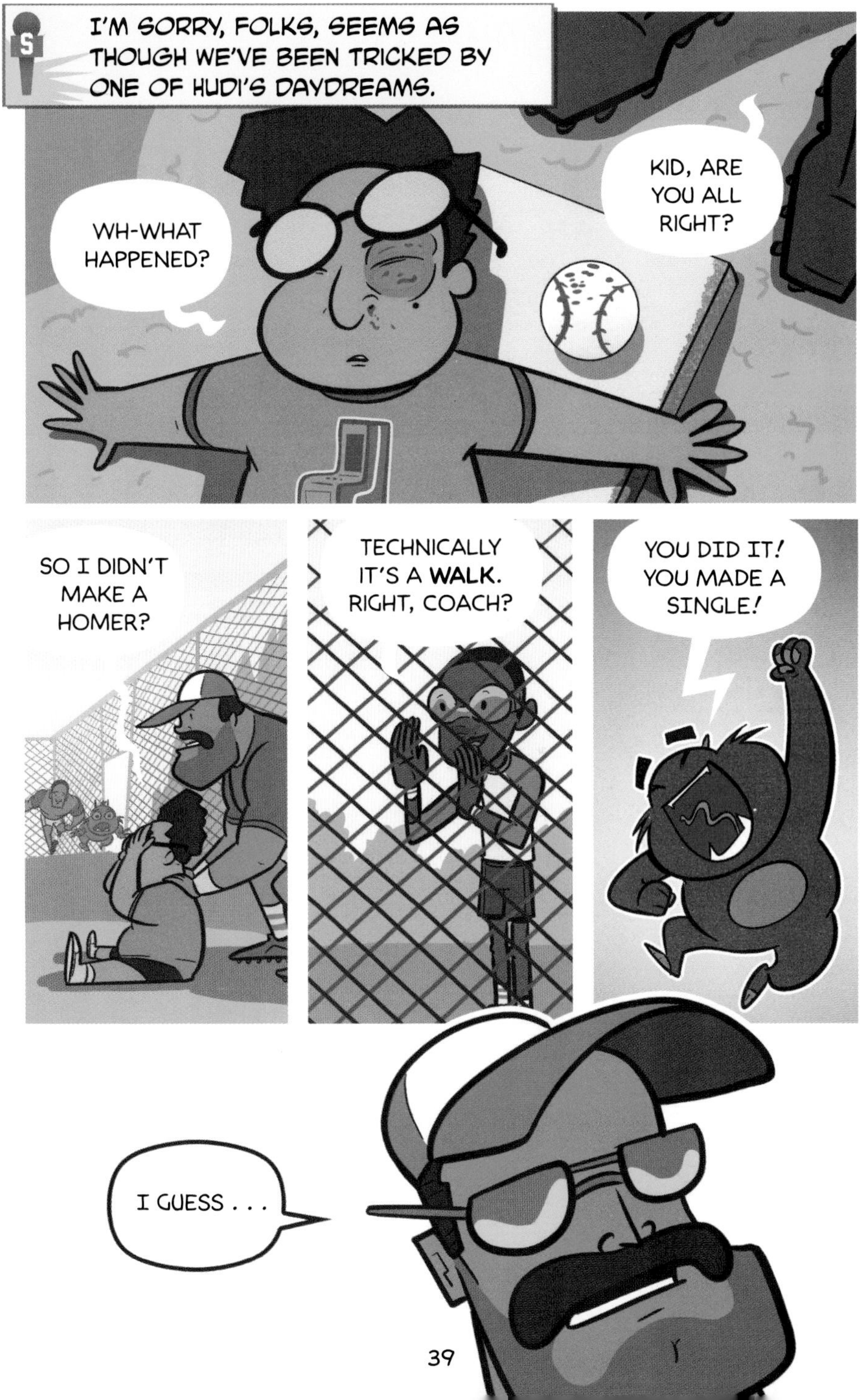
I'M SORRY, FOLKS, SEEMS AS THOUGH WE'VE BEEN TRICKED BY ONE OF HUDI'S DAYDREAMS.
WH-WHAT HAPPENED?
KID, ARE YOU ALL RIGHT?
SO I DIDN'T MAKE A HOMER?
TECHNICALLY IT'S A **WALK**. RIGHT, COACH?
YOU DID IT! YOU MADE A SINGLE!
I GUESS . . .

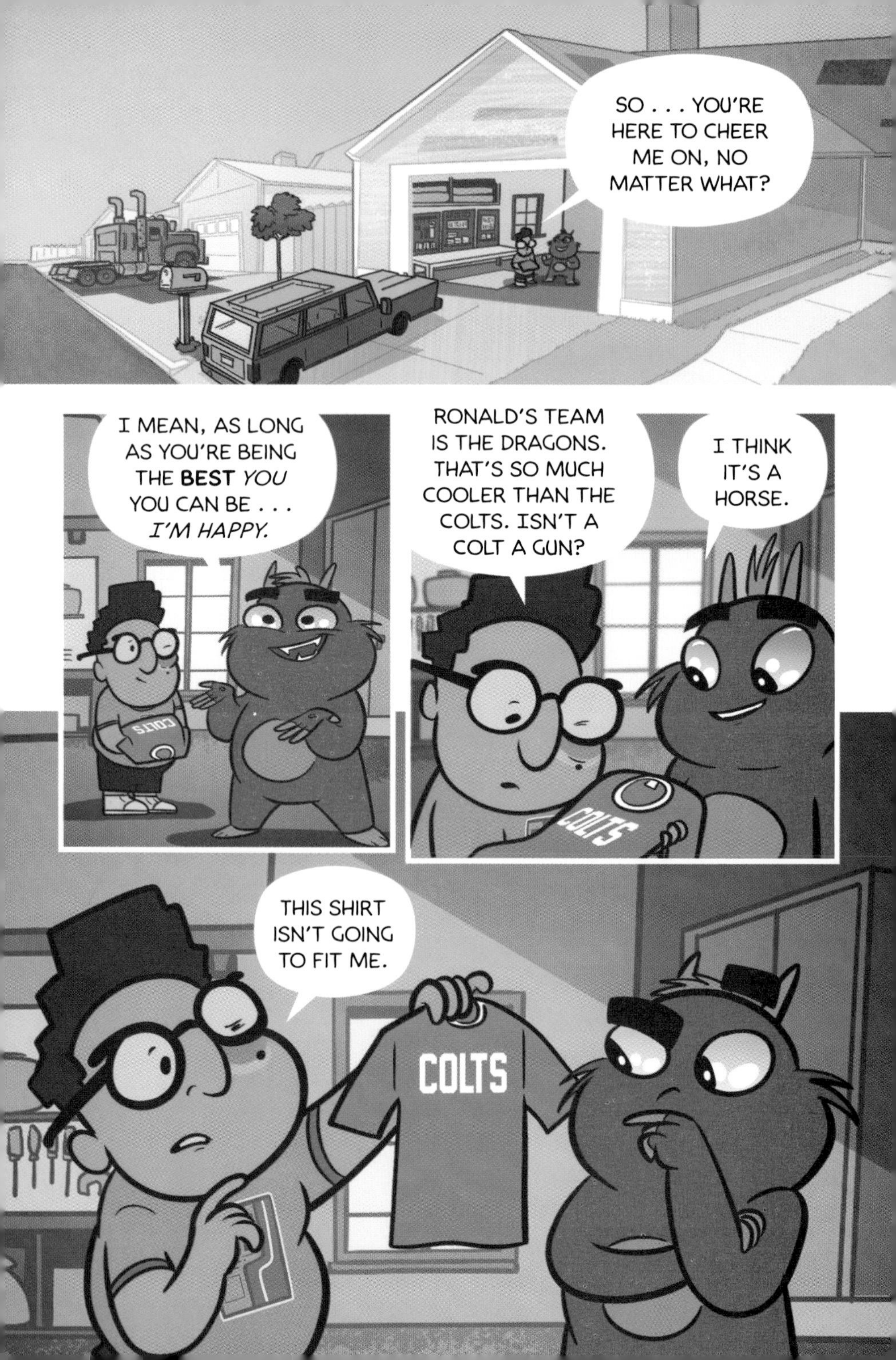
SO . . . YOU'RE HERE TO CHEER ME ON, NO MATTER WHAT?
I MEAN, AS LONG AS YOU'RE BEING THE **BEST** *YOU* YOU CAN BE . . . *I'M HAPPY.*
RONALD'S TEAM IS THE DRAGONS. THAT'S SO MUCH COOLER THAN THE COLTS. ISN'T A COLT A GUN?
I THINK IT'S A HORSE.
COLTS
THIS SHIRT ISN'T GOING TO FIT ME.
COLTS

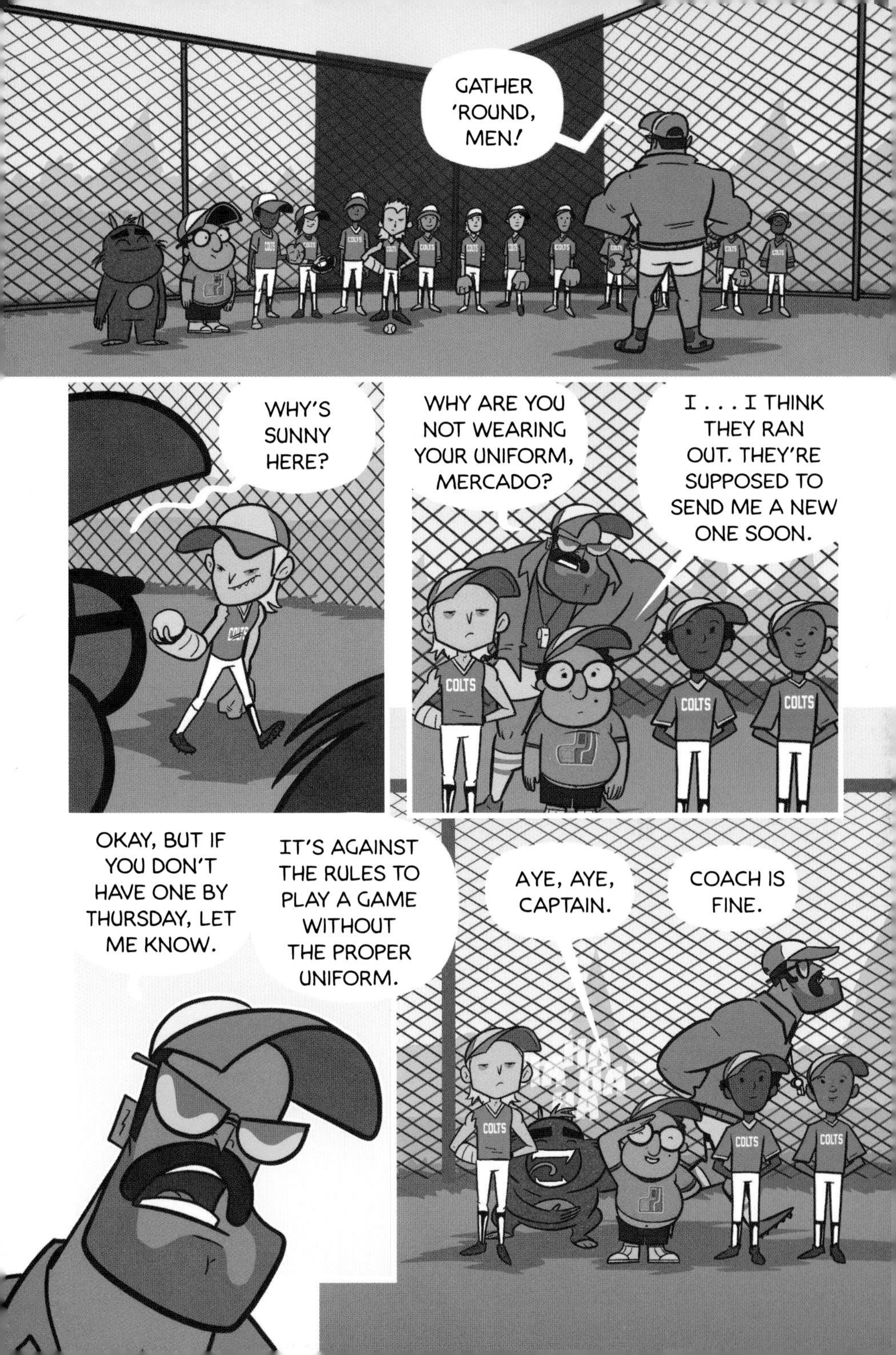
GATHER 'ROUND, MEN!
WHY'S SUNNY HERE?
WHY ARE YOU NOT WEARING YOUR UNIFORM, MERCADO?
I . . . I THINK THEY RAN OUT. THEY'RE SUPPOSED TO SEND ME A NEW ONE SOON.
OKAY, BUT IF YOU DON'T HAVE ONE BY THURSDAY, LET ME KNOW.
IT'S AGAINST THE RULES TO PLAY A GAME WITHOUT THE PROPER UNIFORM.
AYE, AYE, CAPTAIN.
COACH IS FINE.

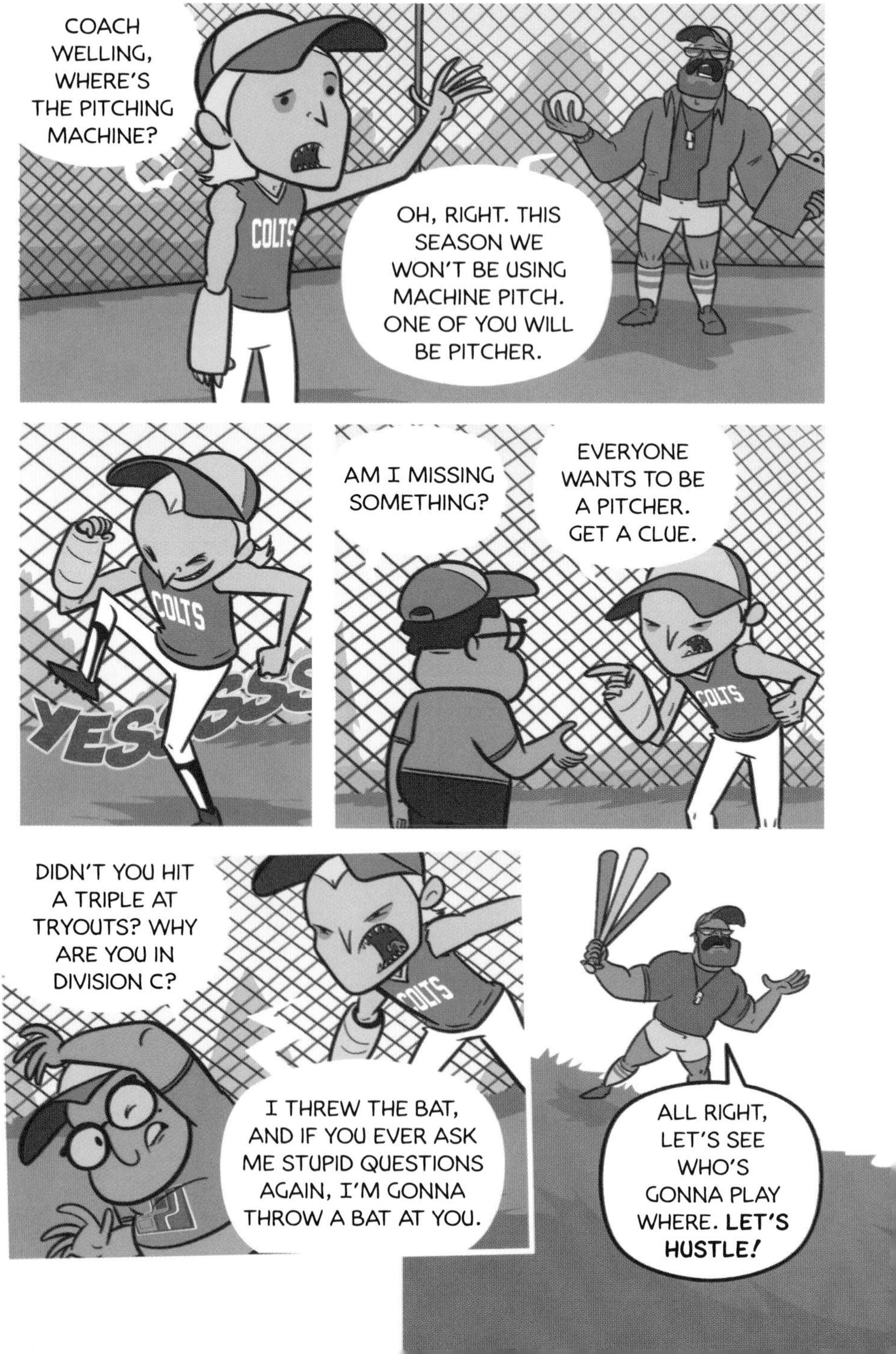
COACH WELLING, WHERE'S THE PITCHING MACHINE?
OH, RIGHT. THIS SEASON WE WON'T BE USING MACHINE PITCH. ONE OF YOU WILL BE PITCHER.
COLTS
YESSSSS
AM I MISSING SOMETHING?
EVERYONE WANTS TO BE A PITCHER. GET A CLUE.
DIDN'T YOU HIT A TRIPLE AT TRYOUTS? WHY ARE YOU IN DIVISION C?
I THREW THE BAT, AND IF YOU EVER ASK ME STUPID QUESTIONS AGAIN, I'M GONNA THROW A BAT AT YOU.
ALL RIGHT, LET'S SEE WHO'S GONNA PLAY WHERE. LET'S HUSTLE!

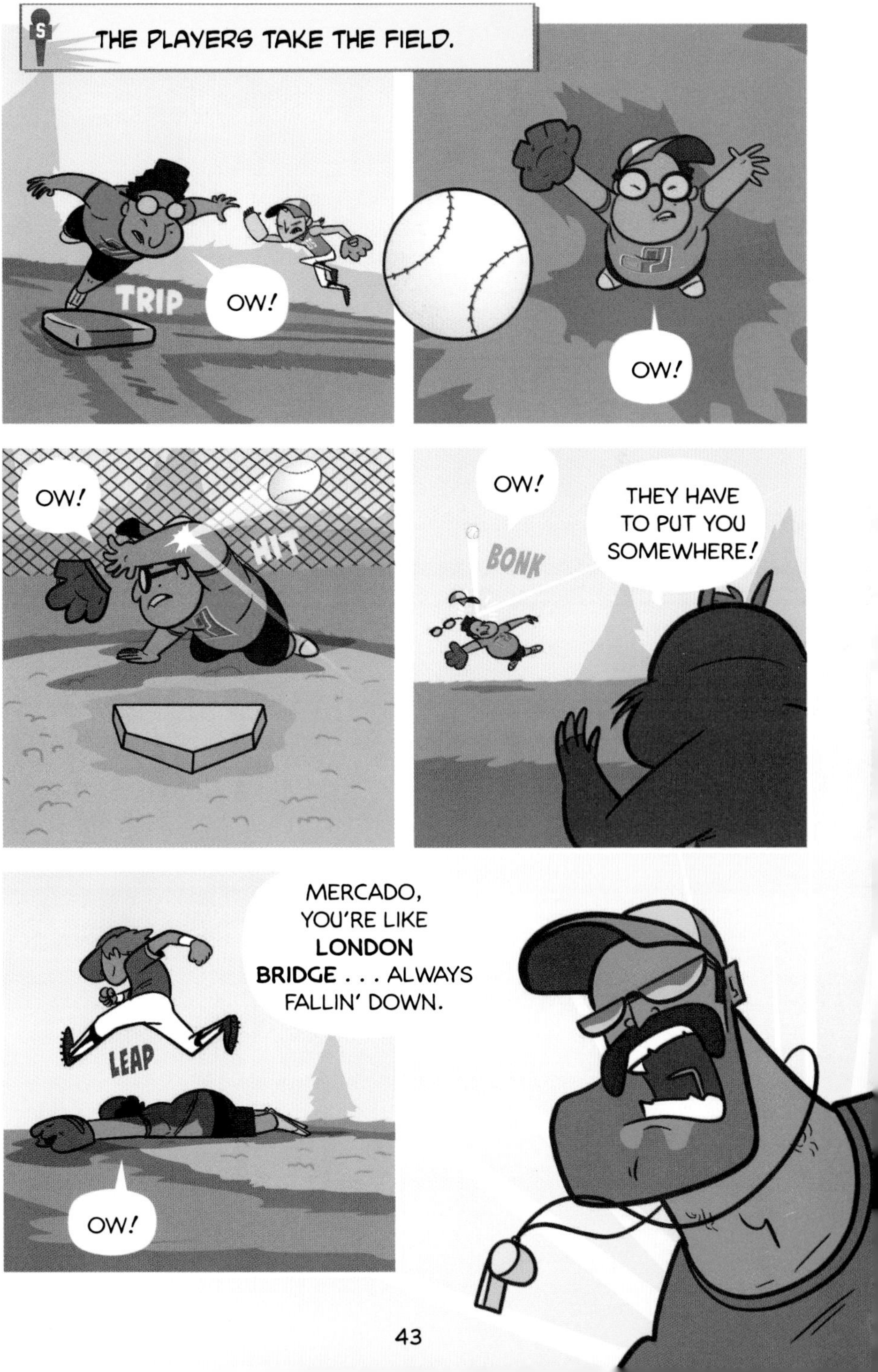
THE PLAYERS TAKE THE FIELD.
TRIP
OW!
OW!
OW!
HIT
OW!
BONK
THEY HAVE TO PUT YOU SOMEWHERE!
LEAP
MERCADO, YOU'RE LIKE **LONDON BRIDGE** . . . ALWAYS FALLIN' DOWN.
OW!

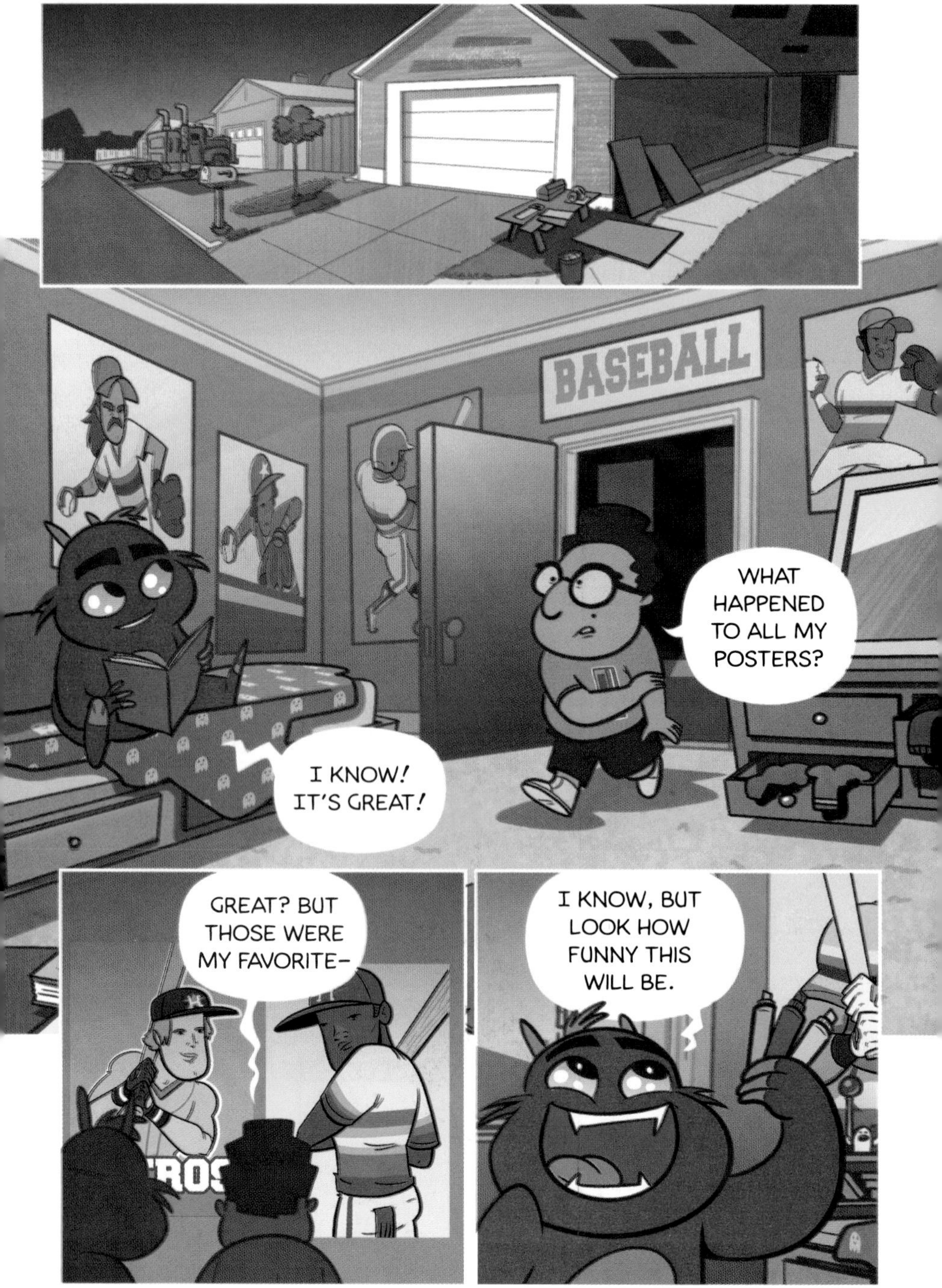
BASEBALL
WHAT HAPPENED TO ALL MY POSTERS?
I KNOW! IT'S GREAT!
GREAT? BUT THOSE WERE MY FAVORITE-
I KNOW, BUT LOOK HOW FUNNY THIS WILL BE.

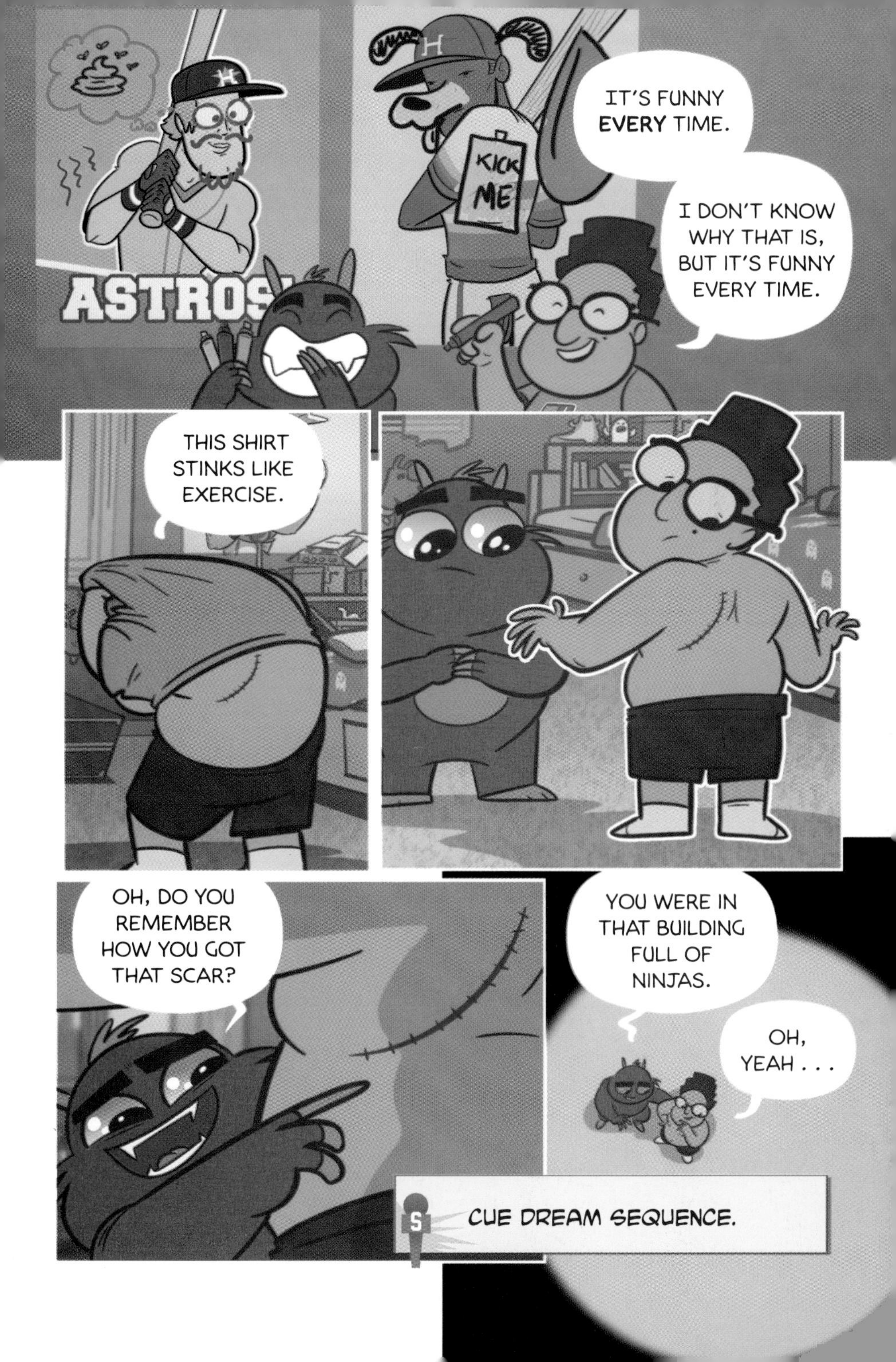
ASTROS
KICK ME
IT'S FUNNY EVERY TIME.
I DON'T KNOW WHY THAT IS, BUT IT'S FUNNY EVERY TIME.
THIS SHIRT STINKS LIKE EXERCISE.
OH, DO YOU REMEMBER HOW YOU GOT THAT SCAR?
YOU WERE IN THAT BUILDING FULL OF NINJAS.
OH, YEAH . . .
CUE DREAM SEQUENCE.

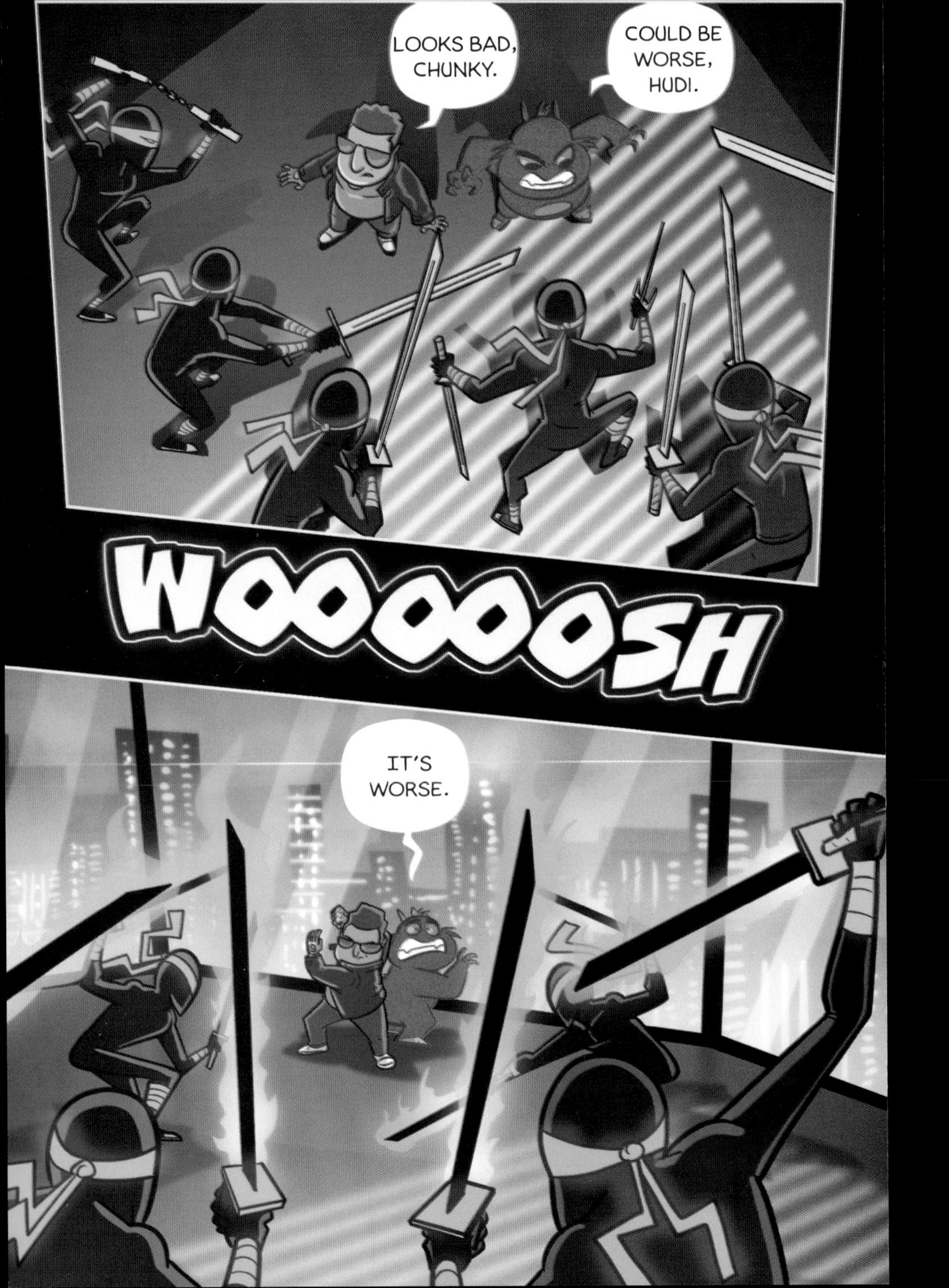
LOOKS BAD, CHUNKY.
COULD BE WORSE, HUDI.
WOOOOOSH
IT'S WORSE.

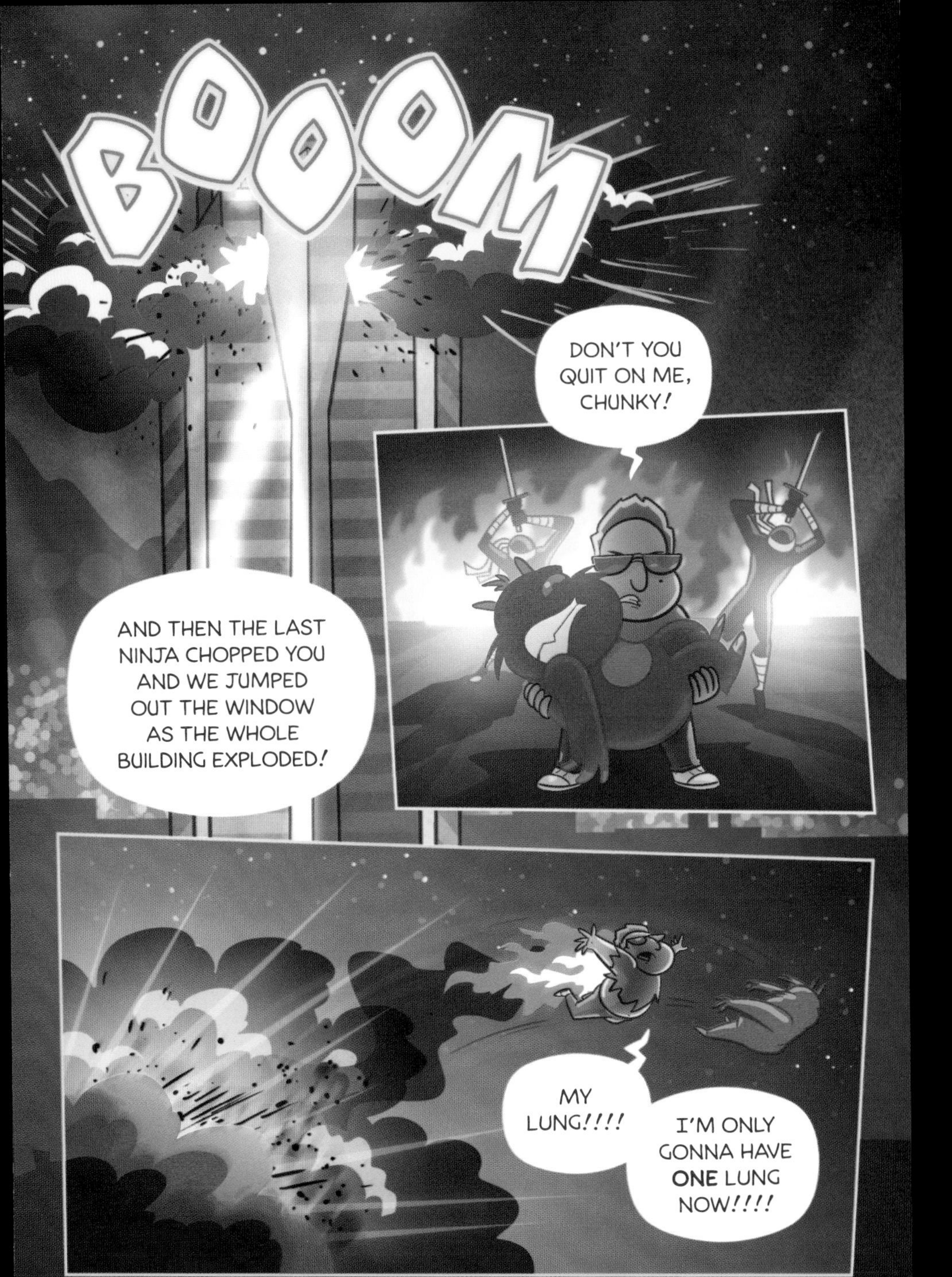
BOOOM
DON'T YOU QUIT ON ME, CHUNKY!
AND THEN THE LAST NINJA CHOPPED YOU AND WE JUMPED OUT THE WINDOW AS THE WHOLE BUILDING EXPLODED!
MY LUNG!!!!
I'M ONLY GONNA HAVE **ONE** LUNG NOW!!!!

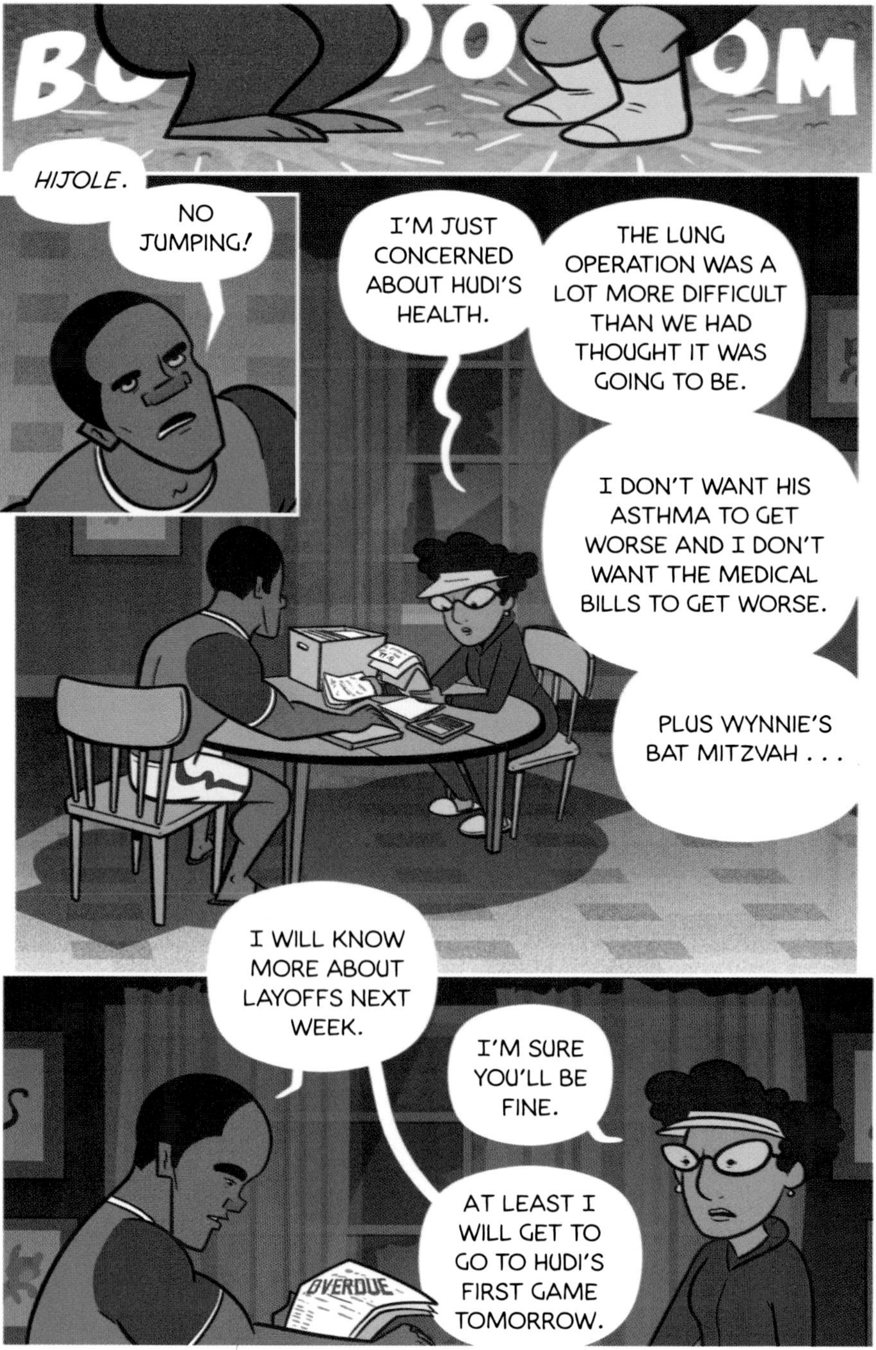

BOOOOOOM
HIJOLE.
NO JUMPING!
I'M JUST CONCERNED ABOUT HUDI'S HEALTH.
THE LUNG OPERATION WAS A LOT MORE DIFFICULT THAN WE HAD THOUGHT IT WAS GOING TO BE.
I DON'T WANT HIS ASTHMA TO GET WORSE AND I DON'T WANT THE MEDICAL BILLS TO GET WORSE.
PLUS WYNNIE'S BAT MITZVAH . . .
I WILL KNOW MORE ABOUT LAYOFFS NEXT WEEK.
I'M SURE YOU'LL BE FINE.
AT LEAST I WILL GET TO GO TO HUDI'S FIRST GAME TOMORROW.
OVERDUE

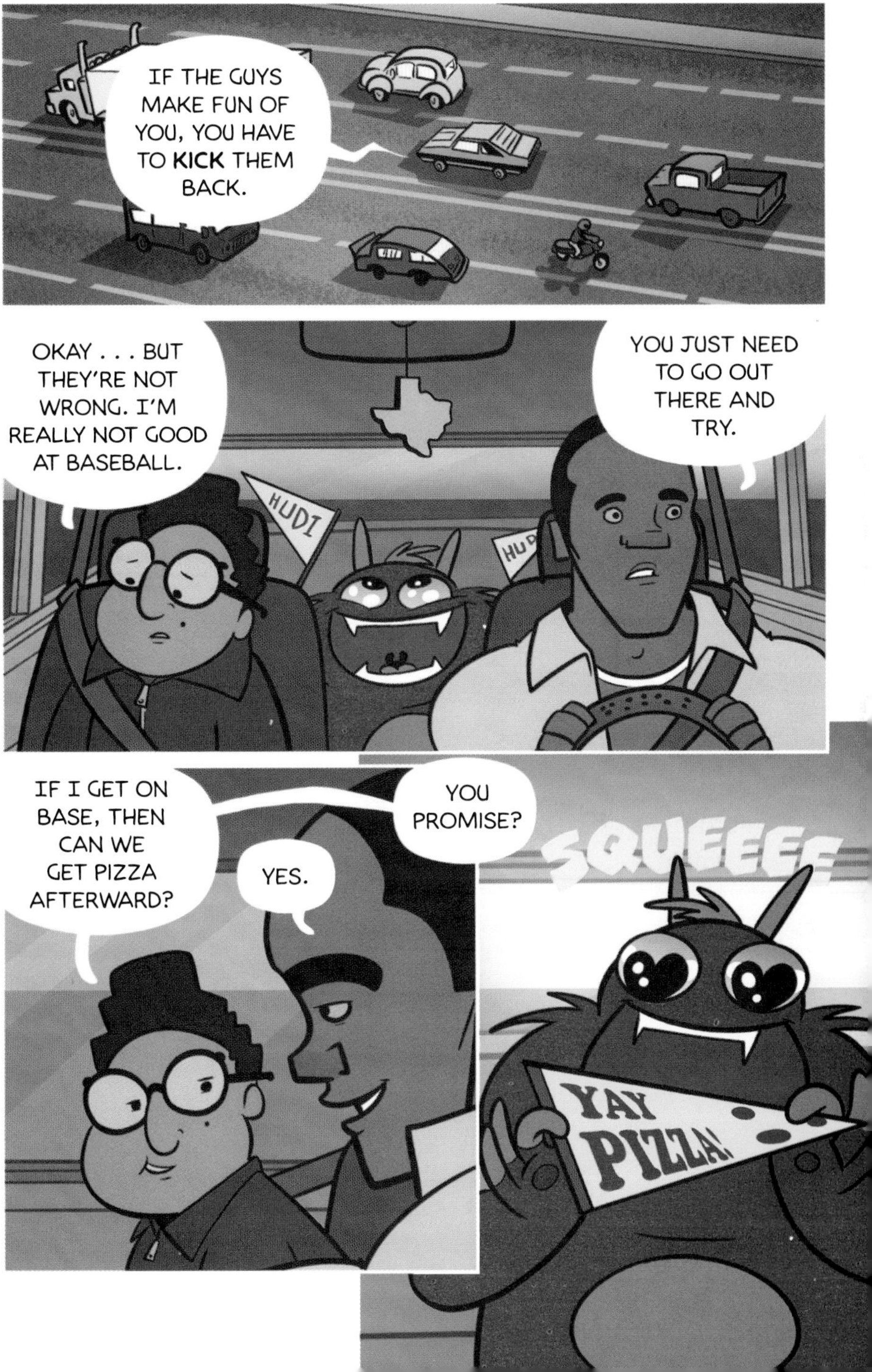
IF THE GUYS MAKE FUN OF YOU, YOU HAVE TO **KICK** THEM BACK.
OKAY . . . BUT THEY'RE NOT WRONG. I'M REALLY NOT GOOD AT BASEBALL.
YOU JUST NEED TO GO OUT THERE AND TRY.
HUDI
IF I GET ON BASE, THEN CAN WE GET PIZZA AFTERWARD?
YOU PROMISE?
YES.
SQUEEEE
YAY PIZZA!

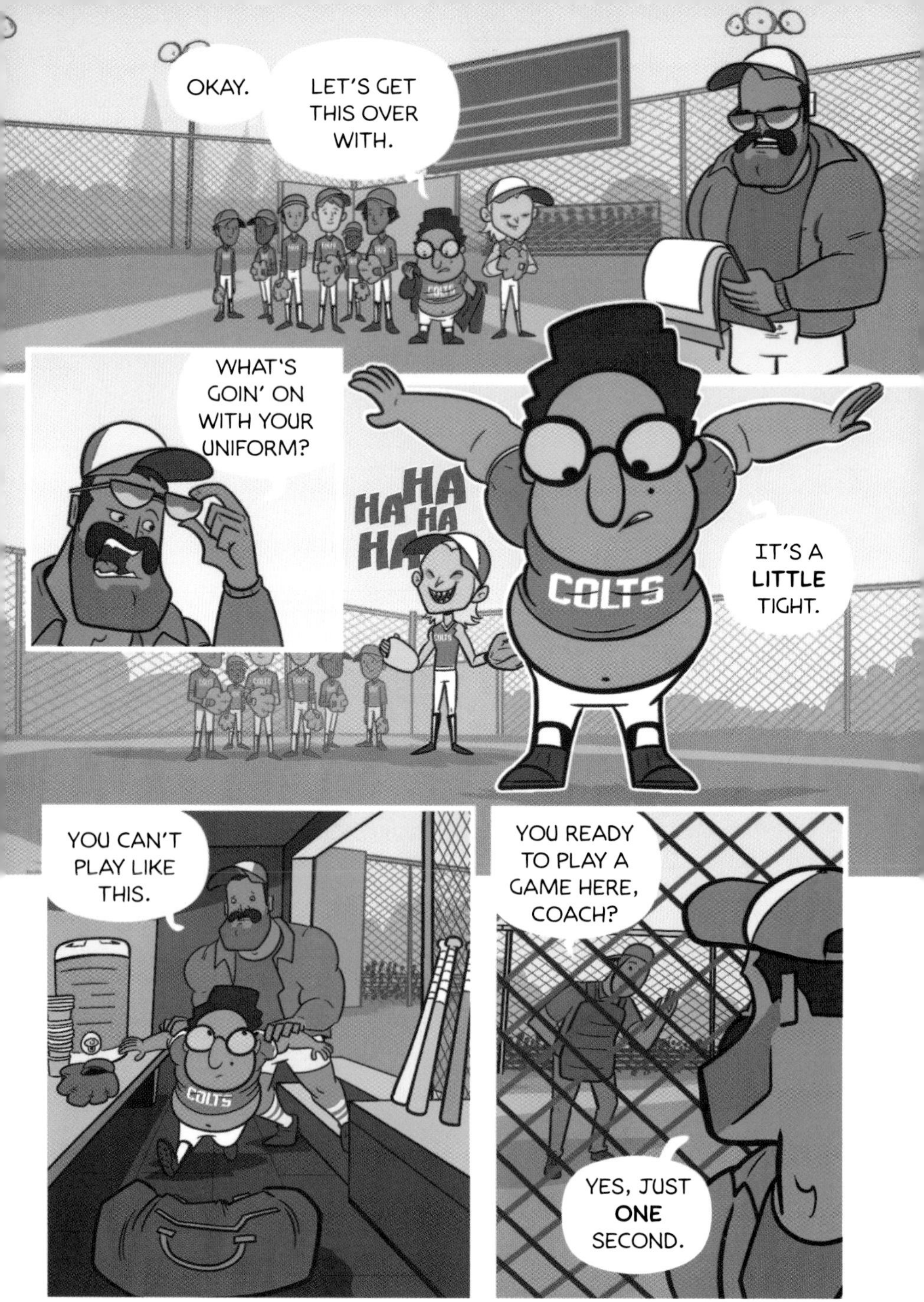
OKAY.
LET'S GET THIS OVER WITH.
WHAT'S GOIN' ON WITH YOUR UNIFORM?
HA HA HA HA HA
IT'S A **LITTLE** TIGHT.
COLTS
YOU CAN'T PLAY LIKE THIS.
YOU READY TO PLAY A GAME HERE, COACH?
YES, JUST **ONE** SECOND.

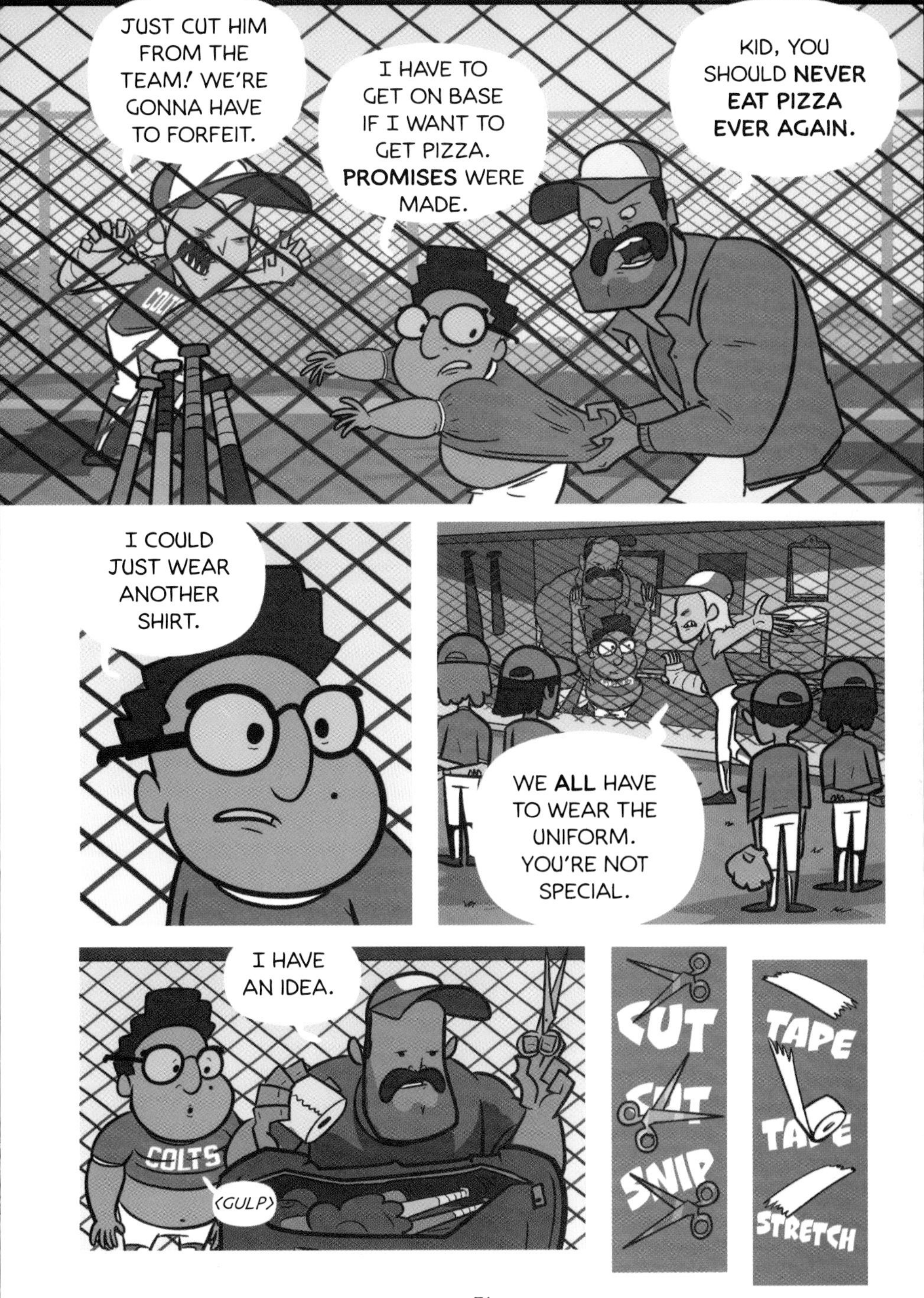
JUST CUT HIM FROM THE TEAM! WE'RE GONNA HAVE TO FORFEIT.
I HAVE TO GET ON BASE IF I WANT TO GET PIZZA. PROMISES WERE MADE.
KID, YOU SHOULD NEVER EAT PIZZA EVER AGAIN.
COLTS
I COULD JUST WEAR ANOTHER SHIRT.
WE ALL HAVE TO WEAR THE UNIFORM. YOU'RE NOT SPECIAL.
I HAVE AN IDEA.
COLTS
<GULP>
CUT
SNIP
TAPE
STRETCH

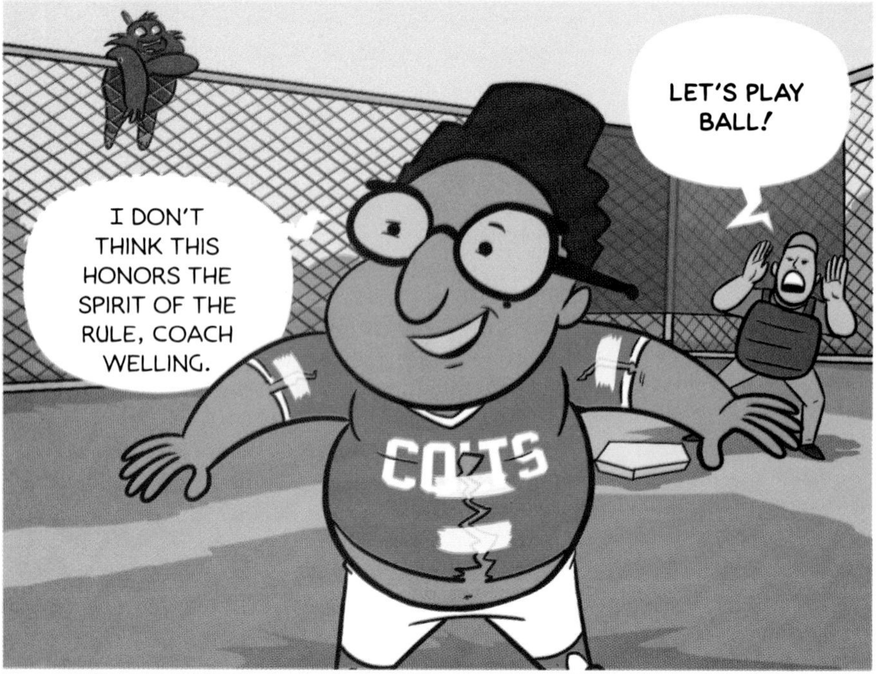
I DON'T THINK THIS HONORS THE SPIRIT OF THE RULE, COACH WELLING.
LET'S PLAY BALL!
COLTS

IT'S THE FIRST GAME OF THE SEASON, COLTS VS. PIRATES, AND SUNNY HAS BEEN CHOSEN TO BE THE TEAM'S PITCHER.

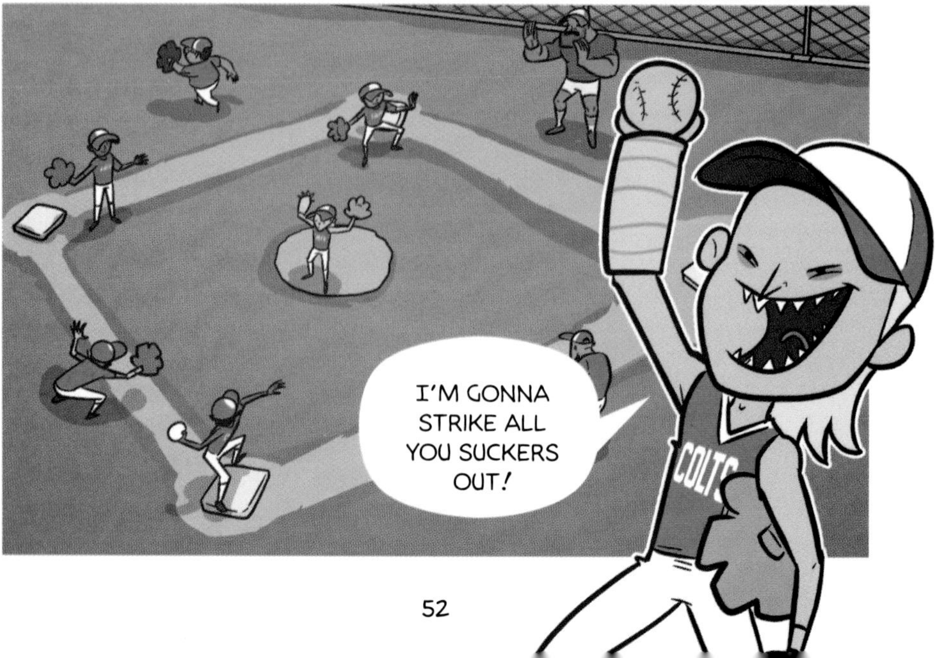
I'M GONNA STRIKE ALL YOU SUCKERS OUT!
COLTS

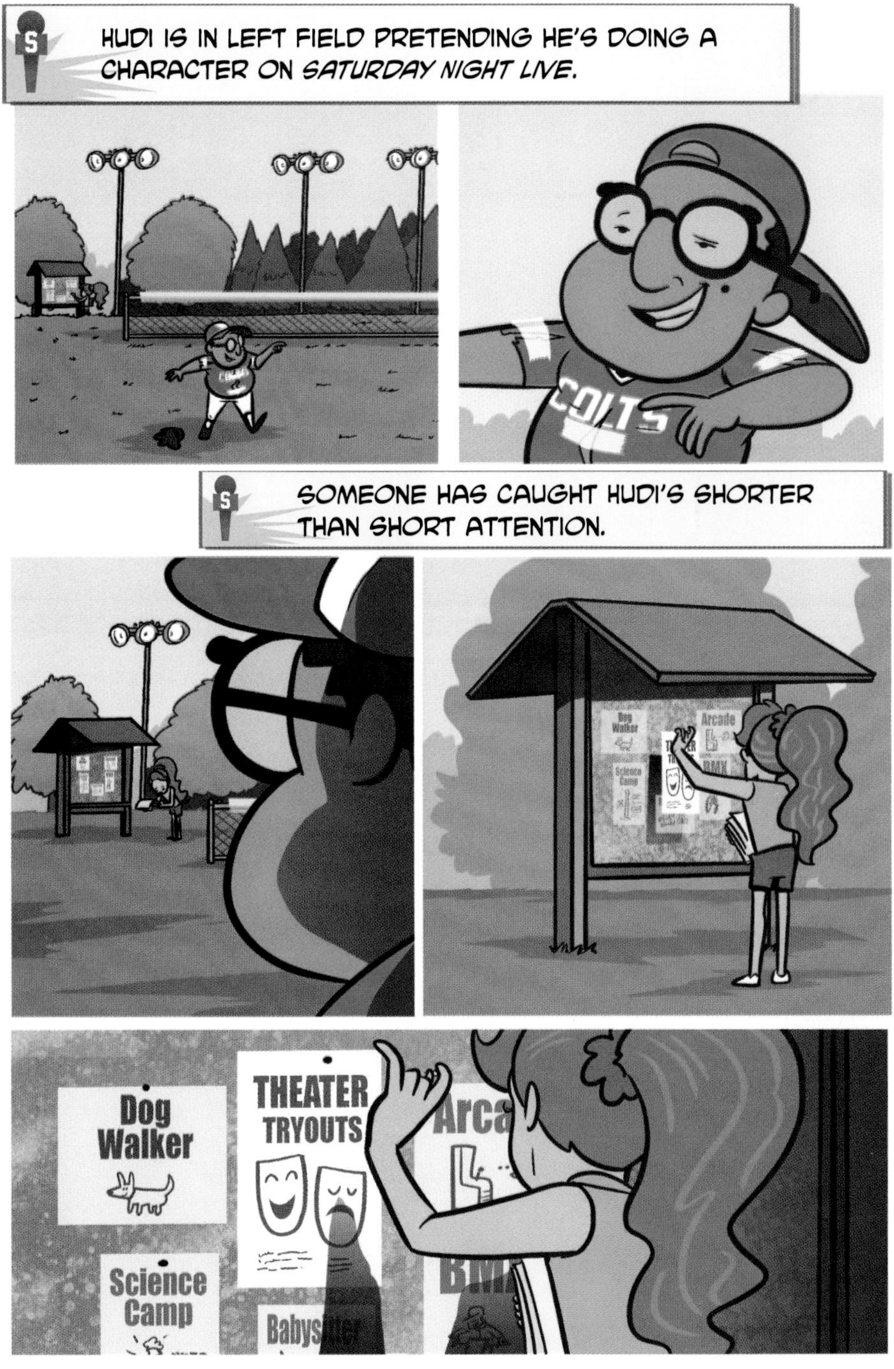
HUDI IS IN LEFT FIELD PRETENDING HE'S DOING A CHARACTER ON *SATURDAY NIGHT LIVE.*
COLTS
SOMEONE HAS CAUGHT HUDI'S SHORTER THAN SHORT ATTENTION.
Dog Walker
Arcade
Science Camp
Dog Walker
THEATER TRYOUTS
Arca
Science Camp

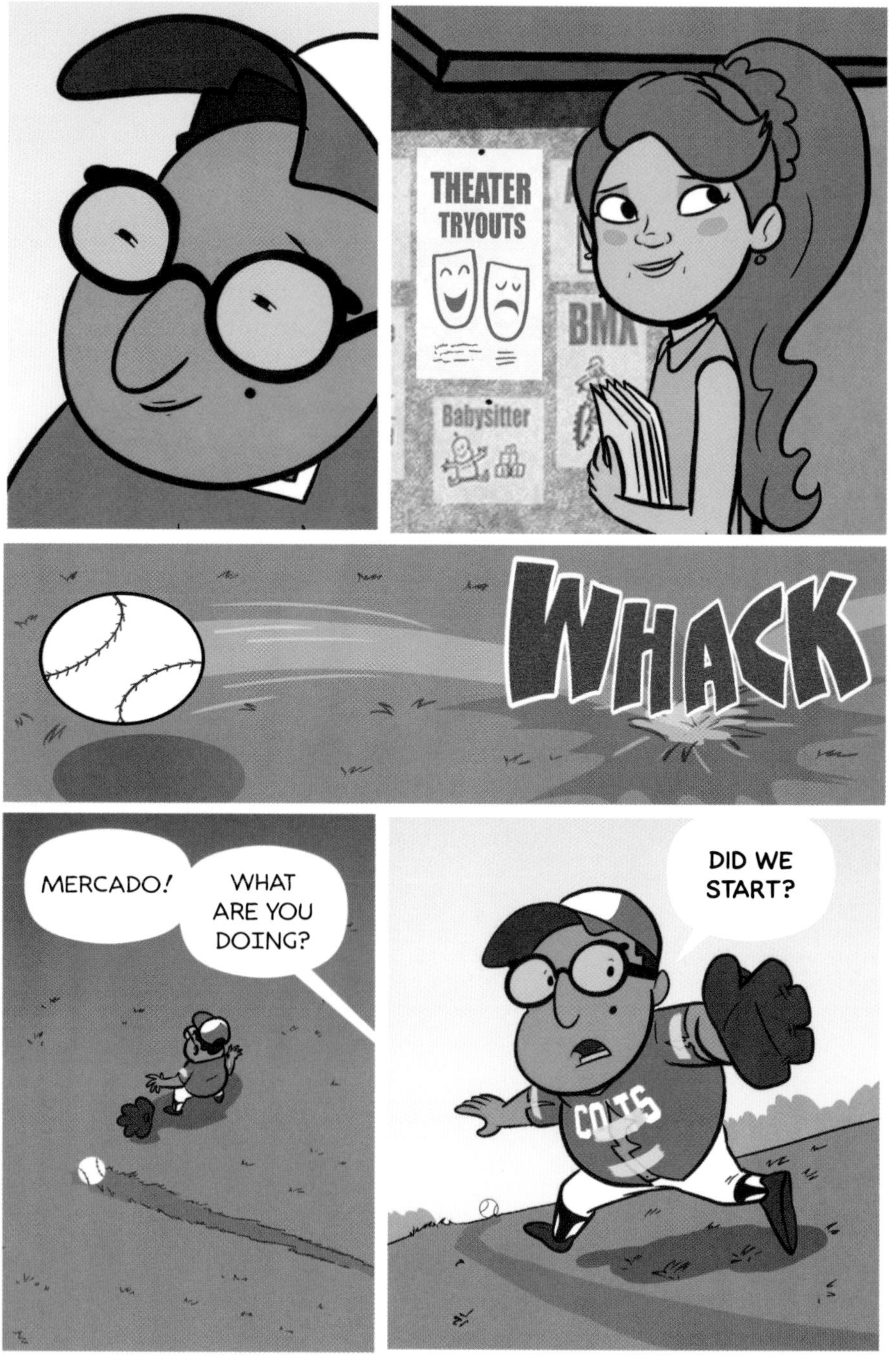
THEATER TRYOUTS
BMX
Babysitter
WHACK
MERCADO!
WHAT ARE YOU DOING?
DID WE START?
COLTS

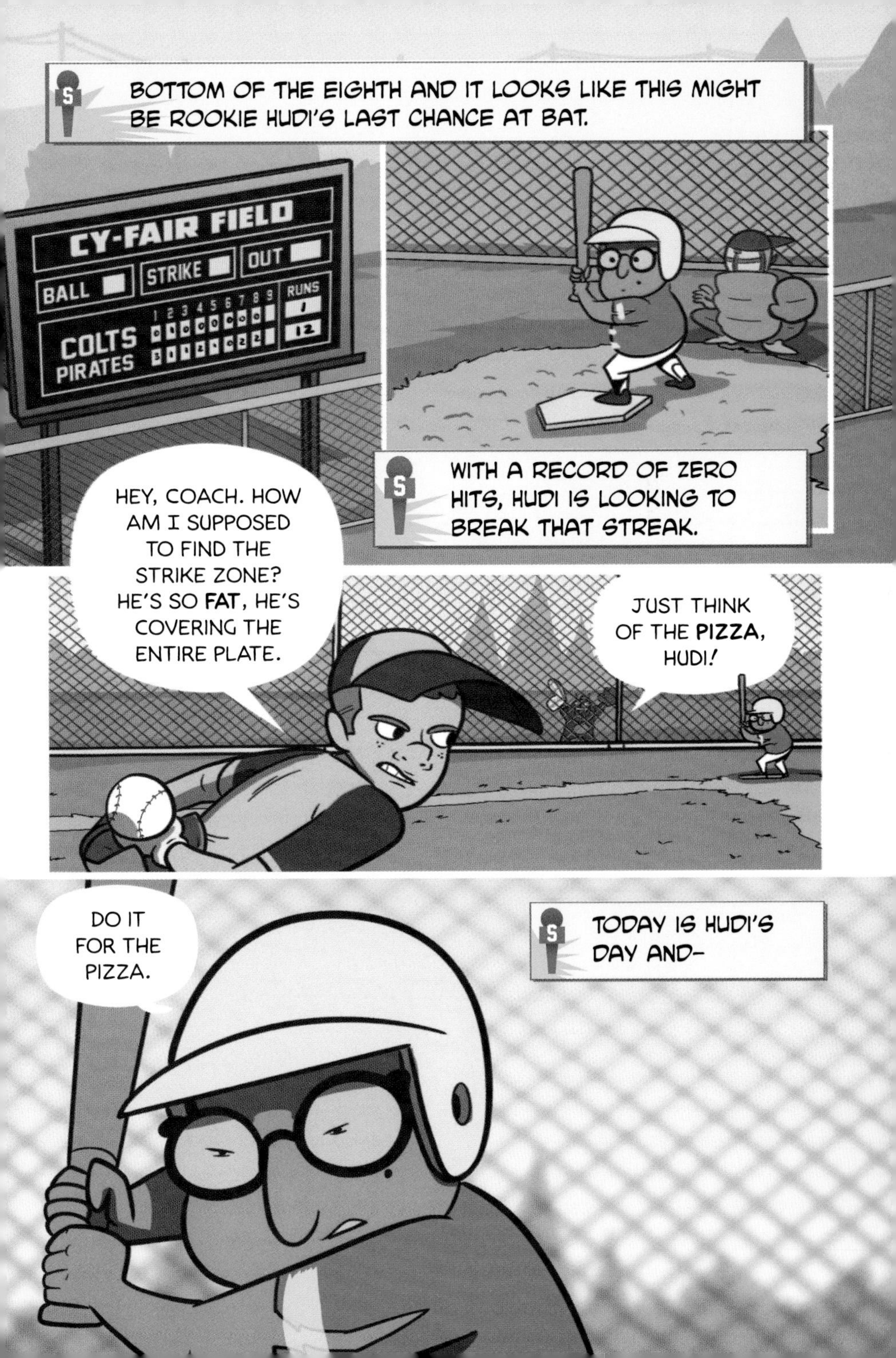
BOTTOM OF THE EIGHTH AND IT LOOKS LIKE THIS MIGHT BE ROOKIE HUDI'S LAST CHANCE AT BAT.
CY-FAIR FIELD
BALL
STRIKE
OUT
RUNS
COLTS
PIRATES
WITH A RECORD OF ZERO HITS, HUDI IS LOOKING TO BREAK THAT STREAK.
HEY, COACH. HOW AM I SUPPOSED TO FIND THE STRIKE ZONE? HE'S SO **FAT**, HE'S COVERING THE ENTIRE PLATE.
JUST THINK OF THE **PIZZA**, HUDI!
DO IT FOR THE PIZZA.
TODAY IS HUDI'S DAY AND–

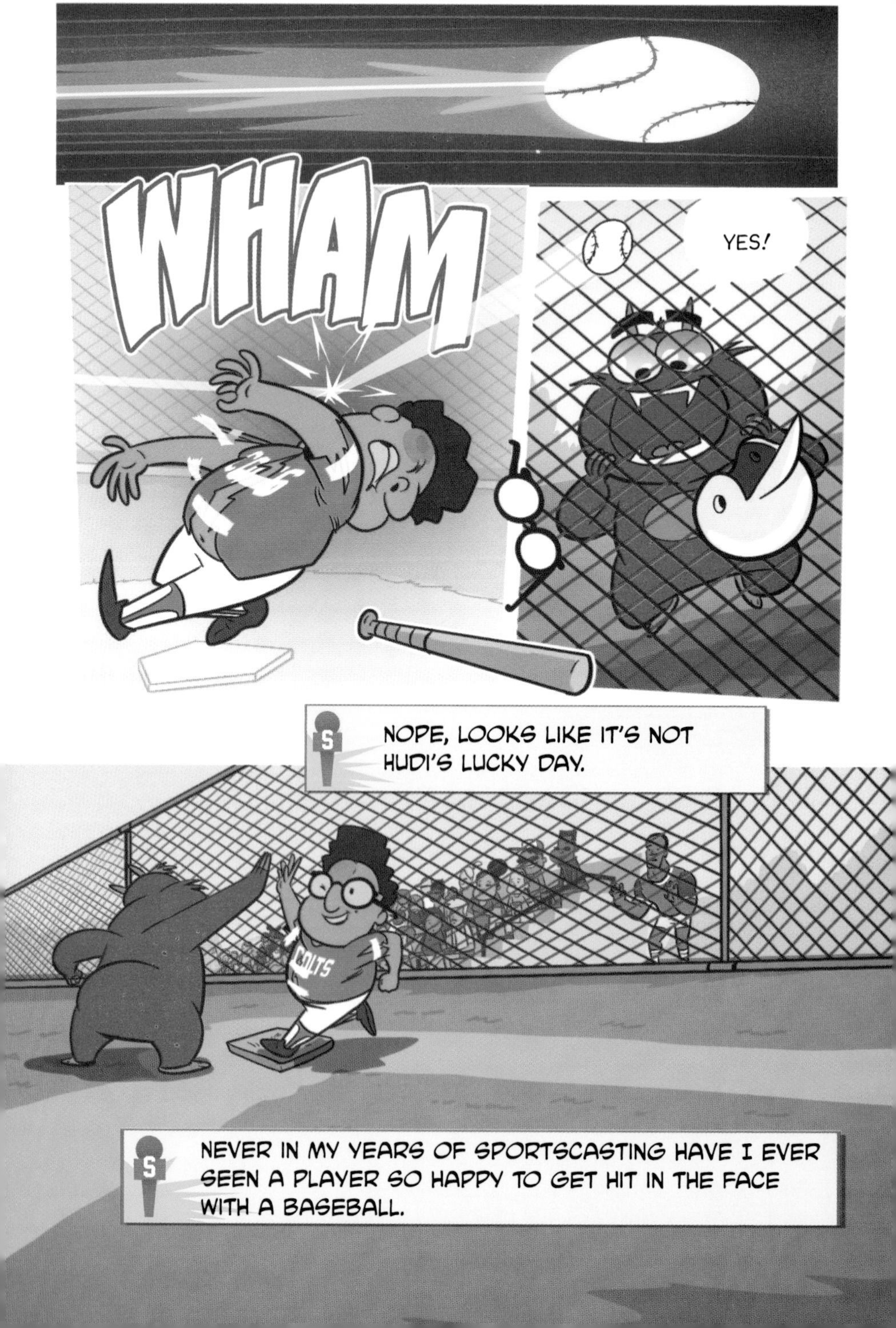
WHAM
YES!
NOPE, LOOKS LIKE IT'S NOT HUDI'S LUCKY DAY.
COLTS
NEVER IN MY YEARS OF SPORTSCASTING HAVE I EVER SEEN A PLAYER SO HAPPY TO GET HIT IN THE FACE WITH A BASEBALL.

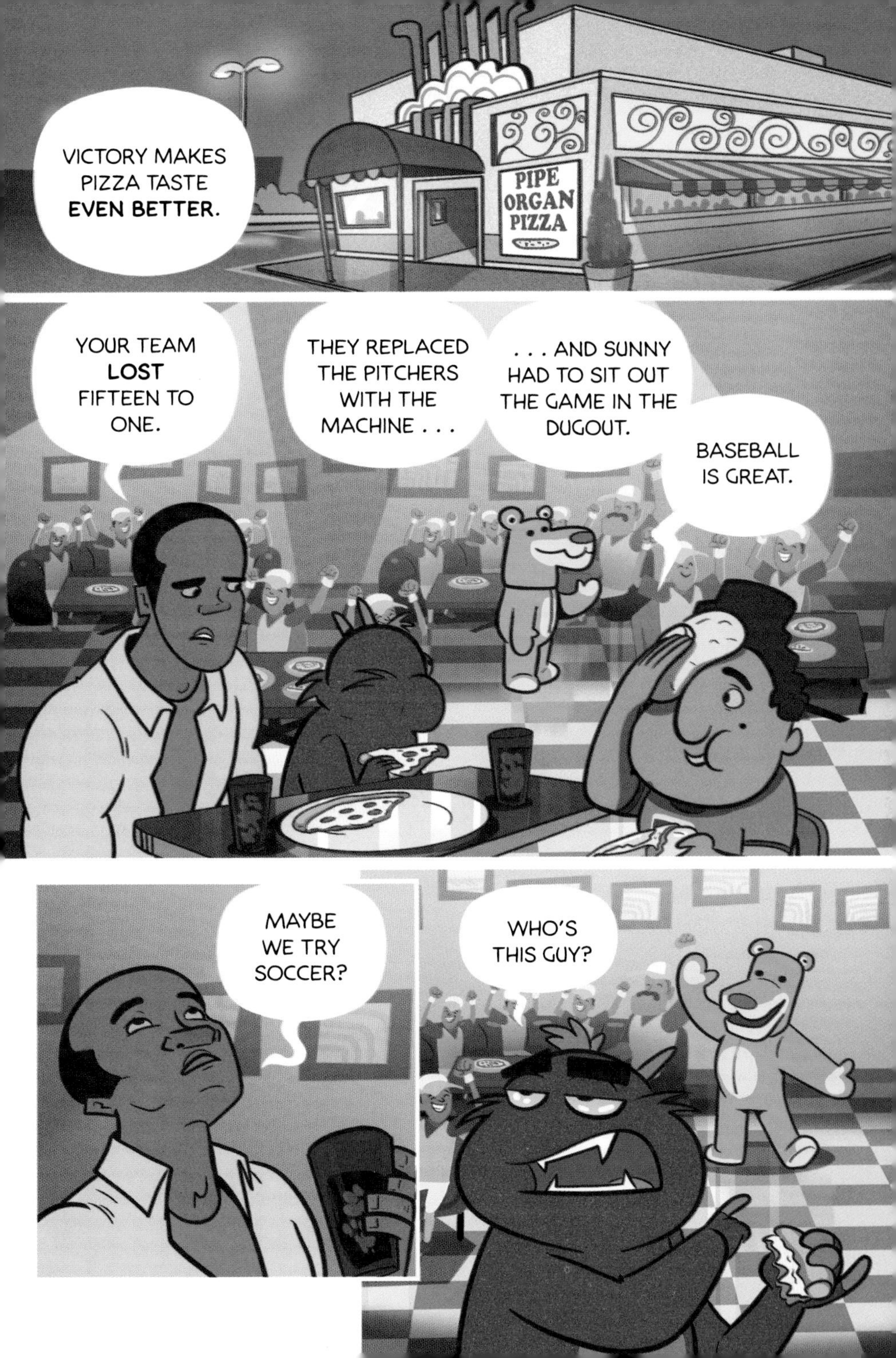
VICTORY MAKES PIZZA TASTE **EVEN BETTER.**
PIPE ORGAN PIZZA
YOUR TEAM **LOST** FIFTEEN TO ONE.
THEY REPLACED THE PITCHERS WITH THE MACHINE . . .
. . . AND SUNNY HAD TO SIT OUT THE GAME IN THE DUGOUT.
BASEBALL IS GREAT.
MAYBE WE TRY SOCCER?
WHO'S THIS GUY?

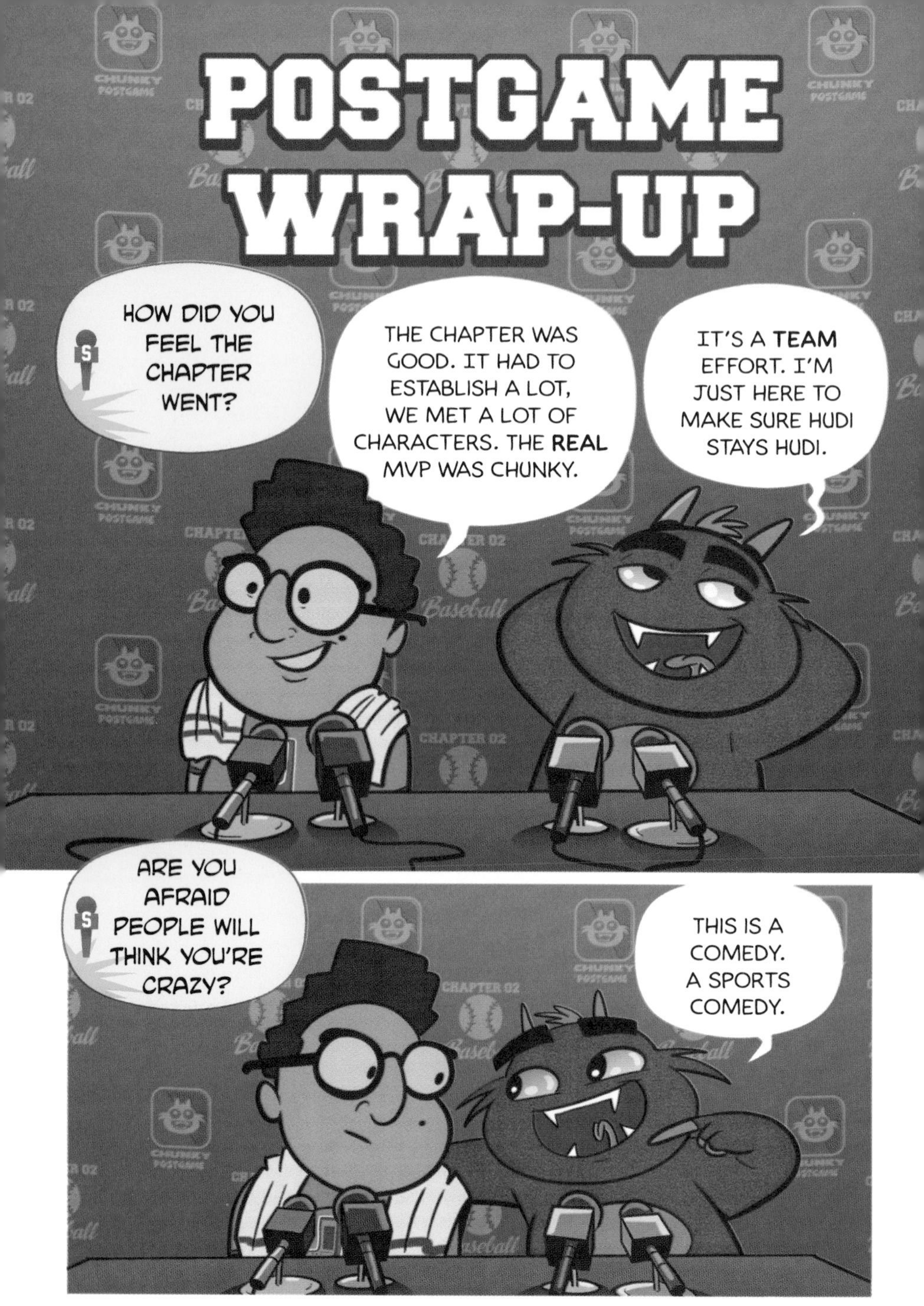
POSTGAME WRAP-UP
HOW DID YOU FEEL THE CHAPTER WENT?
THE CHAPTER WAS GOOD. IT HAD TO ESTABLISH A LOT, WE MET A LOT OF CHARACTERS. THE REAL MVP WAS CHUNKY.
IT'S A TEAM EFFORT. I'M JUST HERE TO MAKE SURE HUDI STAYS HUDI.
ARE YOU AFRAID PEOPLE WILL THINK YOU'RE CRAZY?
THIS IS A COMEDY. A SPORTS COMEDY.

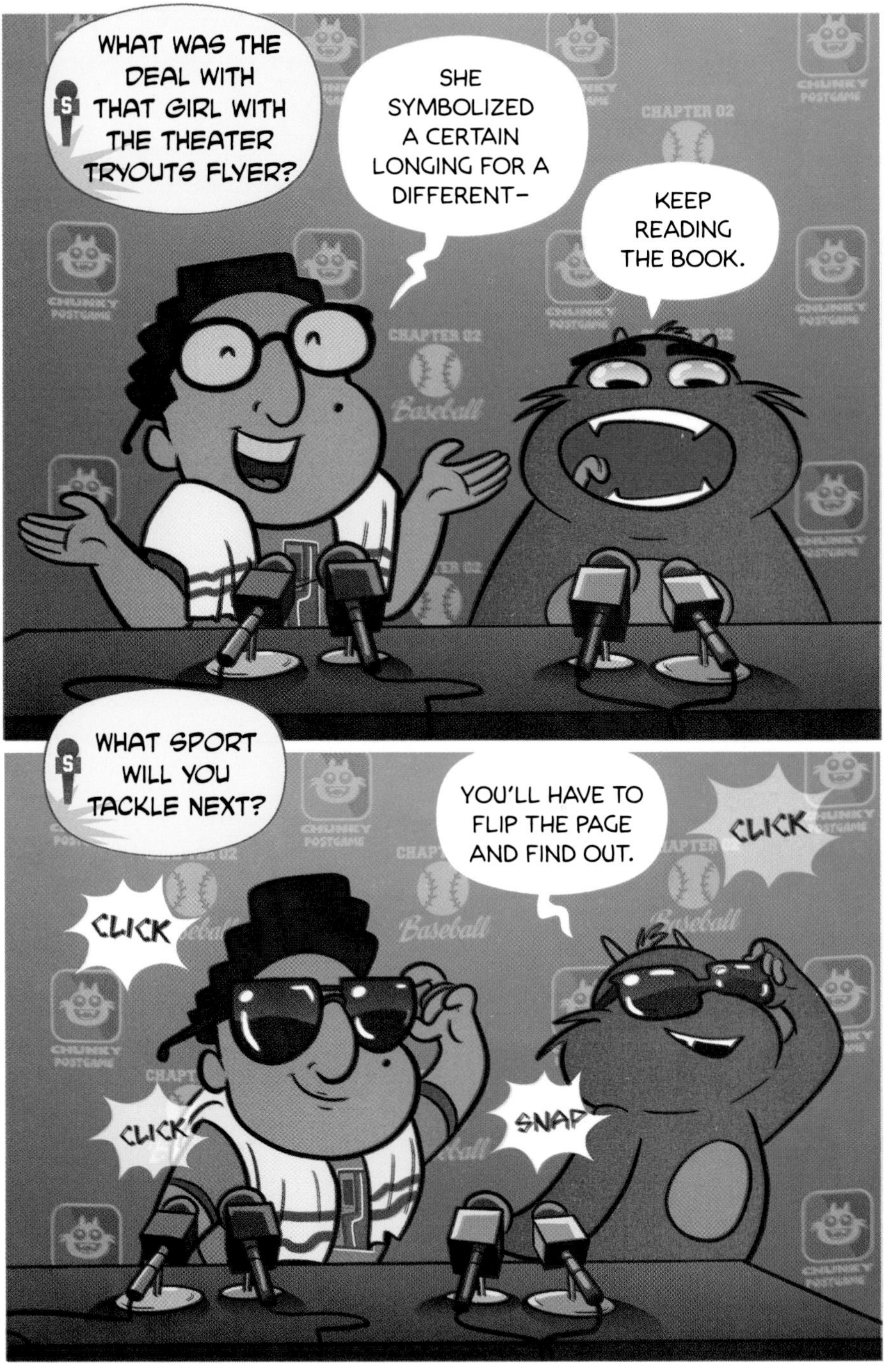
WHAT WAS THE DEAL WITH THAT GIRL WITH THE THEATER TRYOUTS FLYER?
SHE SYMBOLIZED A CERTAIN LONGING FOR A DIFFERENT–
KEEP READING THE BOOK.
WHAT SPORT WILL YOU TACKLE NEXT?
YOU'LL HAVE TO FLIP THE PAGE AND FIND OUT.
CLICK
CLICK
CLICK
SNAP

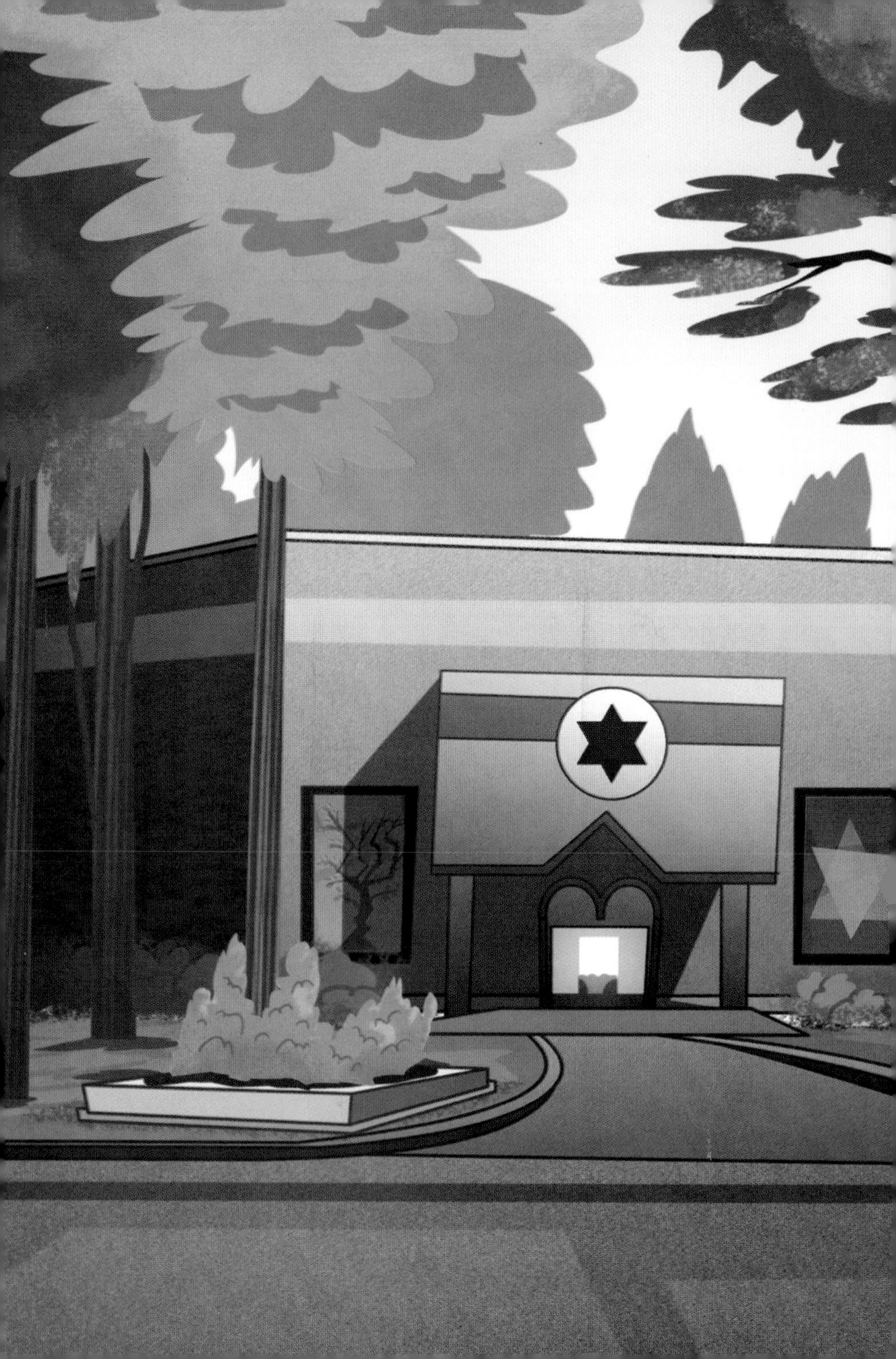

CHAPTER THREE
Soccer

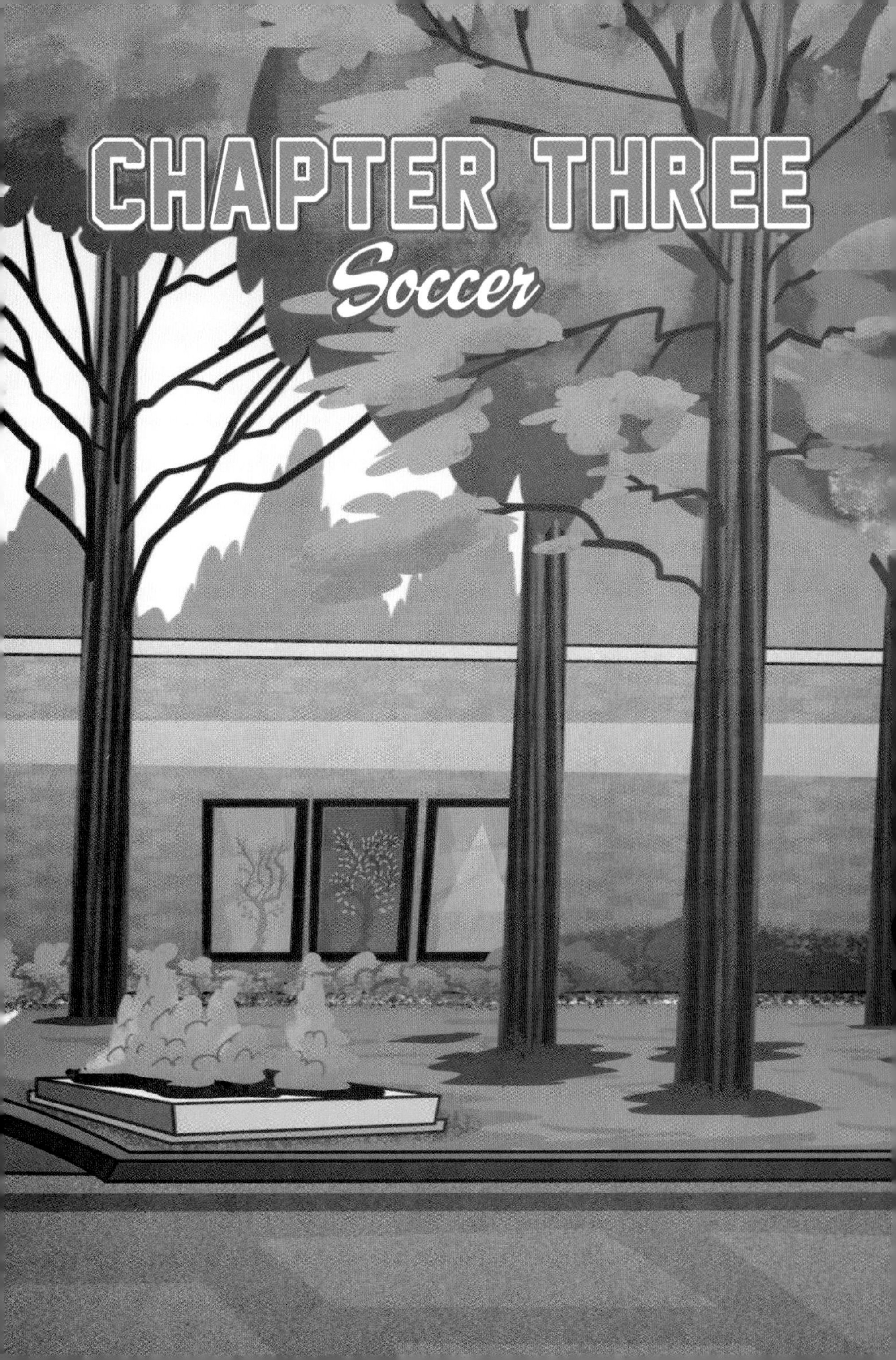

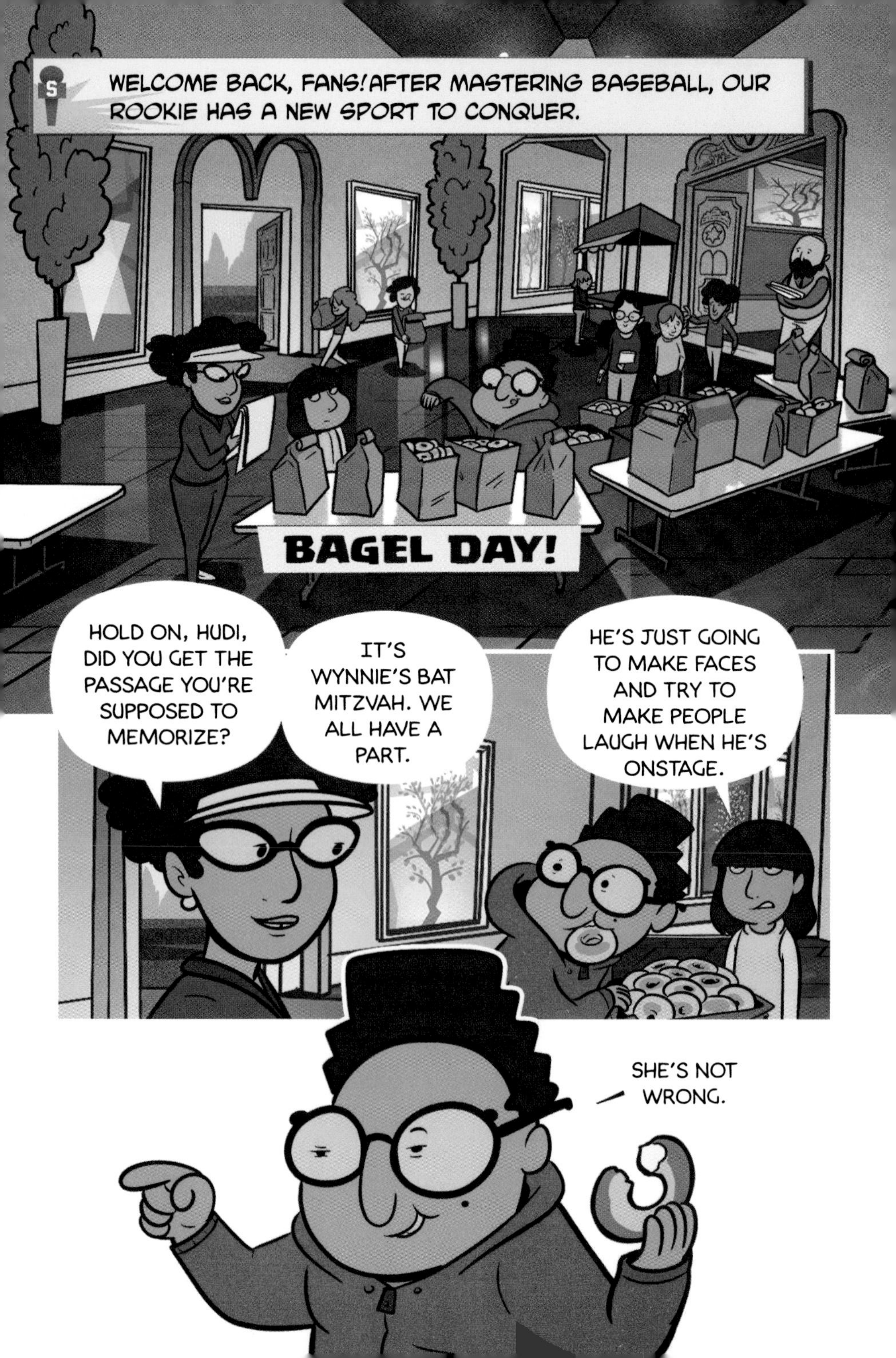

WELCOME BACK, FANS! AFTER MASTERING BASEBALL, OUR ROOKIE HAS A NEW SPORT TO CONQUER.
BAGEL DAY!
HOLD ON, HUDI, DID YOU GET THE PASSAGE YOU'RE SUPPOSED TO MEMORIZE?
IT'S WYNNIE'S BAT MITZVAH. WE ALL HAVE A PART.
HE'S JUST GOING TO MAKE FACES AND TRY TO MAKE PEOPLE LAUGH WHEN HE'S ONSTAGE.
SHE'S NOT WRONG.

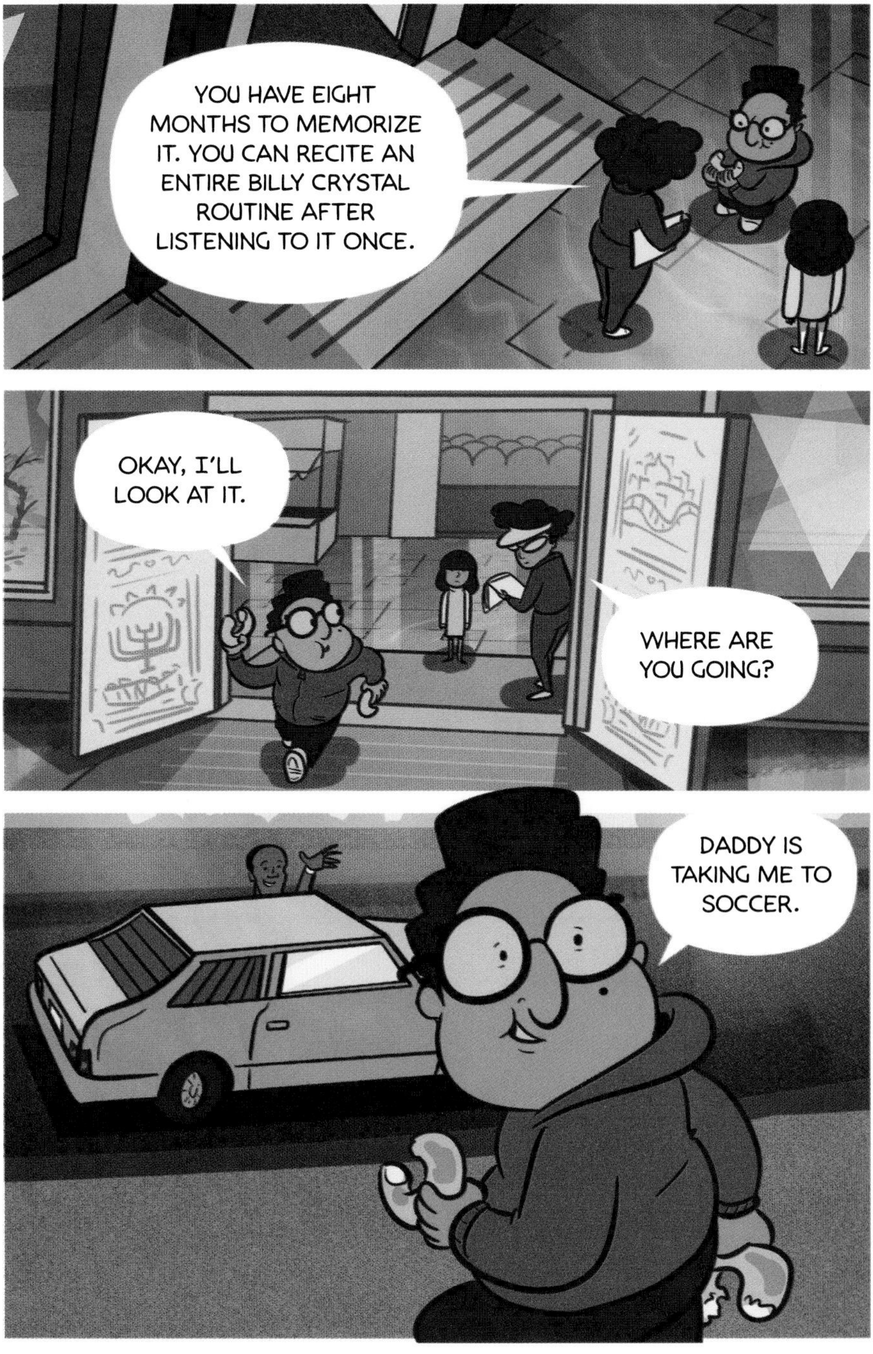
YOU HAVE EIGHT MONTHS TO MEMORIZE IT. YOU CAN RECITE AN ENTIRE BILLY CRYSTAL ROUTINE AFTER LISTENING TO IT ONCE.
OKAY, I'LL LOOK AT IT.
WHERE ARE YOU GOING?
DADDY IS TAKING ME TO SOCCER.

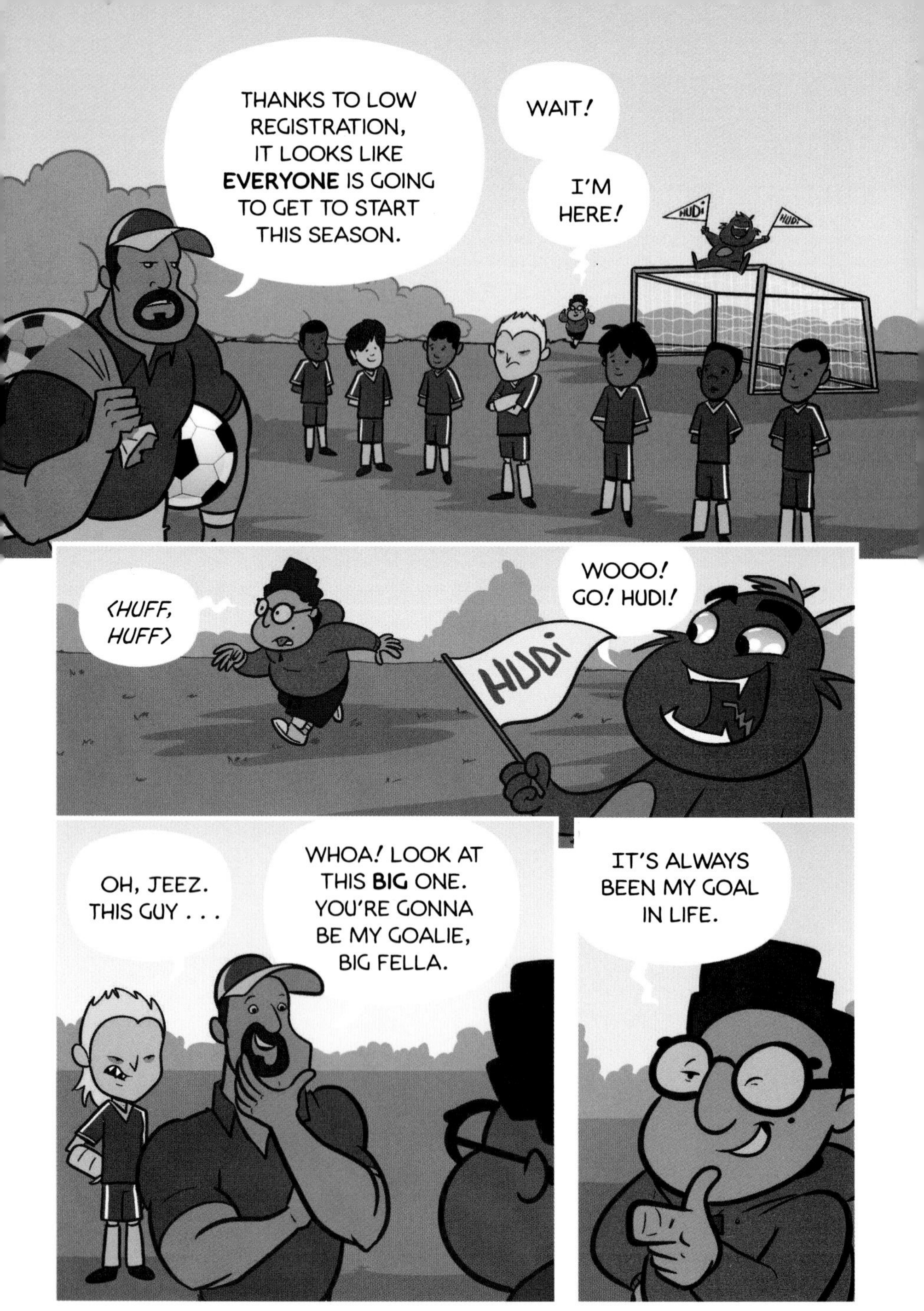
THANKS TO LOW REGISTRATION, IT LOOKS LIKE **EVERYONE** IS GOING TO GET TO START THIS SEASON.
WAIT!
I'M HERE!
HUDi
HUDi
<HUFF, HUFF>
WOOO! GO! HUDI!
HUDi
OH, JEEZ. THIS GUY . . .
WHOA! LOOK AT THIS **BIG** ONE. YOU'RE GONNA BE MY GOALIE, BIG FELLA.
IT'S ALWAYS BEEN MY GOAL IN LIFE.

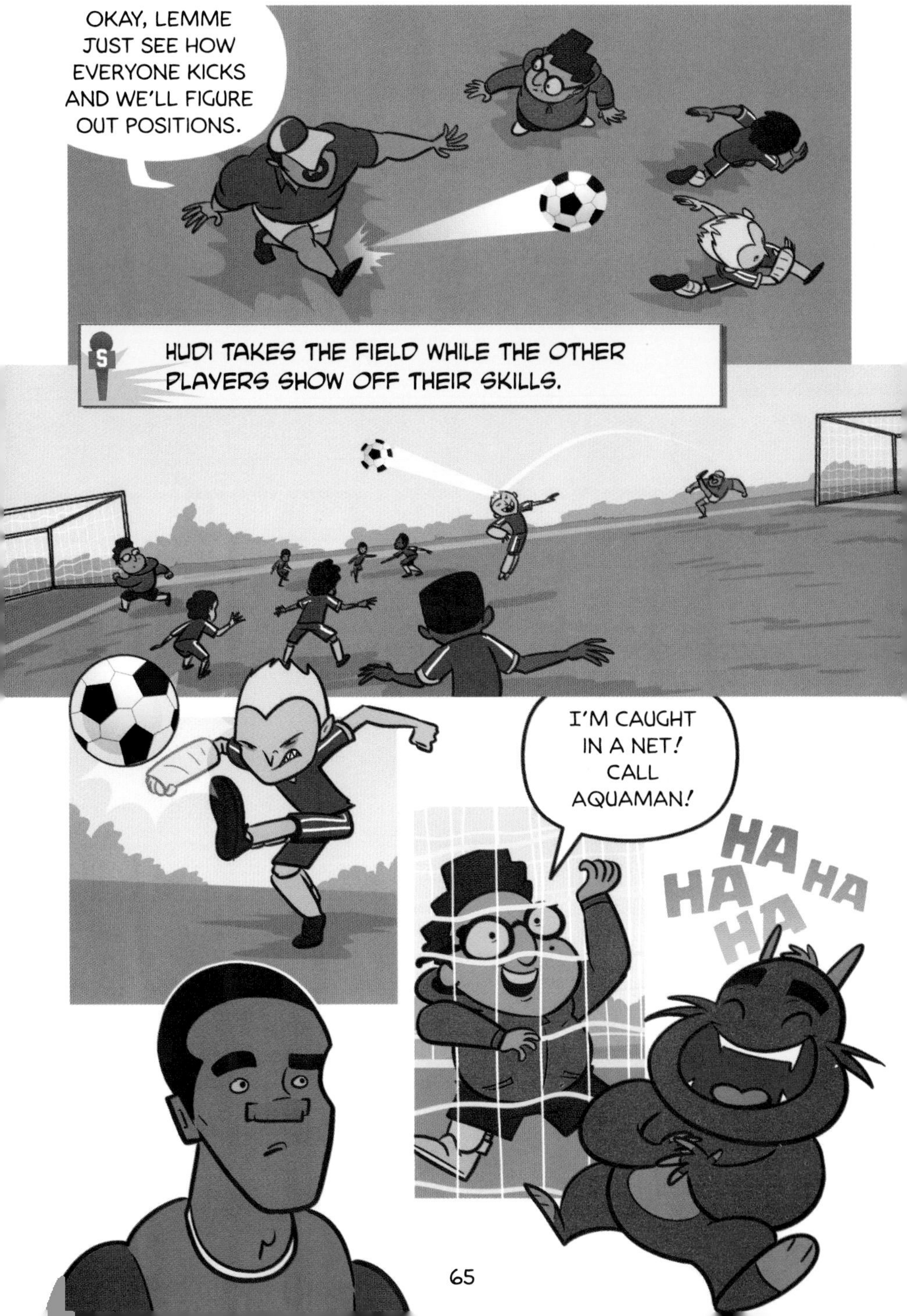
OKAY, LEMME JUST SEE HOW EVERYONE KICKS AND WE'LL FIGURE OUT POSITIONS.
HUDI TAKES THE FIELD WHILE THE OTHER PLAYERS SHOW OFF THEIR SKILLS.
I'M CAUGHT IN A NET! CALL AQUAMAN!
HA HA HA HA

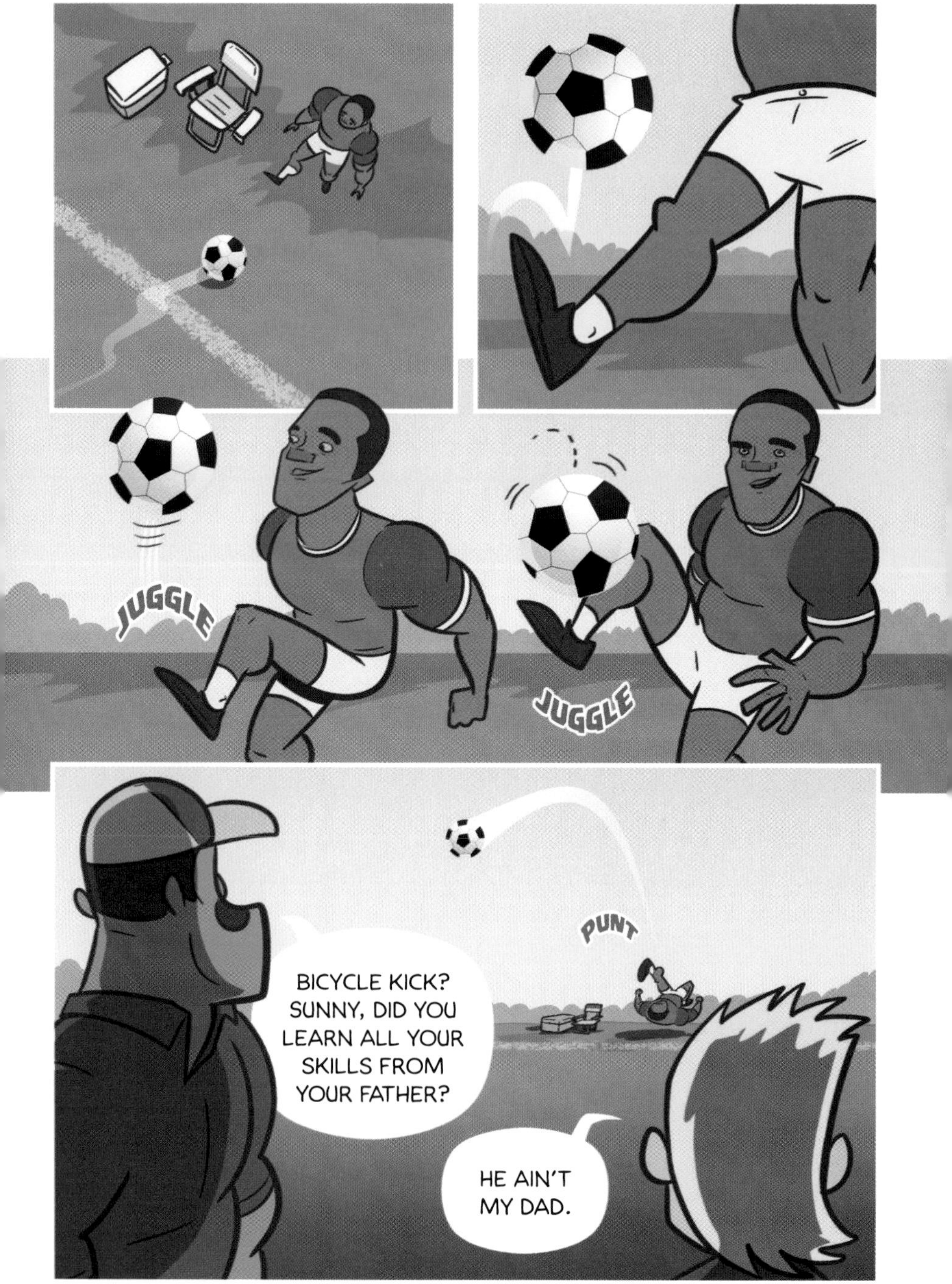
JUGGLE
JUGGLE
PUNT
BICYCLE KICK? SUNNY, DID YOU LEARN ALL YOUR SKILLS FROM YOUR FATHER?
HE AIN'T MY DAD.

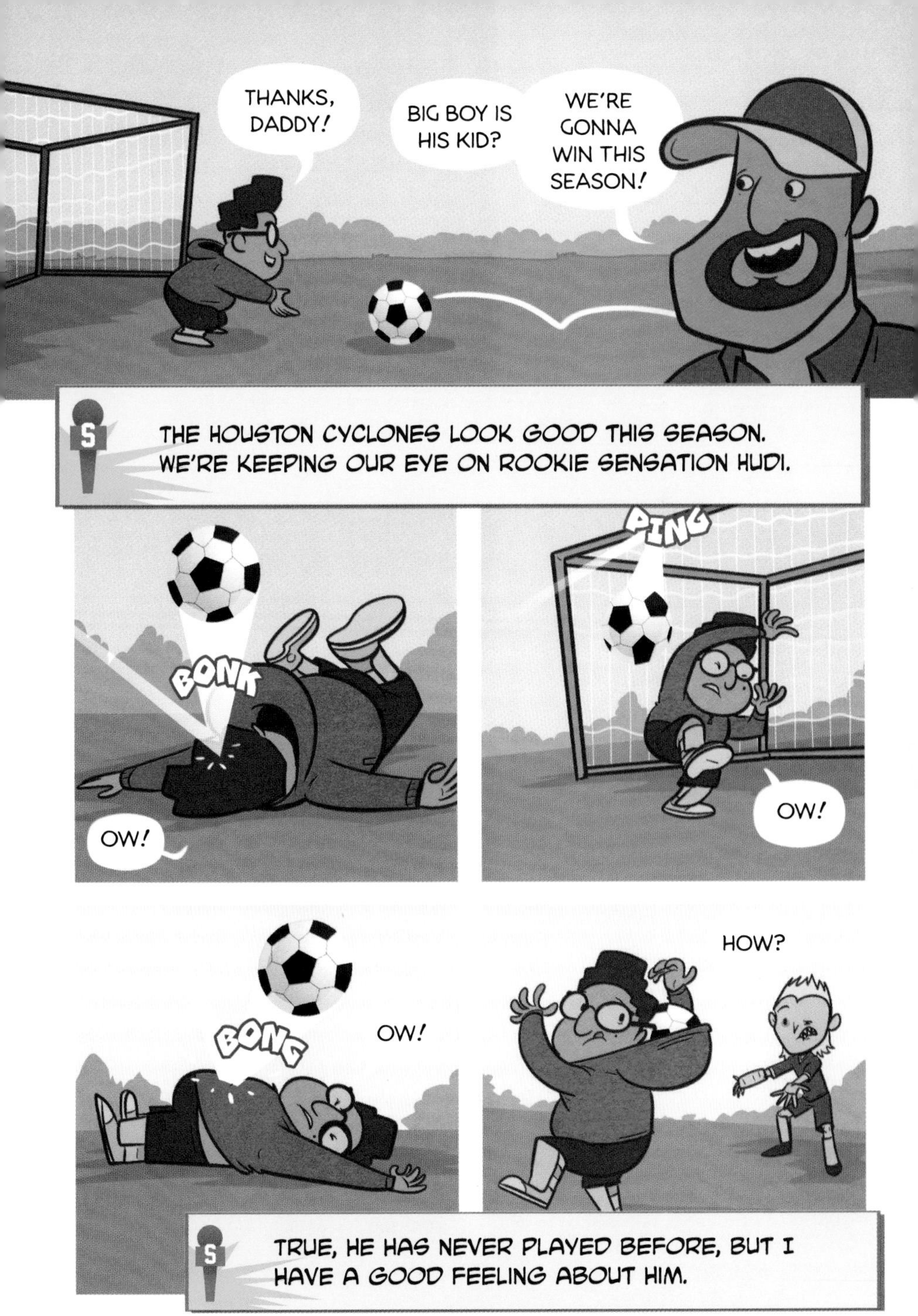
THANKS, DADDY!
BIG BOY IS HIS KID?
WE'RE GONNA WIN THIS SEASON!
THE HOUSTON CYCLONES LOOK GOOD THIS SEASON. WE'RE KEEPING OUR EYE ON ROOKIE SENSATION HUDI.
BONK
OW!
PING
OW!
BONG
OW!
HOW?
TRUE, HE HAS NEVER PLAYED BEFORE, BUT I HAVE A GOOD FEELING ABOUT HIM.

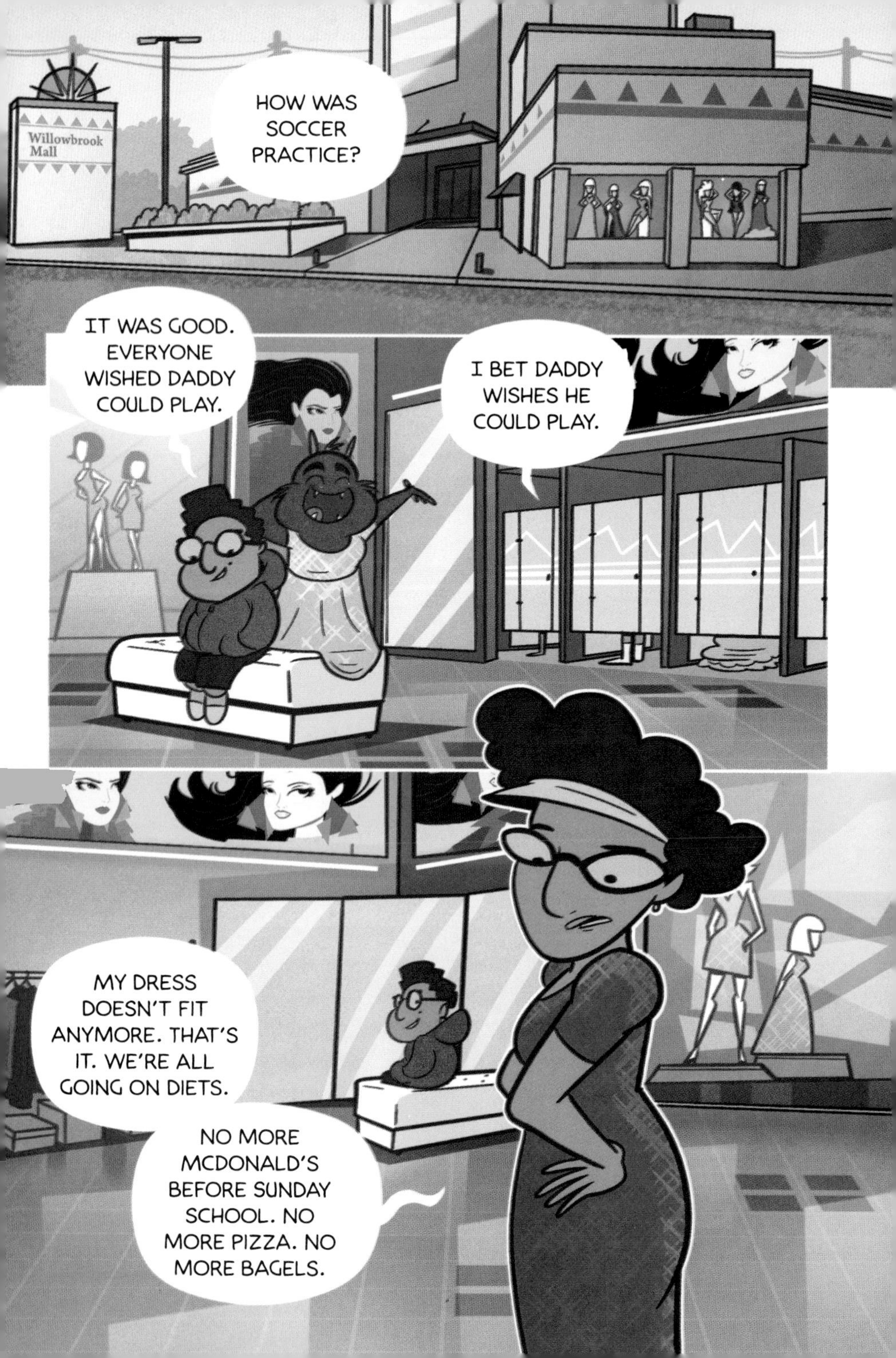
Willowbrook Mall
HOW WAS SOCCER PRACTICE?
IT WAS GOOD. EVERYONE WISHED DADDY COULD PLAY.
I BET DADDY WISHES HE COULD PLAY.
MY DRESS DOESN'T FIT ANYMORE. THAT'S IT. WE'RE ALL GOING ON DIETS.
NO MORE MCDONALD'S BEFORE SUNDAY SCHOOL. NO MORE PIZZA. NO MORE BAGELS.

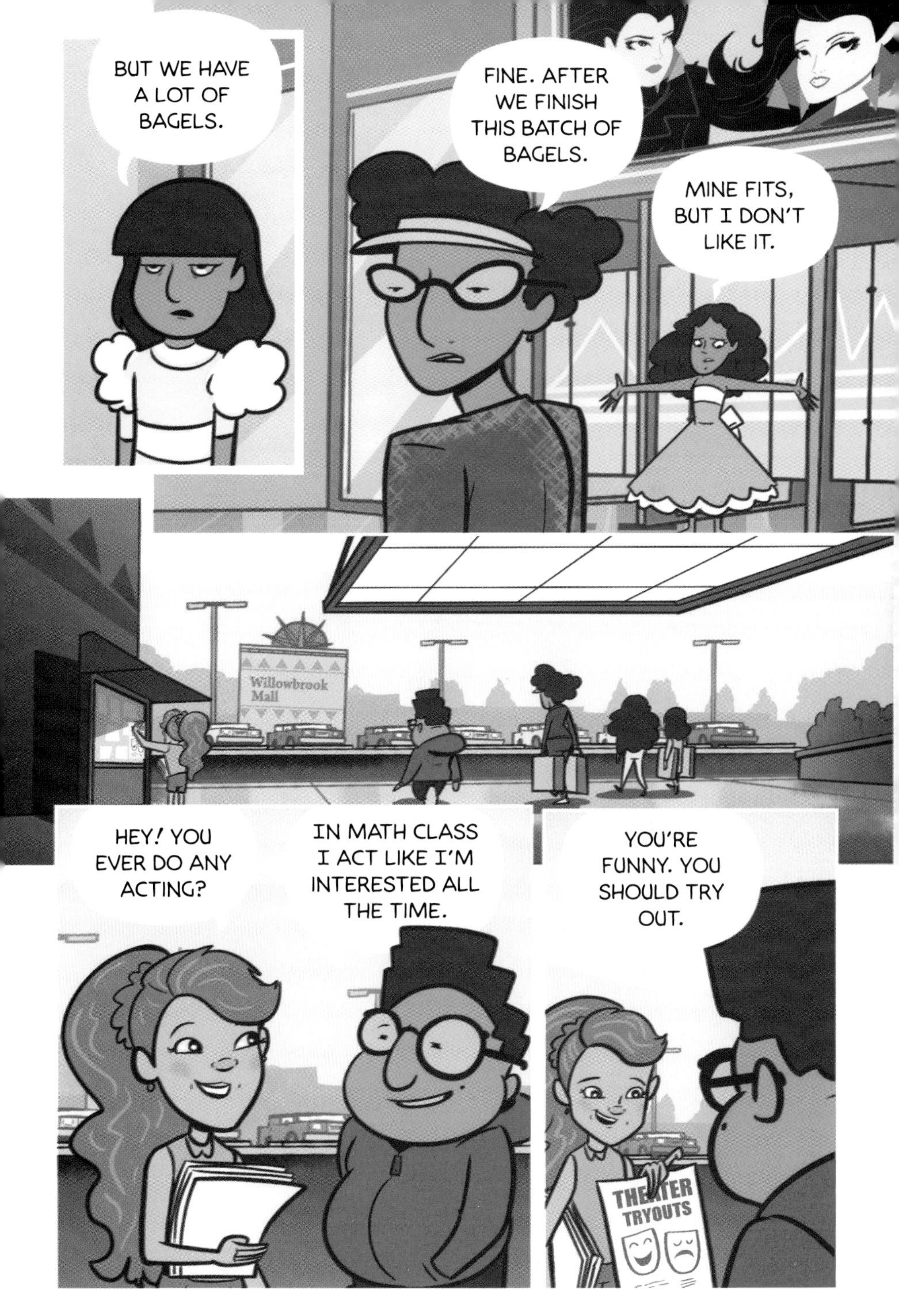
BUT WE HAVE A LOT OF BAGELS.
FINE. AFTER WE FINISH THIS BATCH OF BAGELS.
MINE FITS, BUT I DON'T LIKE IT.
Willowbrook Mall
HEY! YOU EVER DO ANY ACTING?
IN MATH CLASS I ACT LIKE I'M INTERESTED ALL THE TIME.
YOU'RE FUNNY. YOU SHOULD TRY OUT.
THEATER TRYOUTS

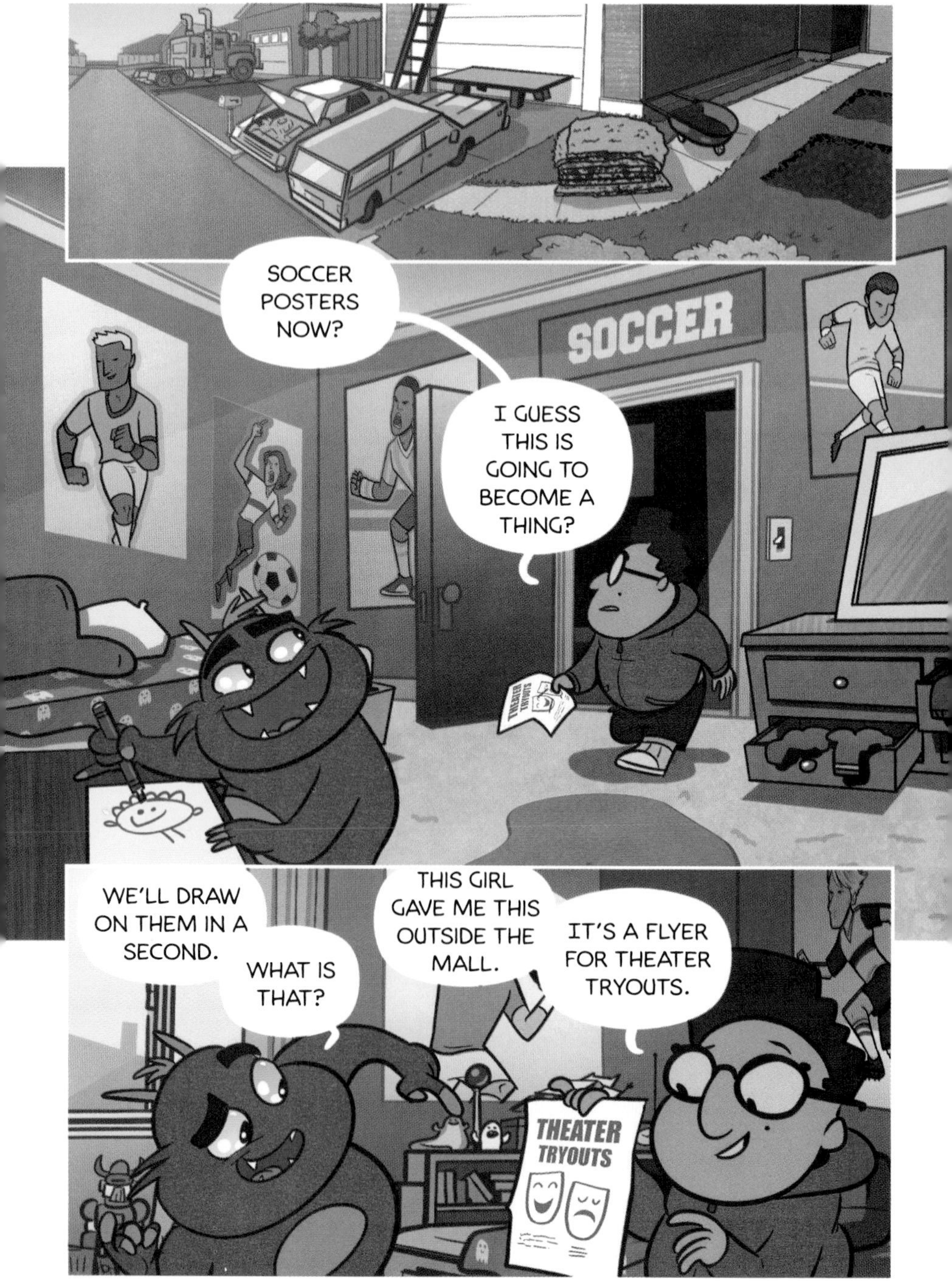
SOCCER POSTERS NOW?
SOCCER
I GUESS THIS IS GOING TO BECOME A THING?
THEATER TRYOUTS
WE'LL DRAW ON THEM IN A SECOND.
WHAT IS THAT?
THIS GIRL GAVE ME THIS OUTSIDE THE MALL.
IT'S A FLYER FOR THEATER TRYOUTS.
THEATER TRYOUTS

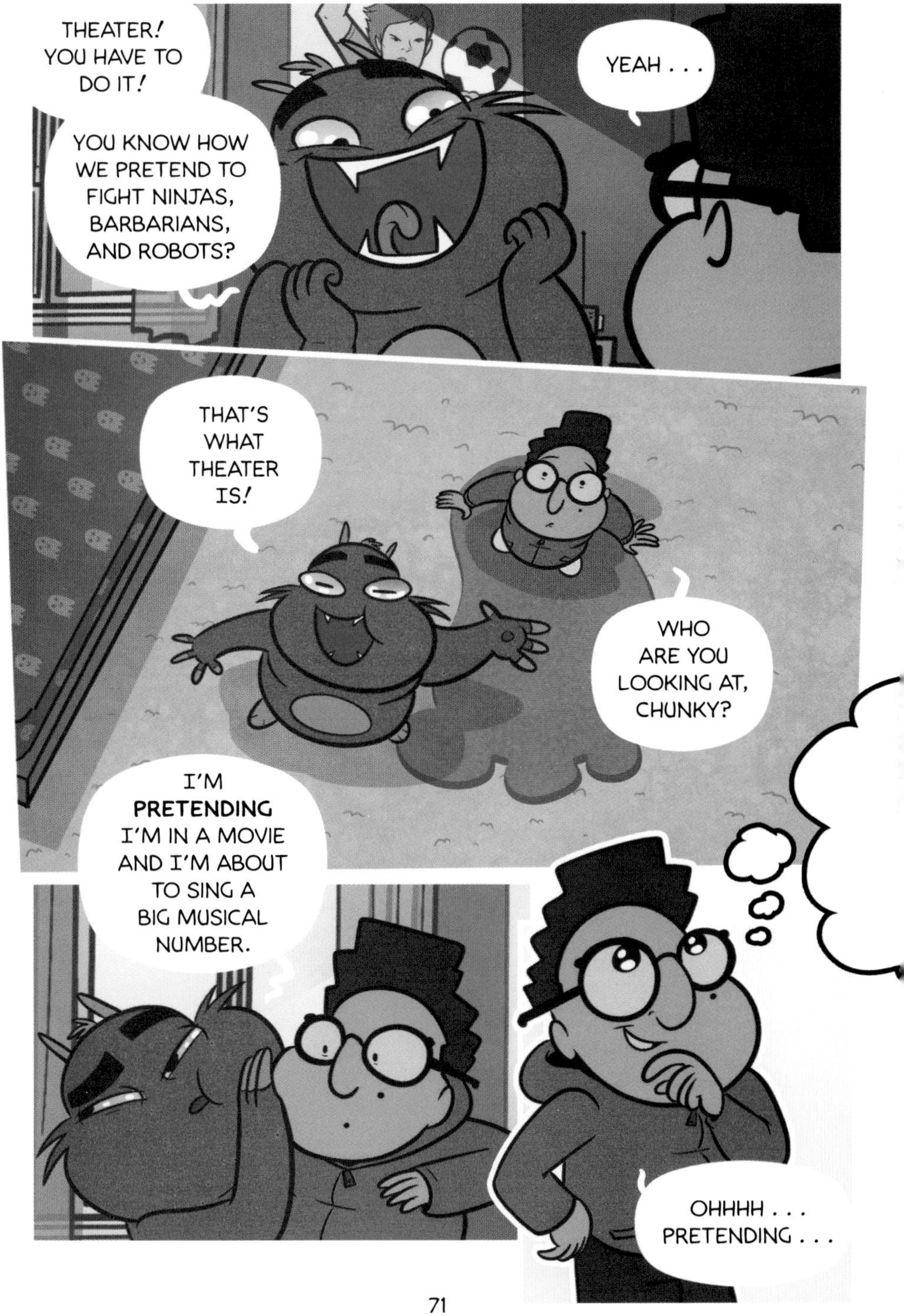
THEATER! YOU HAVE TO DO IT!
YOU KNOW HOW WE PRETEND TO FIGHT NINJAS, BARBARIANS, AND ROBOTS?
YEAH . . .
THAT'S WHAT THEATER IS!
WHO ARE YOU LOOKING AT, CHUNKY?
I'M **PRETENDING** I'M IN A MOVIE AND I'M ABOUT TO SING A BIG MUSICAL NUMBER.
OHHHH . . . PRETENDING . . .

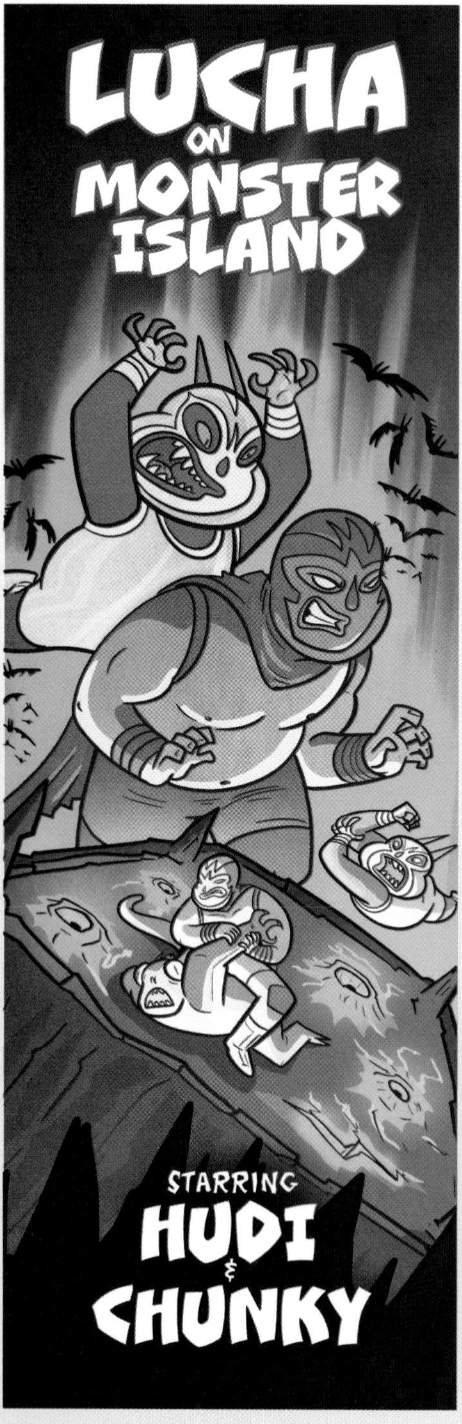
LUCHA
ON
MONSTER
ISLAND
STARRING
HUDI
&
CHUNKY

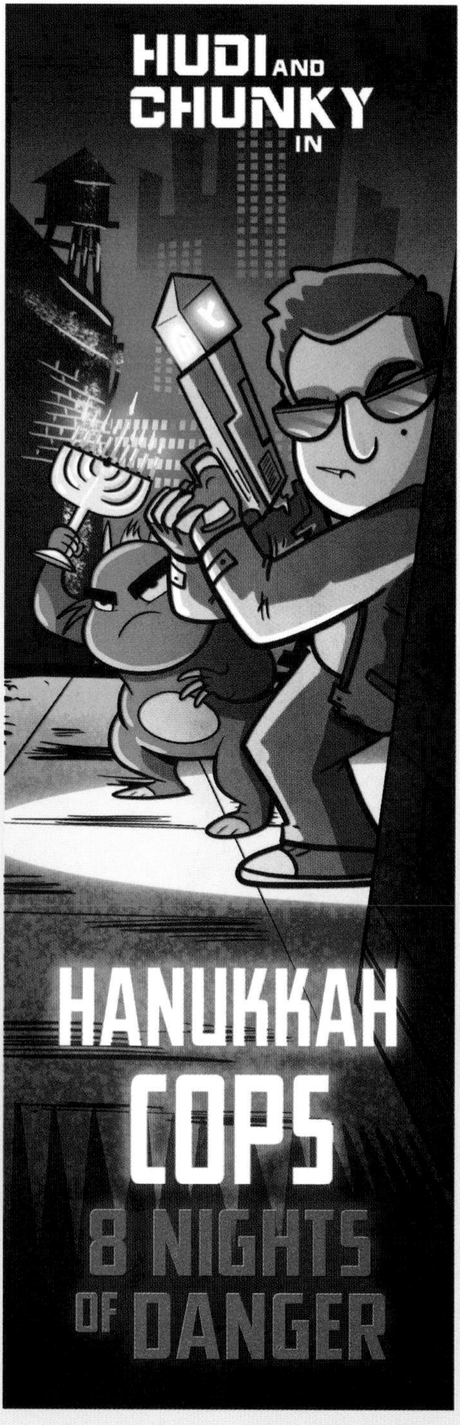
HUDI AND
CHUNKY
IN
HANUKKAH
COPS
8 NIGHTS
OF DANGER

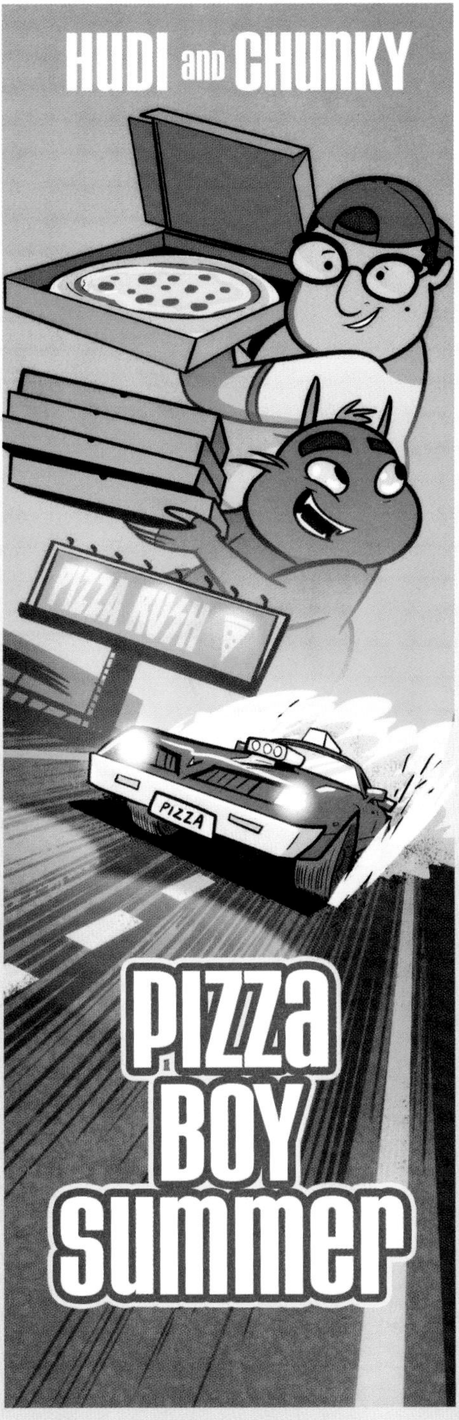
HUDI and CHUNKY
PIZZA RUSH
PIZZA
PIZZA BOY SUMMER

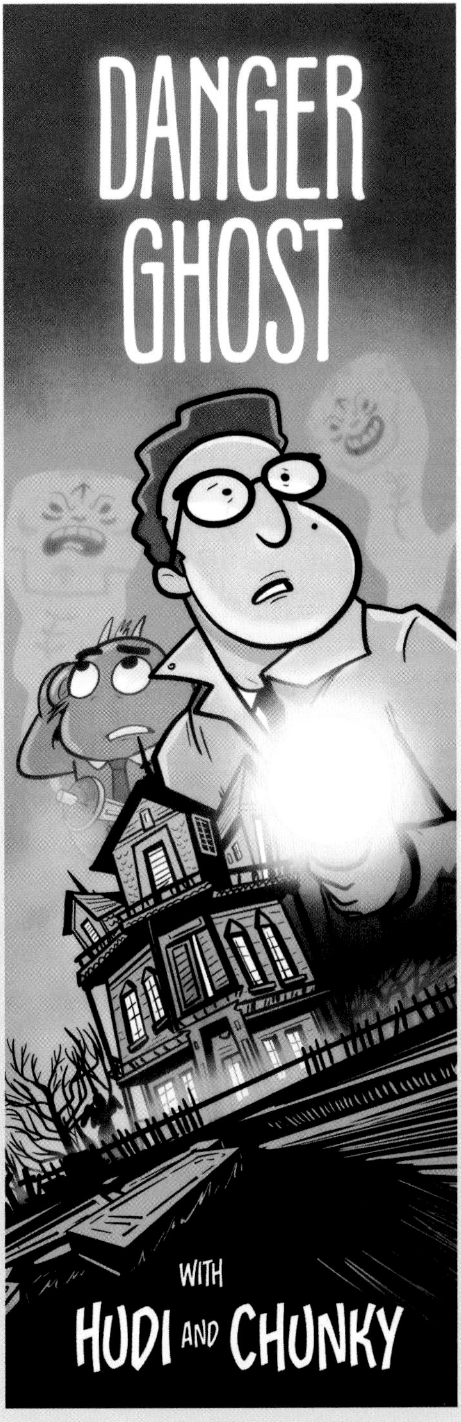
DANGER GHOST
WITH
HUDI AND CHUNKY

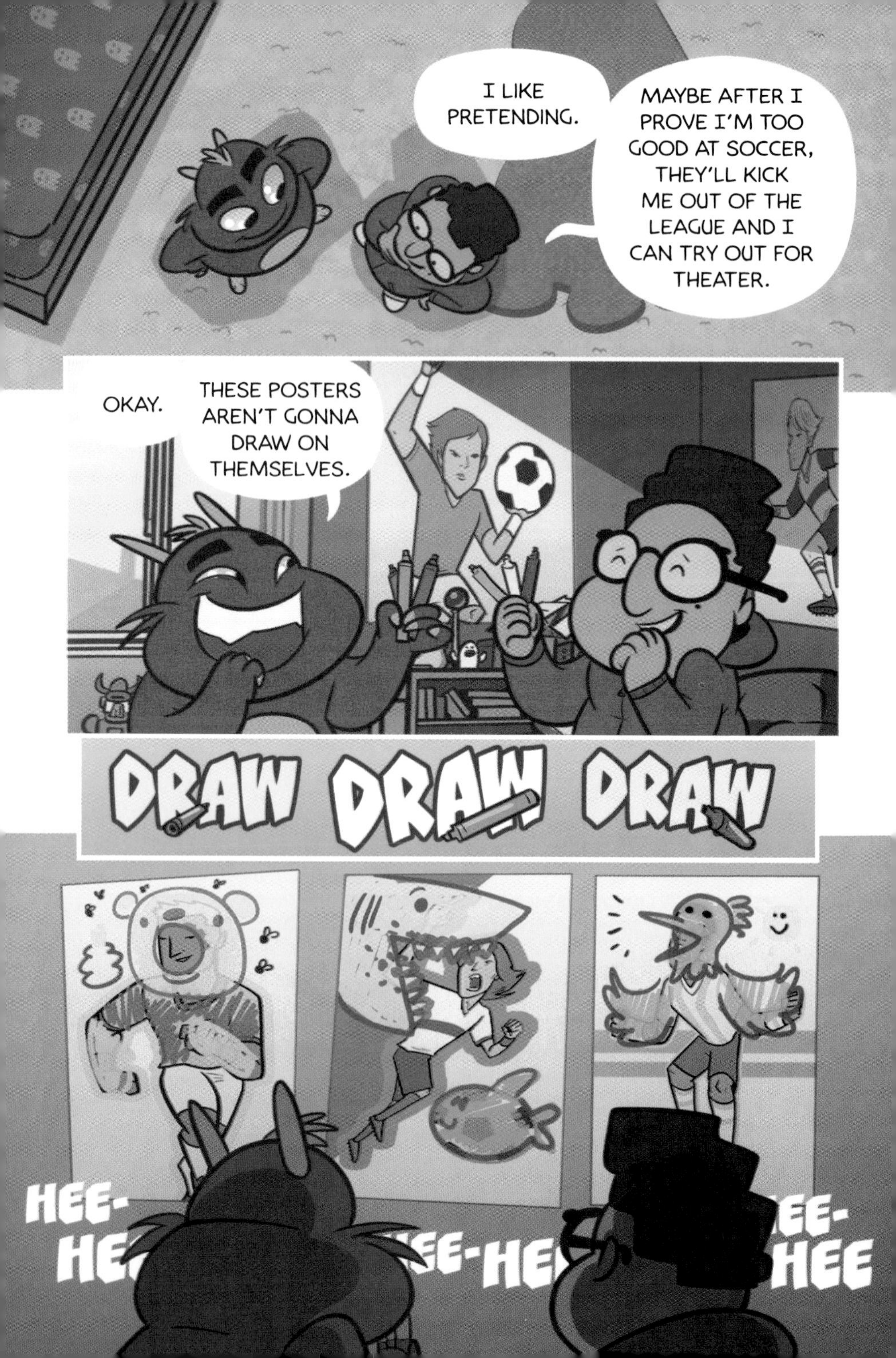
I LIKE PRETENDING.
MAYBE AFTER I PROVE I'M TOO GOOD AT SOCCER, THEY'LL KICK ME OUT OF THE LEAGUE AND I CAN TRY OUT FOR THEATER.
OKAY.
THESE POSTERS AREN'T GONNA DRAW ON THEMSELVES.
DRAW DRAW DRAW
HEE-
HEE-HEE-HEE-

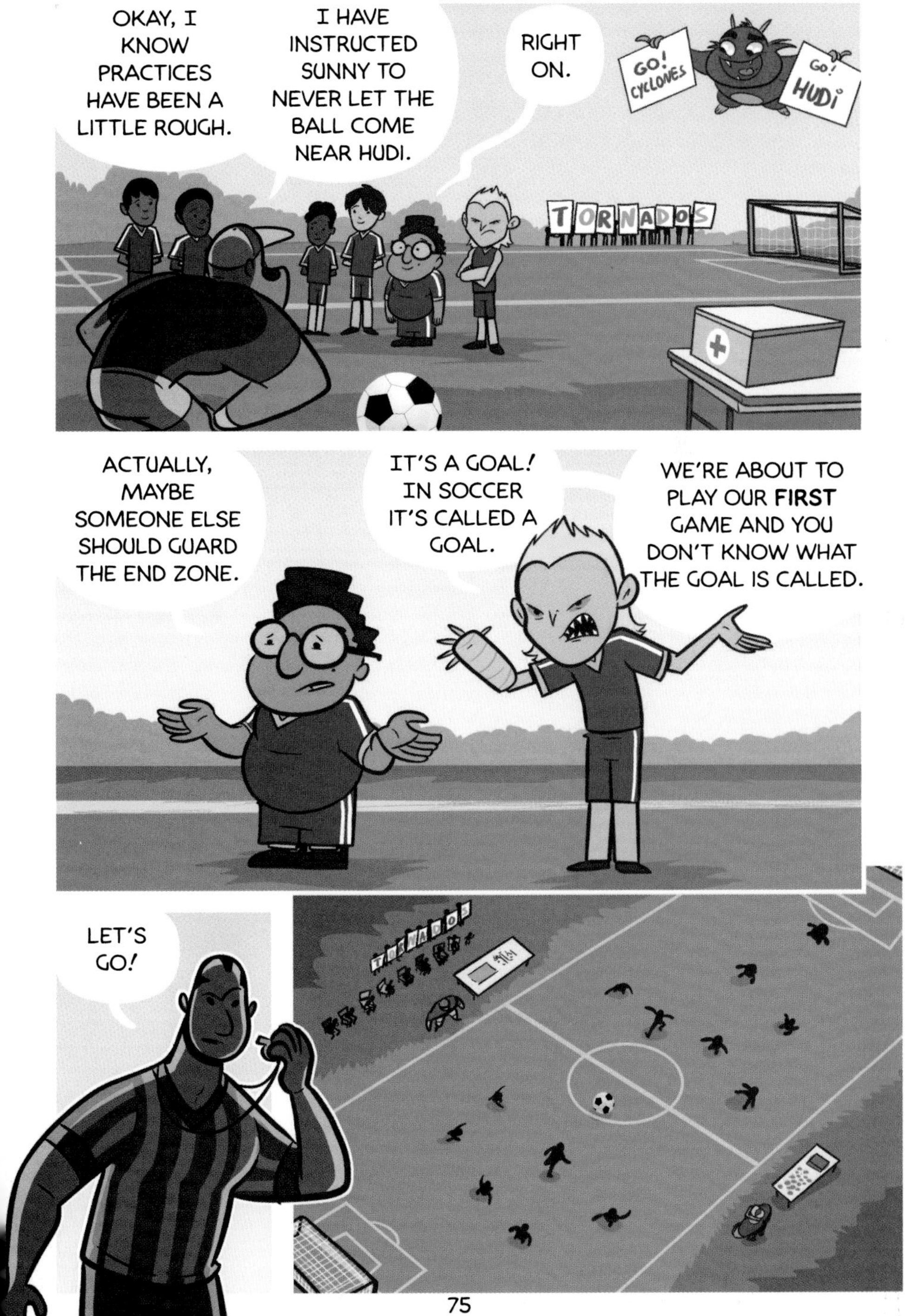
OKAY, I KNOW PRACTICES HAVE BEEN A LITTLE ROUGH.
I HAVE INSTRUCTED SUNNY TO NEVER LET THE BALL COME NEAR HUDI.
RIGHT ON.
GO! CYCLONES
GO! HUDI
TORNADOS
ACTUALLY, MAYBE SOMEONE ELSE SHOULD GUARD THE END ZONE.
IT'S A GOAL! IN SOCCER IT'S CALLED A GOAL.
WE'RE ABOUT TO PLAY OUR **FIRST** GAME AND YOU DON'T KNOW WHAT THE GOAL IS CALLED.
LET'S GO!

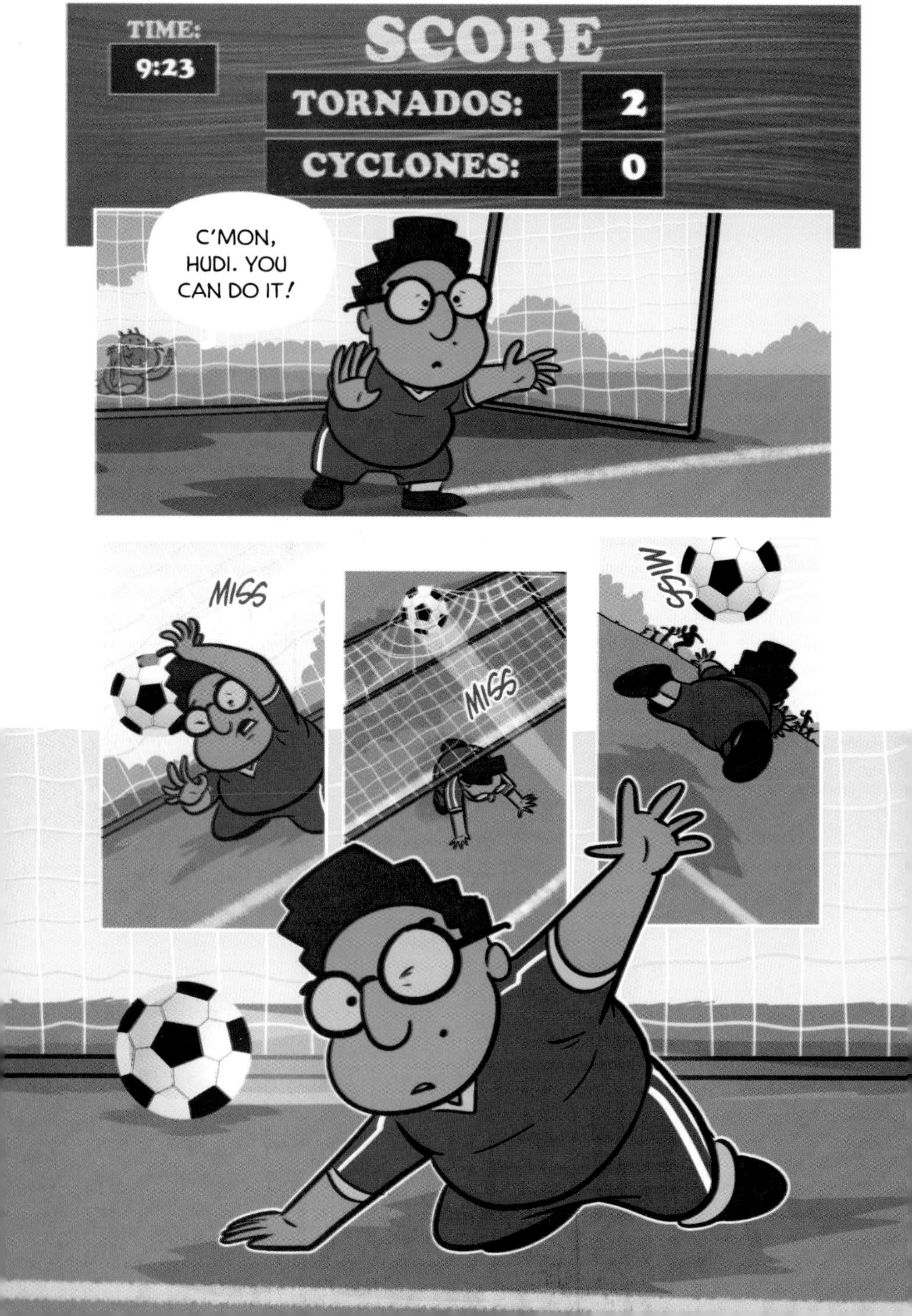

TIME:
9:23
SCORE
TORNADOS: 2
CYCLONES: 0
C'MON, HUDI. YOU CAN DO IT!
MISS
MISS
MISS

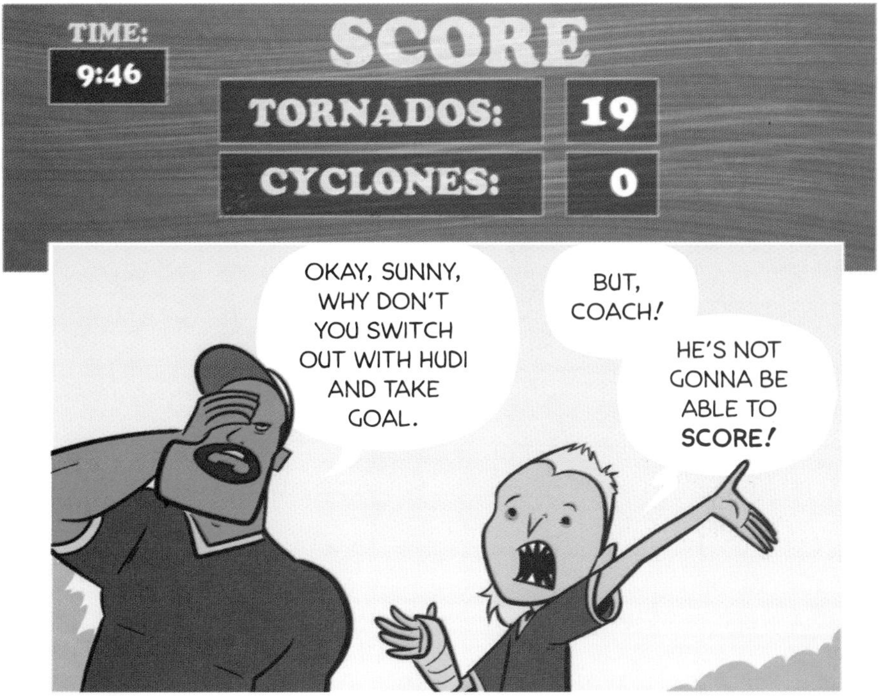
TIME:
9:46
SCORE
TORNADOS: 19
CYCLONES: 0
OKAY, SUNNY, WHY DON'T YOU SWITCH OUT WITH HUDI AND TAKE GOAL.
BUT, COACH!
HE'S NOT GONNA BE ABLE TO SCORE!

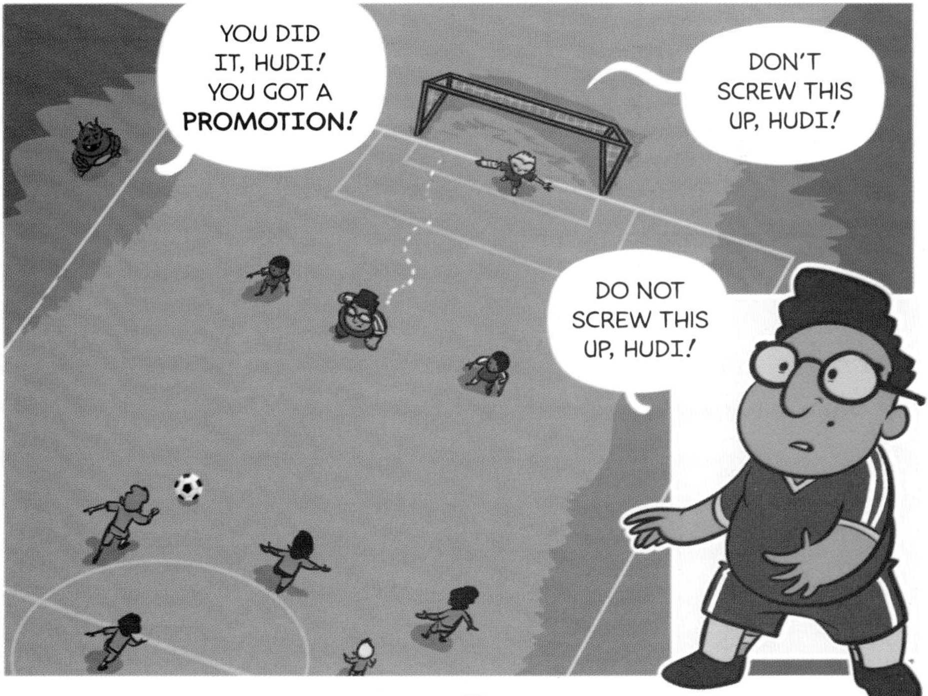
YOU DID IT, HUDI! YOU GOT A PROMOTION!
DON'T SCREW THIS UP, HUDI!
DO NOT SCREW THIS UP, HUDI!

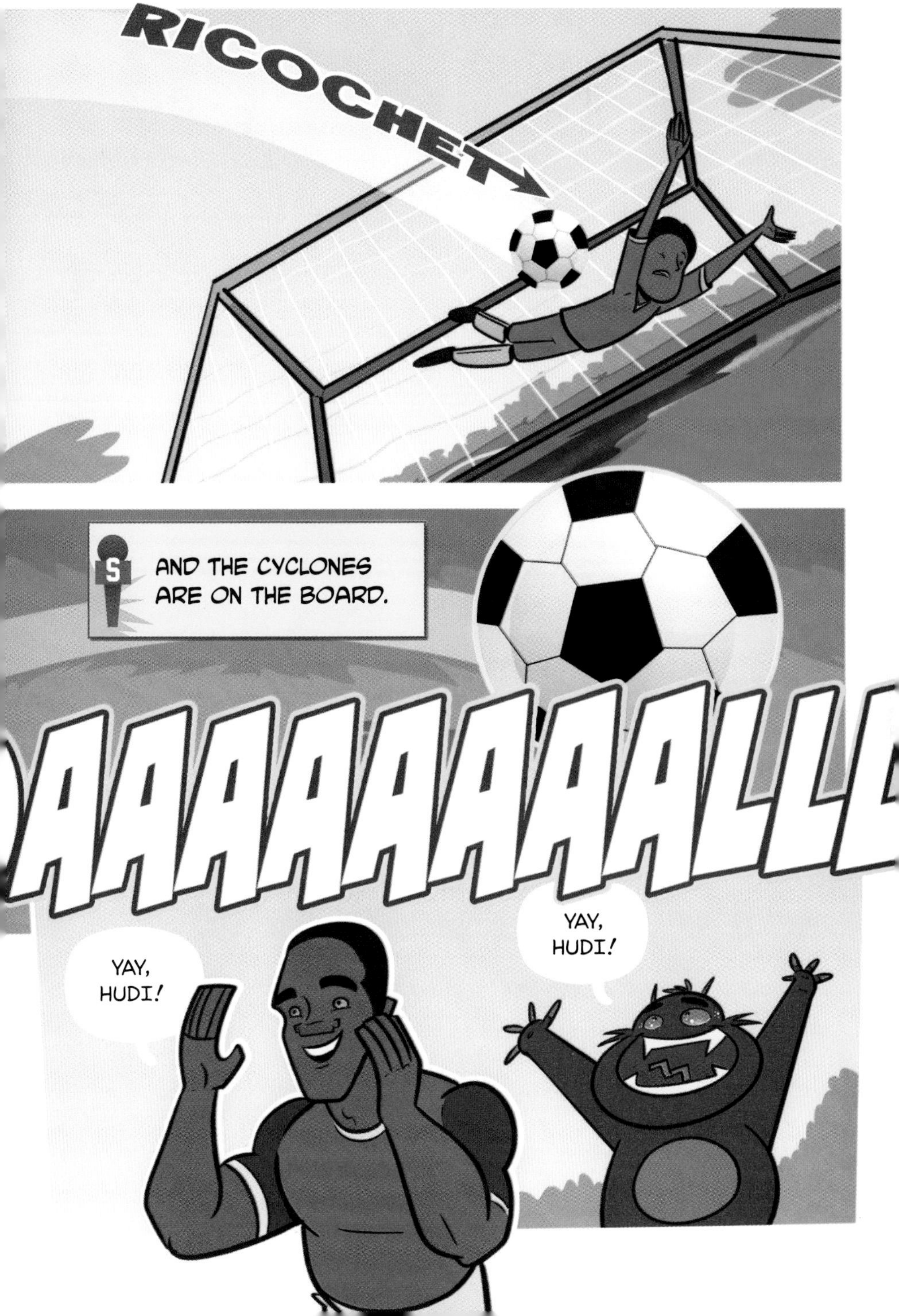
RICOCHET
AND THE CYCLONES ARE ON THE BOARD.
AAAAAAAAALLL
YAY, HUDI!
YAY, HUDI!

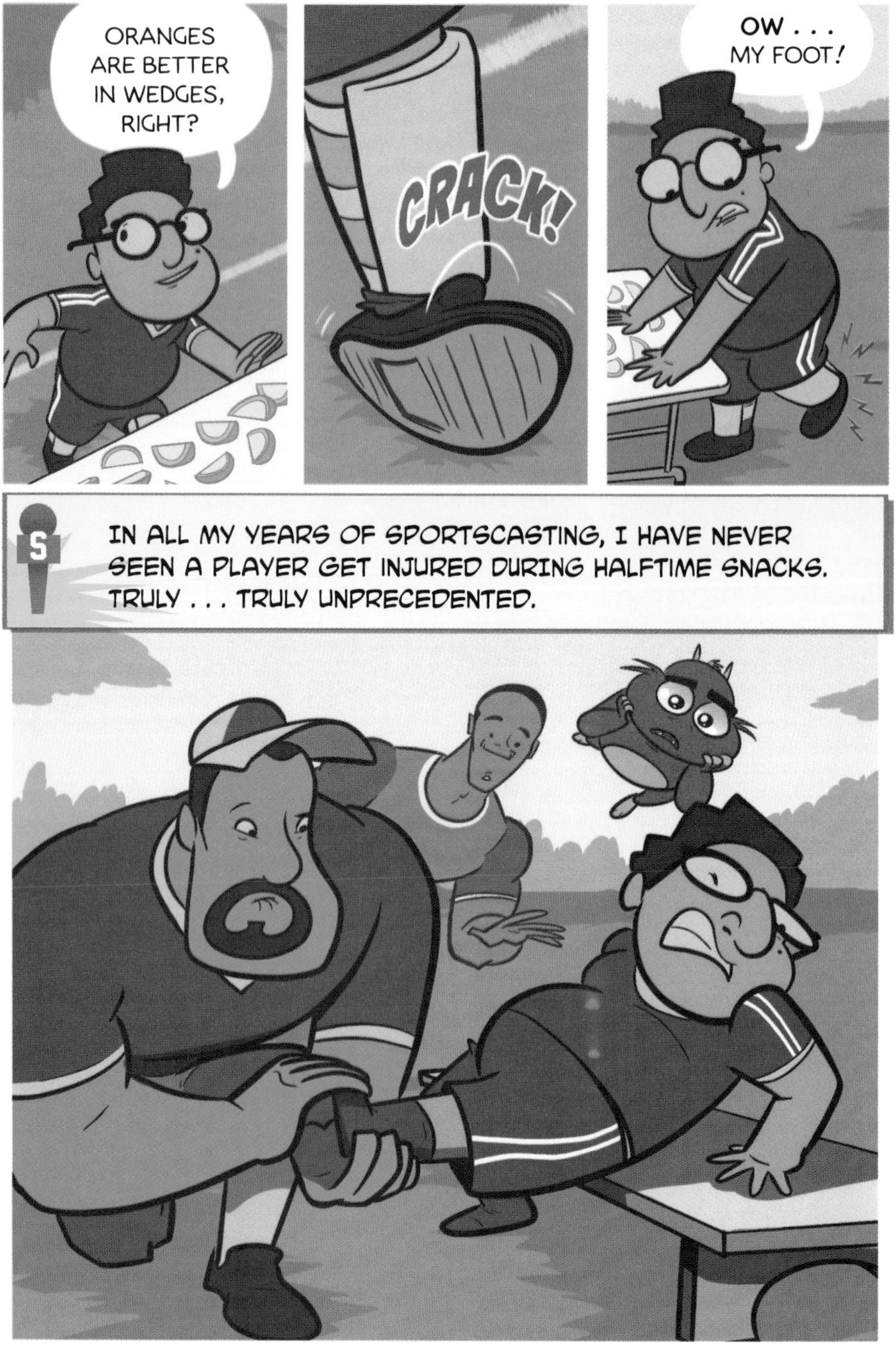
ORANGES ARE BETTER IN WEDGES, RIGHT?
CRACK!
OW . . . MY FOOT!
IN ALL MY YEARS OF SPORTSCASTING, I HAVE NEVER SEEN A PLAYER GET INJURED DURING HALFTIME SNACKS. TRULY . . . TRULY UNPRECEDENTED.

83

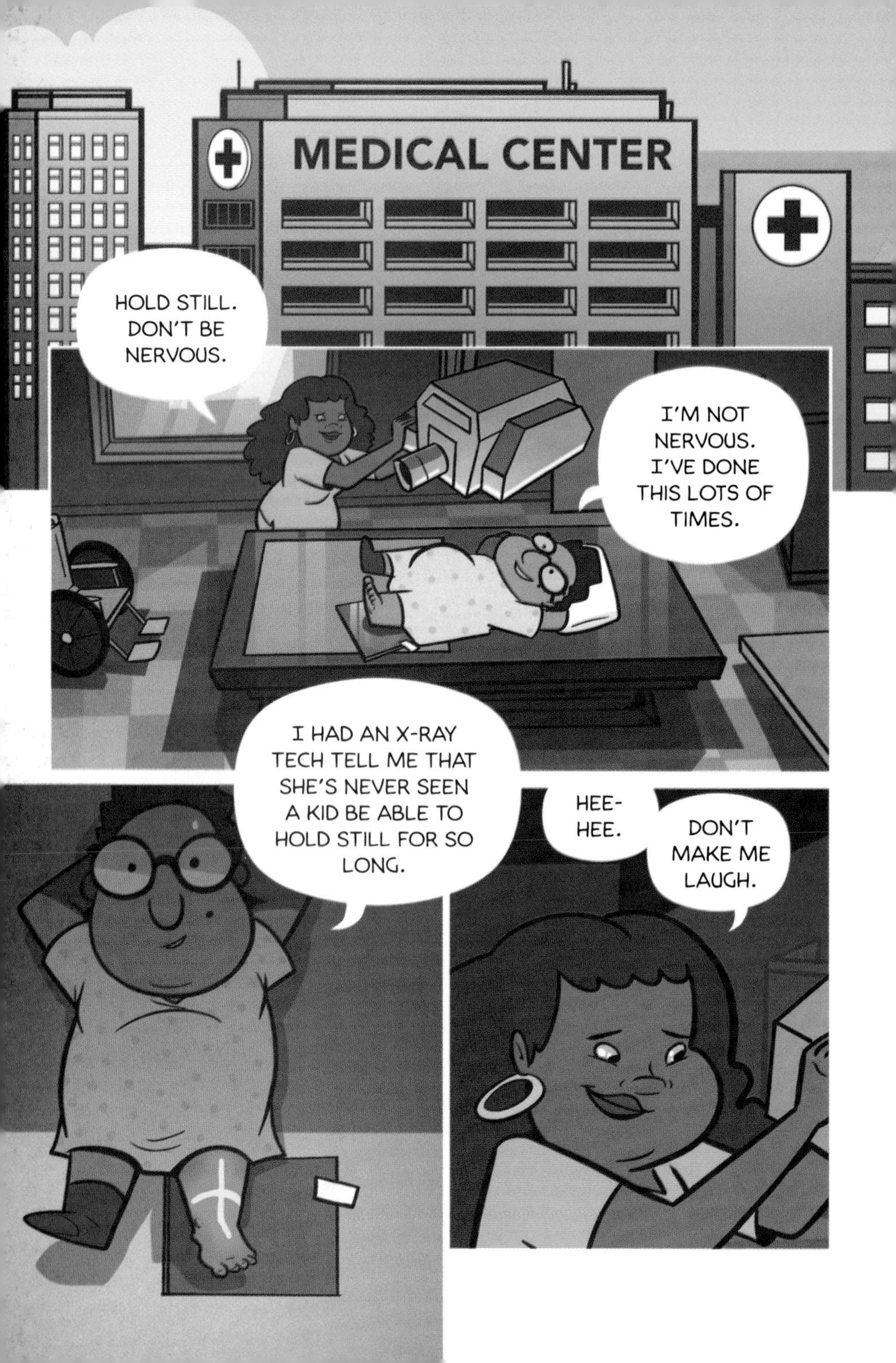
MEDICAL CENTER
HOLD STILL. DON'T BE NERVOUS.
I'M NOT NERVOUS. I'VE DONE THIS LOTS OF TIMES.
I HAD AN X-RAY TECH TELL ME THAT SHE'S NEVER SEEN A KID BE ABLE TO HOLD STILL FOR SO LONG.
HEE-HEE.
DON'T MAKE ME LAUGH.

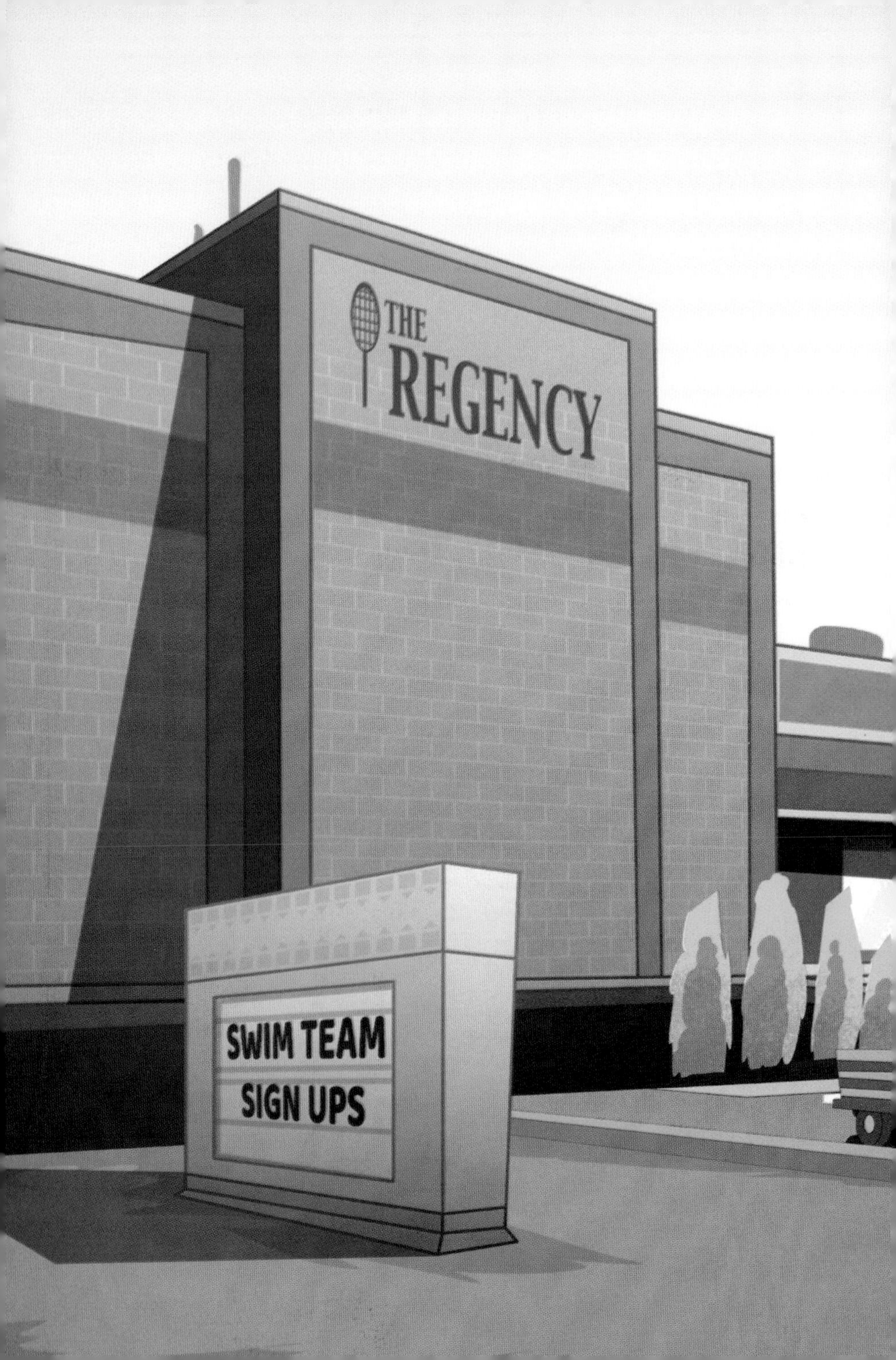
THE REGENCY
SWIM TEAM
SIGN UPS

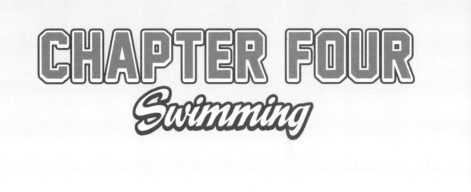

CHAPTER FOUR
Swimming

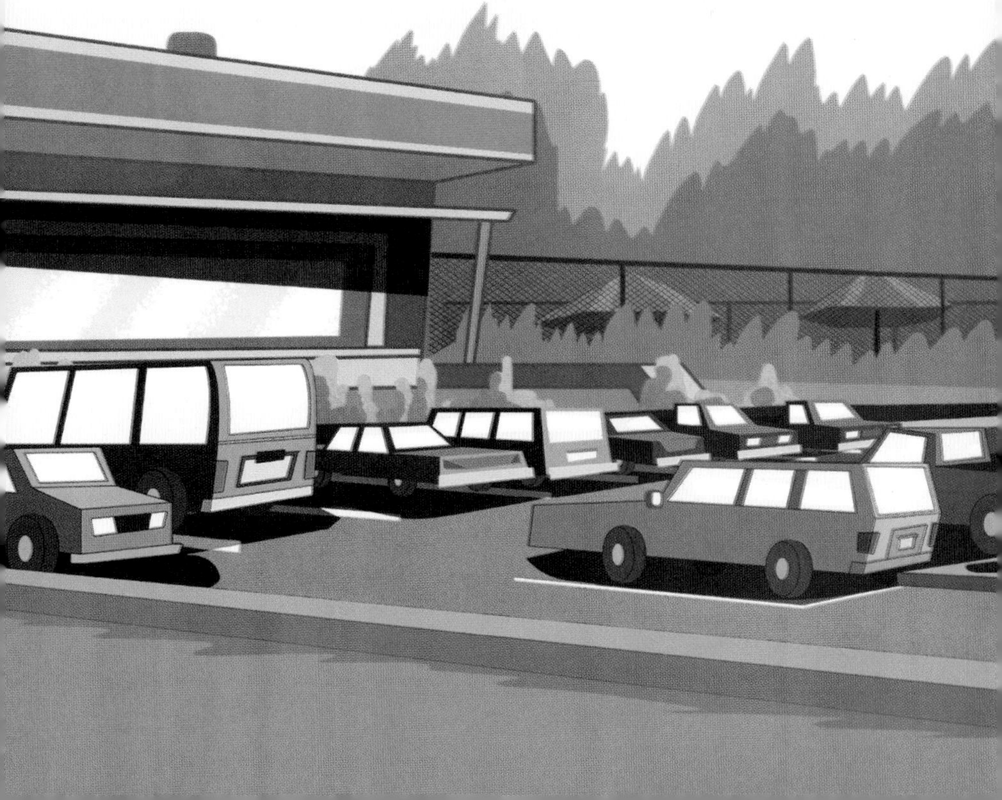

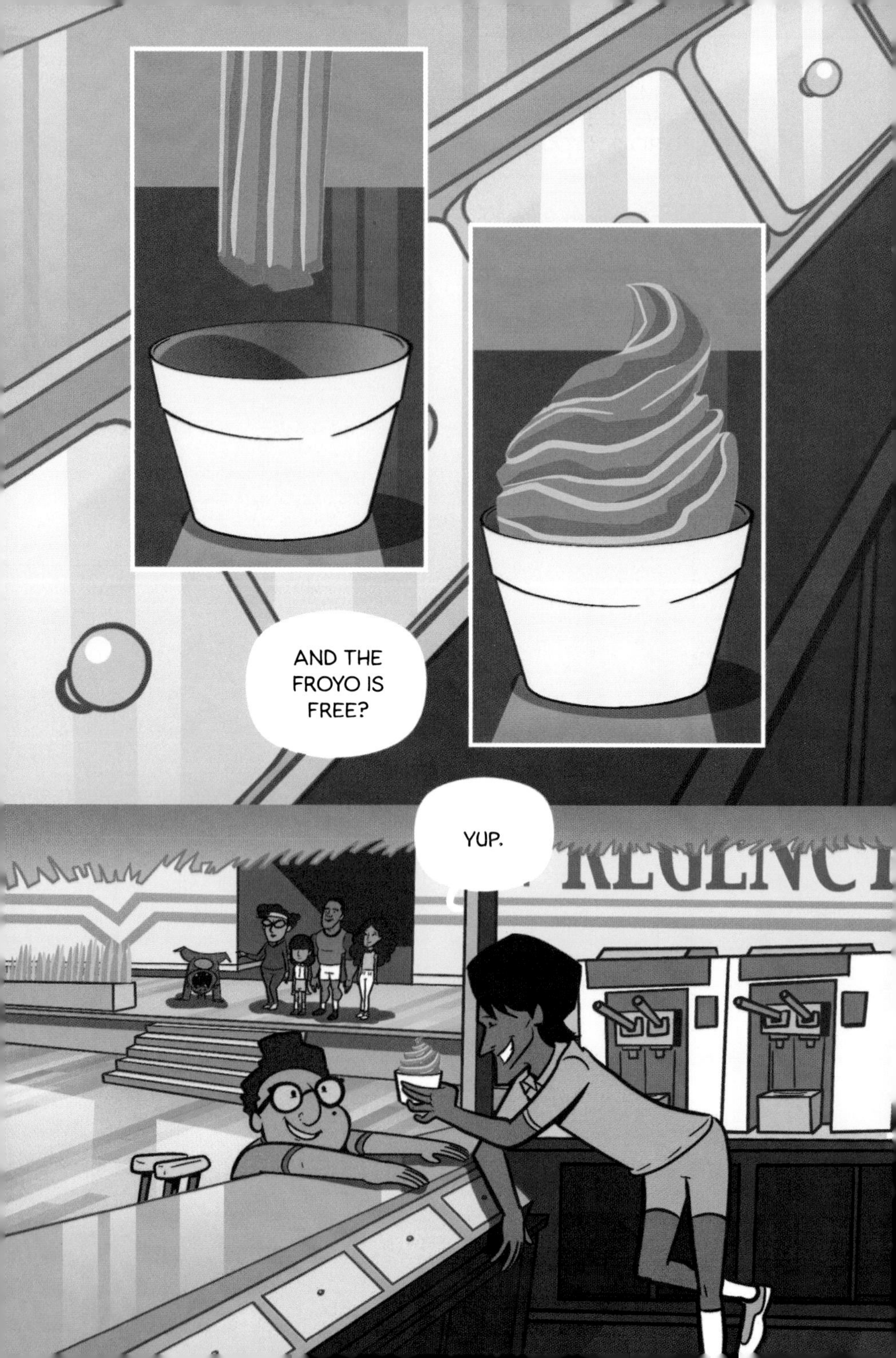
AND THE FROYO IS FREE?
YUP.

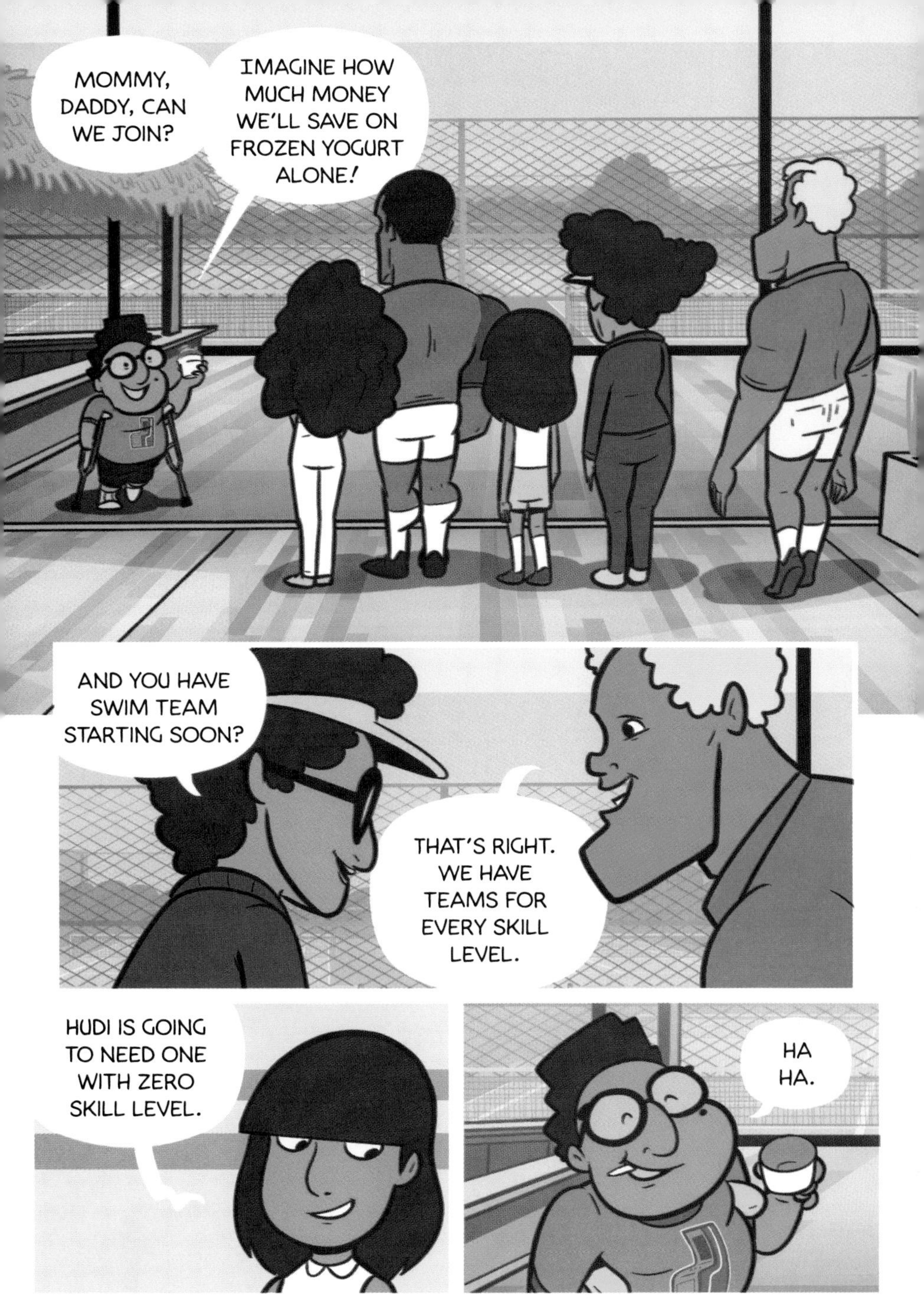
MOMMY, DADDY, CAN WE JOIN?
IMAGINE HOW MUCH MONEY WE'LL SAVE ON FROZEN YOGURT ALONE!
AND YOU HAVE SWIM TEAM STARTING SOON?
THAT'S RIGHT. WE HAVE TEAMS FOR EVERY SKILL LEVEL.
HUDI IS GOING TO NEED ONE WITH ZERO SKILL LEVEL.
HA HA.

96

97

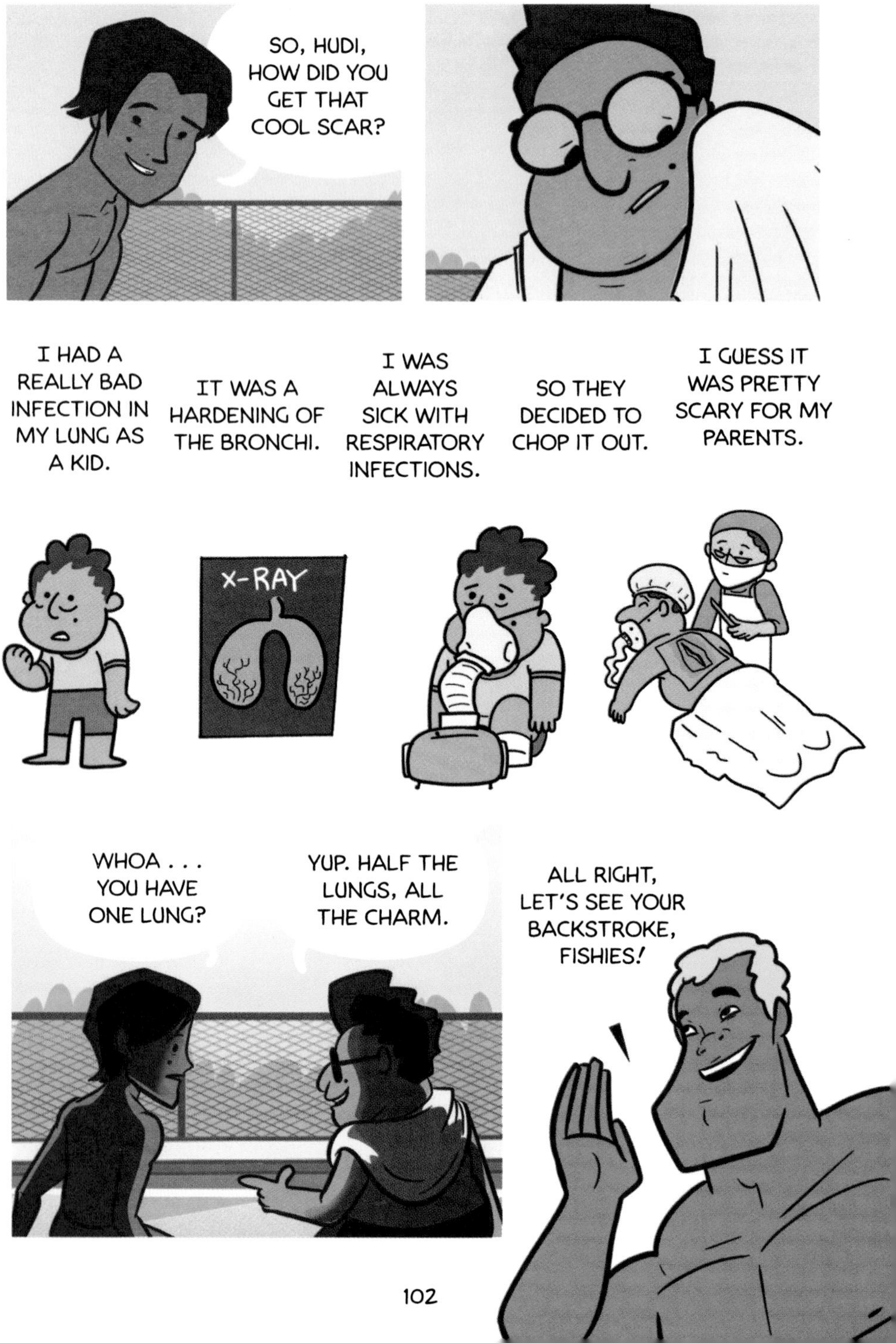
SO, HUDI, HOW DID YOU GET THAT COOL SCAR?
I HAD A REALLY BAD INFECTION IN MY LUNG AS A KID.
IT WAS A HARDENING OF THE BRONCHI.
I WAS ALWAYS SICK WITH RESPIRATORY INFECTIONS.
SO THEY DECIDED TO CHOP IT OUT.
I GUESS IT WAS PRETTY SCARY FOR MY PARENTS.
X-RAY
WHOA . . . YOU HAVE ONE LUNG?
YUP. HALF THE LUNGS, ALL THE CHARM.
ALL RIGHT, LET'S SEE YOUR BACKSTROKE, FISHIES!

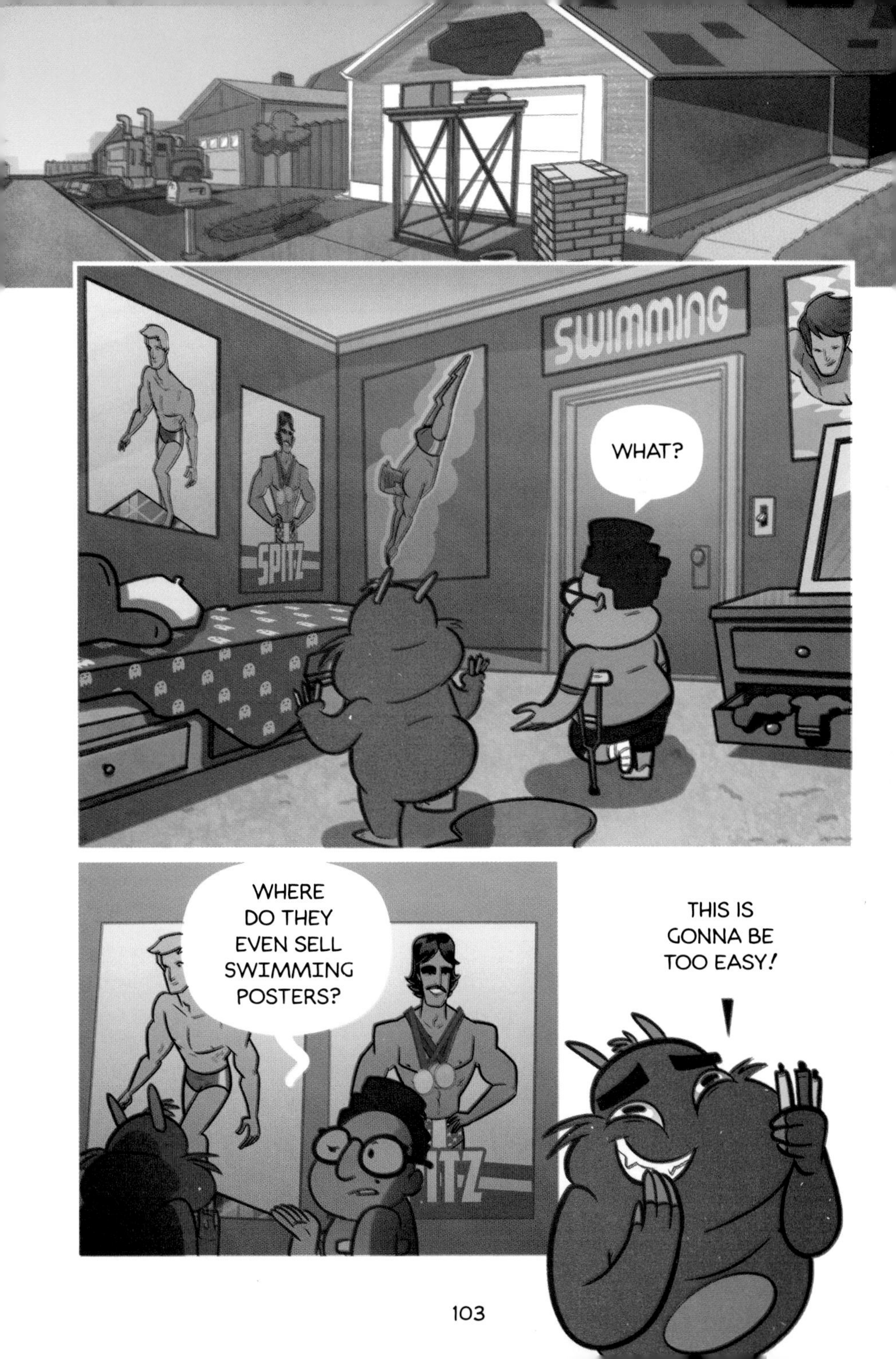
SWIMMING
SPITZ
WHAT?
WHERE DO THEY EVEN SELL SWIMMING POSTERS?
THIS IS GONNA BE TOO EASY!

"IF SOMETHING EMBARRASSING LIKE THAT EVER HAPPENS, LIVE ON TV AND IN FRONT OF A BIG AUDIENCE . . . "

"THE ONLY WAY OUT IS TO PRETEND LIKE YOU DID IT ON PURPOSE AND START DOING A CRAZY DANCE UNTIL THE BAND STARTS PLAYING ALONG WITH YOU."

HA HA HA HA HA

EMERGENCY CRAZY DANCE. SOUNDS LIKE A PLAN.

ONCE YOUR FOOT HEALS, WE SHOULD PRACTICE PRATFALLS.

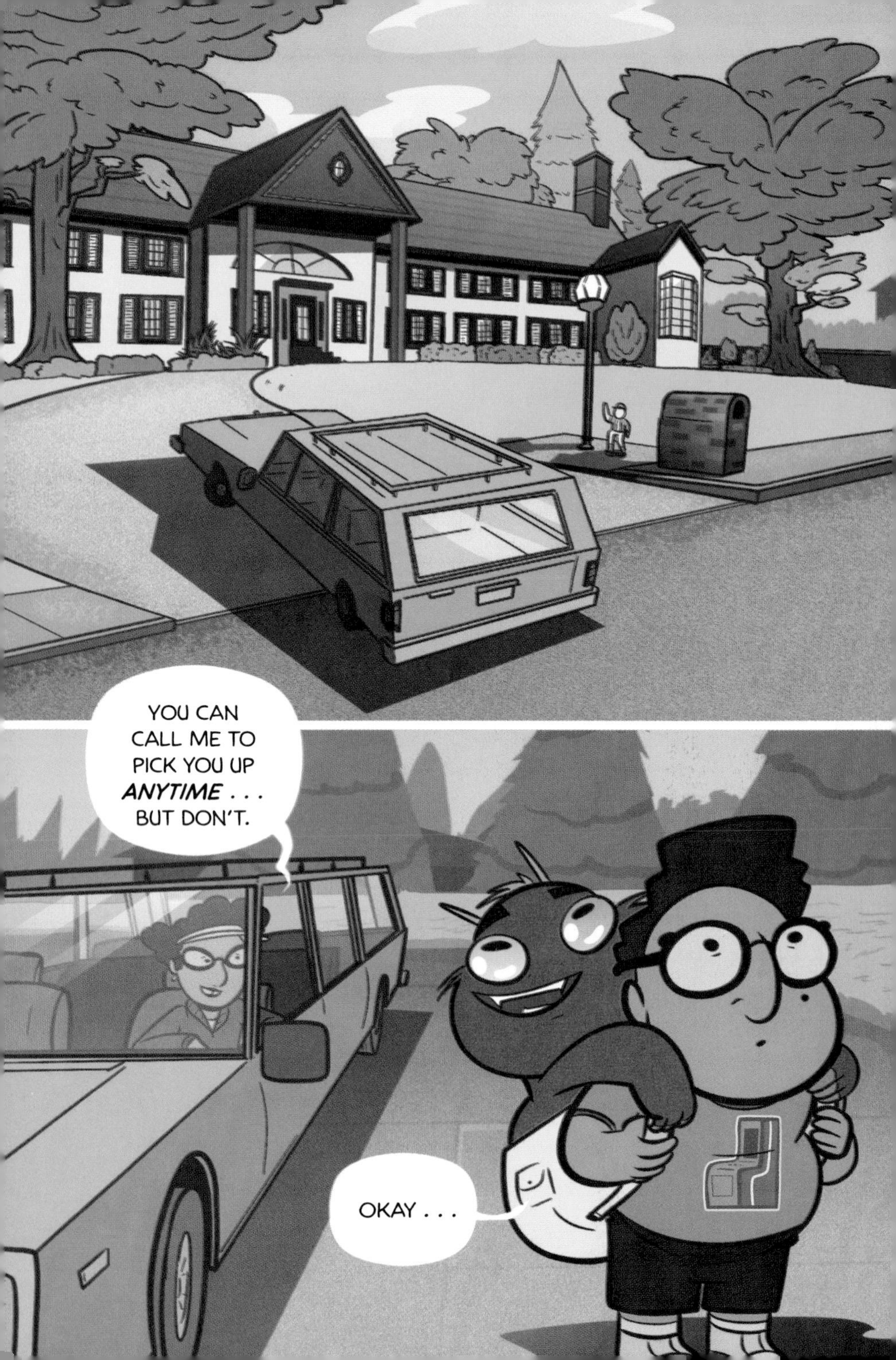
YOU CAN CALL ME TO PICK YOU UP *ANYTIME* . . . BUT DON'T.
OKAY . . .

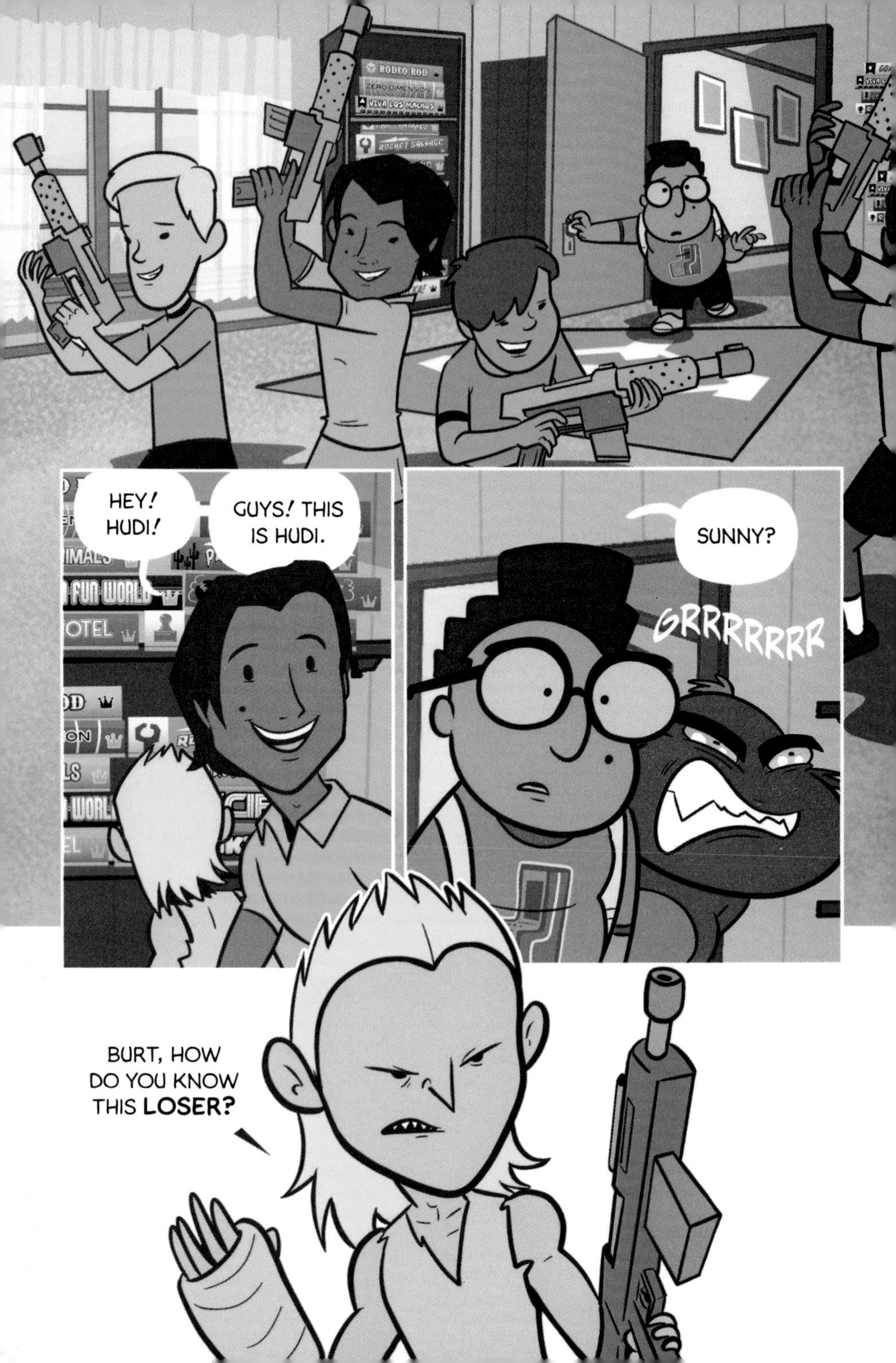

RODEO ROD
ZERO DIMENSION
VIVA LOS MACHOS
ROCKET SALVAGE
HEY! HUDI!
GUYS! THIS IS HUDI.
SUNNY?
GRRRRRRR
BURT, HOW DO YOU KNOW THIS LOSER?

113

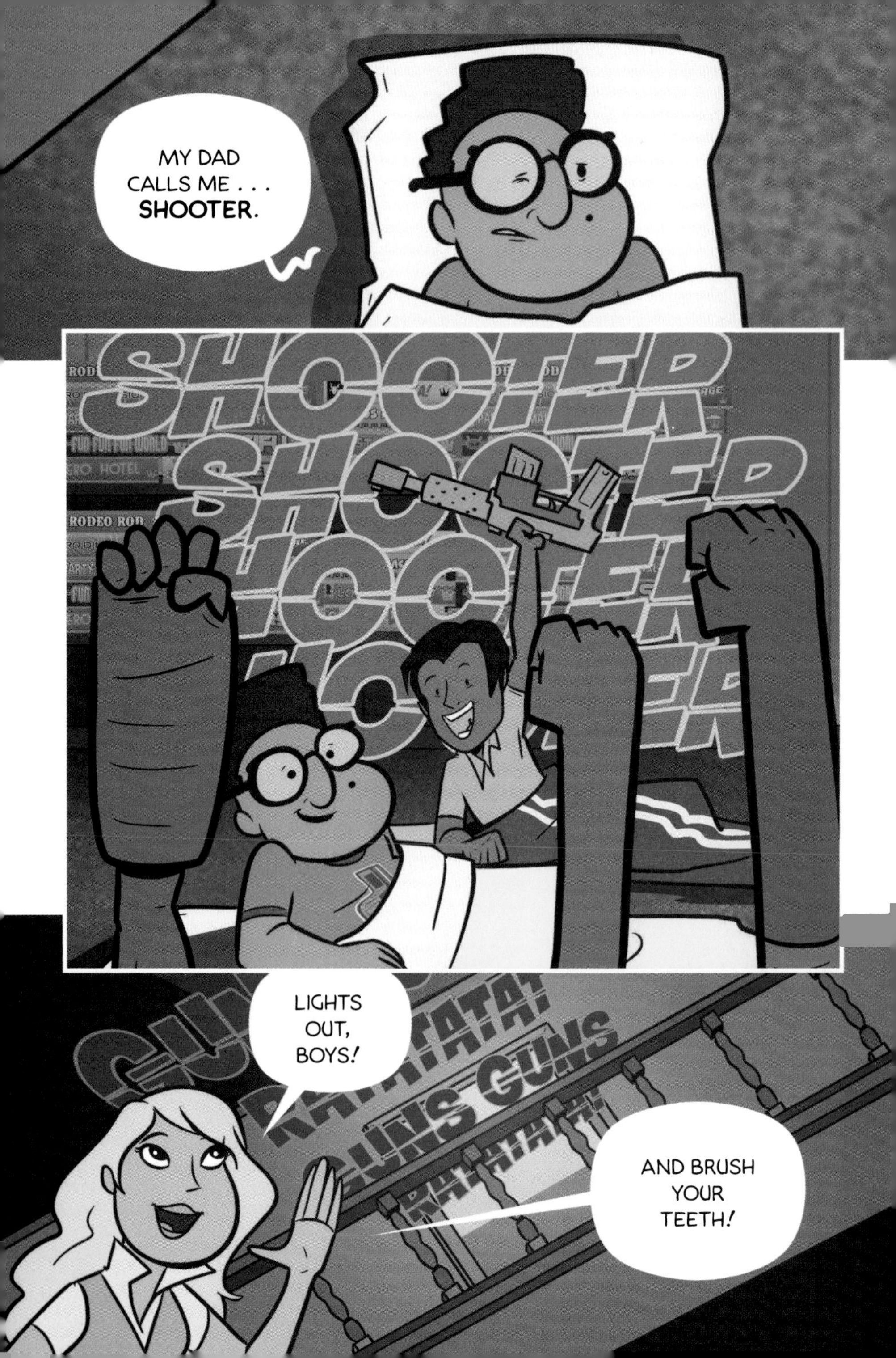
MY DAD CALLS ME . . . SHOOTER.
SHOOTER SHOOTER SHOOTER SHOOTER
LIGHTS OUT, BOYS!
AND BRUSH YOUR TEETH!

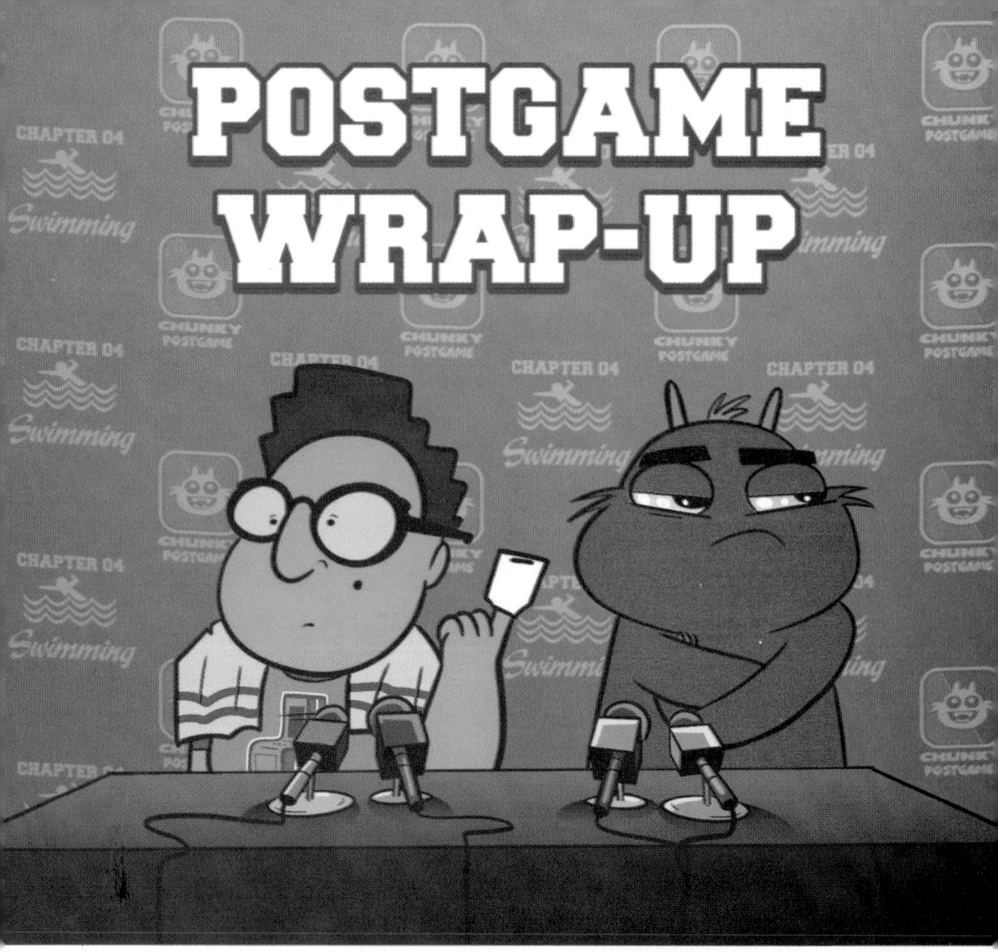
POSTGAME
WRAP-UP
CHAPTER 04
Swimming
CHUNKY
POSTGAME

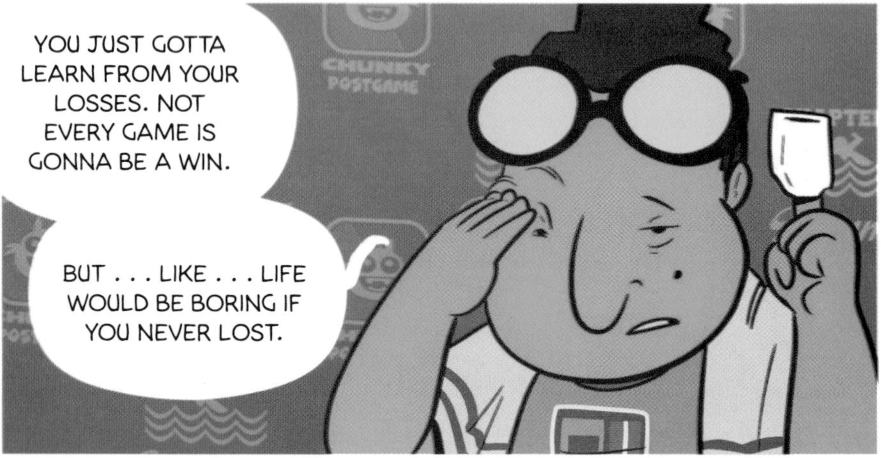
YOU JUST GOTTA LEARN FROM YOUR LOSSES. NOT EVERY GAME IS GONNA BE A WIN.
BUT . . . LIKE . . . LIFE WOULD BE BORING IF YOU NEVER LOST.

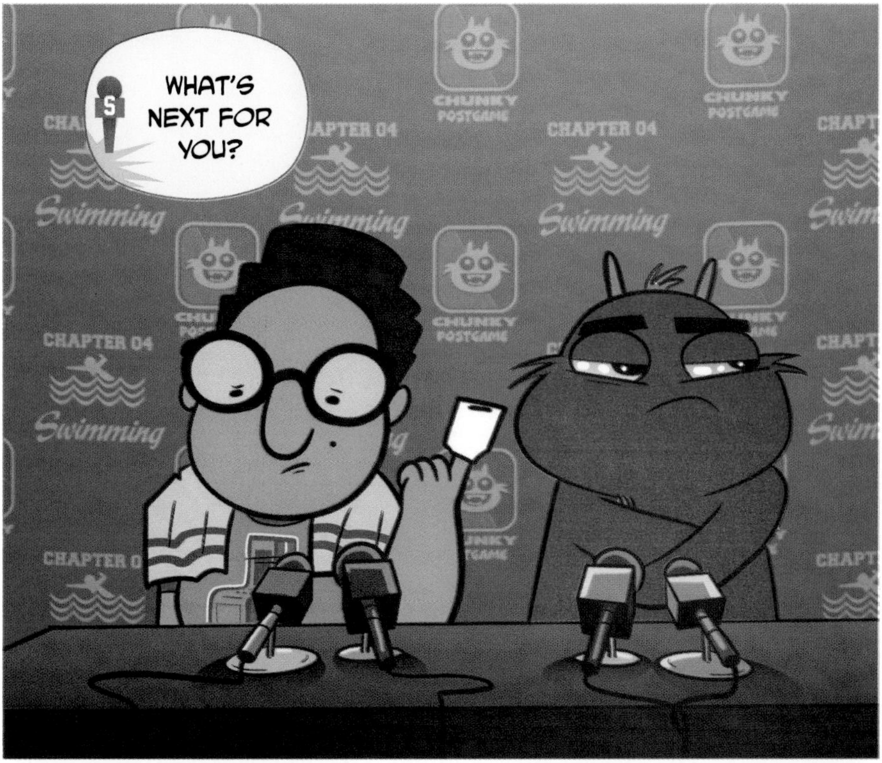

WHAT'S NEXT FOR YOU?

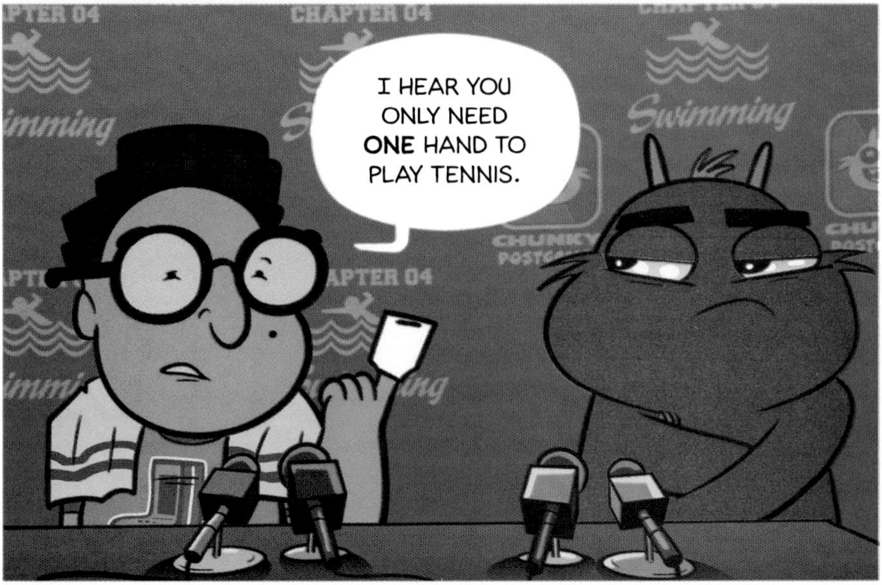

I HEAR YOU ONLY NEED **ONE** HAND TO PLAY TENNIS.

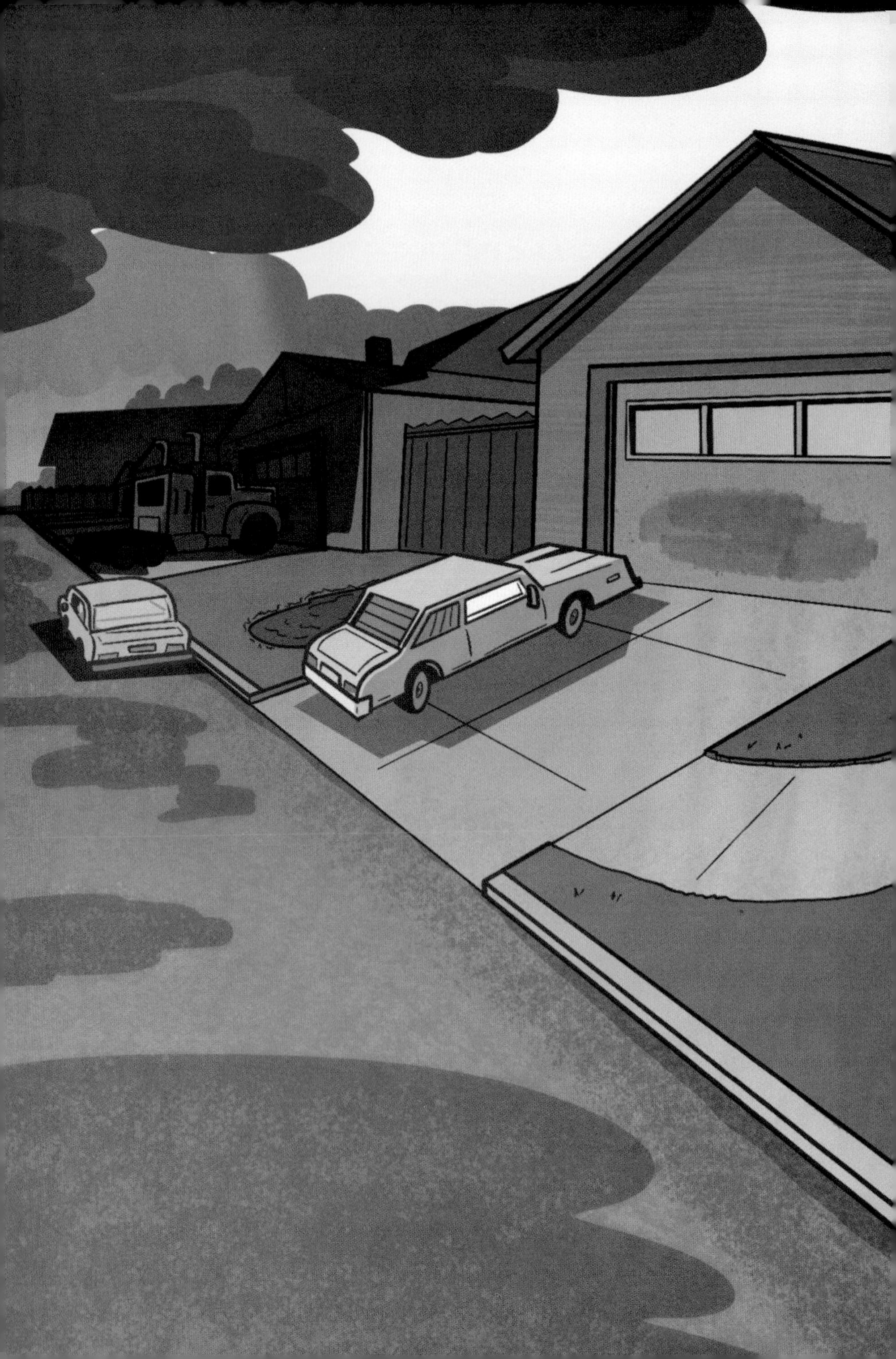

CHAPTER FIVE
Tennis

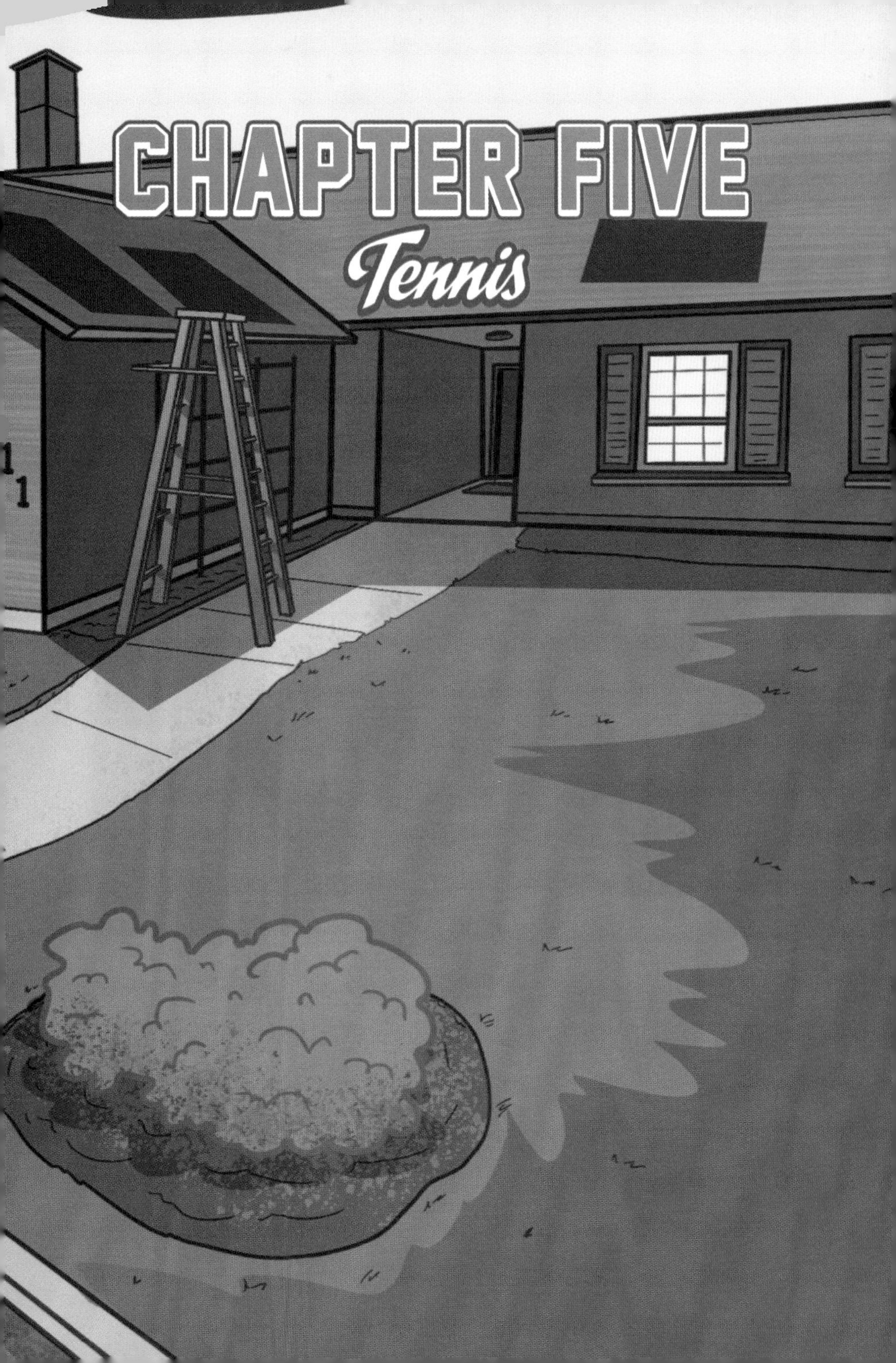

129

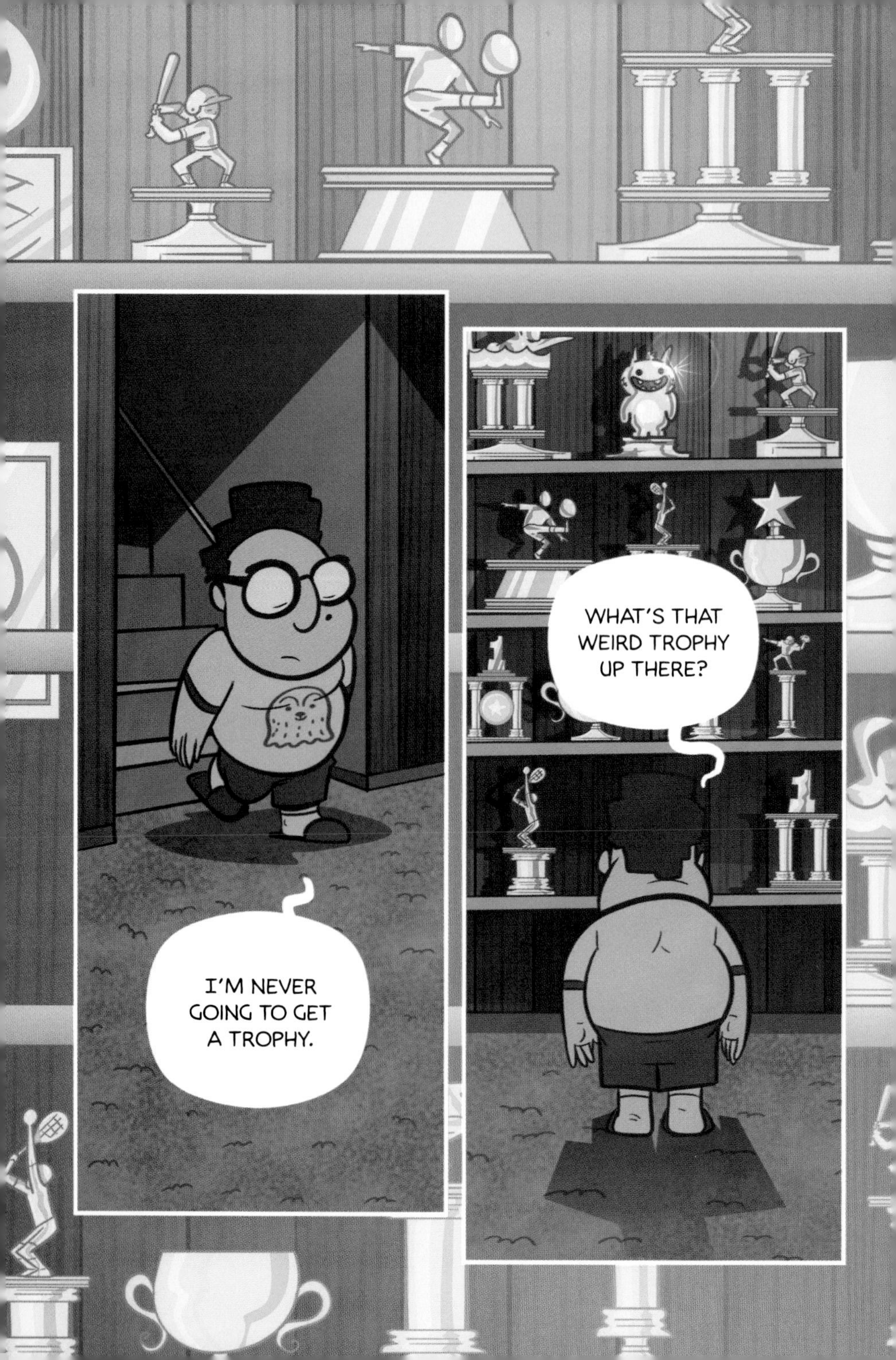
I'M NEVER GOING TO GET A TROPHY.
WHAT'S THAT WEIRD TROPHY UP THERE?

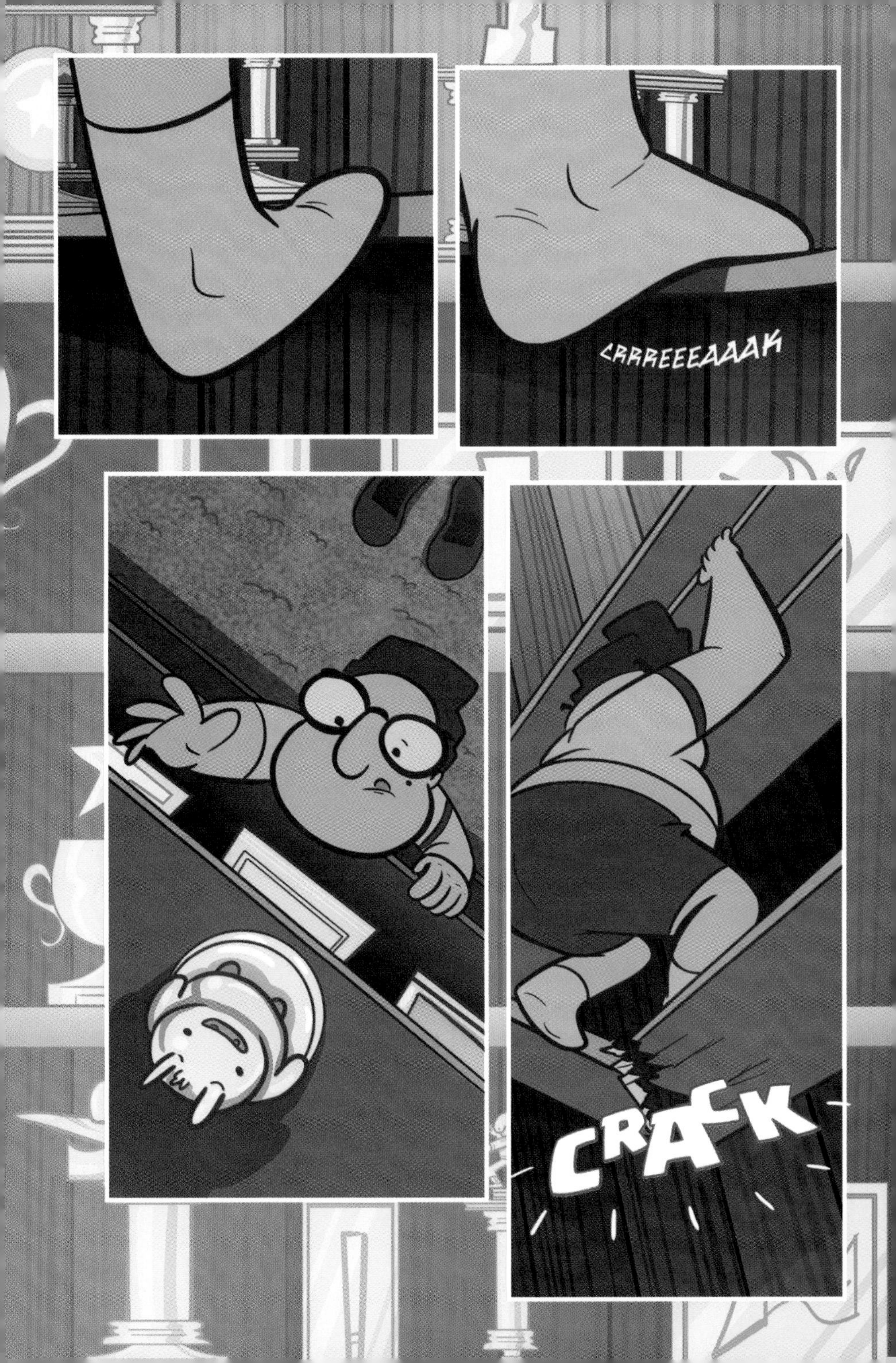
CRRREEEAAAK
CRACK

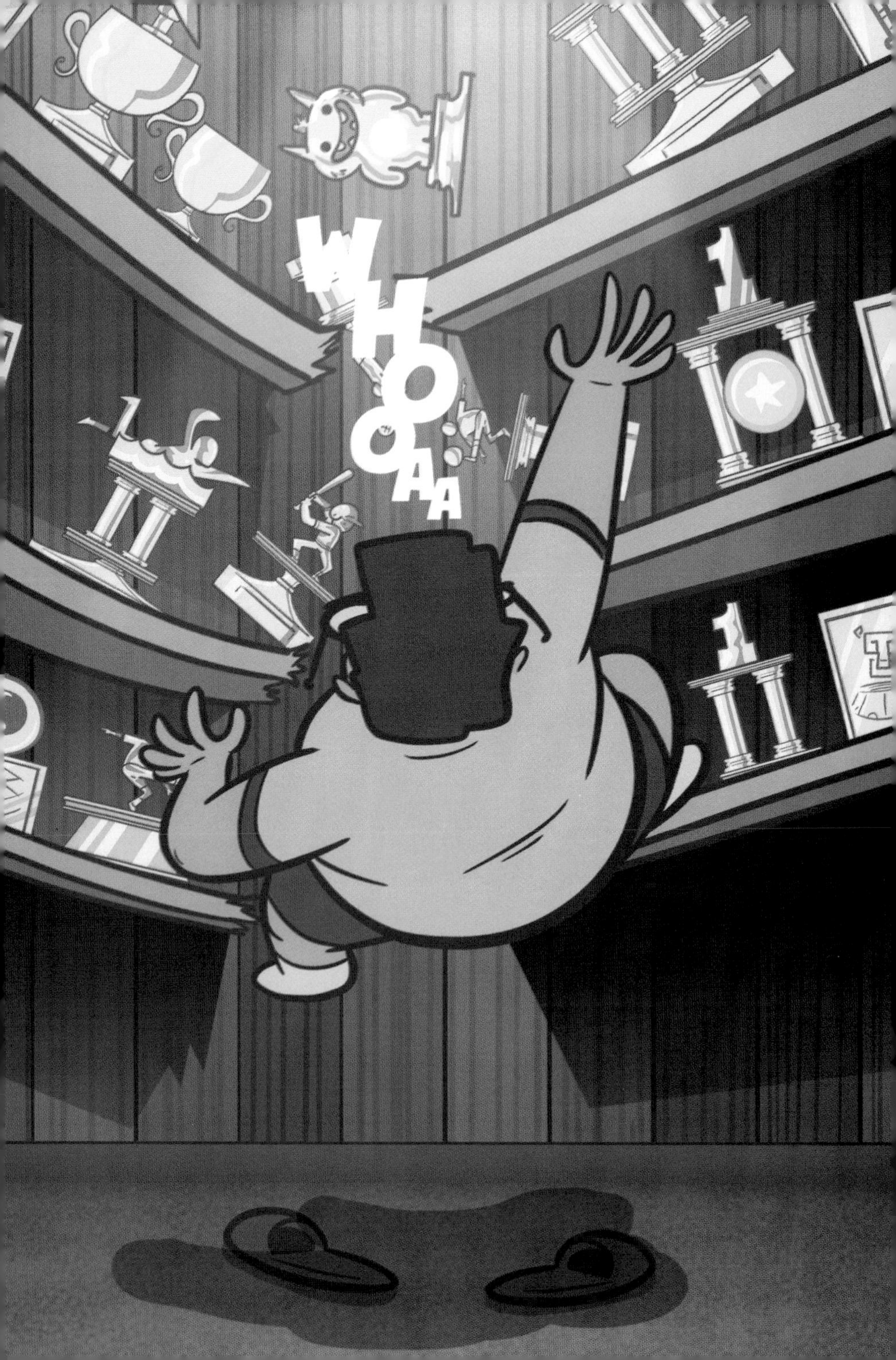
WHOOAAA

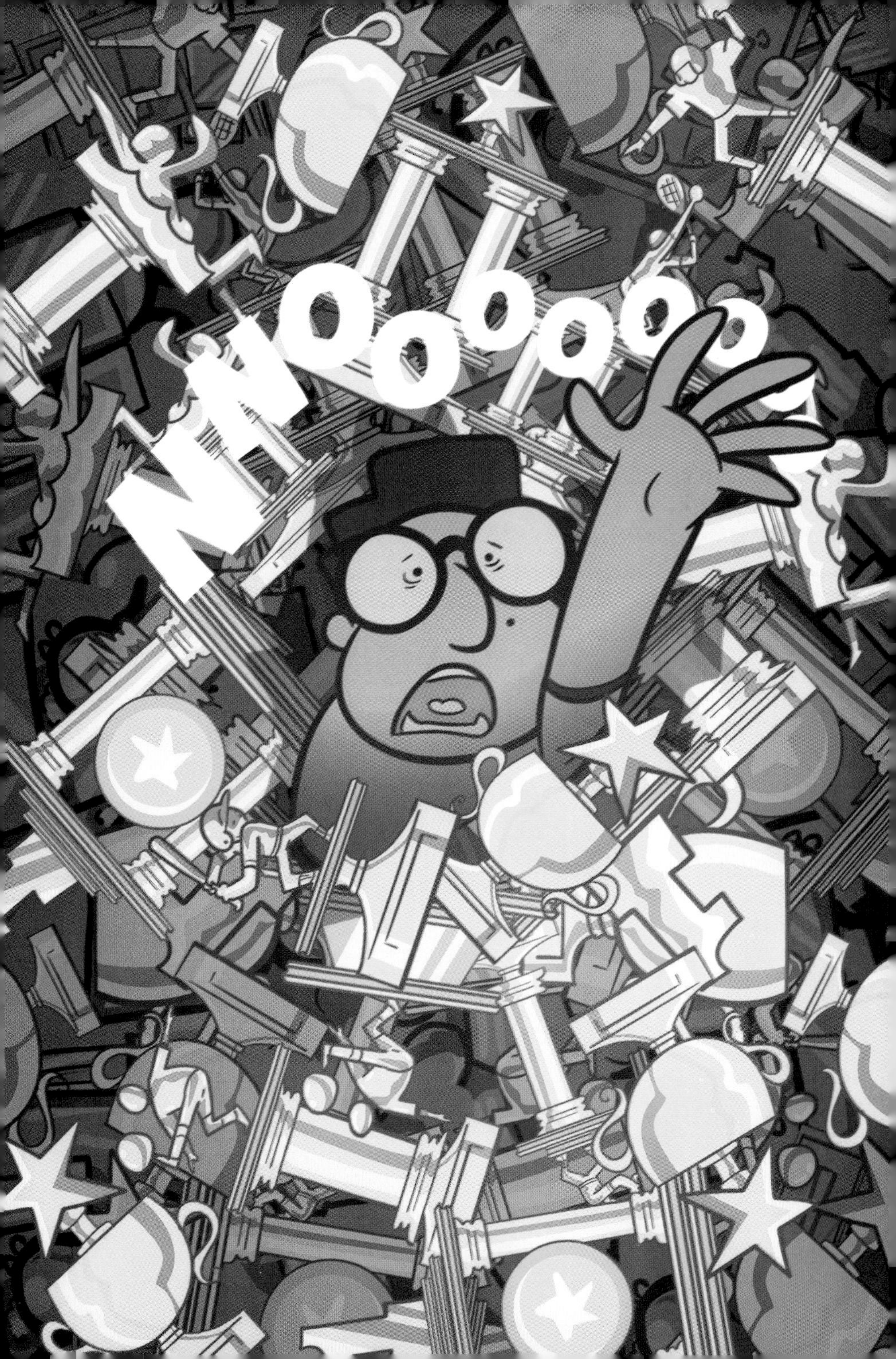
NOOOOOO

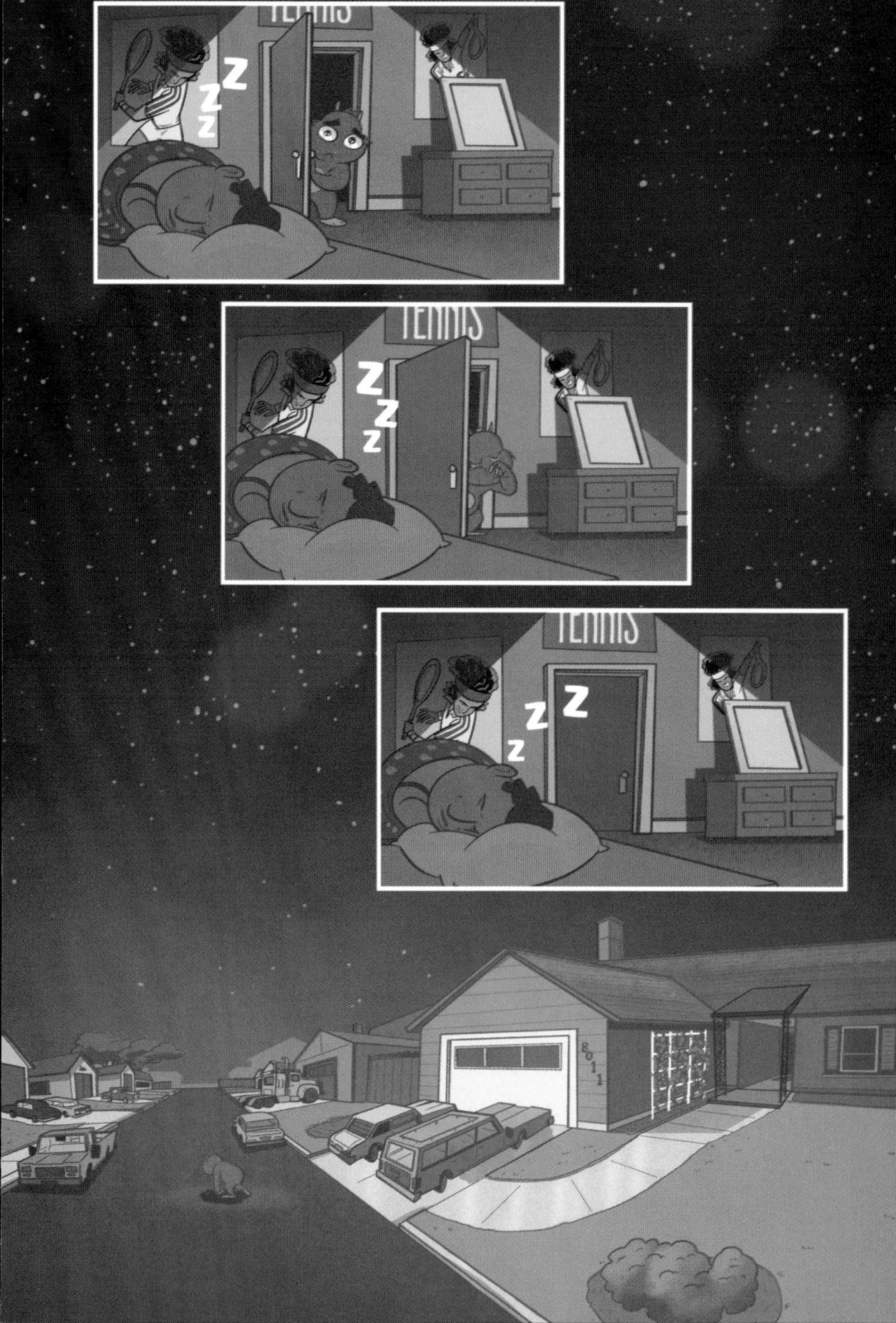
Z Z Z
TENNIS
Z Z Z
TENNIS
Z Z Z
8011

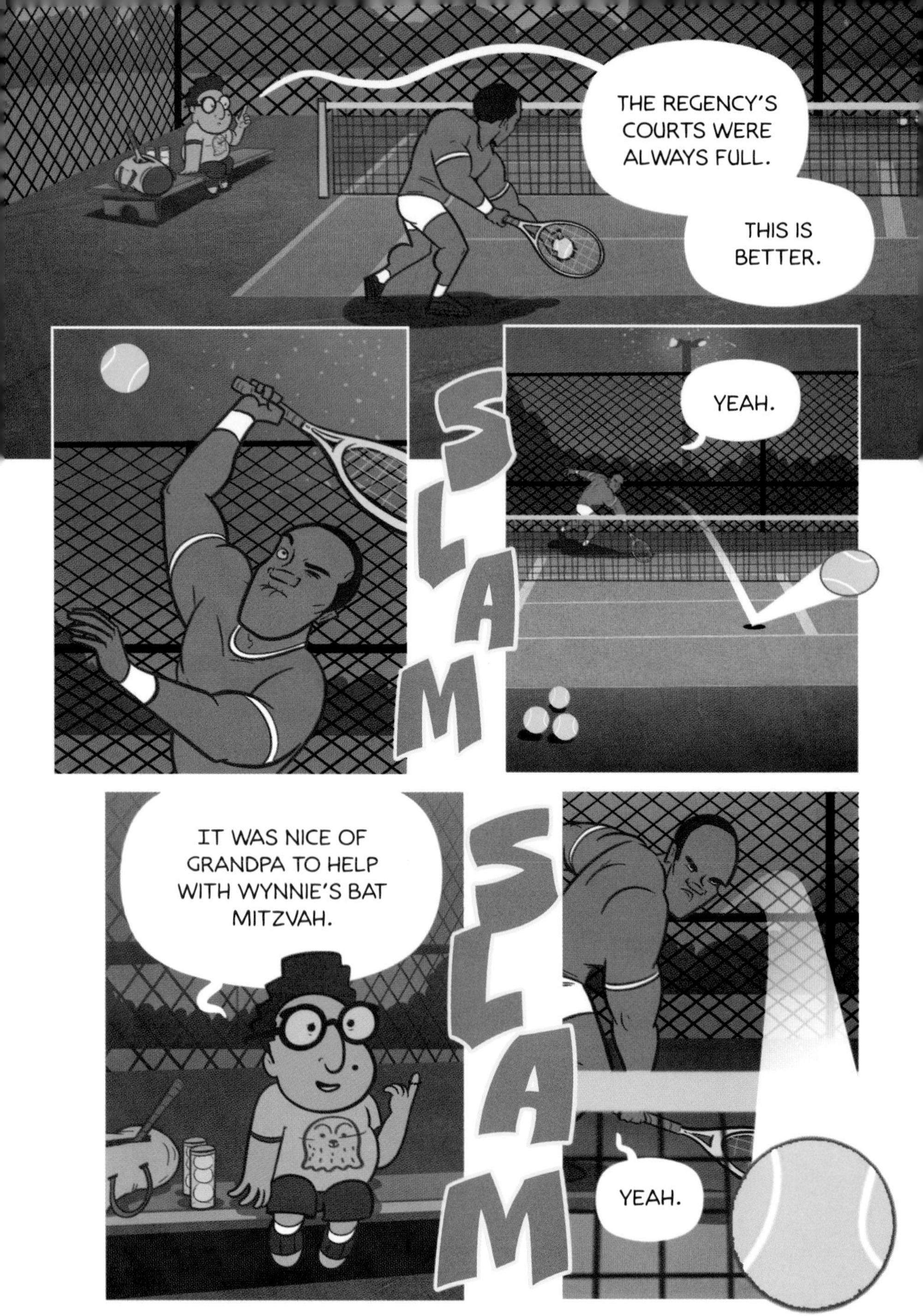
THE REGENCY'S COURTS WERE ALWAYS FULL.
THIS IS BETTER.
YEAH.
SLAM
IT WAS NICE OF GRANDPA TO HELP WITH WYNNIE'S BAT MITZVAH.
SLAM
YEAH.

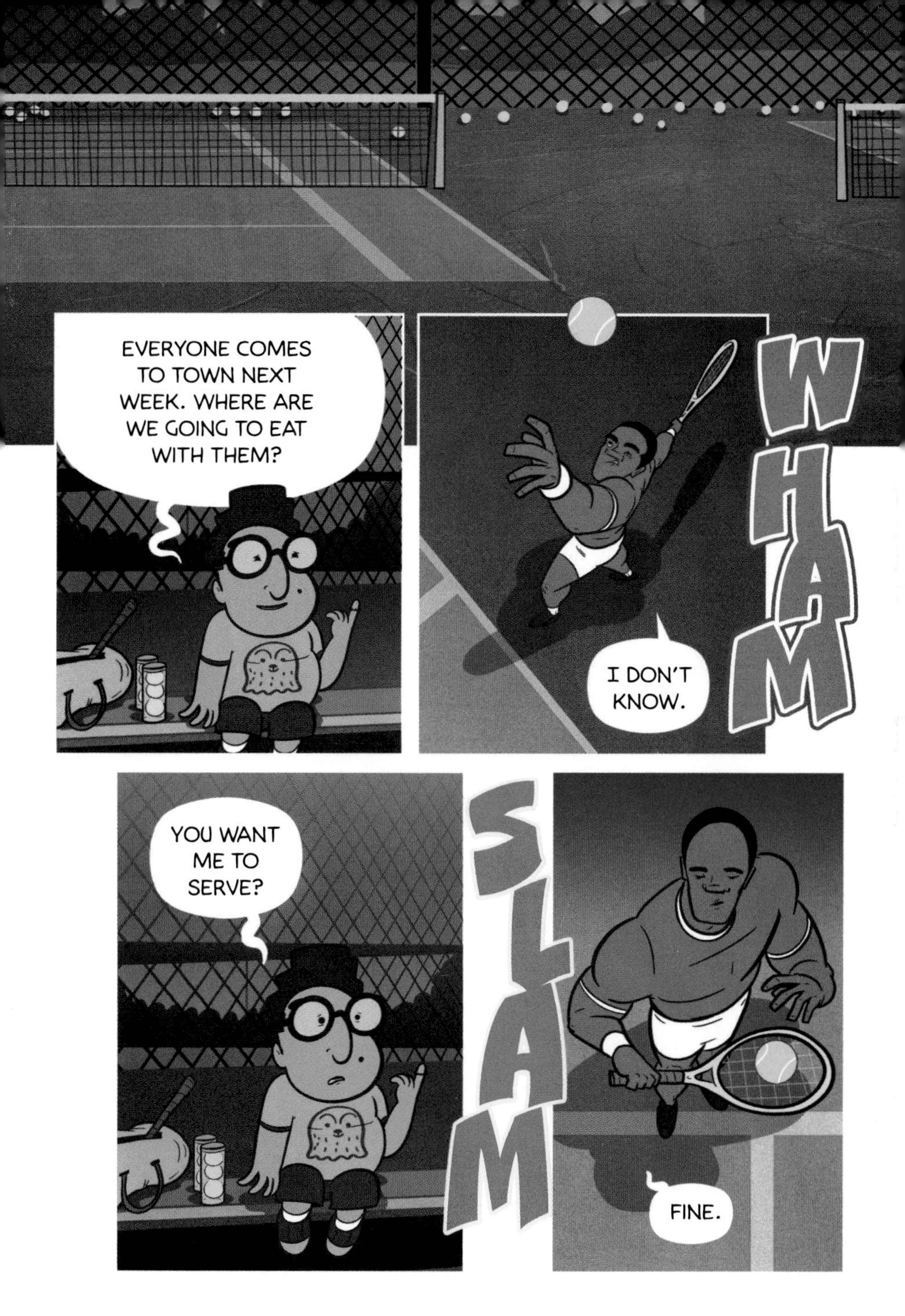
EVERYONE COMES TO TOWN NEXT WEEK. WHERE ARE WE GOING TO EAT WITH THEM?
I DON'T KNOW.
WHAM
YOU WANT ME TO SERVE?
SLAM
FINE.

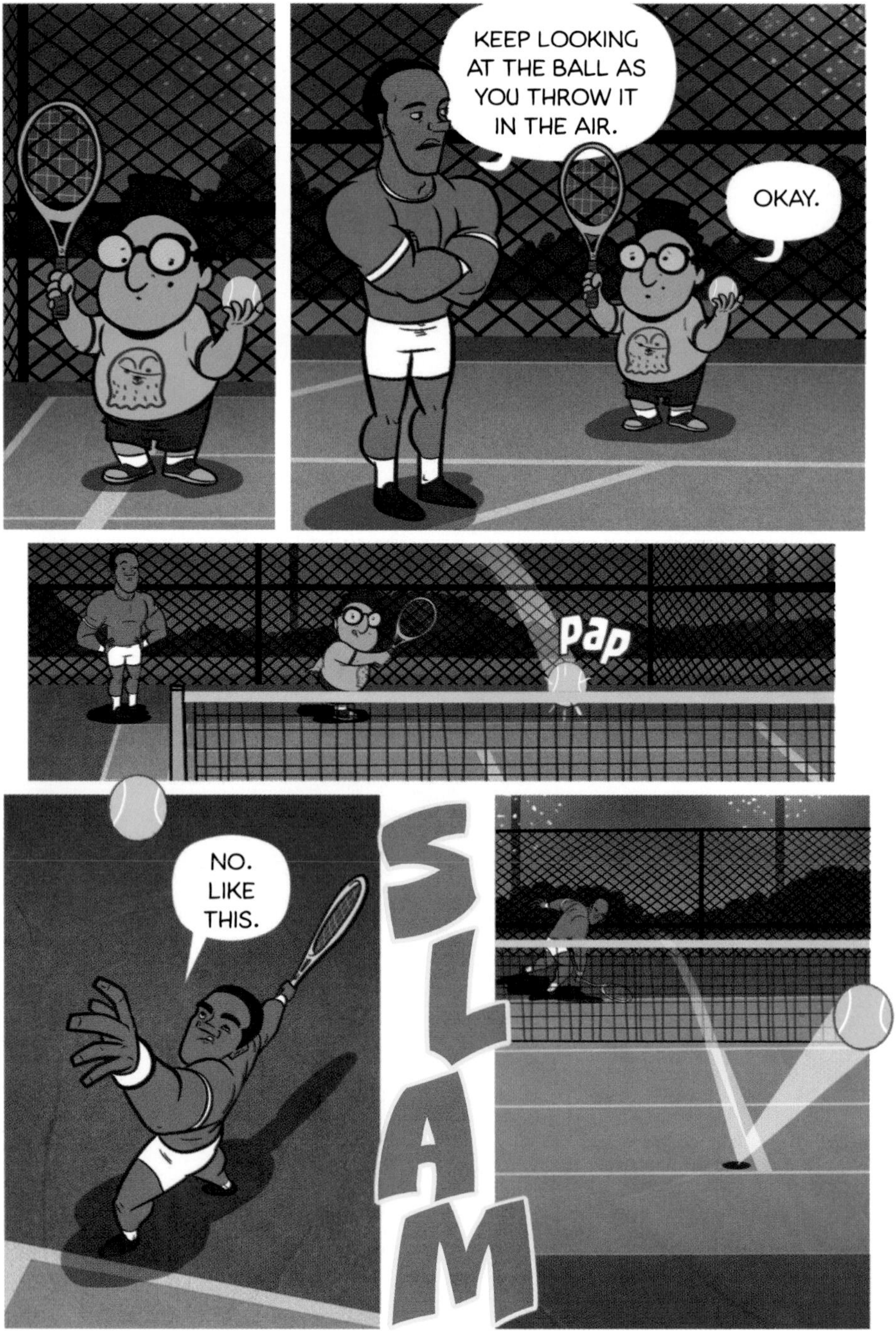
KEEP LOOKING AT THE BALL AS YOU THROW IT IN THE AIR.
OKAY.
PAP
NO. LIKE THIS.
SLAM

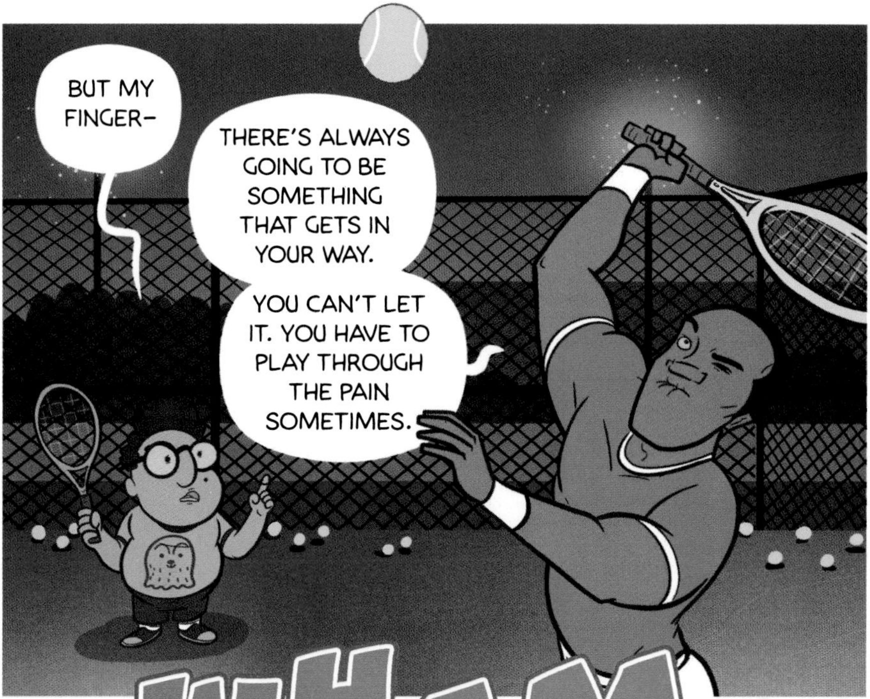
BUT MY FINGER–
THERE'S ALWAYS GOING TO BE SOMETHING THAT GETS IN YOUR WAY.
YOU CAN'T LET IT. YOU HAVE TO PLAY THROUGH THE PAIN SOMETIMES.

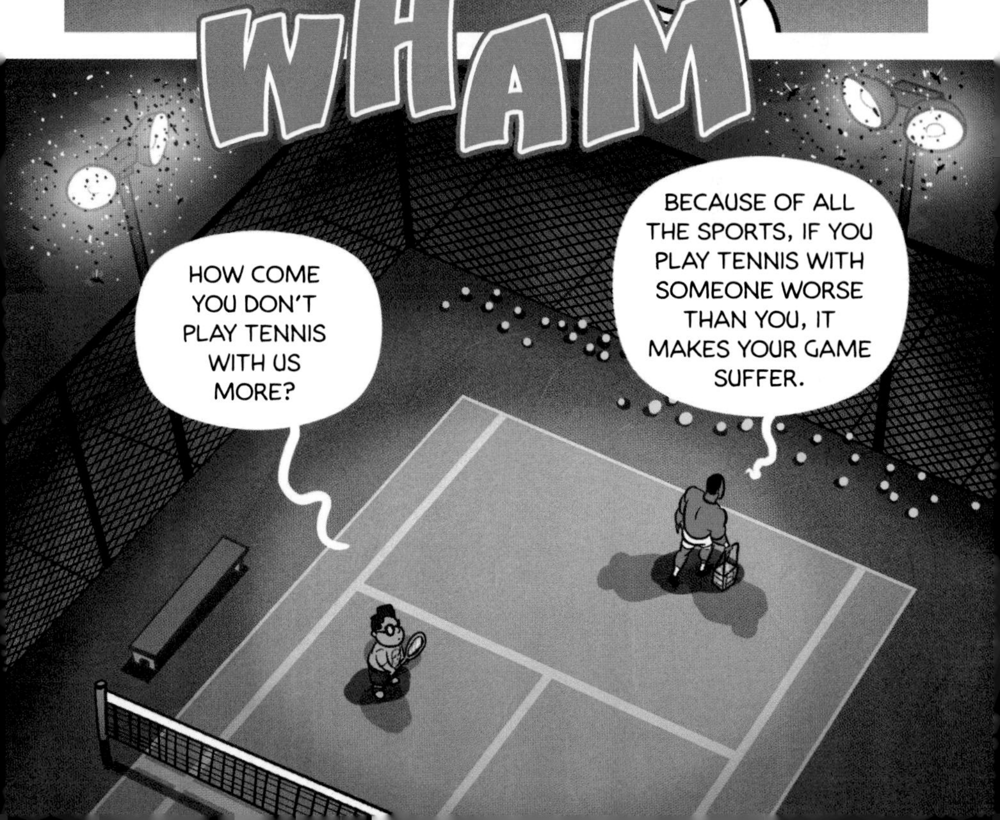
WHAM
HOW COME YOU DON'T PLAY TENNIS WITH US MORE?
BECAUSE OF ALL THE SPORTS, IF YOU PLAY TENNIS WITH SOMEONE WORSE THAN YOU, IT MAKES YOUR GAME SUFFER.

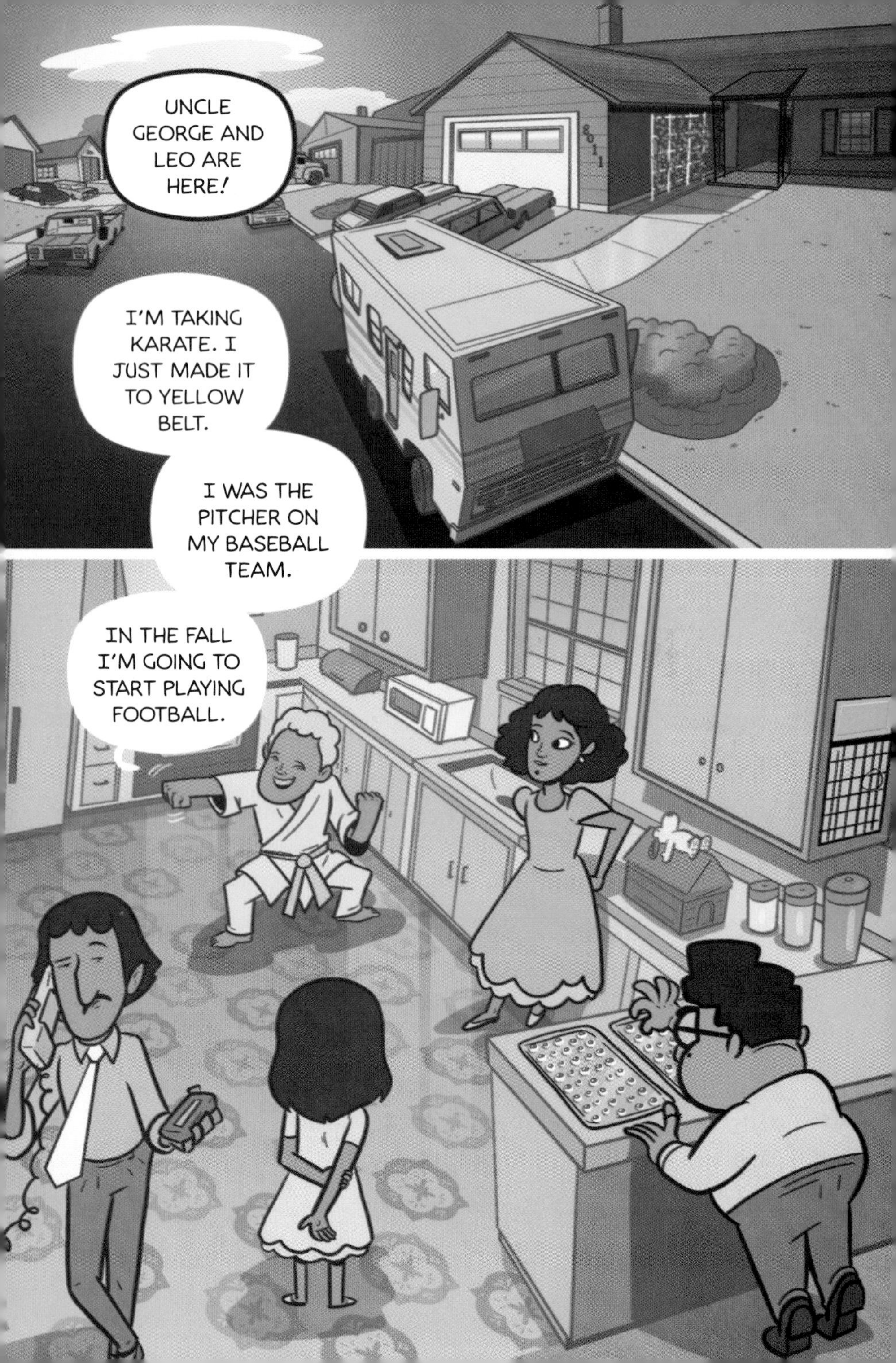
UNCLE GEORGE AND LEO ARE HERE!
I'M TAKING KARATE. I JUST MADE IT TO YELLOW BELT.
I WAS THE PITCHER ON MY BASEBALL TEAM.
IN THE FALL I'M GOING TO START PLAYING FOOTBALL.
8011

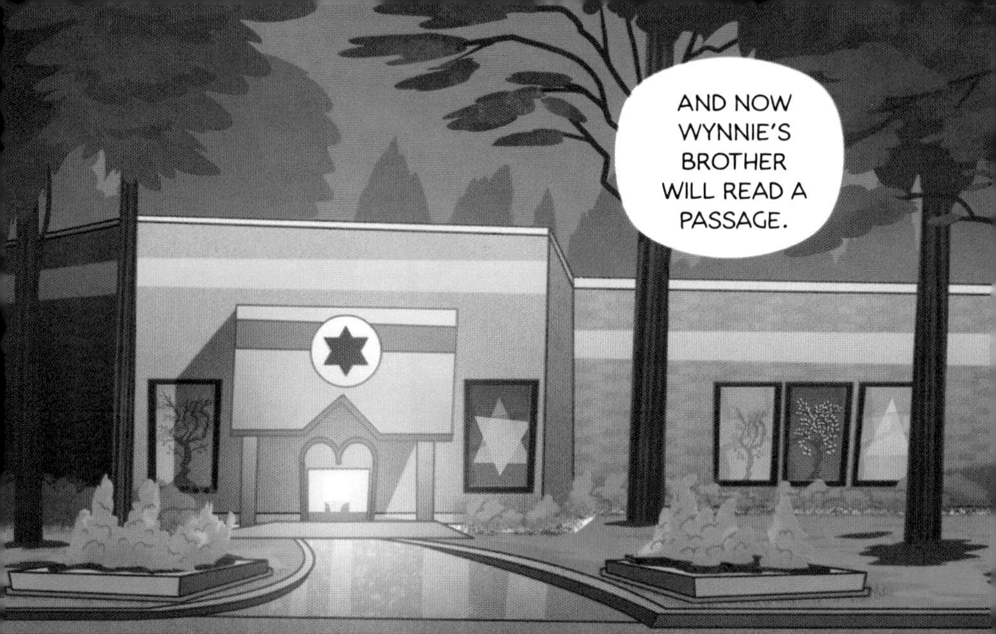
AND NOW WYNNIE'S BROTHER WILL READ A PASSAGE.

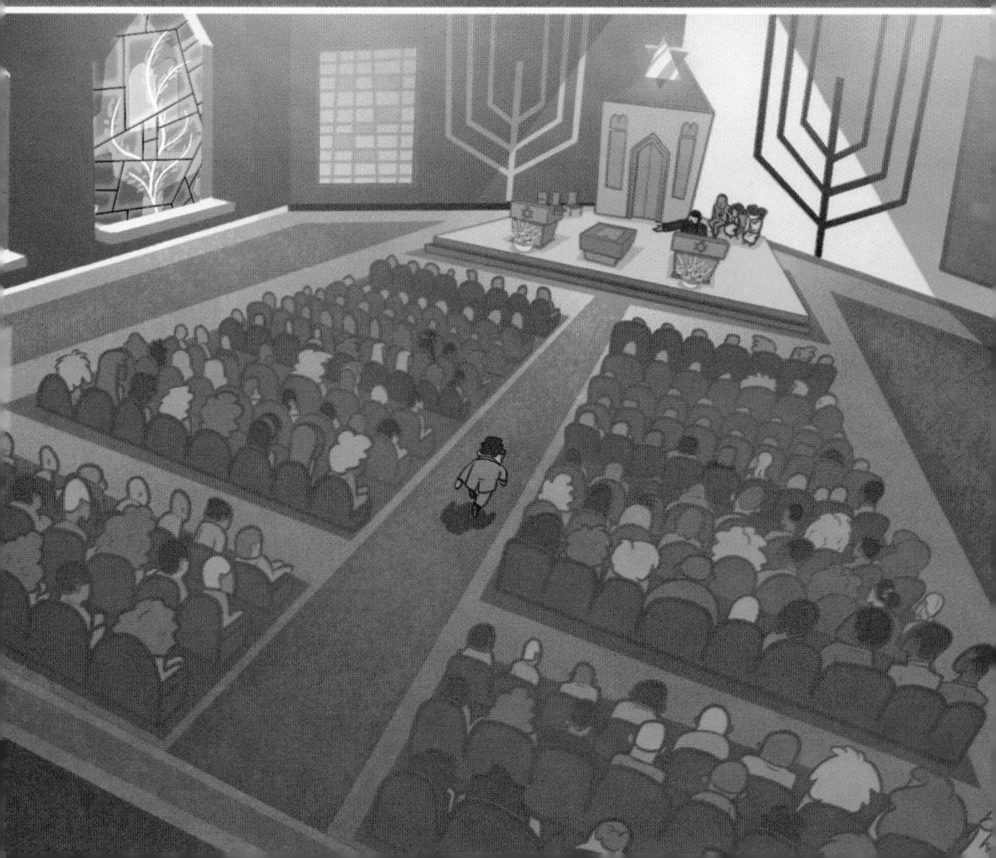

CHUCKLE   GIGGLE   CHUCKLE

GUFFAW BELLY LAUGH GUFFAW

153

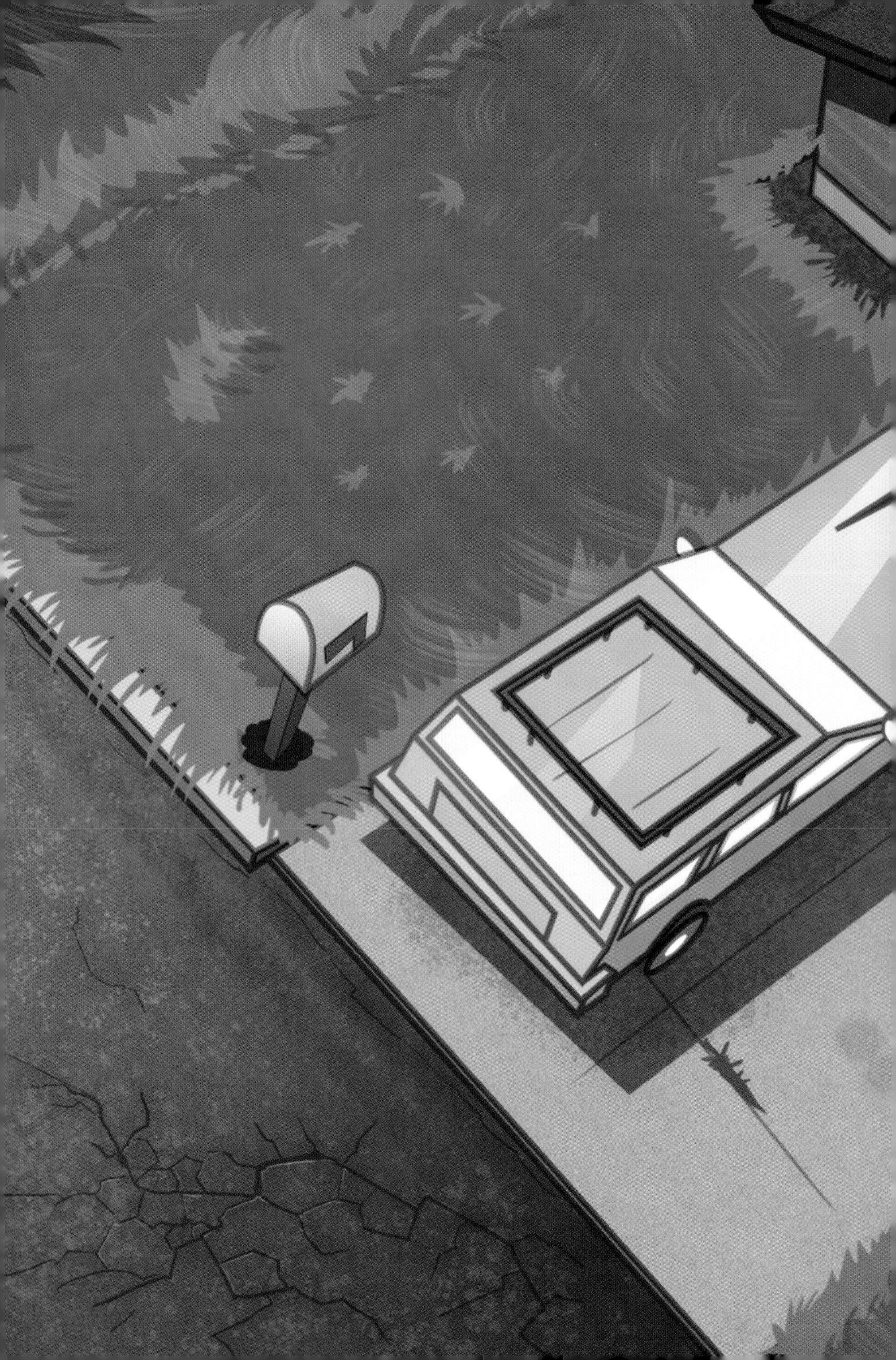

CHAPTER SIX
Football

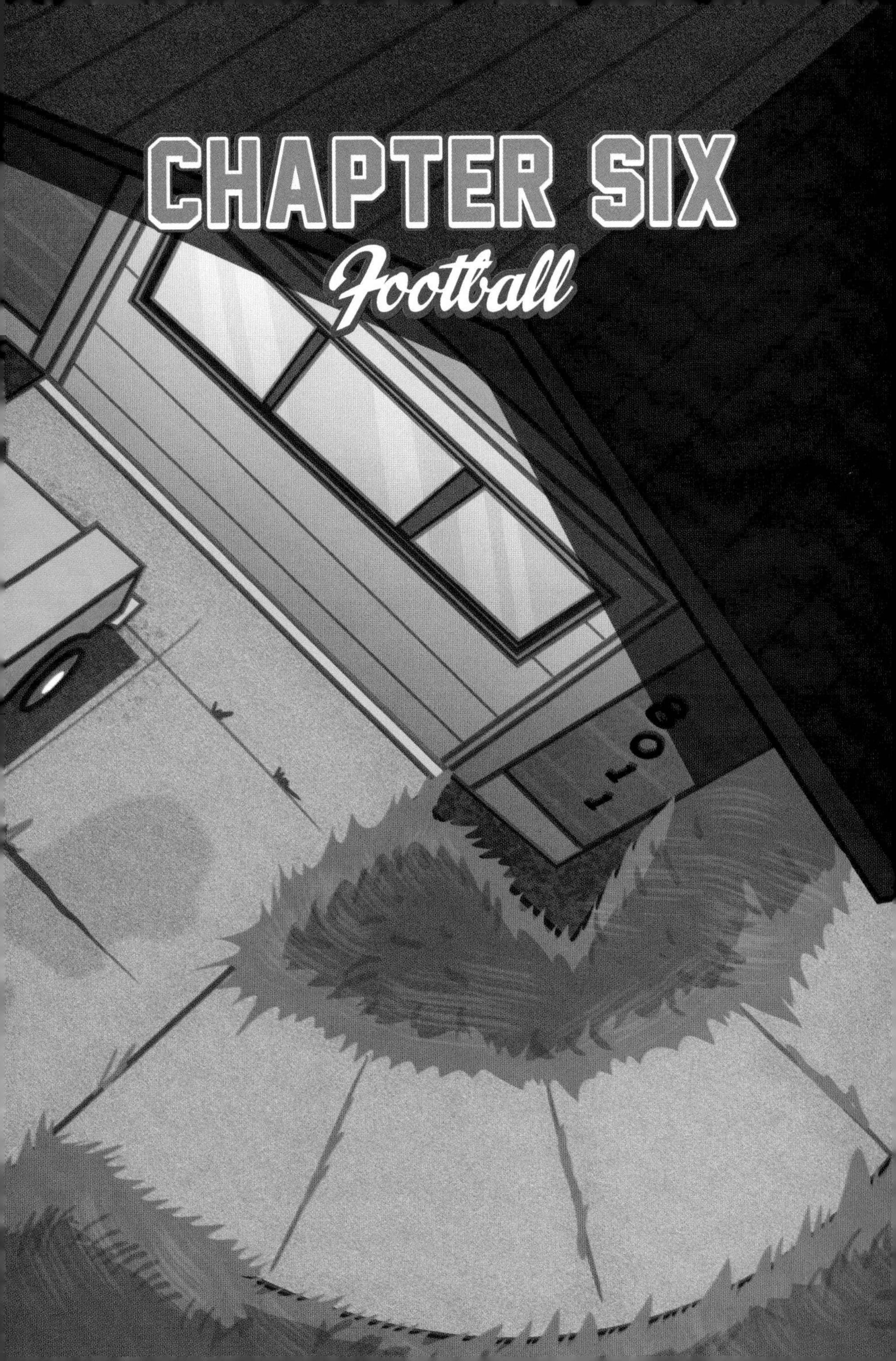

157

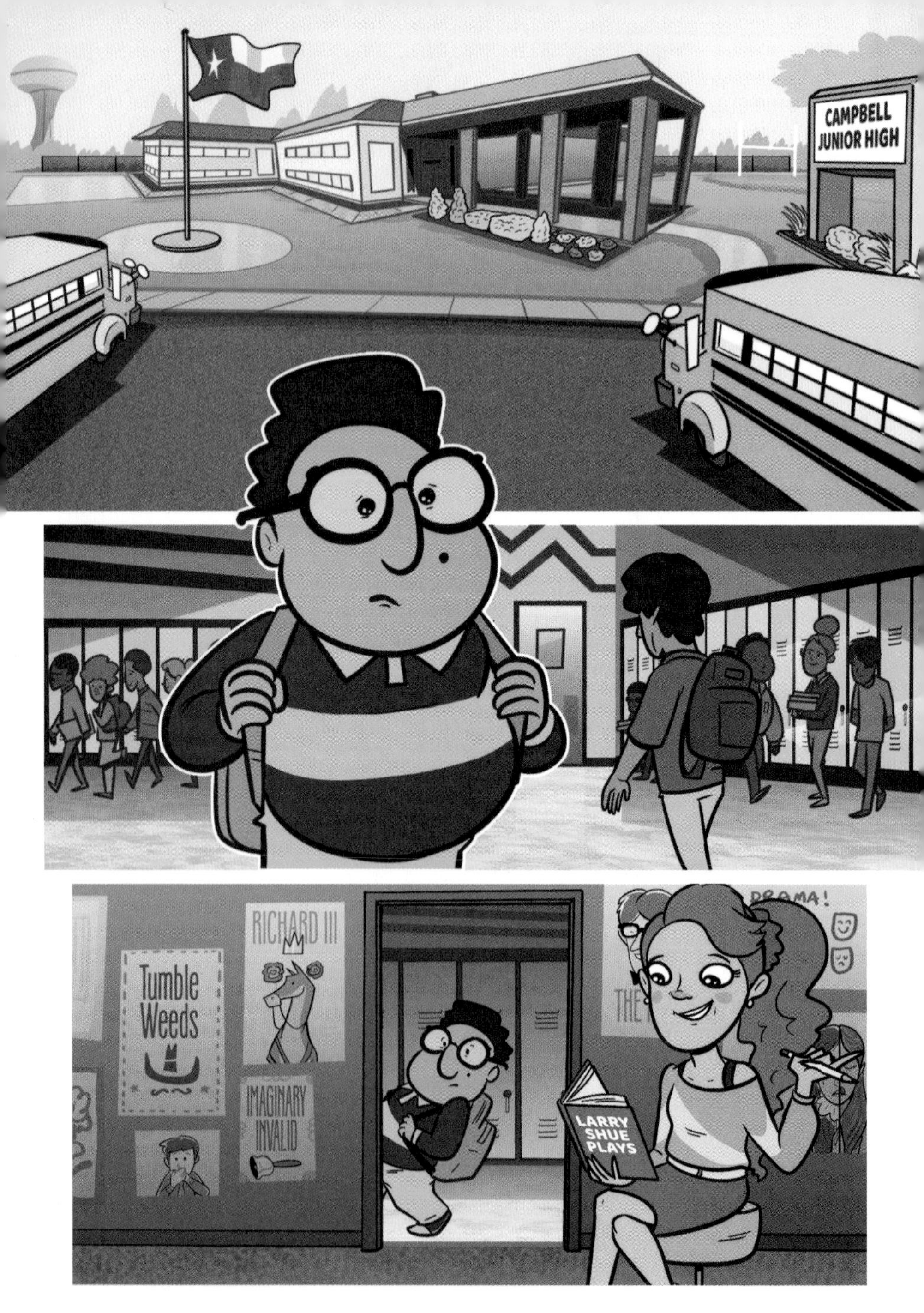
CAMPBELL
JUNIOR HIGH
RICHARD III
Tumble
Weeds
IMAGINARY
INVALID
DRAMA!
LARRY
SHUE
PLAYS

159

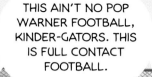

THIS AIN'T NO POP WARNER FOOTBALL, KINDER-GATORS. THIS IS FULL CONTACT FOOTBALL.

IF YA **CAN'T** HANDLE THAT, THEN YA BEST GET WALKING NOW AND SAVE US ALL A HECK OF A LOTTA TIME.

BIG MAN, YOU AIN'T GOT SCHOOL PRIDE?

THE GYM UNIFORM DOESN'T **FIT** ME, COACH.

HAH! FATSO!

SHUT UP, SUNNY!

THESE UNIFORMS WERE MADE FOR **LITTLE BABIES.**

NOT BIG MEN LIKE THIS GUY.

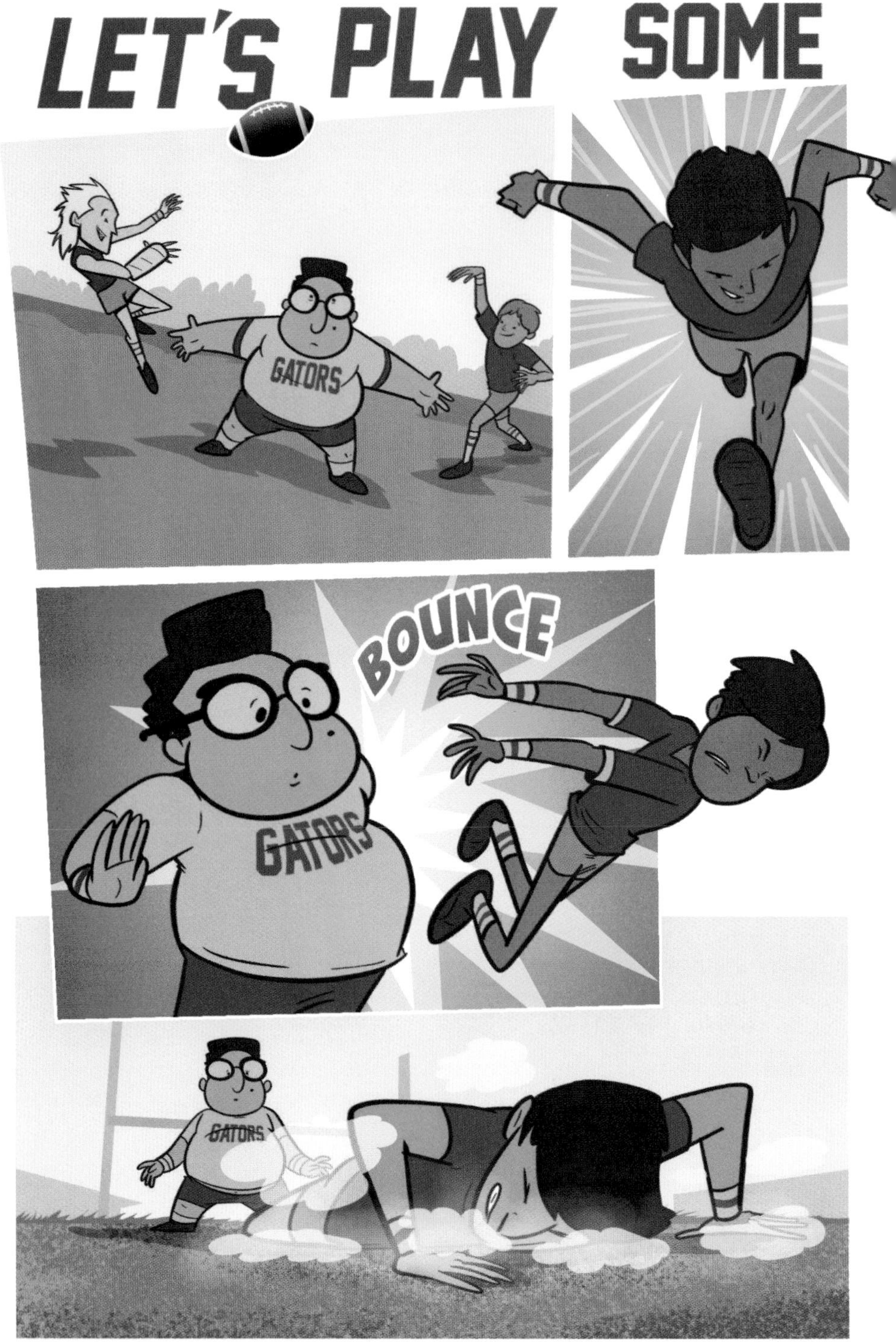
LET'S PLAY SOME
GATORS
BOUNCE
GATORS
GATORS

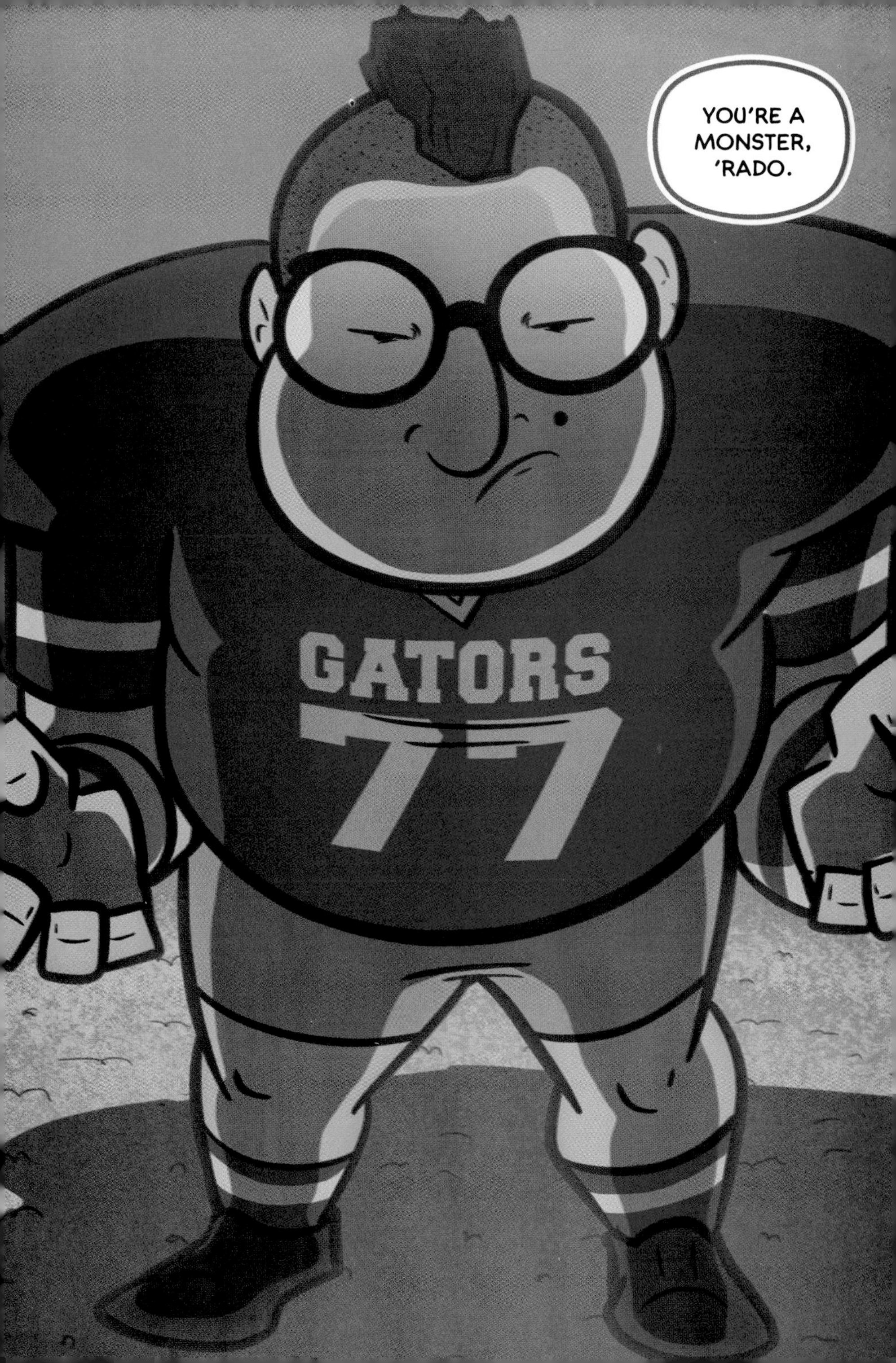
YOU'RE A MONSTER, 'RADO.
GATORS
77

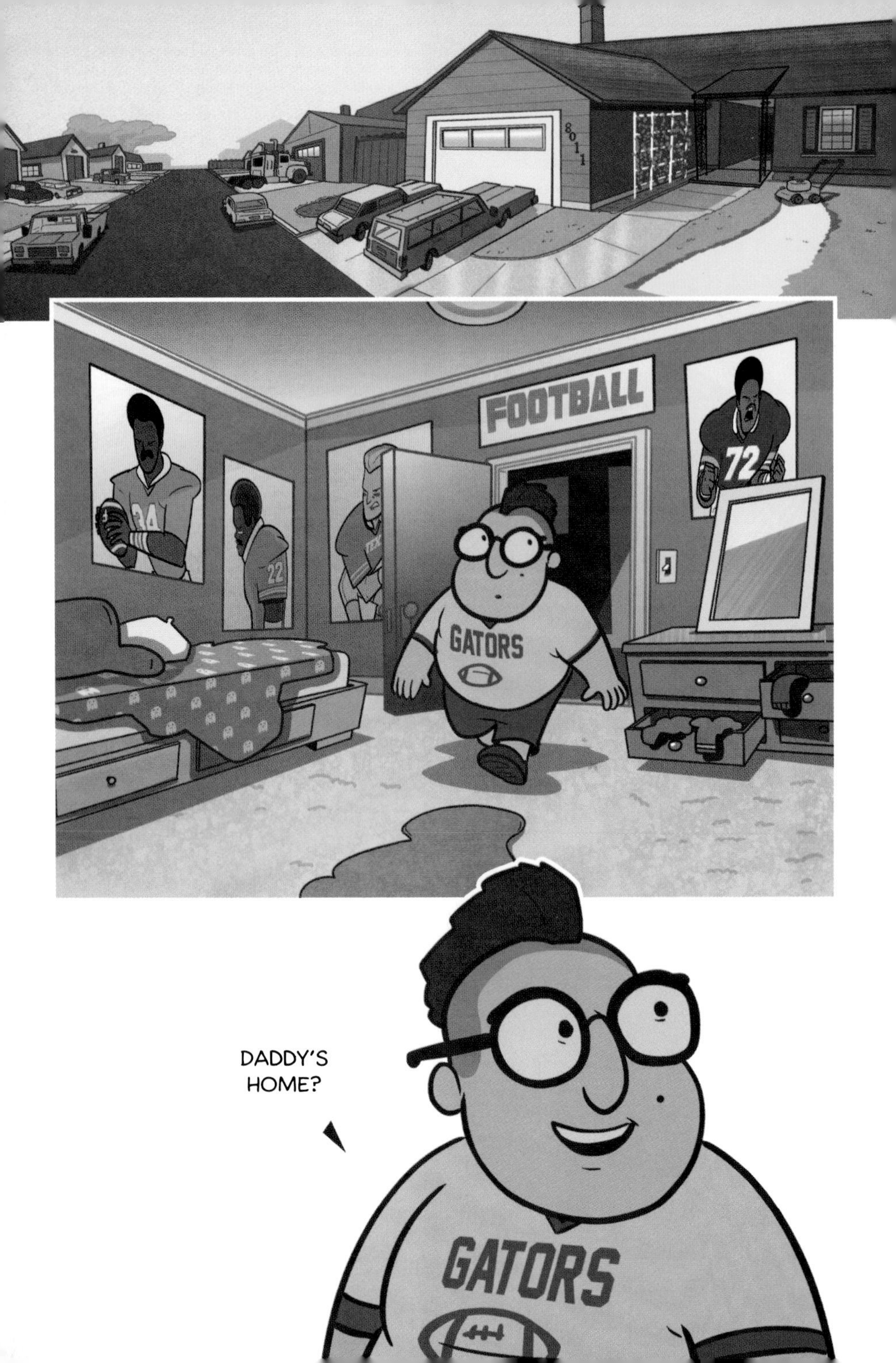
8011
FOOTBALL
72
GATORS
DADDY'S
HOME?
GATORS

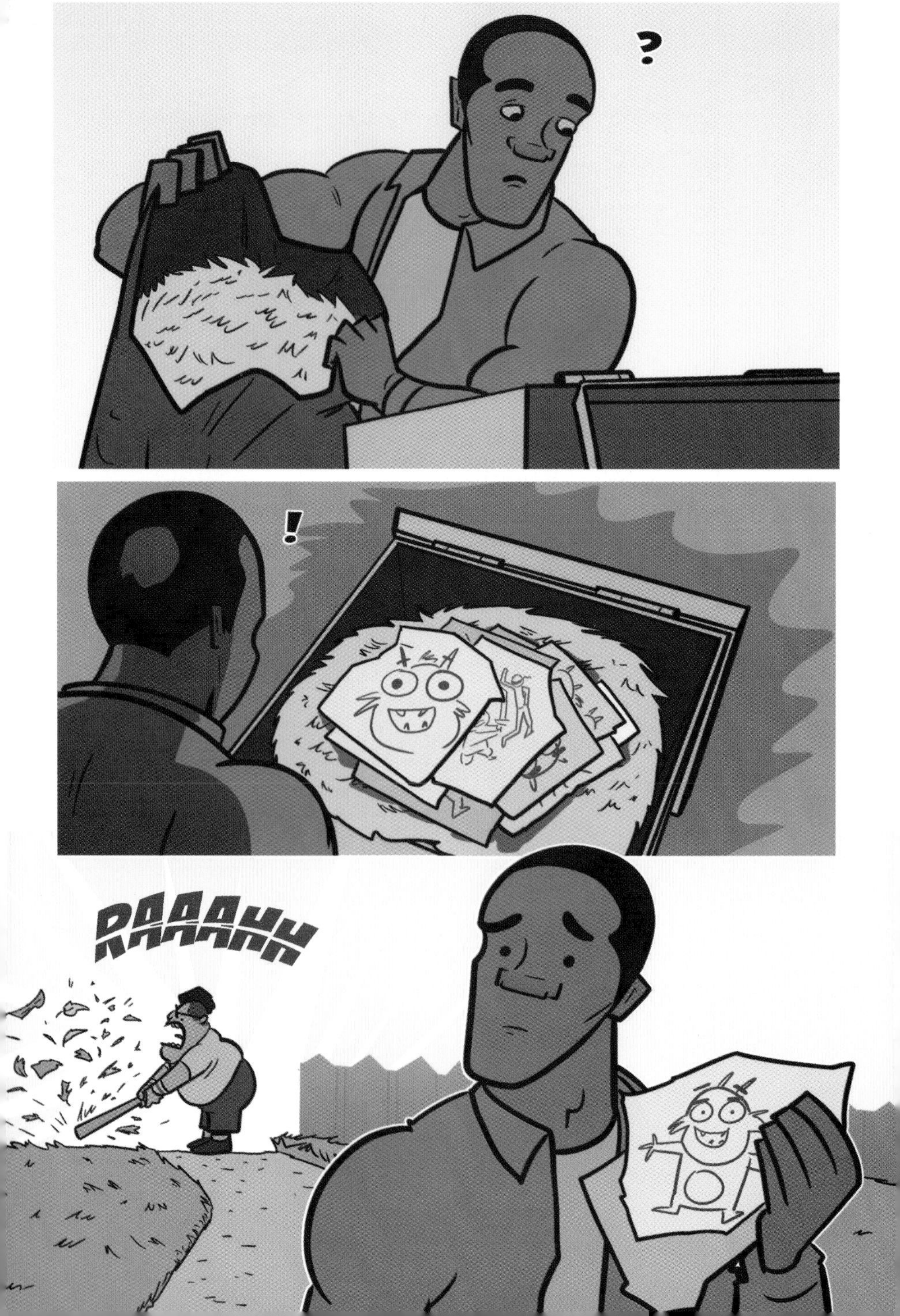
?
!
RAAAHH

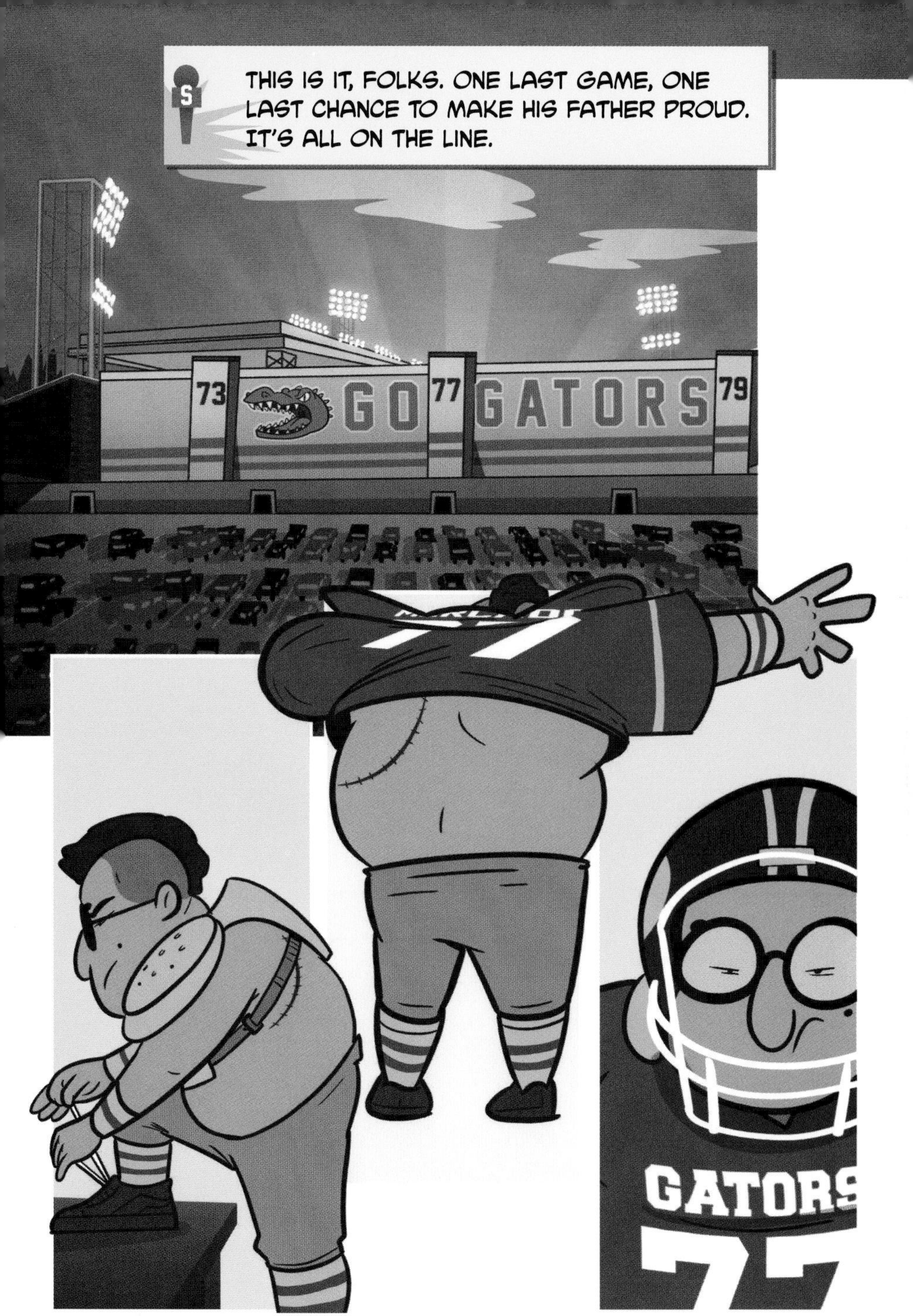
THIS IS IT, FOLKS. ONE LAST GAME, ONE LAST CHANCE TO MAKE HIS FATHER PROUD. IT'S ALL ON THE LINE.
73
GO
77
GATORS
79
GATORS

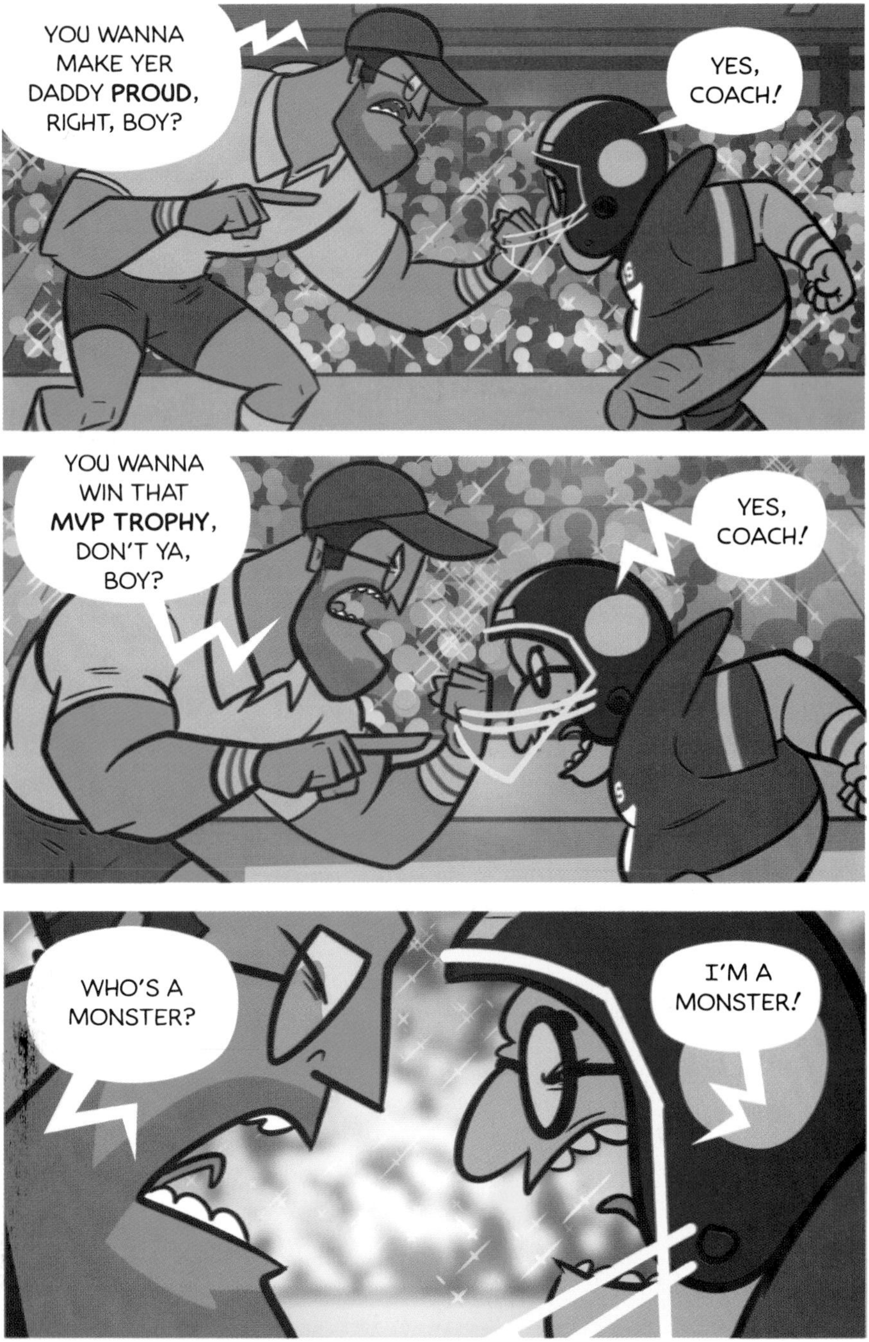
YOU WANNA MAKE YER DADDY **PROUD**, RIGHT, BOY?
YES, COACH!
YOU WANNA WIN THAT **MVP TROPHY**, DON'T YA, BOY?
YES, COACH!
WHO'S A MONSTER?
I'M A MONSTER!

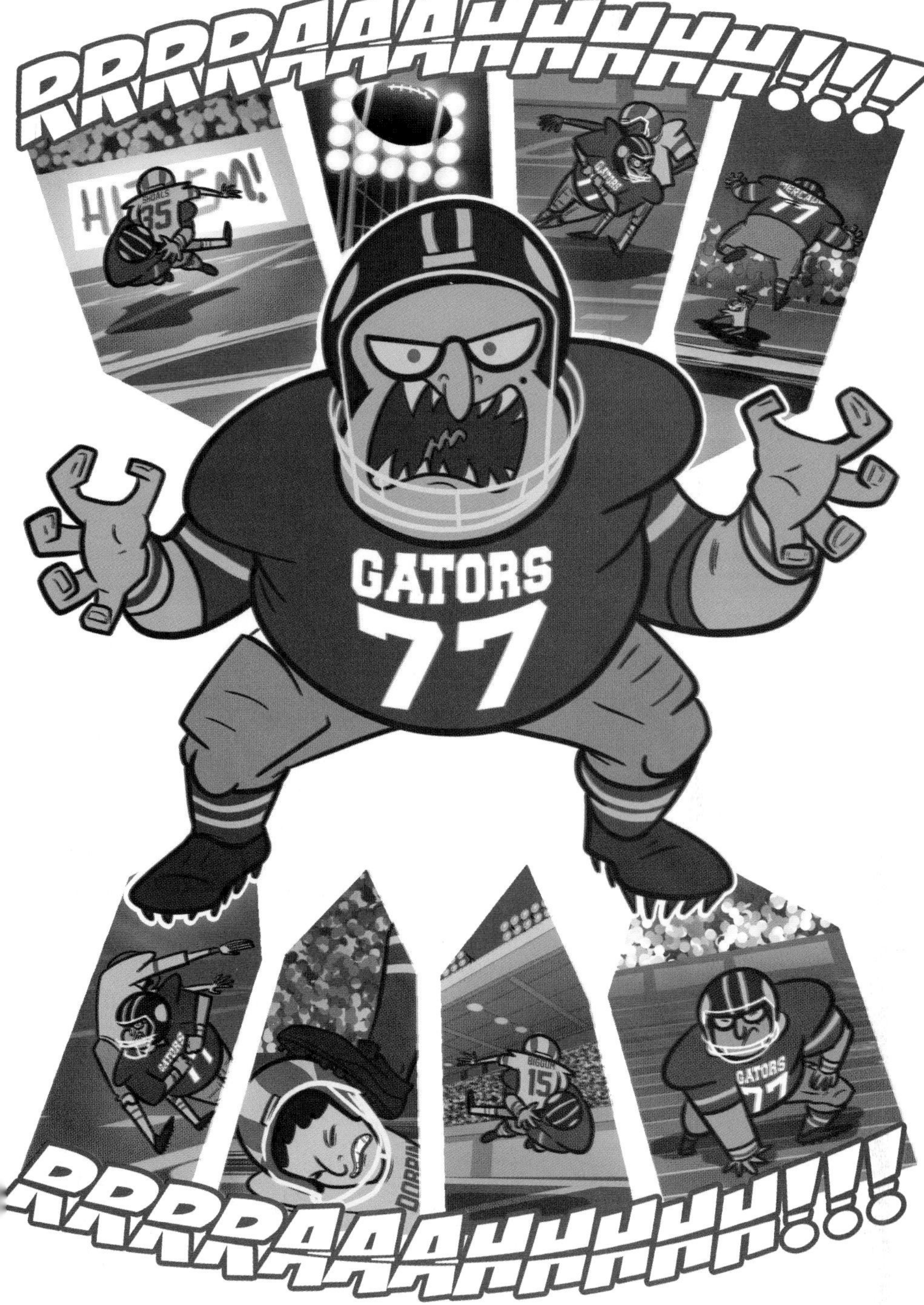
RRRRAAAHHHHH!!!!
GATORS
77
RRRRAAAHHHHHH!!!

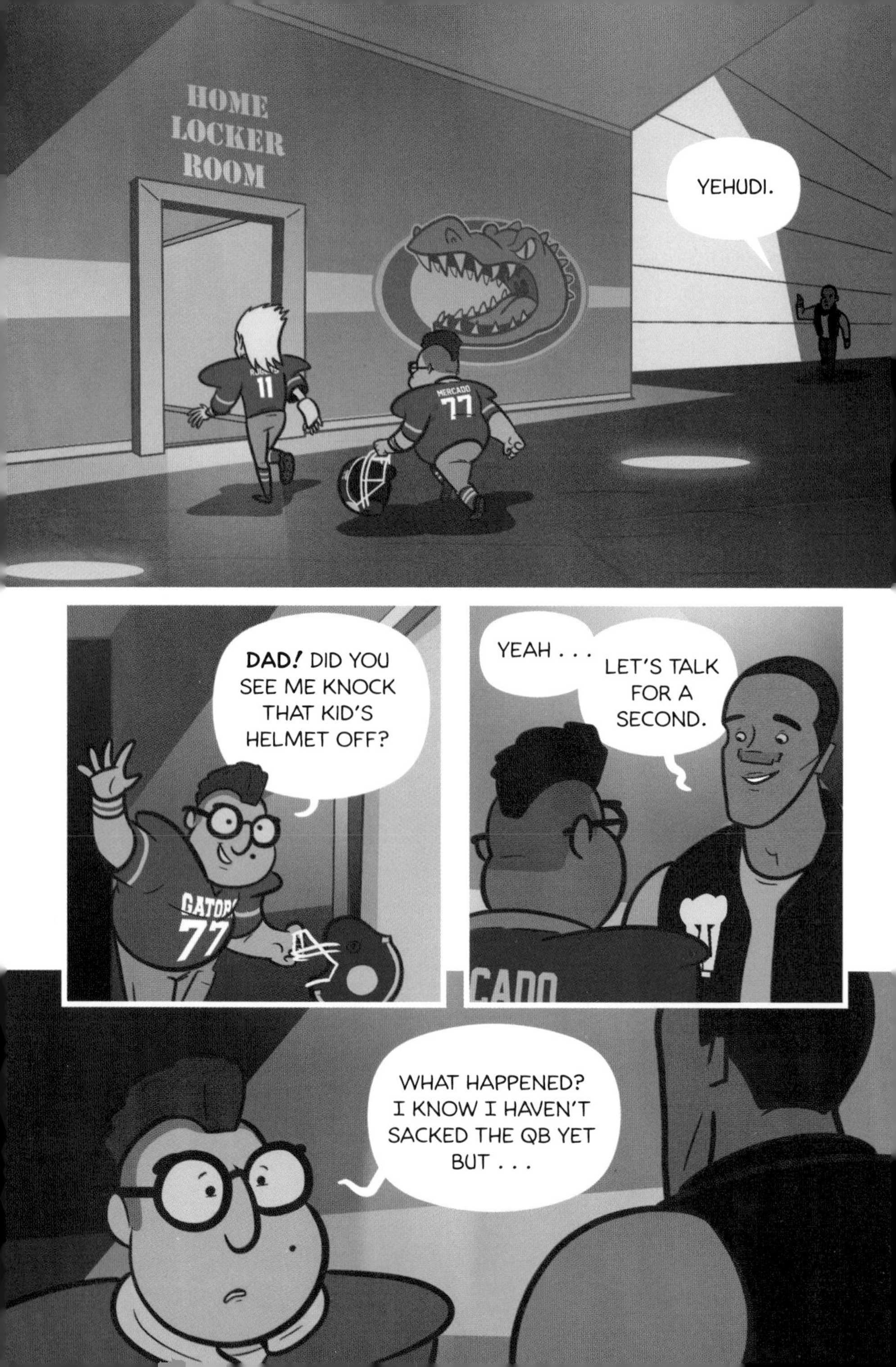
HOME
LOCKER
ROOM
YEHUDI.
MERCADO
77
11
DAD! DID YOU SEE ME KNOCK THAT KID'S HELMET OFF?
GATOR
77
YEAH . . .
LET'S TALK FOR A SECOND.
CADO
WHAT HAPPENED? I KNOW I HAVEN'T SACKED THE QB YET BUT . . .

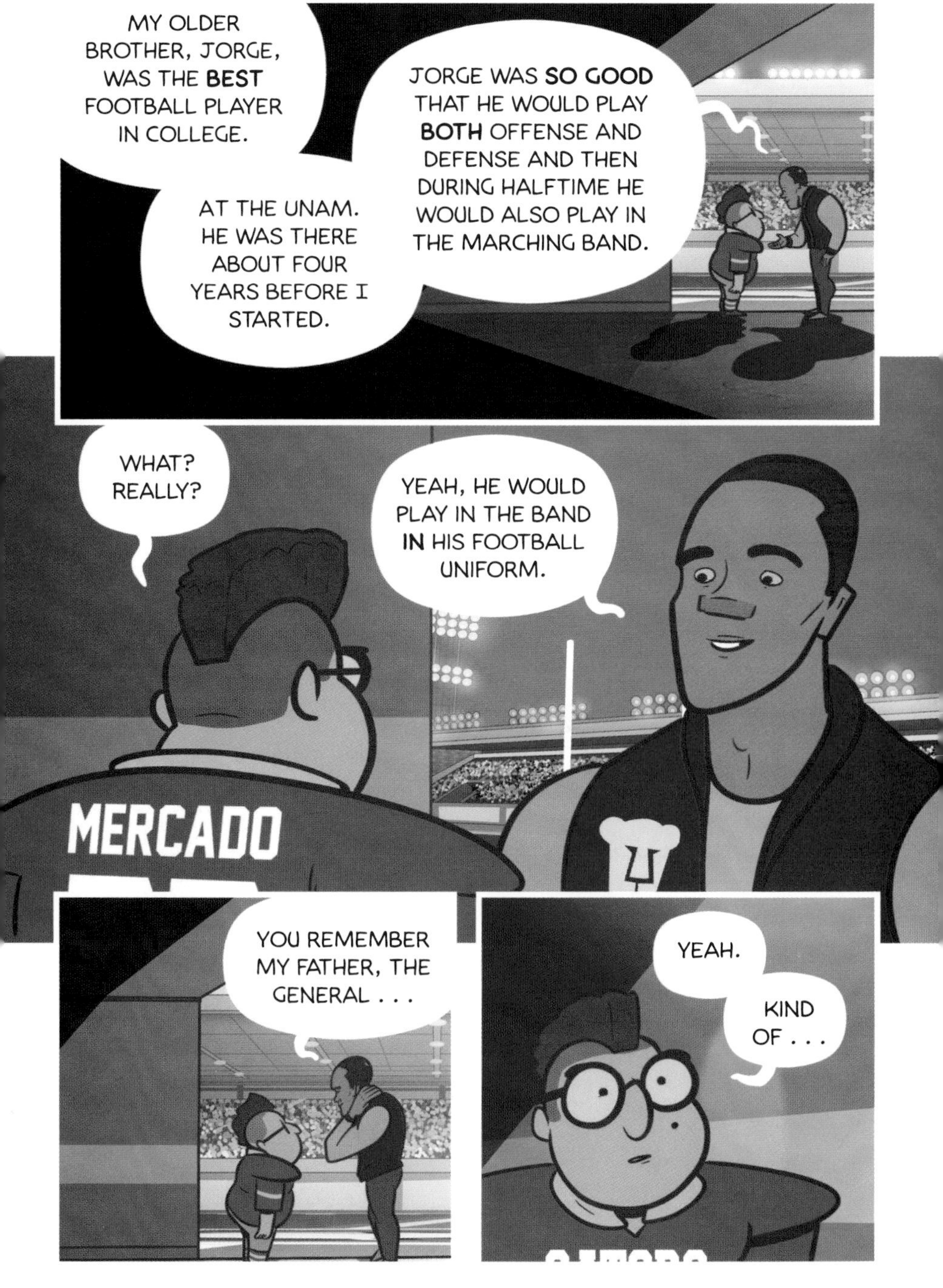
MY OLDER BROTHER, JORGE, WAS THE **BEST** FOOTBALL PLAYER IN COLLEGE.
AT THE UNAM. HE WAS THERE ABOUT FOUR YEARS BEFORE I STARTED.
JORGE WAS **SO GOOD** THAT HE WOULD PLAY **BOTH** OFFENSE AND DEFENSE AND THEN DURING HALFTIME HE WOULD ALSO PLAY IN THE MARCHING BAND.
WHAT? REALLY?
YEAH, HE WOULD PLAY IN THE BAND **IN** HIS FOOTBALL UNIFORM.
MERCADO
YOU REMEMBER MY FATHER, THE GENERAL . . .
YEAH.
KIND OF . . .

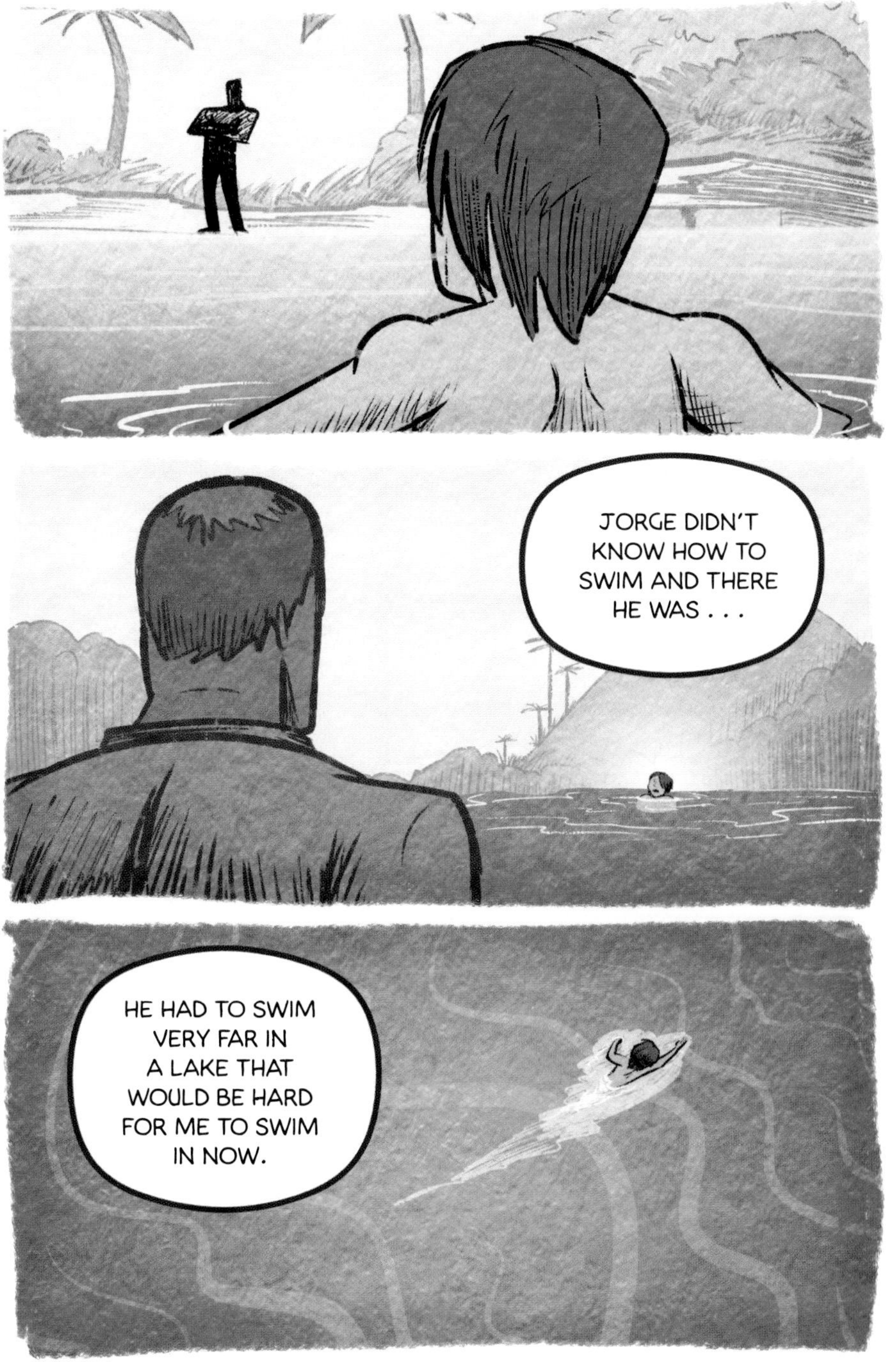
JORGE DIDN'T KNOW HOW TO SWIM AND THERE HE WAS . . .
HE HAD TO SWIM VERY FAR IN A LAKE THAT WOULD BE HARD FOR ME TO SWIM IN NOW.

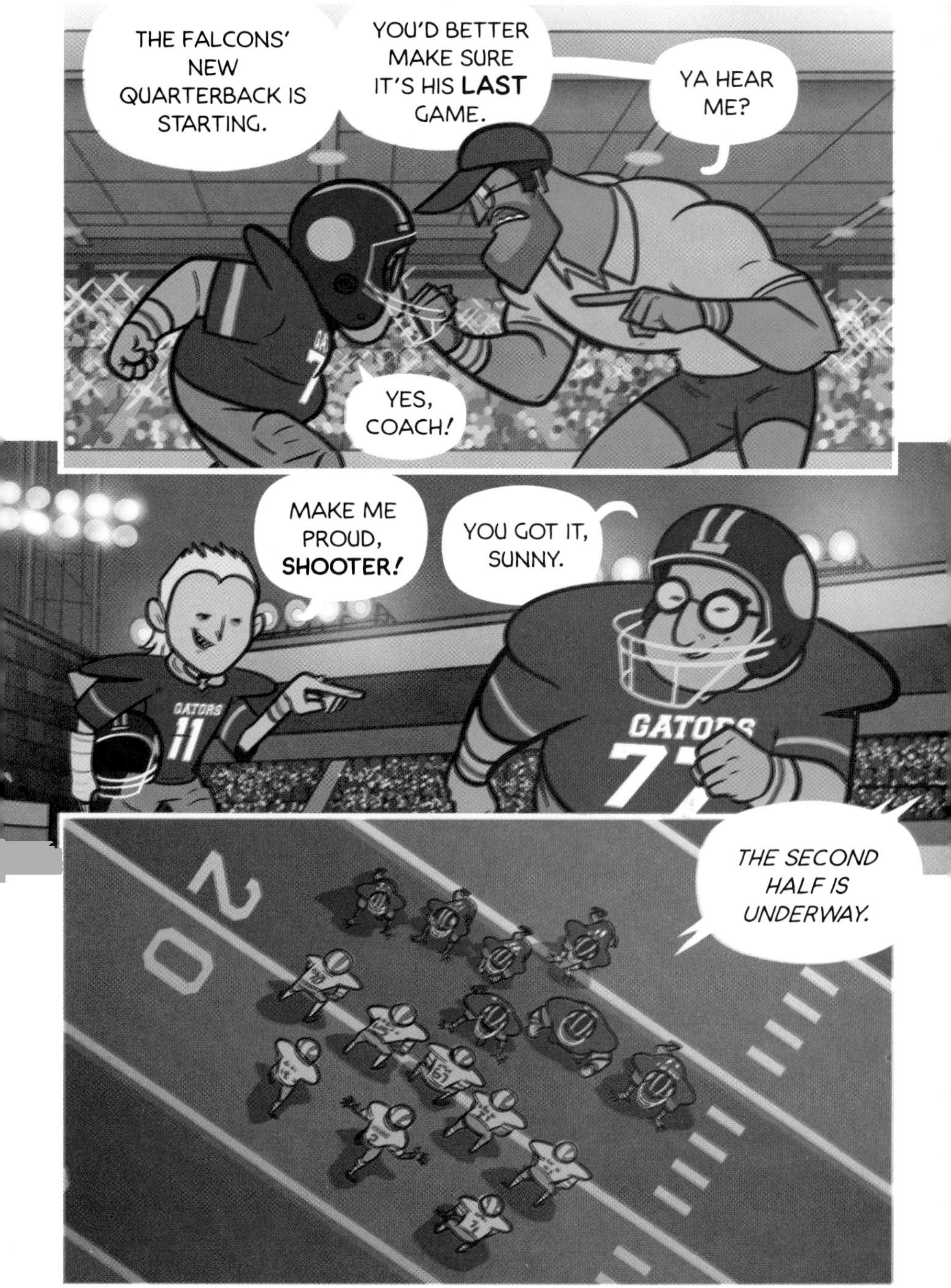
THE FALCONS' NEW QUARTERBACK IS STARTING.
YOU'D BETTER MAKE SURE IT'S HIS **LAST** GAME.
YA HEAR ME?
YES, COACH!
MAKE ME PROUD, **SHOOTER!**
YOU GOT IT, SUNNY.
GATORS
GATORS
THE SECOND HALF IS UNDERWAY.

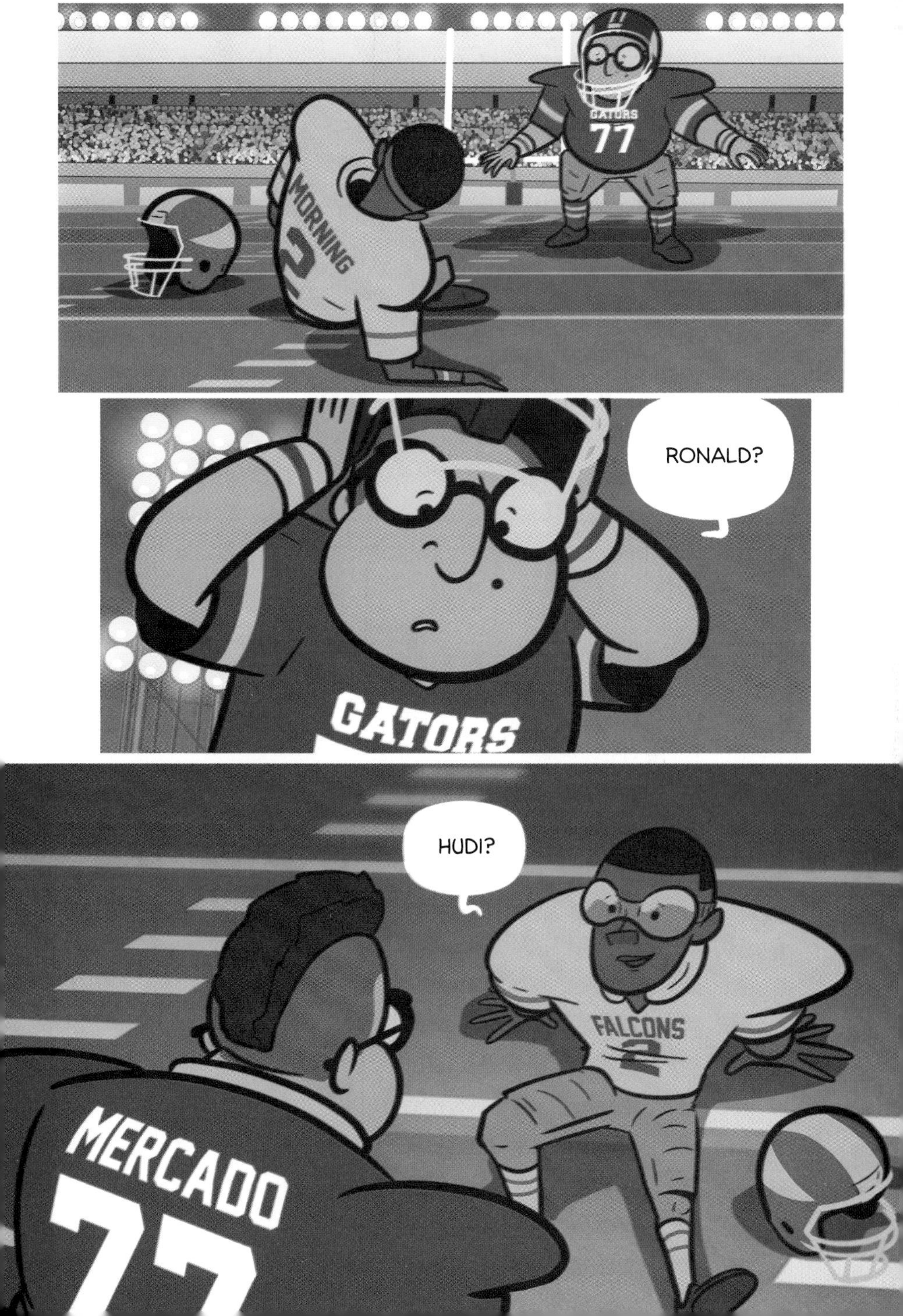

GATORS
77
MORNING
2
RONALD?
GATORS
HUDI?
FALCONS
2
MERCADO
77

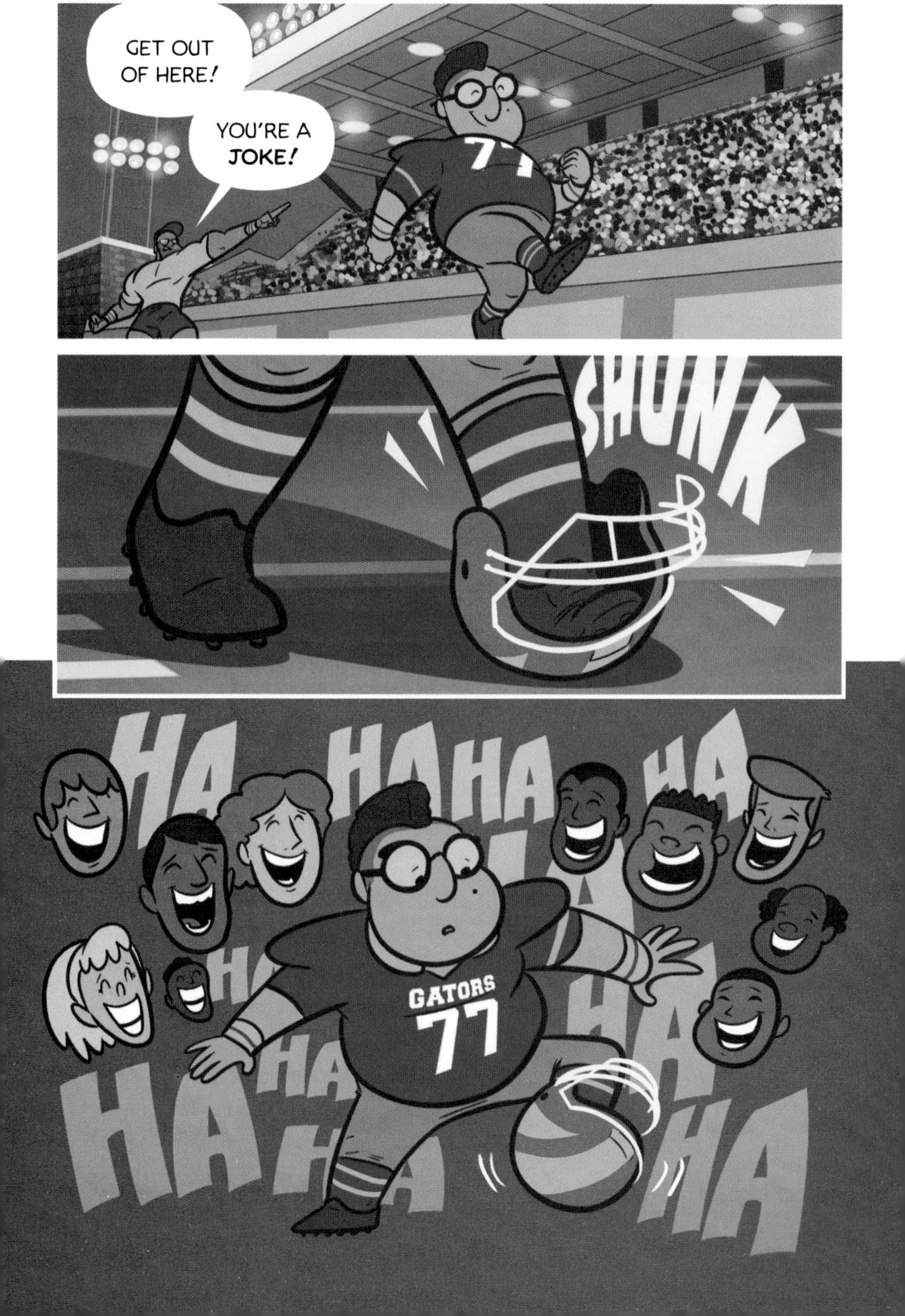

GET OUT OF HERE!
YOU'RE A JOKE!
SHUNK
HA HAHA HA
HA
HA
HA
HA
HA
HA
GATORS 77

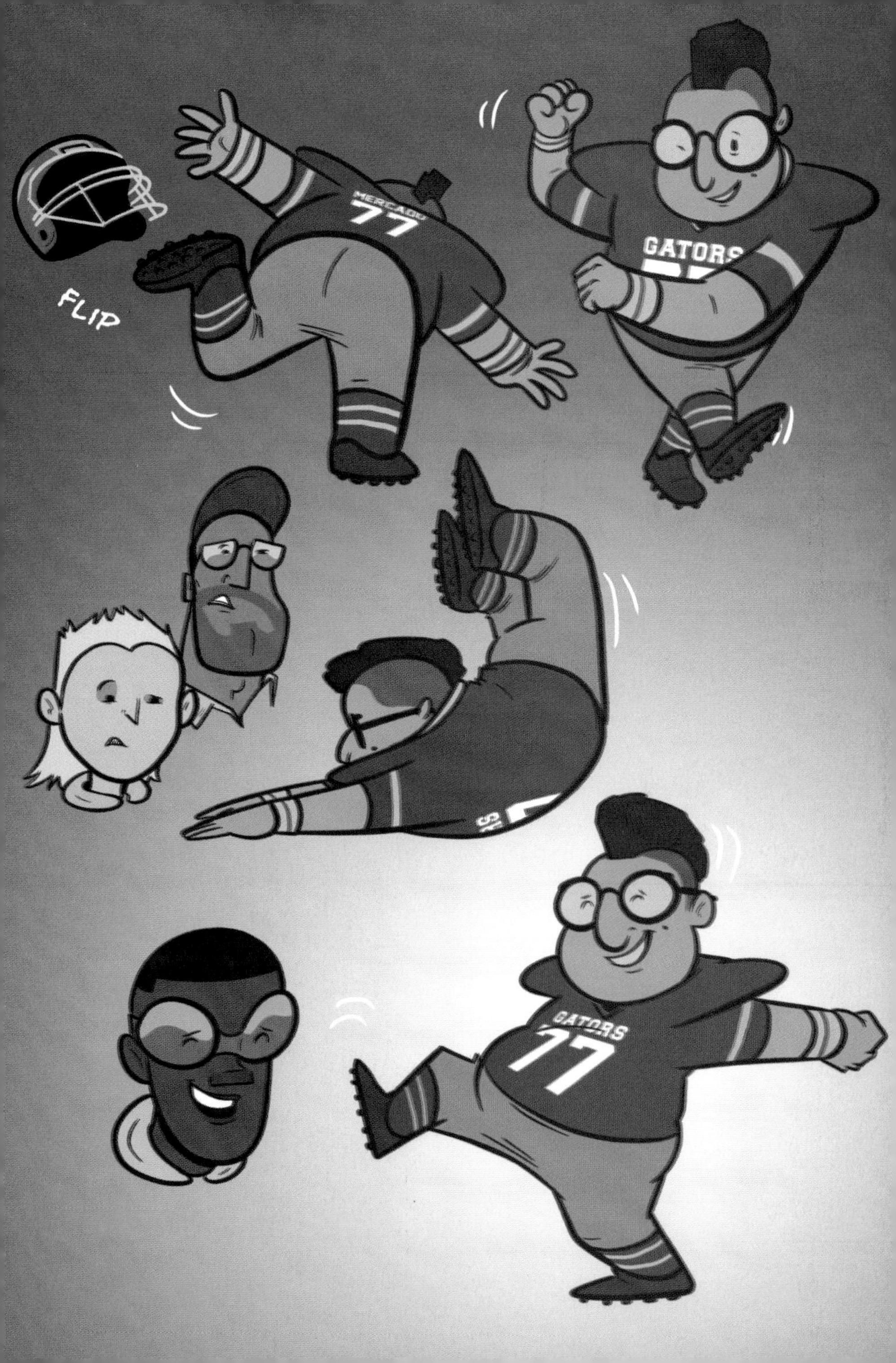

FLIP
MERCADO
77
GATORS
GATORS
77

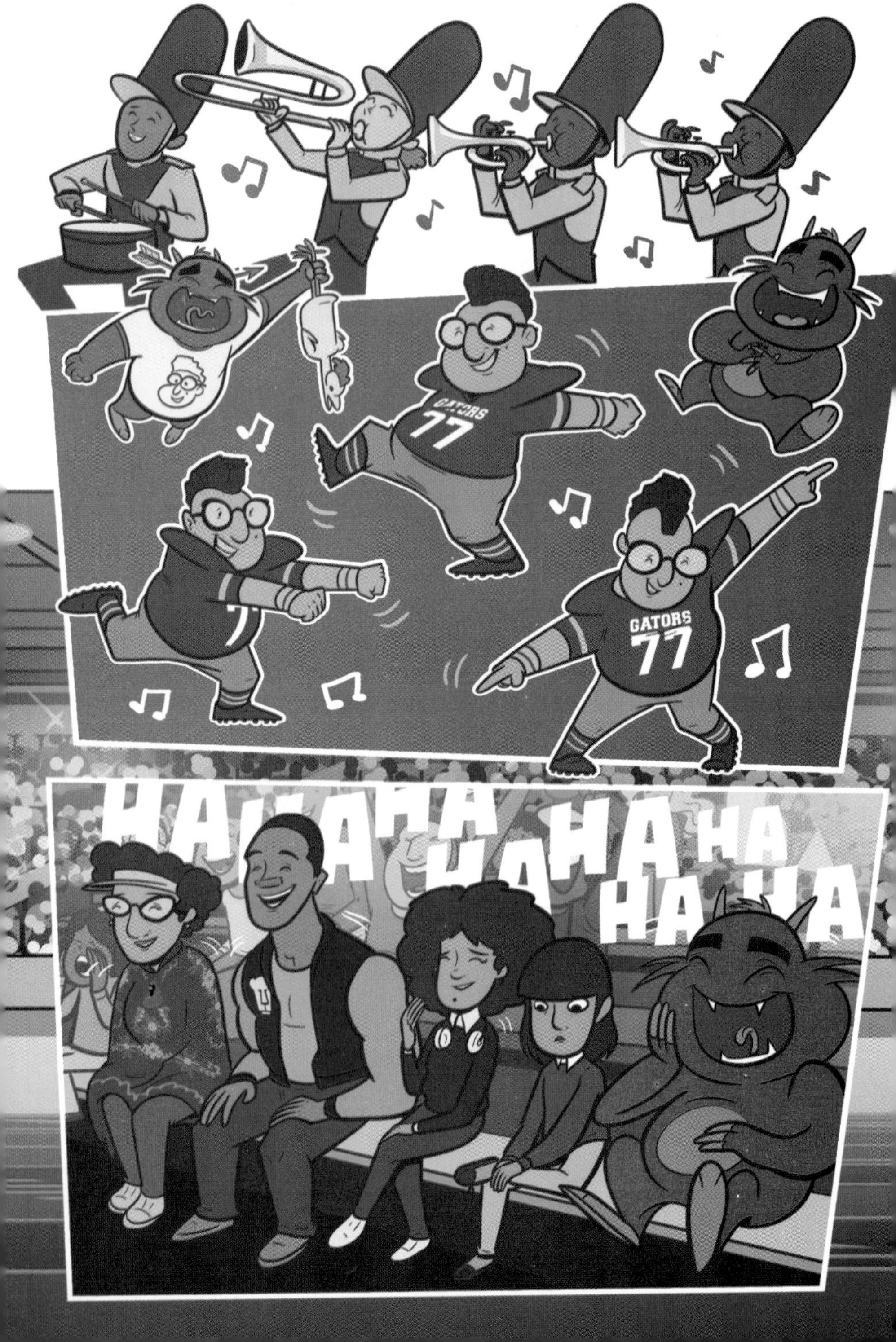
GATORS
77
GATORS
77
HA
HA
HA
HA
HA
HA

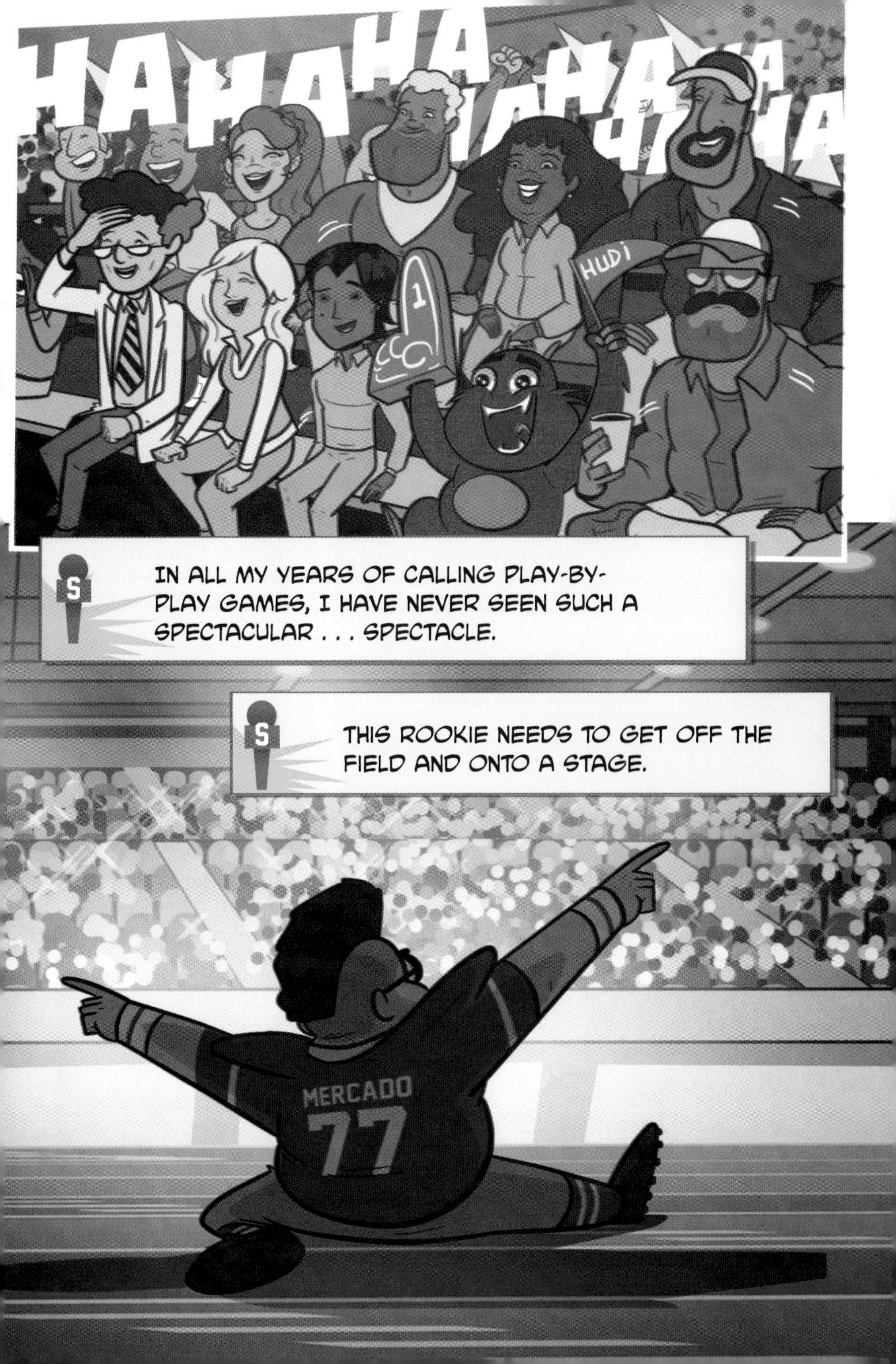
HAHAHAHAHAHAHAHA
HUDi
IN ALL MY YEARS OF CALLING PLAY-BY-PLAY GAMES, I HAVE NEVER SEEN SUCH A SPECTACULAR . . . SPECTACLE.
THIS ROOKIE NEEDS TO GET OFF THE FIELD AND ONTO A STAGE.
MERCADO
77

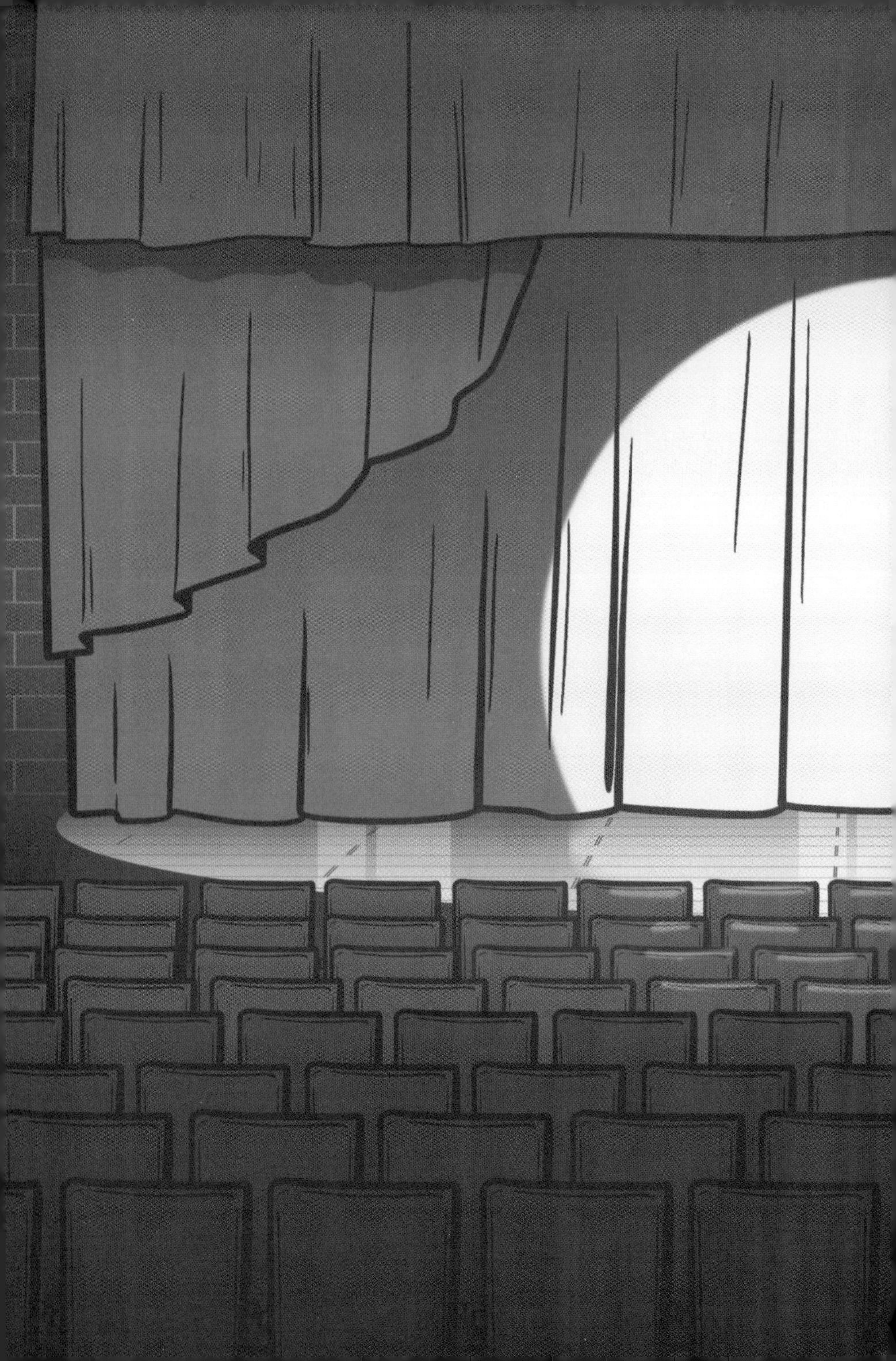

CHAPTER SEVEN

Theater

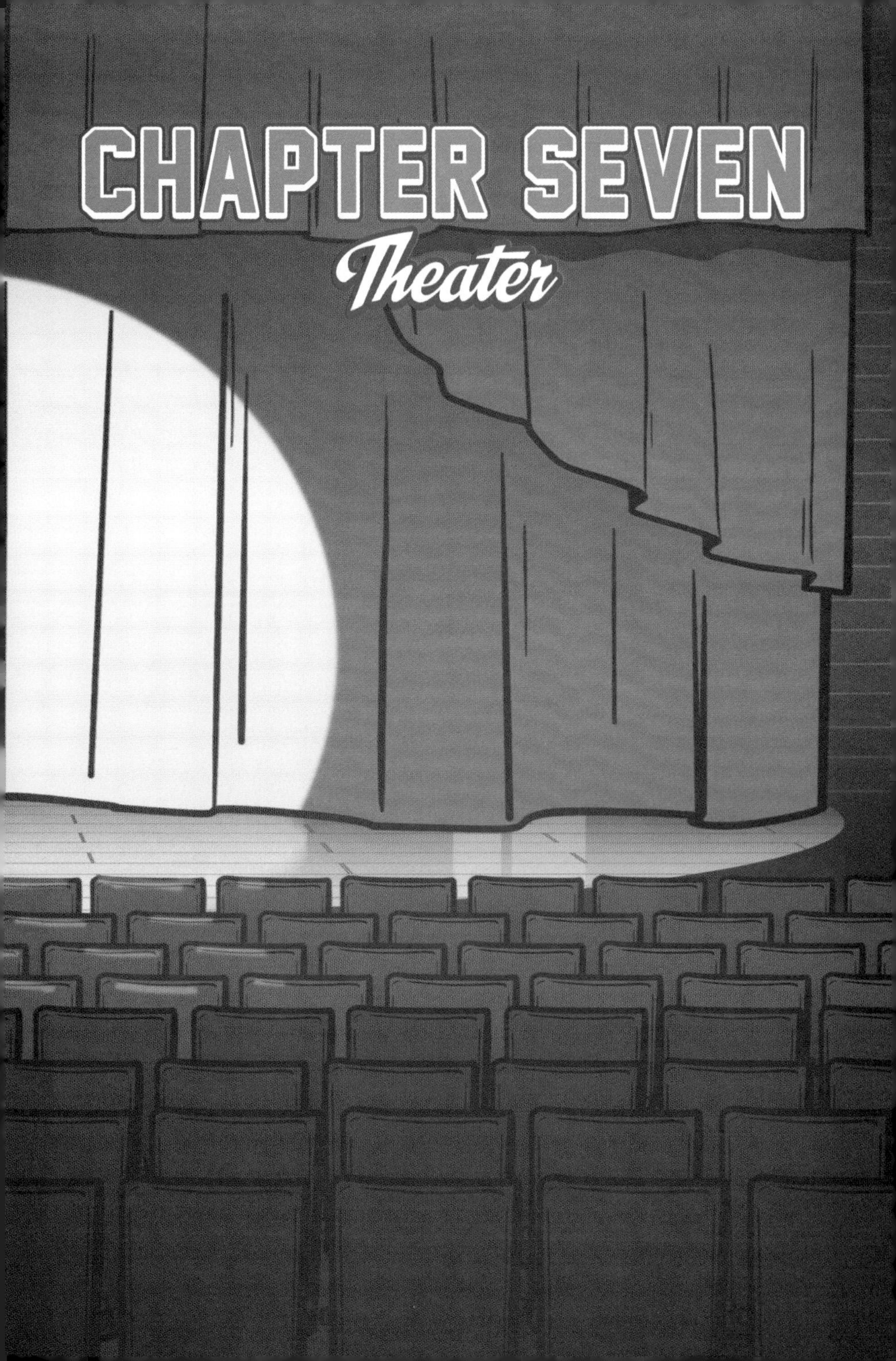

HELLO, MRS. MILLER. MY NAME IS YEHUDI MERCADO AND FOR MY AUDITION I'LL BE DOING . . .
. . . EDDIE MURPHY'S MONOLOGUE FROM THE DECEMBER FIFTEENTH, 1984, EPISODE OF *SATURDAY NIGHT LIVE*.

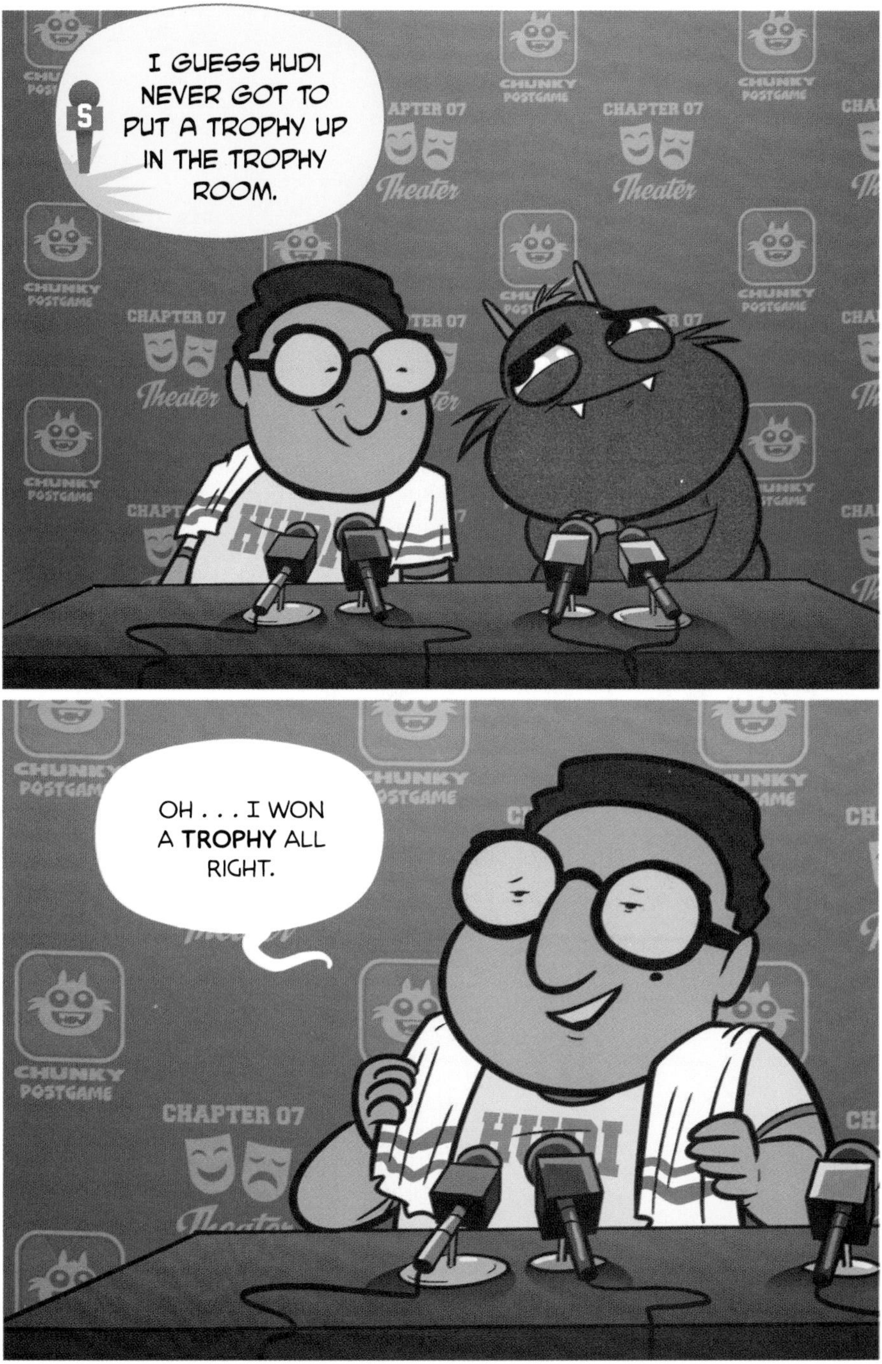
I GUESS HUDI NEVER GOT TO PUT A TROPHY UP IN THE TROPHY ROOM.
OH . . . I WON A **TROPHY** ALL RIGHT.

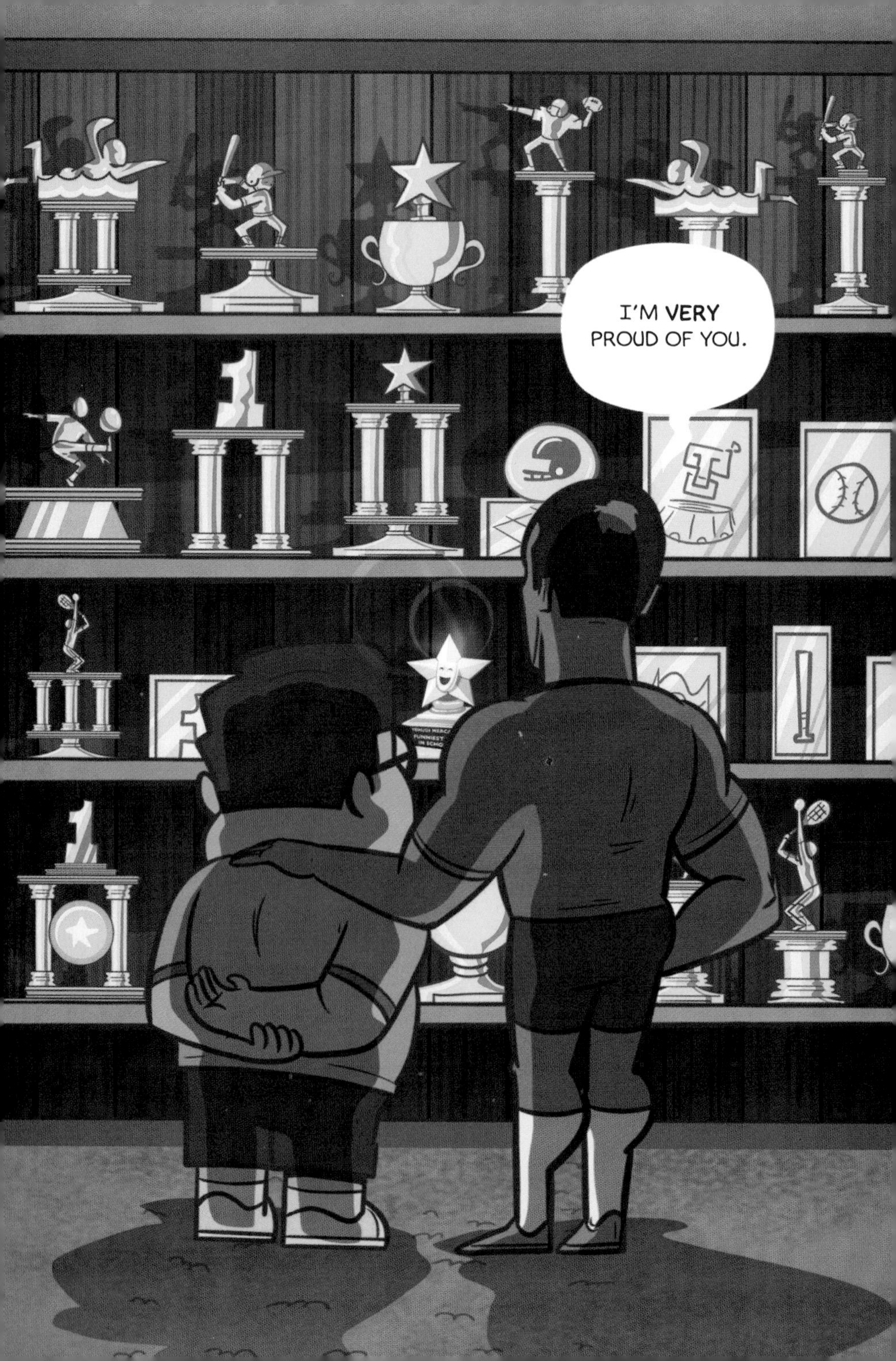
I'M **VERY** PROUD OF YOU.

AUTHOR'S NOTE

First of all, my parents want you to know that they weren't *that* pushy.

I want to thank them profusely for all the support they've shown me my whole life. They always encouraged my artistic pursuits. My father, while being a great athlete, is also an amazing artist. So we always had art supplies all over the house and I was never without a sketch pad or a fist full of markers.

All the health issues in the book are real. All the trips to the emergency room and the hospital really happened. Dr. Plumb was the doctor who performed my lung operation. I only remember flashes of that time. The whole operation and the recovery took me out of school for half a year. I actually had to repeat the first grade, which really bothered me, because I had done all the reading and homework from home—thanks to my mother, who was a teacher.

I continued with football until the eighth grade, but I never really loved it. Texas football was very brutal, and some of those drills are now outlawed. But there was one incident where I hurt my arm, and that's when it hit me. I didn't want to risk injuring my drawing hand because art meant way more to me than sports. I may not be a sports fan, but I do love sports movies.

Yehudi's father at Wynnie's Bat Mitzvah celebrating his US citizenship.

Being "Chunky" isn't about being fat. Being Chunky is about feeling like you don't fit in. As a Mexican Jewish kid with loads of health problems growing up in Houston, Texas, I never felt like I fit in anywhere. It wasn't until I discovered theater that I felt like I finally found my people. In high school I tried out for all the plays. I was playing leads by sophomore year. I went to speech tournaments and competed in various categories like mime, duets, and monologues. My senior year I played Richard III in the UIL (University Interscholastic League) One-Act Play Contest and we went all the way to state. I guess making theater into a sport was a very "Texas" thing to do.

This book is dedicated to my high school drama teacher, Mrs. Marylyn Miller. That's the back of her head on page 195. She passed away in 2012. She helped shape me into the person I am; she let me write and direct plays and always cheered me on. I never would have had the confidence to do what I now do for a living if it weren't for Mrs. Miller.

Find that thing that sparks your imagination. Find your people. Find your Chunky.

Special thanks to
Ben Rosenthal
Raina Telgemeier
Dave Scheidt
Charlie Olsen
Eileen Anderson
the Hoodis family
the Warfields
the Pueblitzes
and
Katherine Tegen

Yehudi in junior high on the Campbell Gators football team.